A Wedding at the Paragraph Ranch

Kay Ellington &
Barbara Brannon

BOLD
FACE
BOOKS

LUBBOCK, TEXAS
WWW.BOLDFACEBOOKS.COM

Cover Design by Greg Simanson

This is a work of fi ction. Names, characters, places, brands, media, and incidents are either the product of the author's imagination or are used fi ctitiously. Any resemblance to similarly named places or to persons living or deceased is unintentional.

www.facebook.com/TheParagraphRanch
www.ParagraphRanch.com

Print ISBN 978-1-935619-22-2
EPUB ISBN 978-1-935619-23-9
Library of Congress Control Number: 2015914601

For our siblings
by birth and by marriage

Contents

Prologue 7

1   The Platform 9

2   Party Favorite 16

3   Something Borrowed, Something Blue 32

4   The Big D 46

5   A Day of Labor 58

6   Brags and Sags 67

7   All the Ships Come In 75

8   Generations 86

9   Friday Night Lights 90

10 On the Road Again 99

11 Climate Change 107

12 A Pound of This, a Pound of That 113

13 Social Climbing 124

14 Getting Over the Color Green 137

15 Going to the Candidates' Debate 148

16 Texas Writers Offline 160

17 Sí, Se Puede 176

18 Fashion Sense 191

19 Railroaded   204

20 Hide and Seek   216

21 Skeletons in the Closet   233

22 Día de los Muertos   258

23 Election Returns   272

24 Engagements   283

Acknowledgments   289

All chapter epigraphs are from *Etiquette in Society, in Business, in Politics and at Home,* by Emily Post (Mrs. Price Post); illustrated with private photographs and facsimiles of social forms (New York: Funk & Wagnalls, 1922). As Mrs. Post prefaced her 627-page bible of social customs, "To you my friends whose identity in these pages is veiled in fictional disguise it is but fitting that I dedicate this book."

Prologue

Alice
Thursday, August 28, 2008

THAT DURNED GRANDFATHER *clock makes more racket than I ever realized back at the home place. Maybe I just didn't pay attention to its sound out there, where it was stuck in a corner in the living room. But I hear it now. Strikes ever' blessed fifteen minutes. And practically a whole church hymn on the hour.*

Not that I resent what it reminds me of. The kids gave it to us as a present on our fiftieth wedding anniversary, me and Wilton, six years ago. We didn't have the heart to tell 'em we already had four clocks in the house that chimed the hour. It was a thoughtful gesture.

Now that I've got nothin' on my hands but time, in this crackerbox house they call a patio home, I hear that dadgum clock all day and all night long and it's about to drive me slap crazy. Days like this I miss working in the fields with him, miss cookin' dinner in that old house on the hill, hot as blazes, waitin' for the school bus to stop at the gate, kids to come in and do their chores and homework. I miss Penny's smart sewing, Buddy's football games, Dee Anna with her feet slung over the side of the armchair, readin' a book.

Hard to believe Penny's oldest is gettin' married. Time does fly. It seems like yesterday that Wilton proposed to me our senior year . . . said I do out in that country church that summer, brought me out here to set up housekeeping. We didn't have two nickels to rub together. But we were happy enough. I shore do miss him. Wish he was here for this wedding. It's bound to be the first of many.

1
The Platform

To begin with, before deciding the date of the wedding, the bride's mother must find out definitely on which day the clergyman who is to perform the ceremony is disengaged, and make sure that the church is bespoken for no other service. If it is to be an important wedding, she must also see that the time available for the church is also convenient to the caterer.

Sundays, and days in Lent, are not chosen for weddings, and Friday being a "fast" day in Catholic and very "high" Episcopal churches, weddings on that day, if not forbidden, are never encouraged.

—Chapter XXI, "First Preparations before a Wedding"

DEE BENNETT MAINTAINED her posture in the vibrating leather chair at Claxton's only nail salon, leaving the pen and yellow pad balanced in her lap and opening one eye just a slit—the way you'd peek between slats of the blinds to spy without being noticed—to see what the chatter was all about. It wasn't like she went in for a pedicure every week. More like never, in fact—and just as she was settling in to appreciate the full benefit of a lavender-and-sea-salt scrub with complimentary wine-a-rita and drift off into a massage-induced daydream about the gala evening ahead at Max's gallery, a cacophony of female voices invaded her oasis. Twentysomethings, she estimated. A little older than Abby, whom she couldn't imagine prattling on about polish colors and signature cocktails as though the salon were a public slumber party.

She had no desire to eavesdrop on their talk, but it was becoming harder to ignore with every round of gossip they batted across the aisle of thronelike chair stations.

"I'm tellin' you, it was the wedding from *hay*-ull," one of the young women confided gleefully. "We're all lined up on the beach, trying to keep the wind from blowing sand in our eyes, and the groomsmen are sweating bullets. And here she comes down through the dunes with her chocolate Lab and he's standing there with his Doberman—"

The others cackled, and the one on the far end leaned over to interrupt. "I can't believe they really went through with it!"

"—and the Best Dog gets loose, goes after the Lab, knocks the bride on her butt, and, um, *consummates* things right in front of everybody!" By now they were all in stitches.

"Can you say *Mutt* of Honor?" another of the voices added, cracking up.

The wine-a-ritas had kicked in, Dee guessed. She closed her eyes again, tried to get back to her happy place. One that didn't involve copulating canines.

"No destination wedding for me, sorry," the girl on the end said. "If I'm spending big money on a vacation it's gonna be to get *away* from my crazy family."

With that sentiment, Dee couldn't have agreed more. She gave up on trying to relax and returned her attention to the legal pad in front of her as the Asian nail tech lathered her calves with lotion.

Platform, she inked at the top of the blank page, underscoring the word as if that would make the goal clearer. An agent friend-of-a-friend in New York had advised her to build an online presence before starting to shop her book around. "Blogging is white-hot," she'd said. Dee was so far behind in this new digital world of 2008, the woman had had to explain the word. "Weblog. Web *log.* A lot of people like this stuff they call social media—you know, MySpace, Facebook. But I can assure you, not one book was sold in 2007 from some writer posting a picture of what they cooked for dinner last night. Blogs like Velveteen Rabbit, Lifehacker, Boing Boing—that's what gets authors noticed. Start blogging and find a media outlet to link to you, and we'll get this book of yours placed with a publisher in no time. Easy-peasy."

Dee wasn't so sure about that last part, but she was willing to give it a try.

Moving back to Claxton, laying claim to her birthplace, and carving out her path as a full-time writer had not exactly been *easy-peasy* either so far, Dee thought. Coming home under trying circumstances had tapped into a mix of feelings about growing up on the farm, about friends and community, and even romance. The summer's turn of events had unearthed a loyalty to the home place that she would never have predicted. At least her transition from Tar Heel academic to Texas cotton farm owner provided plenty of fodder for a *blog*.

She'd even been successful in landing a media outlet for "The Paragraph Ranch," as she'd titled her musings about writing and rural life. She made a bullet point on the page and wrote down the title. Granted, her online angel was nothing more than the home-town *Claxton Courier,* which had finally launched a website a few months earlier. Claxton.com had been one of the first initiatives of the new editor, whiz kid Shannon Thomas, a Texas Tech alum and the first female to hold the job in the newspaper's eighty-eight-year history. Thomas had been brought in from the paper's home office in Big Spring to replace Norton Loveland, editor since Dee's high school years. Dee had taken Mama to Norton's retirement party and had seized the opportunity to pitch her idea to the new editor. "Sort of an online freelance column," Dee had described it. "First-person." "Oh," Thomas had replied. "A blog. Sure, let's talk about it."

The Asian woman patted Dee's legs with a dry towel then reached over for a pair of steaming, moist ones. "You get pedicures lot?" she asked.

"No," Dee replied. "I have this thing I have to go to this weekend."

"What kind of thing?" she asked, wrapping hot towels tightly around each of Dee's calves, creating a sensation that soothed her to the point of letting down her customary reserve.

"A wedding," Dee said.

"You getting married?" the pedicurist asked brightly, silencing the salon and turning all eyes in Dee's direction.

"Congratulations!" said a perky voice from the middle of the pack across the aisle. Dee looked up to fully appreciate the hot-pink T-shirt with the word *Bridezilla* bedazzled across the chest. "I'm getting married, too, and these are my bridesmaids." She swept her arm across the room in a grand gesture of ownership.

"No!" Dee said, a little flustered. "*I'm* not getting married. I'm going to my niece's wedding." The idea of marrying again herself—a few months from her looming fortieth birthday—left Dee cold.

"Where is your wedding?" the bride-to-be asked, oblivious. "I'm Ashley, by the way."

"Dallas," Dee answered. "My niece's wedding is getting married in Dallas. I mean, my niece is getting married in Dallas. This Sunday."

"Sunday?" one of the bridesmaids blurted out. "Isn't that—"

Bridezilla Ashley cut her off. "Mine's in Cancun. *If* everyone gets there. It's never a good sign if Jim Cantore shows up forty-eight hours before your big day."

"Relax, it's going to be fine," said another of the young women. "I'm Heather, the maid of honor. Don't pay our horror stories any mind."

"Really, Heather—you're not exactly putting *my* mind at ease!" said Ashley, giggling.

Dee smiled, nodded, and didn't return the introductions. As a college professor—make that former college professor, she corrected herself—she'd learned to be cordial but not chummy with her undergraduates. Best to keep your cool and your distance.

She returned her gaze to her notes and began to draft an outline. But instead of crafting her blog she found herself calculating living expenses. Come September 1, there'd be no predictable deposit of a faculty salary into the bank, as there'd been for the past seven years. On the farm account, crop insurance wouldn't pay off on the cotton for a while yet, and the sorghum had only begun to sprout. She could eventually cover her car payment, insurance, utilities, gas, and basics with that, without dipping into the reserves she'd put away, though she might have to use her few savings to get by in the short term. She subtotaled the column. Health insurance was another matter—she'd nearly fainted from sticker shock when she learned the figure for her continuing coverage. With the presidential election coming up, Dee secretly pinned her hopes on the candidate who was leading the charge on affordable health care—even though Barack Obama didn't seem the most popular candidate in West Texas, by a long shot. But that could still go either way, and right now, she needed a steady income. Soon.

In the background, one of the bridesmaids was detailing another reception gone wrong with a hot air balloon getting stuck in a forest in Colorado, while Heather followed that tale by recalling a nasty zip line incident in Costa Rica.

Dee wondered if she could keep getting by with the public library's Wi-Fi for a little bit longer, delaying the $75 a month that high-speed satellite Internet was going to cost. Or maybe she could consolidate her trips into town more efficiently, save some on gas. She did the math in longhand while the bridesmaid at the far end asked if they'd heard about the honeymoon couple stranded on a disabled cruise ship.

She was relieved that Madison's wedding would be taking place on dry land. Though given Penny's penchant for pageantry, not even an inland setting or her older sister's months of micromanagement were guaranteed to forestall disaster. The biggest wild card was always their mother. Mary Alice Bennett had been uncharacteristically cooperative and calm these past weeks, since Dee had come home to Claxton for good. That calm made Dee nervous.

At this point in the game their frocks hung pressed and ready, their hotel reservations were set, and the big day was almost upon them. There was only her blog to finish, and Max's gallery opening tonight, before they hit the road for the Big D.

The thought of Max made her blush. Or was it cringe? She could kick herself for being so stupid. Why hadn't she invited him to go with her? They'd been out to dinner twice now since their sizzling-hot evening under the stars a few weeks earlier. She accepted the conspiratorial, congratulatory looks in town that had started to imply they were a couple, or at least headed that direction. And she certainly liked the way the sight of Max's tanned face, his salt-and-pepper hair and moustache, and his tall, trim, jeans-clad figure made her pulse quicken. Was it the awkward prospect of an overnight trip, or her reluctance to involve anyone in more of her family's drama, that had made her hesitate?

She'd told him she'd be totally preoccupied taking care of Mama, but she sensed he knew better. Max got along quite well with Mary Alice Bennett and would actually have been an asset during a high-stress time. So what made her hold back in asking her handsome cowboy to escort her to the wedding? And most inscrutable of all, as her sister put it, when so many guests went to great lengths to snag a suitable plus-one, what woman in her right mind who had such an eligible date would ever, ever want to go to a wedding *minus* one?

The pedicure portion of her grooming done, Dee gave up her pen and notes and prepared to surrender her hands to the nail tech's ministrations. As she made her way to the manicure station, her toes splayed in foam dividers, a slender figure in motion, talking animatedly on a cell phone, appeared in the sunlight's glare just inside the storefront.

A waft of fragrance occupied the room in the same way the woman's silhouette filled the doorframe. Dee thought she recognized the scent as a Chanel number—Nine? Five? She couldn't keep them straight. Her fashion sense was practical and classic, but it didn't always extend to brand recognition.

Before Dee's eyes could adjust to the afternoon glare or she could take her seat, the redhead in bright red Capri pants, striped boat-neck tunic, and slingbacks slipped into the station in front of her and barked at the manicurist, "I broke a nail. I'll pay you ten dollars to fix it right now." The woman never paused in her phone conversation. "Tell him not to be late," she ordered to the other end of the line.

Finding no opening to challenge the line-breaker, Dee slipped into another chair and waited, pretending to be taking notes. Lapses of manners never failed to arouse her indignation, but she wasn't about to act on this one. A saying of her late father's came to mind. *You can't outpiss a skunk, Dee Anna, so just leave it be.*

The redheaded woman continued loudly, "I'm here now. I drove myself."

Dee couldn't help herself. She stole a quick glance through the front windows, making out the late-model silver Acura MDX that she was pretty sure hadn't been in the handicap spot five minutes earlier.

Her nail repaired swiftly, the woman stood up and handed the nail tech a twenty. "I'm on my way to the mayor's office right now," she said more evenly, cell cradled on her shoulder with one hand, the other palm out for change. "Trust me, this is *going* to happen." And with that last blast of certitude, the interloper was gone.

2
Party Favorite

Those who keep their visiting list in order have comparatively little work. But those who are not in the habit of entertaining on a general scale, and yet have a large unassorted visiting list, will have quite a piece of work ahead of them, and cannot begin making it soon enough.

In the cities where a Social Register or other Visiting Book is published, people of social prominence find it easiest to read it through, marking "XX" in front of the names to be asked to the house, and another mark, such as a dash, in front of those to be asked to the church only, or to have announcements sent them. . . . In country places and smaller cities, or where a published list is not available, or of sufficient use, the best assistant is the telephone book.

—"How the Wedding List Is Compiled"

CLAXTON'S BRICK-PAVED downtown streets had emptied of activity as usual on a Thursday afternoon, Dee noted as she pulled her Subaru into a choice spot near the Windstream Gallery and stepped out in the new strappy dress sandals that showed off her coral-pink toes. At five, when the courthouse and government offices shut down, nearly everything else did too, and on top of that folks were probably getting a head start on the Labor Day weekend. She hoped, for Max's sake, that a respectable number of guests would stick around and brave the triple-digit heat to congratulate him, view the photographs she'd helped him hang the night before, and buy a few books and prints.

Dee opened the door softly and paused inside the big open space before calling his name, to absorb the full effect in a moment of complete quiet. The large, matted black-and-white images showed beautifully in contrast to the dove-gray walls. The sun cast prism accents like jewels through bevels in the old window glass. The industrial interior perfectly suited Max's artistry with the lens, for this exhibition of windmill photos. Not the old-fashioned kind, though there were a couple of those, but the towering twenty-first-century turbines that now generated energy across the West Texas landscape. The exhibition was stunning. She exhaled the breath she hadn't realized she was holding.

She hadn't realized Max had been watching, either.

His voice reverberated in the cavernous space. "What do you think?" he asked, palms raised to indicate the show as he emerged from the loft and strode toward her. He didn't wait for an answer but instead enfolded her in his arms. "Never mind that. No one will notice a thing tonight except how lovely you look." He kissed her lips urgently, and she half-closed her eyes to fully enjoy the moment.

"You clean up pretty well yourself," she said, running a clear-varnished fingernail down the side of his rugged cheek, past the moustache she was truly becoming fond of, down to the throat of his white linen shirt. She knew he was flattering her plain appearance, though she did think the simple black sundress set off with turquoise and coral beads was a good choice for the evening. She was proud of the tan she'd gained working out on the farm these past weeks, and the golden lights that had appeared in her straight brown hair. Not bad for thirty-nine. Not bad for a single-again mom. Or maybe it was just that Max made her feel vital again, appreciated.

"Well, we did it," he sighed, dropping his arm to her waist and indicating the gallery around them. "I'm really grateful for the collaboration on the project. I think it's going to be a huge success."

"You deserve it," Dee said. "Especially after everything you went through to get those photos!" They shared a laugh about the summer's misadventures.

Max turned to look her in the eyes again. "Listen, Dee, I imagine things are going to get busy here in a second, but I was hoping . . . "

"Hoping what?"

"Hoping when all the excitement dies down, and you get back from that wedding shindig, we might plan a little getaway—"

"Oh, Max, that sounds like fun, but I just don't know how things will go, with so much to do out at the home place, Abby starting back to college, and Mama still not a hundred percent—and I have to find a job. I—oh, good grief, why am I babbling? I'm just not used to things changing so fast." She kicked herself again for hesitating.

He chuckled. "I sort of like *this* kind of change." He kissed her again, lightly, leaving her breathless for more. She heard the gallery door open and realized their moment alone had come to an end. Before turning to welcome his guest, Max added, "If I don't see you much during the evening, it might be I'm being monopolized by the mayor. He got an e-mail today from this campaign manager named Charlie something-or-other who wants his candidate to make a big announcement here tonight. Tax or railroad commissioner or something. I said sure, no problem."

Just like Max to be so laid-back, so generous. Even after everything he'd been through, himself. "Knock 'em dead, Miller. I'll be fine," she said.

* * *

The room seemed to fill faster than the town swimming pool on opening day. Guests trickled in at first, then poured in and flowed around the exhibits in a steady stream, stopping long enough to shake the host's hand, then accumulating at the bar. That was it, Dee thought. The availability of liquor by the drink, a recent development in Claxton, surely made art events like this a more popular draw than she'd ever remembered in her small hometown. Of course she had to give Max and his reputation full credit for attracting a crowd. But folks seemed to be sticking around and really having a good time, and for that she credited the wine and beer.

Dee pushed through the crush of schoolteachers and cowboy poets, women's-clubbers and plein-air artists, farmers and shop-keepers and oilmen and lawyers and bankers pressing inside, to the makeshift bar of opened wine bottles and two-liter sodas. She filled a clear plastic cup halfway with Chardonnay and scanned the crowd for her host and date and pretended to be listening to the Claxton Community College jazz quartet's uneven strains of "Don't Get Around Much Anymore."

The first familiar face to greet her, however, was her cousin Ruby Lee Bargeron, well-endowed proprietor of Ruby Lee's Treasure Chest in neighboring Poplar Grove. "Hey, there, P-h Dee," Ruby Lee gushed, holding her champagne flute out of range as she gave Dee a warm one-arm hug. "How are things out at the home place? And how's Auntie Alice?"

"Quiet for the moment! And Mama's been improving, but she's all in a tither until this wedding business is over and done with."

"Well, I for one am looking forward to it. You know how I love a big party! And speaking of, I'm doing some recruiting tonight for the Red Hat Society Fall Style Show. You still have our date on the calendar for October, right?"

"Yep, sure thing."

"Any chance I could get you back on stage again?"

"When hell freezes over," Dee shouted over the chatter to make her sentiment unmistakable. The whole reason she'd agreed to hold the event at the farm in the first place was that serving as host was the surest way she could think of to avoid getting roped into any other role.

She and Ruby Lee shared a laugh over that memory. "Well, I'm gonna go over here and say hi to Margaret Strickland, kiddo," said Ruby Lee. "I'll see you in Dallas on Sunday!"

She had to hand it to Max for his way of making the unlikeliest of alliances work. She noted the tattooed hipsters making small talk with the Chamber of Commerce manager in front of a Max Miller original, the close-up of a giant propeller blade on a truck. Next to them were Jane from Jesse Jane's Roadhouse and a woman Dee assumed to be her partner but hadn't yet met. Jane waved to Dee across the gallery, but Dee, unable to thread through the masses, just waved back apologetically. Also among the crowd were several of the members of the Write Stuff writing group—his unabashed Max Miller groupies ever since he had wowed them with a session on how to use images with their writing.

"Introduce me," said a male voice from over Dee's shoulder.

She turned to face a blond-haired guy who looked to be her age, maybe a little younger, bottle of Lone Star in hand. She was at a loss, though he looked a little familiar. "I'm sorry . . . "

"No, my bad." He pointed to himself slightly with the beer bottle. "Hank Hardeberger. New at Claxton High. Biology. I was interested—I, um, came out to your place with the writing group when they put up your sign this summer."

"Oh, right!" Dee said, recalling that Cynthia, the librarian and group organizer, had fielded several inquiries after running a notice in the library newsletter. The writers' group was scheduled to resume its weekly gatherings next week.

"So, I see some of your writer friends are here tonight," said Hank. "Not to mention the Man of the Hour, your beau there."

"Oh, my beau? Oh, yes, well, I—"

"I'm a writer too. Creative nonfiction, I guess you'd call it. Nature writing. I'd be keen to meet the locals." Hank flashed her an earnest smile.

"Well by all means come do that!" Dee cocked her head to motion him over though a gap that had opened in the crowd. "I take it that means you're not one of them. Locals, that is."

"Austin. Just finished my master's, needed a job. Claxton made it worth my while."

Dee steered him to where Summer Jones hung with the hip crowd, looking eager to shed her identity as manager of the Subway restaurant for an evening. Dee had also spotted JoAnn, J. D., and Cynthia earlier but had lost track of them now. "Hey, Summer, how's it going?"

"Oh, hi, Dr. Dee!" Summer giggled, maybe the effect of the beer. "Just great—I've been cranking out the chapters, how 'bout you?"

Dee raised her eyes skyward with a wry grin, dodging the question. "Busy settling in. And speaking of settling in, did you get a chance to meet Hank, who's new to the high-school faculty?"

Summer gave Hank's hand a hearty shake. "Welcome! I think we spoke at Dee's gate-raising out at the farm. Are you going to join the Write Stuff?"

"I hope so."

"What do you write?"

"Nature, outdoors, that sort of thing," he replied. "My undergraduate degree's in education, but I went for science in grad school. I've published a few essays."

"Cool! We'll start meeting again Tuesday night at the public library. Our group is small but fun. And diverse, I guess you could say. We're all ages, all genres."

As if on cue a Latina woman, short and squarely built, clad in black T-shirt, jeans, and boots, appeared behind the group, tentatively edging her way in until Summer took notice.

"Teresa! You made it!" said Summer.

"Teresa—hi," said Dee. "I didn't know you'd be here!" It hadn't even occurred to her that Mama's home health aide—a dedicated young writer struggling to find her voice—would have come to the gallery opening. She chided herself for not thinking to invite Teresa, but was glad to see Summer apparently taking her under her wing.

"I wanted to come see Max's pictures," Teresa said so softly Dee could hardly make out her words in the din.

"Well, I'm glad you did," said Dee, leaning close for Teresa to hear. "If it wasn't for you there might not have been any book to launch tonight." That seemed to please the shy twenty-year-old immensely. "I could never have taken the time away from caring for Mama to help Max out."

"Can I tell you something, Dee?" Teresa said out of earshot of the others.

"What's up?"

"I think you might have some trouble with your mother tomorrow," she said.

Dee sighed. "What else is new?"

"You know how she is always going on about her therapy."

Dee nodded.

"Well, she really been having a hard time getting up and down from chairs and — and — "

"Go ahead and say it. The toilet."

"Yes, the toilet. She's struggling almost as much as she did when she had the casts on her wrists. And she doesn't want anybody to know it."

Dee digested this bit of information. It made sense that her mother had been hiding the extent of her infirmity. Things had been too smooth, too easy.

"So Dee, I get a little idea — I get kind of a hunch she gonna try to stay home and not go to this wedding."

Dee blew air out between her teeth. "Okay . . . well, I surely do appreciate your telling me." She mulled over the possibilities in her mind. If Mama refused to travel to Dallas for Madison's wedding, it wouldn't be the end of the world, but it might come close.

"I think your sister would not be happy about this." Teresa hit the nail on the head.

"I'll see what I can figure out," Dee answered, wondering if she shouldn't drop everything and go on over to her mother's place this very second, get to the bottom of things.

"Where have you been hiding?" she heard Max say to her, and turned to find him readying to introduce her to the mayor of Claxton. "Sid Shelton, Dee Bennett," he said. "Claxton native and writer par excellence. Back to make Caprock County home again."

But before Dee could answer, before she could even muster a hello, the mayor glanced over her head. "Excuse me, Max, I think that's Charley Hensley with Rowdy McCorrigan's campaign. It's so nice of you to let McCorrigan say a few words. Be right back."

The mayor brushed past her. Max shrugged and said under his breath, "Guess he's not running for reelection."

"Pity," she replied. "With all that charm he'd be a shoo-in."

Max smiled and moved closer to her, placing a hand on her shoulder blade. He searched into her eyes and mouthed, "You know I'm glad you're here."

She forced a smile, unable to push Teresa's concerns from her mind. "Hey, it's the hottest ticket in Claxton tonight," Dee said, wiping the bead of perspiration from her nose and preparing to drain the rest of her Chardonnay, when the mayor backed into her, jolting her elbow and spilling the wine down the front of her dress.

Hizzoner, clueless, pivoted and said, "Max, I want you to meet Charley Hensley." A tall, sleek, red-haired woman, resplendent in flawless silk blouse and red leather skirt, took a step toward Max and offered her hand. Her nails, fire-engine red, were perfect.

Charley? All thought of her mother's woes fled from Dee's mind. Ms. Broken Nail. *That* was the Charley who'd hijacked Max's gala for political purposes? A tendril of distaste sprouted immediately in Dee's mind like a weed.

Close on Hensley's heels—*four-inch* heels, Dee estimated—was an equally imposing figure who turned heads in the room with his familiar six-foot-five frame and hero's wave. Ronald "Rowdy" McCorrigan had last spent time in Claxton when quarterbacking the 1977–78 Cougars to the state championship. Dee, though she hardly claimed to follow Texas's cult of football, knew a little of his history from her brother, Buddy. As a junior, McCorrigan had been recruited by every Division I college in the country before loyally signing with the University of Texas Longhorns. As a tea-sipper, he set school records, was nominated for a Heisman, and brought home a Cotton Bowl trophy. Then, drafted by the Houston Oilers, McCorrigan did not find pro ball to be kind to him, and he was jinxed by one injury after another before retiring in the mid-nineties. He stayed in the Space City long enough to make a wealth of connections in the oil and gas and real estate industries and had spent the past decade as a lobbyist in Austin. Recalling the earlier portraits of McCorrigan's handsome mug that had made the papers from time to time, Dee considered that the man's receding hairline and furrowed brow had rendered him less like a god but more like a statesman. He still commanded attention.

Dee recalled that he'd thrown his hat in the ring for a seat on the Texas Railroad Commission this year—an elected body that had nothing to do with trains and everything to do with the energy industry. But what was he doing in Caprock County? she wondered. There surely couldn't be enough votes at stake to stump here.

Claxtonites crowded around McCorrigan to shake his hand, cadge an autograph, and try to squeeze in a remembrance, but Hensley was as formidable as a backside guard leading the wing on a sweep, ushering the candidate to an improvised clearing that became a de facto dais for Max, the mayor, McCorrigan, and herself. Dee found herself suddenly sidelined at the back of the jazz band, behind the upright bass player.

"May I have your attention please?" Mayor Shelton said. He repeated the question in a louder voice to quiet the crowd. Someone tapped a glass with a fork. "Thank you," he said when everyone was silent.

"First, I just want to thank Max Miller for sharing this special night with all of us," he began. Everyone applauded. A few of the cowboy poets whistled. "I appreciatecha coming out for such a *warm* reception this evening." Chuckles.

The mayor put on a pair of reading glasses and pulled out a piece of paper. "For ten years, Earl Maxwell Miller has been a part of this community, photographing everything from reunions to ribbon cuttings, weddings to windmills," he said. "More recently, his studio and gallery have been an important part of our downtown revitalization. And he's produced this beautiful new coffee-table book"—he held up a copy—"that shines the spotlight on our growing wind industry. So, on behalf of all the proud citizens of Claxton, I'd like to say thank you, and keep up the good work!"

The crowd clapped again as the mayor gripped Max's forearm in a hearty handshake. Max waved but seemed to shrink from the praise. Who could blame him, thought Dee—he was about to have his thunder stolen, big time.

"There's another fellow here tonight . . ." Shelton glanced over at McCorrigan, who did not seem to resist being singled out. A murmur went up from the crowd, and there was a scatter of applause.

"He's asked to say a few words, and can't stay for long," the mayor continued, "because as you know he's running for office, and he has another appearance later this evening. You all know him as a high school, college, and professional football star. But he's also a family man, a Little League coach, a husband, and a deacon in his church. It is my great pleasure to introduce to you the next railroad commissioner for the State of Texas—Rowdy McCorrigan!"

The candidate waved. Cameras snapped and flashed. From the direction of the door two members of a television crew pressed forward, mic and shoulder-mounted videocam in the vanguard as McCorrigan offered his matinee idol's perfect smile. A chant of *Row-dee! Row-dee!* began in the back and gained momentum, until the candidate motioned for quiet.

"Thank y'all for coming," McCorrigan said. "And congratulations to Max Miller for a wonderful show opening tonight. This studio and gallery are such an asset to downtown Claxton."

He paused to allow the room to settle down. "It's not easy for a small business to be successful these days . . . with all of the Washington regulations . . ." A few catcalls filtered from the attendees. McCorrigan laughed and said, "I hear you. Texans are tired. Too many taxes, too much bureaucracy, too much government." Some of the cowboy types whooped.

"Too much dependence on foreign oil," he continued, louder. "You and I know that there's plenty of oil right here in West Texas, if Washington will just get out of the way with all of this unnecessary red tape—I'm sorry, but we can't hold up energy independence over something like the mating sanctuary of the lesser prairie chicken." He elongated his words in sarcasm, and several in the audience laughed. Dee happened to catch the expression on Hank Hardeberger's face. He did not appear amused.

"But, we're not going to let that happen, are we?" he said. "With your help and prayers, we will stop the folks from Austin from acting like they're in Washington. In fact, that's why I'm here tonight. I have a very special announcement."

A murmur rippled through the crowd.

McCorrigan ratcheted up his volume. "I will be running my fall campaign from right here in Claxton. West Texas values are what made this state great, Claxton and Caprock County are what inspired me to serve our state, and I am proud to host my statewide campaign from Claxton, Texas."

Dee wondered why he hadn't run his primary campaign from Claxton too. Perhaps spring values were different from fall values, she thought. But she had to admit little understanding of the machinations of campaigns. Politics was something she was very glad she'd never had any dealings with.

"And with your help, and God's grace—" McCorrigan was almost yelling now— "we will prevail in November. Thank you! And God bless you, and God bless *Texas!*"

The crowd broke out in applause and whistles, and Charley Hensley steered McCorrigan and the mayor toward the door as the two men shook hands along the way. Dee finally made her way around the bass player to stand beside Max just as the campaign manager looked back over her shoulder and said, "Max, hon, I'll meet you in the morning, about nine. Thanks for everything."

"You bet," Max said, and waved.

When no one remained within earshot, Dee asked, "What was that about?"

"Sid asked me to show Charley around," Max said.

"The mayor wants you to show Charley around?" Dee parroted.

"Yes, she's looking for office space, and she doesn't know the town, and Sid asked if I could help, and I said, sure. No big deal. And hey, I'd love to have you come along."

She gave him a regretful look. "Wish I could, Max, *hon.* But you know where I have to be."

* * *

Dee, exhausted and her one glass of Chardonnay long worn off, slumped into her Subaru. By the time she'd snapped her seat belt and started the ignition, the guilt had sunk in. Abby was leaving Claxton tomorrow for her sophomore year at Smith College, and Dee had spent the past week completely focused on Max.

As she drove beneath the flashing traffic lights of an after-hours Claxton, the epiphany came to her, and she slapped the steering wheel in silent conversation. That was her reason for not asking Max to the wedding, and she shouldn't regret it. Her sole motive in moving back to Texas had been to master being a part of a family, to mend the fences she'd left in a burning heap two decades earlier. She hadn't even unpacked her boxes, though, before she'd relegated her only daughter to the back burner, passing her over for a man she barely knew.

Granted, Abby was a free spirit herself. In the days since she and the new boyfriend, Ian, had shown back up in Claxton, heading cross-country in a rattletrap van, she'd seemed more than happy to putter around the garden and kitchen, look in on her grandmother, bide her time till Labor Day. The kids had gone to Mama's tonight, in fact, keeping her company and cooking her dinner rather than coming to the show. But what if Dee *had* given Abby her undivided attention? How much closer might they have grown during their short time together?

Approaching the city limits, Dee relaxed her cross-examination and recriminations with herself. If Dee hadn't sacrificed her job and come to Claxton to live, Abby wouldn't even have been here to cook one of her famous stir-frys for her grandmother. Maybe that would be enough . . . maybe just by carrying on the tradition in this old farmstead no one else wanted, Dee would bring the family together. As she drove toward the top of the hill and the weathered, white wooden house, she felt a little like a lone pioneer on an isolated frontier, hoping someday other settlers would come.

Ian's gray van was parked out front, a sign they were back from town safely. Dee was relieved that their New Mexico purchase had gotten them this far, and hoped it would suffice for Dallas and points east. At least she wouldn't be getting up in the wee hours to take them to catch the Greyhound bus this time.

A floodlight had been rigged in the back of the house. Ian was up on a ladder doing something to the window, which stood about eight feet off the ground. He was attaching some kind of metal box. As Dee walked around toward the steps at the kitchen door, Abby came out on the raised porch and greeted her with "Surprise!"

Which was one word Dee never relished hearing from her daughter.

"It cools like a dream," Abby said to Ian as he descended from the ladder with the floodlight under his arm.

"What did you do?" Dee said.

"We found you an air conditioner on Craigslist," Abby said.

"Who's Craig?"

"Mm, not sure about that part," Abby said. "It's a free classified service. People just go online and list their stuff to sell. We bought this window unit for forty dollars from a guy in town."

"It's totally quiet and portable," Ian said. "We installed lots of these this summer in the pueblos around Albuquerque."

"Will it make the power bill go up?" Dee said.

"Hardly at all," Ian replied. "That was a concern on the reservations too, but these new energy-efficient units impact your utilities ten to fifteen dollars a month tops."

"That's not bad," Dee said.

"Plus, it's portable," he added, "if you decide to move it to another room."

Abby said, "The living room is already cooler. Y'all come on in."

"That old swamp cooler is pretty useless when the temperature hits a hundred," Dee admitted. "I'm sorry it's been so uncomfortable here all month. Ian, if you'd been able stick around till September, you'd see just how beautiful the weather on the plains can be. It's not always an oven."

"No big deal, Mom," Abby said. "I'm just glad that you let us do something to change things. Gramma Alice never would let anyone help her."

"I didn't exactly *let* you, but since it's a definite improvement, I appreciate the initiative."

"So, about Gramma Alice," Abby began. "She might be having second thoughts."

"About?"

"About traveling tomorrow. I got the feeling—we got the feeling—"

Dee picked up on the subtle signal that Abby was still trying to be respectful with family matters around Ian. "It's okay. Ian's heard plenty of your grandmother's hard-headed notions already." Ian nodded, untroubled, but said nothing. Dee liked this guy more every day.

Abby continued, "We got the feeling there might be a huge diva moment coming."

"When's she gonna blow?" Maybe August had gone by so uneventfully because Dee and Mama had each been absorbed in acclimating to new living situations. Mary Alice, always strong-minded and often crotchety, had been through a lot since Wilton Bennett died back in December, and leaving the home she'd occupied for more than half a century had to be a sobering reality. Dee tried to remember to cut her mother some slack.

"You just might get stood up by your wedding date," said Abby. "I think she's considering staying home tomorrow."

Did Mama have no idea what kind of disruption such a last-minute decision would cause? They'd discussed the options fully already, while there was still something they could have done to accommodate her. Mama could have gone to stay with Penny a week ago, rested up if she thought the full-day trip would be too hard on her. She could've asked Dr. Taylor for a stronger prescription. Or Madison could've at least had some advance notice that her only surviving grandparent wouldn't be able to attend her wedding, and Dee could also have made arrangements for Teresa to stay over the holiday weekend. But no, Mama had had her heart set on going, and that was that. Now, wouldn't it be just like her to back out at the last minute because the occasion wasn't about *her*? Dee wasn't going to have Mama ruin Maddy's big day. Penny would be hard enough to deal with. But not Mama too. "Thanks for the warning," she said.

"Is there anything Ian and I can do? Do you think Gramma Alice would ride with us?"

Dee considered the van's seventy-at-seventy air and the quarter of a million miles on its engine. "It's okay. You all get an early start just like you'd planned, and I'll deal with Gramma Alice."

"Okay, if you're sure."

"We'll work it out." In her mind, though, Dee *wasn't* so sure. She probably wouldn't sleep well tonight for fretting about it. "Now, is there anything you need?" she asked Abby as she reached for her purse.

"We're really okay for cash, Mom. But there are a couple of little favors—since you asked."

Uh-oh, Dee thought. Always the other shoe.

"Will you pick up my bridesmaid's dress at the alterations shop? They didn't have it quite finished, and they don't open till ten."

"No problem," Dee said. There, that hadn't been difficult. And she was quite pleased that Abby had shed her weight gain to the point that, a month after the dress had been delivered and fitted, when she'd tried it on yesterday, it needed taking in.

"And . . ." Abby hesitated. "My new apartment doesn't take cats. Can you keep Cori until we figure out something else?"

That request wasn't too hard either. She'd halfway expected it. "Sure," Dee said. "I can use the company around here."

"Looks to me like you have plenty of company with Mr. Max Miller," Abby said with a sly grin.

Abby's remark caught Dee off guard, so she offered up a stock answer. "Now that we're through collaborating on his book, that situation will probably change."

"Seems like you've been collaborating on a lot more than the book already," Abby said.

Dee kicked off her sandals and put up her feet, regaining some perspective regarding Max. "Summer's over," Dee said. "Time for me to get serious about the next chapter in my life. I have a lot of work to do around here, and I need to find a job."

"Maybe your friend Cynthia at the library can hook you up," Abby said. "She seems pretty hard-wired around here. By the way, how was the show?"

"Jam-packed with people—a great success," Dee said. She omitted mention of the redheaded stranger and her candidate.

"So I just have one question," Abby said, abruptly changing the subject. "Why isn't Max going with you to the wedding?"

Dee was taken aback, but not for long. "I didn't ask him to."

"Why not?" Abby said, sinking into the leather couch next to her mother as Ian waved good night and headed down the hallway to Buddy's old room, which now doubled as Dee's home office too.

"Weddings are about family," Dee said. "I need to be available to help Mama and Penny. And you." She reached an arm around her only child and hugged her close.

"You better save some of that help for tomorrow," Abby said. "I'll be fine. But you're going to have your hands full with Gramma Alice," she added before yawning, stretching, and turning in, leaving Dee to her thoughts. Which went something like, *Let the games begin.*

3
Something Borrowed, Something Blue

The most lavish trousseau imaginable for the daughter of the very rich might be supposed to comprise:

House Linen

One to six dozen finest quality embroidered or otherwise "trimmed" linen sheets with large embroidered monogram.

One to six dozen finest quality linen sheets, plain hemstitched, large monogram.

One to six dozen finest quality linen under-sheets, narrow hem and small monogram.

Two pillow cases and also one "little" pillow case (for small down pillow) to match each upper sheet. . . .

Two to ten dozen finest quality, extra large, face towels, with Venetian needlework or heavy hand-made lace insertion (or else embroidered at each end), and embroidered monogram.

Five to ten dozen finest quality hemstitched and monogrammed but otherwise plain, towels.

Five to ten dozen little hand towels to match the large ones.

One to two dozen very large bath towels, with embroidered monogram, either white or in color to match the border of towels.

Two to four dozen smaller towels to match.

One tablecloth, six or eight yards long, of finest but untrimmed damask with embroidered monogram on each side, or four corners. Three dozen dinner napkins to match. (Lace inserted and richly embroidered tablecloths of formal dinner size are not in the best taste.)

One tablecloth five to six yards long with two dozen dinner napkins to match. . . .

In addition to the above, there are two to four dozen servants'
sheets and pillow cases (cotton); six to twelve woolen blankets, six
to twelve wool filled quilts, four to six dozen towels, and one or
two dozen bath towels; six to twelve white damask (cotton or linen
and cotton mixed) tablecloths and six to twelve dozen napkins, all
marked with machine embroidery.

Two to six dozen kitchen and pantry towels and dishcloths complete the list.

— "The Trousseau"

SHORTLY AFTER FIVE Dee heard footsteps and the creak of
linoleum in the kitchen. Soon she smelled coffee brewing and threw
on her robe.

"Sorry," Ian said as she wandered into the kitchen, bleary-eyed, a
frayed beige towel around his shoulders. "I hope I didn't wake you."
His short blonde Afro was still wet from the shower, and he smelled
of a fresh mixture of Zest and peppermint.

Dee shook her head and waved away his concern.

"I'm supposed to get Abby up at sunrise," he said, pointing
toward the bedroom down the hall, from which Dee could hear
gentle snoring. He had folded his own bed linens neatly on the
couch beside his backpack.

"Sit," Dee said, motioning to the chairs around the kitchen table.
"You and I haven't had much of a chance to talk, just the two of
us. When you and Abby came through here in June on your way
to Albuquerque, you pretty much worked the whole time, just like
you have this month. I don't think I said thank you enough, for all
of the help."

"You're welcome," he said, "I enjoy it. I mean, I like working with
my hands when I can use something I've learned academically and
apply it practically. Make sense?"

"Yep," Dee said. "I need to learn to do the same thing." She rum-
maged around the cabinets and found a box of Pop-Tarts. "Hungry?"

He shook his head.

She poured herself a cup of coffee and brought her breakfast to the table. "Can I ask you something?"

He nodded, now looking perplexed.

"Abby's going to move in with you when you go back to Massachusetts. That's why she can't take the cat, right? *Your* land-lord doesn't take cats?"

His mouth dropped open and then shut, then he quietly said, "Yes."

Dee put a reassuring hand on his. "It's okay. Despite the impression I might give otherwise, I'm not clueless."

He smiled and then furrowed his brow in seriousness. "When Abby goes back to Smith this fall, she'll need to concentrate on classes, and not try to hold down a job, except maybe part-time. Sharing expenses will enable her to do that."

"If you played any role in persuading her to go back to school," Dee said, keeping her voice low, "I am truly grateful."

He nodded. "I think this year will be a stable one for us, with my externship at the Green Energy Council in Needham, and Abby's classes."

Dee nodded. "Please don't say anything to Abby. I really want her to tell me about all of this on her own terms."

"Sure," he said. "You have my word."

"About what?" Abby said, entering the kitchen with her own backpack. Abby was fully dressed. Dee guessed she hadn't been the only one keyed up about the events ahead of them.

"That Ian will keep an eye on you," Dee said, rising and casually putting an arm around her daughter.

"Good luck with that," Abby said, slipping out of Dee's grasp and heading to the coffee pot. "Time to head 'em up and move 'em out, pardner," she said to Ian, making a lasso motion with one hand and extracting a travel mug from the side pocket of her pack with the other. "I'm taking my coffee to go."

"I'm packed," Ian replied, saluting. "Wagon's ready to roll."

Dee hugged Ian as he rose to join Abby. "Be safe," she said, "and we'll touch base when we get to the hotel tonight."

"We're good. See you there."

*   *   *

Teresa's pursed lips told Dee all she needed to know.

That, and Mama still in her flower-print duster and house slippers, silver hair uncombed, when Dee arrived at nine.

Mary Alice Bennett was lodged firmly in her recliner, a pile of tennis balls and bungee cords at her feet, pretending to watch *The Price Is Right.*

"What's going on?" Dee said, picking up the remote and turning off the TV.

"I was watching that," Mama snapped, without looking at her.

Dee sat down next to Mama in the other matching brown corduroy recliner, pointedly looked at her watch, and said gently, "I thought you had an appointment at the beauty shop right about now. We need to be on the road in about an hour so we can take it easy traveling today." They'd thought of that when they made their plans—if Mama had any difficulty remaining comfortable for a day-long drive, they could always stay over in Mineral Wells or Weatherford and still make it in time for the rehearsal dinner Saturday evening.

Mama picked up the *Baptist Standard* and pretended to read the paper, answering, "I don't need no appointment. I'm not going nowhere."

Teresa shook her head and rolled her eyes, continuing to fold towels on the sofa.

"Mama, what's up? You aren't feeling well?" asked Dee.

"My wrists and arms have been bothering me something fierce since we started that dang twicet-a-day *thurapy*," she said, glaring in Teresa's direction.

"I'm really sorry about that . . . I know it hurts. I remember Dr. Lee said the pain might keep flaring up for a while till you get your muscle tone back."

Mama cut short Dee's bid to commiserate. "Besides, the Sabbath's supposed to be holy. It's bad form to get married on a Sunday. Bad etiquette."

Wow, that was a bolt out of the blue, Dee thought. Since when had *etiquette* mattered to Mary Alice Bennett, the most plain-spoken woman in Caprock County? "Well . . . Madison went to great lengths nearly a year ago to pick the only date that would work for everyone's schedule—including her Uncle Buddy's football games," Dee reminded Mama.

"If they didn't have to invite three hundred people they coulda made it work," Mama pouted. "But I guess the groom's family just didn't think that was good enough for Dallas so-ci-e-ty."

Now Dee thought she was getting closer to the truth. She was pretty sure that somewhere in the tangle of Mama's recalcitrance, ego played as much a role as physical discomfort.

"And I'm for darn sure not going to any wedding stag," Mama continued, her chin jutting out.

"I am," Dee said, cajoling. "I was hoping you'd be my date."

Mama turned to Dee. "I figured you'd take Max Miller," Mama said.

"No," Dee answered. "That's not the plan."

"Is he out of town on business?" Mama asked.

"No."

"Did y'all have a fight?"

"No."

"Then what's goin' on? Did you do something to scare him off?"

"Mama, I've known the man for two months," Dee said. "I'm just not sure I'm ready to include him in important family events."

Mama seemed to consider that premise. "Dee Anna, you might be smart to take it slow. I know you never did date much, and you're pretty inexperienced with men. As evidenced by your ex. The Jew from Jersey."

Oh, here we go again, Dee thought. Just when she was sure they'd put her failed marriage—and her mother's bigotry—behind them. "Which gave us Abby," Dee reminded her. "Who as we speak is halfway to Dallas to be part of the biggest wedding spectacle you're ever likely to witness in this family. You don't really want to miss that, do you?"

Mama seemed to take that into consideration, too, as they heard the grandfather clock in the hall strike the hour. "Shoot," she said.

"What?"

"Now, I guess I've done missed my appointment with Nancy," Mama said. "She's always booked solid on Fridays."

Teresa reappeared, having finished her few housekeeping duties. "I have a friend who will come to your house and do your hair, Miz Bennett. I'll call right now."

"I'll pack your suitcase," Dee said.

"I'll get your dress," Teresa added.

"This doesn't mean that I have said yes to going," Mama said, as the other two scurried about. "But I do need to get my hair done."

*   *   *

Crisis averted, Dee hoped. If Mama's shampoo-and-set worked out quickly, and Dee could finish up her own few errands and gas up Mama's car, they could still make it to the outskirts of the Metroplex, though rush-hour traffic on the Fort Worth side would likely prevent them from going any further for the night.

First, she had a blog post to submit, the piece that would run this weekend while she was away. She'd finished it yesterday morning, but given the success of Max's opening night and the big last-minute local developments, she needed to punch it up. Maybe even scrap it altogether, start with something new. Dee was good at meeting deadlines—she'd had long experience with magazine features and travel pieces—but she'd never had to deal with the twenty-four-hour news cycle of a daily newspaper, much less the real-time demands of the Internet. She wondered if she could pull it off in time.

Dee sped around the corner in Mary Alice's big Ford sedan toward downtown, where the Claxton Public Library occupied half a city block on a side street. There were few vehicles in the lot on a Friday morning during school hours. She parked at the curb, pulling her VIP parking placard from her purse and laying it on the dash. She ran up the steps with her laptop, half-waved in the direction of Gladys the circulation clerk, and settled into a quiet corner to take advantage of the library's Wi-Fi. She knew her login and password by heart, by now.

Within an hour she'd pounded out a serviceable post of 350 words and was checking over her spelling when Cynthia Philpott came her way, wheeling the reshelving cart.

Dee glanced up. "Hey, boss lady, they make you do the scut work these days? Or is it like P.T.—you have to stay in regular shape with the Dewey Decimal System?"

"We're always short-handed in the summers," Cynthia answered, pausing momentarily in her rounds. "We'll have some high school students in the afternoons again after Labor Day. What are you working on?"

"My blog for the *Courier.*"

"Really? I'm so glad the library is making that possible!"

"Yep," Dee said. "Then I have to chauffeur M. Alice to Dallas. Big wedding weekend, remember?"

"Oh, right. Say, I have some scoop for you," Cynthia said, pulling up a chair. "But it's off the record."

"Cynthia," she said. "I'm a blogger, not a reporter."

"Promise it's off the record."

"Okay," Dee said, elongating the "ay" to indicate how absurd she thought it all was.

"In my role as head librarian, people tell me things," Cynthia began. "I don't know why, but they just do. They come in and say, 'Mrs. Philpott, have you heard the 4-1-1 on who drop-kicked who?' They say who. I remind them it should be whom."

"Okay," Dee said, baffled as to where this revelation was going.

"Well," Cynthia said, inhaling deeply and lowering her voice. "You know how Rowdy McCorrigan said last night he was moving his campaign here to get away from Austin-type liberal values?"

"Yes," Dee said, still proofreading.

Cynthia scanned the narrow aisles between shelves for eavesdroppers. "I have it from a reliable source that there might be more to it than that."

"Oh?" Dee said. She tried to think of something more to say while remaining noncommittal. She truly wasn't interested in unconfirmed scuttlebutt about some politician. Any politician. "Claxton's the last place anyone could keep a secret."

"I'm just telling you what I heard." Cynthia stood and returned to her cart.

"Thanks, really," Dee said. "And speaking of hearing things, if you should learn of anything suitable, I am looking for a job. I'm not sure what. But short of Lot-a-Burger, I won't rule anything out."

"I'll bet you can teach courses at the community college," Cynthia said.

"Possibly," Dee said, "but positions are already filled for the fall, and I'm not sure I'm ready to jump right back into academe anyway. I'd kind of like to do something new and different. And more lucrative than teaching adjunct."

"I hear you," Cynthia said. "The city hasn't given us raises in three years. Okay, gal, I'll keep my ear to the ground, and let you know if I hear anything. Are you coming to the writers' meeting Tuesday night?"

Dee hadn't been certain about her future with the Write Stuff, but now she'd just asked a favor and felt obligated. "Sure. Six?"

"You got it."

Dee made the last fix to her blog, which focused on how rewarding it was to experience a gallery showing with world-class photographs *and* legal alcohol in her hometown, not to mention a national sports celebrity relocating his campaign headquarters there. *Rowdy McCorrigan makes his first touchdown in Claxton, Texas, in thirty years—and it's a big one,* she'd written on the fly. It was the kind of present-tense puff piece she could have never gotten away with in her former academic life, which was one reason she was beginning to enjoy it. Blogging was freeing, and she sort of liked that. She might even be good at it. Who knew?

*   *   *

By twelve-thirty she'd washed and filled up the car, stopped by the ATM for cash, put ice in the small cooler with canned sodas and bottled water for her and Mama, and headed back to Mama's place. Teresa, who'd been scheduled only for two hours of housekeeping and therapy duties that morning, was gone.

"Mama, I'm back—let's see your hairdo!" Dee called out.

No answer.

"Mama?" Dee peeked into the kitchen, then the bathroom. She found her mother, finally, in her cool, quiet bedroom, where the blinds were drawn and the lights were off. Mama was neatly dressed in slacks and blouse but stretched out on top of the bed covers, eyes closed, her head propped delicately on the pillow. "You sleeping?"

Mama sighed and said, "Dee, I just don't want to go. I've never been to anything like this without your father. It makes me blue just to think about it. Every wedding, every funeral, every birth, every baptism—we went to them all together."

Dee leaned forward and patted her mother's hand. "I know," she said. "But in times like this, I think you have to ask yourself, what would Daddy want you to do?"

"I still miss him," Mama said, her voice cracking.

"We all do," Dee said. She sat on the side of the bed and stared at the wall, listening to the hum of the air conditioner, a riding mower outside nearby, a train in the distance.

If Mama truly couldn't bring herself to attend this wedding, Dee supposed she'd have to miss it too. She couldn't go traipsing off to Dallas and leave her mother alone for four days. Not in this state of mind. The least she could do would be to keep her company. Maybe there'd be some high-tech way of sending them video of the event. She'd heard of such things. She even wondered, for a fleeting moment, if there was any way to reschedule the wedding in Claxton—out at the farm?—but she quickly grasped the impossibility of that notion.

Dee let her breath out like air from a deflating balloon. So much had changed in the years she'd been away. *Stayed* away. Could she make a go of it? Had she been naive to think she could jump right in, take on all of the challenges she'd fled to begin with? Well, too late now, you damn fool, she chided herself.

Too late. She jumped up. "Oh! Abby's dress!"

"Huh?" said Mama, still not raising her head.

"The shop closes at one today. Oh, crap." Dee ran for the door. Now that *would* be a disaster. How would she get the dress to the wedding now, if she and Mama didn't go? Crap, crap, *crap*.

As soon as her daughter's dress was in her possession, in the nick of time, she dialed Buddy's number. Maybe he'd have some helpful insights. When his mobile number went straight to voice mail, she tried his line at the school instead.

"Field house," answered a teenage voice.

"Can I speak to Coach Bennett?" Dee said.

"Coach's on the bus, ma'am," the boy said. "The varsity's on their way to Forsan."

Right . . . season opener for the Darrell Dust Devils. Whose head coach just happened to be the second winningest coach in Texas high school football history. Not by total games, of course, not yet—anybody would have a long way to go to catch up with the legendary Gordon Wood—but by career percentage. Sports could always put an interesting spin on statistics, Dee thought. Buddy Bennett was only a few wins from surpassing that mark. But he would likely have to rack up a perfect season to make it into the record books.

"Thank you," Dee said, and hung up and dialed Buddy's cell again. She left a message asking if he might be able to come through Claxton on his way tomorrow, though she was certain she'd rambled and was not sure she'd made sense. If only she'd gotten Abby to show her how to use the text feature on that danged iPhone, she'd have been able to include all the details in writing, striking the right tone without panicking anyone or—the one outcome worse than calling Penny right now—throwing Buddy off his game.

Defeated for the moment, Dee stomped back up the short, land-scaped walkway to her mother's place for the third time today. If she had to drive to Dallas and back herself tomorrow, she'd figure out something. For now, she shut the bolt of the front door behind her, stretched out on the couch, and fell into a deep sleep, waking that evening only to call Abby and make cold sandwiches for two glum Bennett women for dinner.

*　*　*

Mama's land line jangled at daybreak the next morning, the sound eluding Dee in unfamiliar surroundings. It stopped after a single ring, and she pulled the covers back over her head. Within minutes, though, another noise, closer by, startled her fully conscious. Her cell phone rang raucously with Buddy's ringtone that Abby had programmed into it—an instrumental version of the Notre Dame fight song. Not exactly soothing music for daybreak. She threw off the quilt, sat up from the bed in Mama's guest room, and swiped the device to answer. "Hello?"

"Good morning, Sunshine." It was Buddy's voice, annoyingly chipper, considering the circumstances.

"You must have won last night," Dee said.

"Twenty-eight to seven. Some game," he replied. "It's always crazy after an away game, too—getting the guys showered, dressed, and back on the bus."

"Great start, Coach. You'll be catching up to that record in no time at this rate."

"Plenty of chance to talk about that later. You got my texts with the details about this morning?"

"Texts?" Dee didn't want admit she hadn't yet figured out the whole text functionality on her new phone. "Right. I've got the dress ready. I guess we'll be seeing you before long?"

"In about twenty minutes. I called to make sure you and Mama are ready to go. I just talked to her."

"Ready? Oh, sure," Dee lied, pulling on a T-shirt while she switched the phone from one shoulder and then to the next. What had he said to get their mother to relent? "You talked her into it?"

"Check your texts . . . gotta run—" and with that the phone cut out.

Shoot, Dee thought. She sure didn't have the patience to figure out the text message thing right this minute. If there was even a shred of hope they could still make it to Dallas, she'd have to scramble. She zipped her jeans, knocked, and opened her mother's bedroom door.

There sat Mama on the edge of the bed, fully dressed, with her purse, a sweater, and a large white gift bag in her lap.

"Mama—I know we hadn't had a chance to discuss this, but Buddy just—"

"I know, I done talked to him."

"Well, hallelujah. Whatever did he say to make you change your mind?"

"He reminded me how the last family wedding I didn't attend turned out."

Dee felt her breath catch. There had been only one family wedding they could have meant. Hers.

Her cell phone rang again, Buddy's crazy ringtone. She answered but could hardly make out his words.

"Sorry for the noise. Can you hear me? I was trying to say, you and Mama get your suitcases and meet me at Winkler Field, seven a.m. sharp." She thought she'd understood him correctly. But what was all that about Winkler Field? Well, they'd know soon enough. Whatever he had in mind, it was better than spending Labor Day weekend moping around this crackerbox with a cranky seventy-four-year-old widow.

*   *   *

Dee and Mama said not another word to each other on the short ride out to Claxton's tiny municipal airport, but Dee's mind was racing the whole time. If Buddy had talked Mama into attending the wedding, why the detour? Why did they need to waste time meeting up with him? Maybe he planned to caravan with them the whole way.

Dee pulled the tan Crown Vic into the dirt driveway of the airport, which was really nothing more than an asphalt landing strip with a wind sock and a metal barn for a hangar. As they rounded the hangar, they both craned their necks around in awe at the sleek white private jet parked on the apron. Dee had seen plenty of crop dusters and other propeller craft out here, back when all the Bennett kids would ride their bikes down Claxton's country lanes and out to the airport for sport. Crop duster this was not.

The jet's dual engines powered down and the airport manager on duty walked out toward it. To Dee the aircraft's elegant lines looked like something out of a James Bond movie. From its stylishly perky nose to its upswept tail, it just looked like it should *star* in something. Its oval side windows reminded her of portrait frames in European museums.

The passenger door opened and an airstair magically unfolded from the jet's side. A heavy-set man in golf shirt, Bermudas, and loafers made his way down the steps, followed by the tall, lanky figure of Buddy Bennett, and greeted the airport manager. Dee registered the curiosity on Mama's face as Buddy and the plane's passenger came over to the car. Dee went to roll down the window on Mama's side, but instead the man opened her door, extended a hand that was obviously intended to help her out, and said, "Mitch Mitchell, Junior. At your service. And you must be Mary Alice Bennett, grandmother of the bride."

Mama was at a loss for words.

Buddy angled in as Mama stepped out onto the graveled parking spot. "Mama, I'm going to get your suitcases and things out of the back, and you go with Mitch here," he said. "Dee, roll that window back up and lock the car. We're riding in style."

Mama found her tongue. "Wilton Eugene Bennett, what on earth is going on? You didn't say nothing about no aer-o-plane. Begging your pardon, Mr. Mitchell."

"Well," said Buddy, "Mitch rode on the team bus with us last night, since his son was starting. When I told him it looked like I was going to have to skip the postgame celebration on account of our early departure for Dallas in the morning, he said he was going to be heading that way himself when we got back. I said I wouldn't put him to any trouble for any of us" — he indicated the plane where his own wife and sons were waving out the windows — "but it probably

A WEDDING AT THE PARAGRAPH RANCH   45

would make for a much more comfortable trip for my mother. And I didn't want you refusing."

"I said hell, Buddy, bring 'em all," Mitch Mitchell added. "Doesn't cost any different to fly eight than to fly one."

Mama nodded her head uncertainly. "I surely do appreciate your generosity, Mr. Mitchell. But I don't know about all this. Dee Anna and I are just fine ridin' in the automobile. We'll stop ever' hour or so to stretch our legs."

Buddy, ever the diplomat with his mother, said, "I understand, Mama. It's no problem. I can just get Abby's dress and we'll be on our way. We'll touch down in Dallas in about half an hour, have a leisurely breakfast, take a little dip in the pool, maybe go to the Zodiac Room at Neiman-Marcus for lunch. We'll meet up with y'all for dinner at what, five o'clock?"

Dee suppressed a smile.

"I been to the Zodiac Room once. Ain't all that," said Mama.

"Suit yourself, Mama," Buddy said, holding up his hands in resignation. "Let me just reach in there and get that dress—"

Mama glared at him. "Dee Anna, you get it. Don't keep the man waiting." And to Mitch Mitchell, "You flying this machine?"

"No, sweetheart, not me," he answered. "My pilot's one of the best in the business, twenty years with American before Mitchell Petroleum hired him away."

"Good," she said. "'Cause if this is going to be my first airplane flight ever, I most surely intend to get there in one piece."

4
The Big D

On leaving their table, the bridal party join the dancing which by
now has begun in the drawing-room where the wedding group
received. The bride and groom dance at first together, and then each
with bridesmaids or ushers or other guests. Sometimes they linger so
long that those who had intended staying for the "going away" grow
weary and leave—which is often exactly what the young couple
want! Unless they have to catch a train, they always stay until the
"crowd thins" before going to dress for their journey. At last the bride
signals to her bridesmaids and leaves the room. They all gather at
the foot of the stairs; about half way to the upper landing as she
goes up, she throws her bouquet, and they all try to catch it. The
one to whom it falls is supposed to be the next married. If she has
no bridesmaids, she sometimes collects a group of other young girls
and throws her bouquet to them.

—"Dancing at the Wedding"

"GULFSTREAM 150," Mitch Mitchell, Junior, explained once
everyone was buckled into their cushiony leather chairs. "Seats eight.
She'll travel nearly 3,000 miles at Mach .75 without refueling. We'll
touch down at Dallas Executive Airport in just under forty minutes."

Dee resisted asking pointed questions about Mitch's business,
but Mama didn't hold back. She didn't have to work hard. During
the brief flight from the time they took off over Caprock County's
crazy-quilt landscape of row crops, playa lakes, and rocky canyons and mesas until the plane's wheels glided across the tarmac

at RBD, they learned that his late father had been an old wild-catter who'd struck it big and had the wisdom to invest wisely. "Word was, my father didn't hesitate to bend the rules," he said with a wink. "But that's all ancient history now." These days the junior Mitchell was one of Darrell High School's most enthusias-tic boosters and didn't mind sharing his good fortune to provide what the team needed. Mama reminded him that her son wasn't one to accept favors, and Mitch acknowledged that Buddy Bennett had never allowed him to furnish anything for the athletic teams without insisting that he support an academic program at an equal level. Mama nodded approvingly.

"And by the way, Mrs. Bennett, I want you to be my guests in my condo this weekend, too," Mitch said. "I'm going out to the lake for some bass fishing, and I won't be needing it."

Mama started to protest, but Dee, whose seat faced hers, tapped her mother's foot under the polished laminate table they shared. They still had time to cancel that Holiday Inn.

*   *   *

If Dee had been wowed by their means of transport to the Big D, she really tried not to let the over-the-top trappings of the wedding weekend go to her head once they arrived. Around Max, she'd hedged about the plans, downplaying the full degree of ostentation and conspicuous display of material wealth she anticipated.

But now that she was here, with the biggest worries behind her, she sorely wished she'd invited him to join her. What a great time they could have had!

She kept such sentiments to herself as the chauffeur deliv-ered them all to Mitch Mitchell's lavishly appointed Arts District high-rise. "Make yourselves at home; enjoy the pool; and there's a restaurant right in the building that delivers, but James will also be on call to take you anywhere you'd like to go," Mitchell said. "And my pilot will be ready for your return Sunday evening." They thanked him in amazement as he left the key with Buddy.

"Can you just *believe* this?" Dee asked, taking in the view of the downtown skyline. "I keep expecting to look around and see J. R. and Bobby standing there."

"This is a lot better than any TV show," said Roxanne, laying a hand on Buddy's shoulder and striking an exaggerated Sue Ellen pose. "My husband moves in pretty influential circles, wouldn't you say?" she joked as the boys went over to check out the video game console.

"Speaking of influential circles," Dee said, "have you all heard the latest from Claxton?"

"Let's see . . . Man Bites Dog?" said Buddy.

"Well, I don't imagine it'll make CNN, but we did have a political candidate move his headquarters to town this week," Dee said. "You might know the name. Rowdy McCorrigan?"

"Huh," he said, nodding his head. "Didn't know he was in politics. But I sure remember him from the team. What's he running for, dogcatcher?"

Mama answered. "Railroad commissioner. I read it in the *Courier* yesterday afternoon," she said.

"Here it is in the *Dallas Morning News* today, too," said Roxanne, picking up the paper from Mitchell's coffee table.

"Well, that's real interesting," Buddy said. "I was a sophomore on the JV the year Rowdy led the Cougars to the state championship. That was a *wild* season." He shook his head.

"How so?" asked Dee, who had been too young to understand much about the game throughout her brother's football years.

"McCorrigan was always the golden boy—a kid from a tool pusher's family who showed promise as far back as Pop Warner days, and by the time he got to high school he was tapped for backup quarterback as a sophomore and started every game as a junior and senior. Won all but one of those. But he wouldn't have been nearly the success he was without his wide receiver senior year, a guy by the name of Ricky Jones. He was a class behind Rowdy and a year older than me. There was some crisis or something in Ricky's family right before the last regular season game—we never knew what—and when he didn't play, that's why I got put in, and played all the way through the postseason. I always wondered what happened to Ricky Jones. You see Rowdy again, tell him I said hi, and ask him if he ever stays in touch."

"I doubt I'll have the chance," Dee said. "But I'll keep it in mind."

Mama jumped in again. "I remember Ricky Jones. Your daddy and I watched him play in a lot of your games—whenever Wilton wasn't getting the crop in toward the end of a season. That colored boy could *run*."

Dee shot her mother a look.

"That African American young man, I mean," said Mama.

Roxanne stepped in to ask about orders for brunch. Pulling up the restaurant menu on her iPhone, she showed it to Mama and asked if she was hungry.

"Goodness," Mama said, peering at the small glass screen. "Is that how they make reservations in Dallas these days?"

"It's an app called Urban Spoon," her daughter-in-law explained. "You use it to choose a restaurant, make a reservation, even find the driving directions. It does everything but make the coffee!"

"My stars. Sure is different from back when I was in school, and I'd take the train from Claxton to Dallas in the summers, go shopping and have lunch at a little diner or lunch counter, then travel on to Mineola to visit my aunts in East Texas. They made like I was comin' from California, they thought it was so far. It was a long trip, and I didn't get to go but once a year," she said wistfully. "My father wasn't one to splurge."

They let Mama carry on about the olden days as each took turns selecting their meal and Roxanne called in their order.

Dee, not one to splurge either, nonetheless went all out for the grilled salmon and a bloody Mary. You only go around once, she told herself. Especially when you got to pretend like you were the Ewings for a day.

* * *

For the evening they dressed in what the invitation had described as "Cowboys casual" for the rehearsal and subsequent dinner. Dee had made her best guess what that meant and played it safe with her same black sundress—spicing it up with the boots and red straw Western hat she'd worn to her last social event, earlier that summer.

As the Bennetts arrived by limousine at the tony ranch estate where tomorrow's nuptials would take place, Penny, visibly relieved, greeted them at the front door in a chic peasant-style dress, her blonde hair perfect in a cool updo. Dee marveled that Penny looked hardly old enough to be the mother of the bride.

"Mama!" squealed Penny as the driver came around to open the door and Buddy helped their mother out. "I'm so glad you're here! And all of you!" Buddy gave his older sister a big hug. "And Dee!"

"Hey, Penny—well, it's quite the showplace for Maddy's big day," Dee said.

"Yes, yes. We were blessed. Come on inside, everyone's getting their seats!"

Dee sensed that Penny was thankful her troops had arrived to balance out those of the groom's family. Inside the enormous, barnlike hall of the estate's chapel, she counted four and a half pairs of bridesmaids and groomsmen, fresh-faced and preppy as though ready for a Greek social. Abby and her cousins Web and Whit, Buddy's boys, rounded out the ranks of attendants. Seated on the front row, poised to play their parts right up until their stand-ins practiced their vows for them, were Dee's twenty-four-year-old niece, Madison—the spitting image of her mother but with the same straight brown Bennett hair that Penny had also been born with—and her intended, Kyle, a handsome, affable-looking guy with a take-charge demeanor.

The wedding planner and the minister led the participants in mastering their roles in the time-honored drama, as the sun's rays dropped ever lower through the double-height windows. The rehearsal over, families began making overtures of acquainting themselves. But everyone was eager to resume festivities at the dinner location, arranged through connections of the groom at a site many Texans considered hallowed ground.

The Dallas Cowboys practice facility at Valley Ranch was open to the public from time to time for exclusive behind-the-scenes guided tours, but its field and meeting rooms, always off limits, remained in constant use during the season except for one time during the week: Saturday nights. Kyle, an assistant brand manager for the team, had arranged for the large observation room overlooking the fifty-yard-line to be decked out as a dining hall and buffet line for sixty. After introductions and toasts, back-office staffers showed groups around the enormous building and answered questions about the upcoming season.

"This is a pretty sweet gig you've got, Kyle," Buddy said to the groom as they looked down on the artificial turf. "How long have you been with the team?"

"Two years," Kyle answered. "I started here right after I graduated from SMU. That's where I met Maddy. We're hard-core Dallas—and hard-core Boys fans too!"

"Coolest party *ever*," said Buddy's son Web, older of the two. Whit, the younger, at fifteen, added, "Wonder if they'll have the Dallas Cowboys cheerleaders at his bachelor party?" Their mother, overhearing, elbowed them with dire warnings about the consequences of even thinking about sneaking out to any party.

As guests filled china plates at the elaborate spread, Mama occupied a prime seat at the head table and held court as grandmother of the bride, a role she was clearly relishing. Dee brought her mother and herself plates of miniature roast beef sandwiches, stuffed red potatoes, bacon-wrapped water chestnuts, crudités, and a variety of fruits and cheeses and pulled out a chair next to her. Buddy brought Mama a glass of tea and set his own plate on the other side of her. From across the table the groom's father, a big-shouldered man with a ruddy face, was getting to know Mama.

"What's it like livin' out there in rattlesnake country?" he asked jovially. "Or, as we used to call it when my boys would come out that way for the cattle sales, the Big Empty?"

Mama replied, "Most folks call it the Big Country, I imagine. But yes, we do have our share of snakes and cactus. And some mighty fine ranches, as you've mentioned."

"Too far from Cowboys Stadium for me, I'm afraid. And too far from the malls for my wife."

Kyle's mother, at his side, smiled sweetly. "Your daughter Penny and I have shared a few shopping expeditions and luncheons this summer, Mrs. Bennett. I think she'd agree!"

"I imagine you're right," said Mama. "I believe Penny and her brood are in their perfect habitat in Dallas. I'm just not cut out for all this *new*."

"You know, everybody says that about Dallas," the groom's father retorted. "That it's all about new business, new buildings, new money. But our family's been in these parts since before statehood. My great-grandfather settled on the Trinity back when there were still Indian raids, and he was one of the first ranchers to run cattle instead of hogs in North Texas."

"You don't say," Mama replied. "Both my mother's and father's people came from East Texas, but my grandfather considered the business opportunities better farther west."

Buddy tried to defuse the escalating one-upmanship. "As a resident of one of the smallest, driest towns in all of Texas, I personally propose that *anywhere* in the Lone Star State is worthy of a toast." He raised his wine glass, and Dee and the others followed suit. Dee watched the interactions with amusement.

Kyle's father seemed unable to accept the olive branch and let it go. "Now, on my mother's side, they were the ones with the real fortune. They arrived from St. Louis and invested in railroads. They—"

Mama cut him off. "That's nice. So did my mother's family—they just lost everthing in the Depression. But you know the thing I've always been proudest of for Maddy and Mindy is that they could sign up for the Daughters of the Republic of Texas anytime they wanted, thanks to my husband's ancestors. His grandfather could claim kin to both Sam Houston *and* William Barret Travis. Now, I ain't one to brag, but I always held that made Wilton Bennett something like Texas royalty, and your Kyle there is about to marry a princess."

Dee bit her lip and took another sip of wine. That moment alone had just made it worth all the hassle of getting here.

Her thoughts turned to her own wedding, when she and Jake had run off to the judge knowing Mama and Daddy wouldn't approve. His parents probably wouldn't have, either, but they were no longer living, and Jake joked that it was his decision now if he wanted to marry a shiksa from Texas. Though neither bride nor groom considered themselves religious, their different traditions certainly complicated matters.

Jake had been well on his way in his academic career—and Dee, as much as she was genuinely smitten with the handsome young assistant professor, had latched onto him as her ticket out of the Big Empty.

Although she had determined not to let Mr. and Mrs. Wilton Travis Bennett spoil the wedding of Dee Anna Bennett and Jacob Elias Kaufmann (as she'd pictured their names engraved, had the relations gone more smoothly) and didn't let anything slip to Mama about the elopement, she'd had to call someone. Only her big brother, Buddy, her staunch advisor and comforter, stood at her side when Dee and Jake were married in the judge's chambers of the McLennan County courthouse.

Dee, musing about football, faith, and family in the Lone Star State and wondering if they weren't all one and the same, heard Penny's voice around the corner. She looked over her shoulder to see her sister in a heated exchange with the wedding director.

"What do you mean, you can't find a backup on a holiday weekend?" Penny hissed under her breath.

The beleaguered woman pointed toward a padfolio in her hand, opening it and flipping over a sheet of paper. "I am so sorry—I'll keep trying. I just wanted you to see how many of my contacts I've been through already. I know you don't want to resort to picking a photographer out of the phone book, not for something as important as your daughter's wedding."

Dee excused herself from the table and approached to listen more closely.

"Damn straight I don't," said Penny. "Madison will die if her photos aren't perfect. Just how serious is your guy's case of strep, anyway?"

Dee inched around the corner.

The woman looked about ready to turn green herself. "I'm still on it—"

"Penny?" Dee interrupted smoothly, careful not to tip the balance. "Everything okay?"

Penny turned to Dee, who could detect an ever-so-slight trembling of her sister's lower lip. "The—the wedding photographer has called in sick," she said. She stuck out her chest and regained her poise. "But I'm sure we'll work something out." She turned to the wedding director again, her voice icy. "*Won't* we?"

Dee gave it about two seconds' thought, then casually let it drop. "I know a photographer," she said to Penny. "And so do you."

Penny snapped back around in her direction. "What? Who?"

"You remember Mama mentioning Max Miller from Claxton, right?" The spark in Penny's eyes showed that indeed, Mama had been talking. "You might have to pay his travel on top of his fee, but I just happen to know he's available." She hoped that was still true. Or that maybe she could ensure it would be.

"Dee, are you serious?" Penny's eyes lit up. "Give me his number!"

*   *   *

The Sunday afternoon ceremony came off without a hitch. That was, if you didn't count the ring bearer, Kyle's four-year-old nephew, stopping mid-march to wave at the groom's father and call out loudly, "Hi, Gand-dad!" The bride was beautiful and the bride's mother held up admirably, Dee thought. And Abby looked splendid in her navy silk dress, even if, as the shortest, she did occupy last place at the end of the row of attendants. She was glad the recession business was done—all they had to do was get through the home stretch.

Dee huddled closer in between Buddy and Mama on the back row, following Max's instructions to the group. "Now, on my cue, I want everyone to smile and say 'Tony Romo'!"

The entire clan, families now united, held their poses for several clicks of the camera. The attendants, on the front row, sparkled in their silver and navy, framing the traditionally attired bride and groom.

"Thanks—that's a wrap," Max said, and at that Penny promptly turned to face the wedding party and families.

"I just want to say." She faltered and began to choke up, put her hand over her heart. "I just want to say the biggest thank-you ever to my wonderful family. And especially to my little sister Dee Anna for coming to the rescue!" She reached up to hug Dee, then blew a kiss at Max. "Now, let's strike up the band and do some dancin'!"

* * *

Dee cornered Max for a brief respite during his last-minute assignment. "I think we're even on favors after this," she teased. "You are certainly no longer in my debt for your book."

"Nope, the scale's tipped the other way now, considering what your brother-in-law agreed to pay for my services and travel. I didn't mind—especially since it got me here with you, even if by the back stairs. Now I owe *you* again." The music started up for a slow tune, and he set the camera down on her table. "Repay you with a dance?"

She let herself be swept into his arms to the gentle waltz rhythm, feeling light and almost graceful as he led with ease. "I wish I'd invited you as my guest," she said. "I wasn't being coy—just overwhelmed, mostly."

"Well, let's see what we can do to ease your mind when we get back," he said, brushing her hair with his cheek. "And speaking of, your brother and sister set me up to fly back with you tonight on Mitch Mitchell's plane. I've got an assignment tomorrow in Claxton, and the puddle-jumper to Abilene wouldn't have gotten me home in time. Plus—it means more time with you."

"I'll look forward to that too, then," she said.

About that time the wedding director called for all the young single women to line up. Dee pointedly returned to her seat beside Ian and Mama as Max grabbed up his camera again. Bridesmaids of all heights gathered near the dais. Five-foot-two Abby, Dee observed, ended up near the back of the pack, but they all knew the bouquet would be intended for Maddy's younger sister Mindy, anyway, who had a longtime boyfriend set to finish up at West Point in the spring.

"One—two—three, here goes!" shouted the bride as she tossed the white-and-silver bouquet backward blindly over her shoulder. For an instant Mindy's outstretched arms looked destined to snag it without difficulty. But a short blur of motion made a last-minute bid for an interception, and Abby knocked the missile foul—right into the lap of her astonished mother, who looked as though it were a grenade that might explode.

"Good catch, Dee Anna," Mama stage-whispered, not softly enough. "Almost as good a catch as that photographer over there."

Dee reddened to the color of her glass of wine as she gamely smiled and held up the flowers to surprised applause. Between gritted teeth she managed to say, "Don't even think it, Mama. I'm about as ready for marriage as *you* are."

*   *   *

The Bennetts and Max made a merry party, flying home to West Texas at sunset after the festivities had ended and the newlyweds had been seen off in a shower of soap bubbles. Abby and Ian had remained in Dallas to spend the night at Penny's before resuming their eastbound travel the next day. It had been a superb wedding all around, and Dee was glad the drama was past them.

Even Mama had indulged in a glass of champagne, Dee recalled, and when her mother was dressed to the nines and let her defenses down, she appeared ten years younger. Or maybe it was just the effect of knowing she'd witnessed the first of the next generation suitably married.

As they touched down again on the bumpy runway of the Claxton field, Dee noticed an unexpected vehicle parked beside the hangar. Colonel Wendell Grover's ancient Hummer, the one he used on hunting trips and had driven out to the Bennett farm for the writers' group once.

The stairs of the plane lowered outward, and Buddy exited first to give everyone else room and help the women down. Wendell, deep in animated discussion with the airport manager, came over to inspect and admire the craft during the pilot's brief refueling stop.

"I heard y'all were coming in on this fancy bird," Wendell said to Dee. "Max wasn't sure how he was going to get back to Claxton when I drove him to the Abilene airport, but my friend here—" he indicated the airport manager— "kept me apprised. I don't mind giving you a ride back downtown, Max," he added.

Max turned to Dee. "I was hoping my date and I might go out for a bite of dinner while we're still dressed for a night on the town," he said, an appreciative look in his eye. "Although Sunday night in Claxton, that might mean barbecue or a hamburger."

"Why, that would be quite lovely, Mr. Miller," Dee said, glad he'd taken note of the coral viscose sheath and pashmina shawl that she'd thought offset her brunette ponytail particularly well. "But I do have to get my mother home before our coach turns into a pumpkin again."

Wendell suddenly came to his senses and said, "You know, Mrs. Bennett, I could give you a lift instead." He seemed also to take belated note of the pearls and elegant silver shantung dress and jacket Mama was wearing—a color that, if it had done little in combination with navy blue to flatter the bridesmaids, had worked miracles for Mama. "Well, if you were willing to ride in Matilda there, I could."

The pleading look Dee sent her mother's way must have registered.

"I'm sure if I can get myself up into the cab of a John Deere, I suppose I can manage that thang, Mr. Grover," Mama said, smiling. "Although you have to agree, after Mr. Mitchell's jet here, it shore is a comedown in the world."

5
A Day of Labor

It is the duty of the ushers to show all guests to their places. An usher offers his arm to each lady as she arrives, whether he knows her personally or not. If the vestibule is very crowded and several ladies are together, he sometimes gives his arm to the older and asks the others to follow. But this is not done unless the crowd is great and the time short.

If the usher thinks a guest belongs in front of the ribbons though she fails to present her card, he always asks at once "Have you a pew number?" If she has, he then shows her to her place. If she has none, he asks whether she prefers to sit on the bride's side or the groom's and gives her the best seat vacant in the unreserved part of the church. He generally makes a few polite remarks as he takes her up the aisle. Such as:

"I am so sorry you came late, all the good seats are taken further up." Or "Isn't it lucky they have such a beautiful day?" or "Too bad it is raining." Or, perhaps the lady is first in making a similar remark or two to him.

—"Seating the Guests"

DEE WOKE ON LABOR DAY morning more refreshed and energized than she'd expected to be, especially after the extra glass of wine she'd had with dinner last night. With all the stress and buildup of the wedding behind her, she opened her eyes at the first hint of daylight, crawled out of bed, stretched, and savored the day's lack of obligation. Max was busy today with a job, and she'd call in a little bit and see how Mama was feeling. But for now only Coriander the cat demanded anything of her. She went to the kitchen, made coffee, and fed the feline. "Little beggar," she said to the cat, reaching down to stroke its spine. "You miss Abby already? Ian too, you say? Well, so do I."

Heading to the front porch with a cup of coffee, she nearly stumbled over the row of unpacked boxes from North Carolina sitting on the hallway floor adjacent to the office she had created in Buddy's old bedroom. The UPS packages were lined up like players on the bench, waiting to be put into the game. The last of her books and files from her campus office, they'd remained there as long as Ian had been using the room. She hadn't really had a chance to establish her work space properly. Maybe today would be the day.

From the front porch's sweeping vista, Dee could make out all the activity of the rising summer day. It felt as though she had stepped into one of those children's books that showed the hills and farms in exaggerated perspective: over there on one slope, cows grazing contentedly beside a red barn, the farmer just now beginning to mow the hay with the tractor; down in the valley, a freight train winding snakelike across a river; and above the farthest rise the sun peeking over, a smile on its yellow face. She'd thought of her childhood home that way, like a storybook, and though it had never been an easy life it had had a certain predictability and rigor that had made her feel safe.

What she meant to make of it now, she wasn't certain. Being in charge—alone—was a very different challenge. Her mother hadn't wanted to abandon that role, the one imposed on her when she became a widow. But she'd discovered it was too much for her. Could Dee do any better?

It was high time to unpack her new life and find out, Dee thought. She dressed in shorts and long-sleeved shirt—just in case she had to deal with spiders—and reached for the hanging handle in the hallway that lowered the foldaway attic stairway. The mechanical hatch opened like that of a puddle-jumper on a tarmac. She unfolded the narrow stair all the way to the floor and stepped aboard.

The flimsy pine steps wobbled beneath her as she climbed into the dusty, cobweb-filled attic space. The light source for the room was a single bulb with a pull chain, which she was glad to see worked. Something scurried from the sudden light.

"Cori?" she called down, wondering if the cat would climb the stairs. That was too much to expect, apparently, so she went back down and carried her up. In an instant the cat's instincts kicked in. Cori crouched low to the floor near the corner, her tail waving slowly in anticipation of the hunt.

Some of the little-used books and files from her university life would have to be stored up here, she figured. There simply wasn't enough closet or shelf space on the main floor. In her childhood she'd been vaguely aware that the unfinished attic had stored stuff like out-of-season clothes, baby furniture, deteriorating quilts, who knew what else. Out of sight, out of mind. When Mama moved out Penny had taken it upon herself to sort the flotsam of their parents' fifty-five years of marriage. Dee hadn't even come up here.

The tower of her castle wasn't too bad, though, now that she looked at it. The steep roofline allowed plenty of headroom in a space considerably larger than the spare bedroom below her. Someone had made a start at finishing out the walls with sheetrock, and there was light and a wall electrical outlet. Granted, the drywall was chipped and cracked in some places, and pink insulation sagged in spots under the roof decking. But the dormer window, once she peeled back the musty muslin curtains, afforded a view that was even more remarkable than the one from the porch. Framing the rolling hills, cotton fields, canyons, and dry creek beds, it invited inspiration.

An idea crossed her mind. She backed down the stairs and dragged up a folding chair and then a portable work table, one Mama had used for picking out peas and the like while she watched TV. The setup made quite a comfortable writing desk, all things considered. She might even try writing today's blog upstairs.

Dee opened the window to air out the space, then hauled up the Hoover to take care of the cobwebs and dust. Soon her new room was looking promising. She'd need an electrician to run more outlets and lights, of course, and she'd need to have the drywall repaired and finished. She'd want to run an Internet connection. She wondered what all those improvements would cost. But it wasn't looking too bad. She was terrifically pleased with herself for stumbling onto her own creative haven.

She wondered what potential the rest of the old homestead might hold for her own statement, her own identity. It hadn't really occurred to her to change anything in what she still thought of as her mother's house. But why not?

For now, it was a start. As she sat to compose her blog on the laptop, gazing out over half of the county, she kept coming back to the concept. Even a rug and new curtains would make a difference, and that wouldn't break the bank. By midmorning the writing nook was pretty warm anyhow, even with the window open. She shut it and carried the laptop back down the staircase, leaving the stairs unfolded for Cori to come back down in her own time.

She was headed to the phone to call and see if Walmart was open on the holiday, when the phone rang as though she'd summoned it. "Hi, Dee, it's Shannon Thomas at the paper. Are you busy right now?"

"Not really," Dee replied. "I've just finished my second cup of coffee and tomorrow's piece. What's up?"

"I need a favor today," Shannon said. "I need someone to cover a late-breaking event, ASAP. I'd pay the going freelance rate plus mileage. I know you're only contracted for the blog, but you're an excellent writer, you know the community, and I think you can handle this."

Any new source of funds intrigued Dee, though when it came to hard news she hesitated to tackle an unfamiliar beat. "With the caveat that I have no real experience as a reporter—what did you have in mind?"

"Rowdy McCorrigan's campaign manager just called me at home to make sure we planned to cover the Labor Day barbecue they're putting on at noon, and I don't have anyone available. Margaret's out of town with her new grandbaby, and Phil's taking pictures of the VFW parade in Poplar Grove."

"Didn't the *Courier* do a piece Saturday?"

"We ran the press release," Shannon said. "But Hensley wants us to write a story. She said she's even got Max Miller to shoot photos."

Mm-hmm. Now Dee knew why Max was occupied today. "Okay, I'm in." She thought about the rug and curtains. "*If* you're paying holiday rates."

"Deal," Shannon said, "A hundred dollars, but you'll have to come into the office and file your story before five. I'm here at least until then."

Dee could visualize the new attic accoutrements already.

*   *   *

The Patriotic Picnic was a slightly less than bustling venue on Labor Day afternoon in the corner of Terrell Park. Across the street the municipal pool was packed with squealing children on its last open day this year, but Dee figured that many other folks had taken their families to the lake or were traveling elsewhere.

Red-white-and-blue striped bunting, McCorrigan yard signs, and big banners that read FREE HOT DOGS decorated a series of folding tables under the pavilion. Dee took a seat in a folding chair under a shade tree and began writing her observations in her new reporter's notebook she'd just picked up at Walmart.

Charley Hensley, she noted, prowled the scene with some kind of small device in her ear and a walkie-talkie in her hand. Not much demand for high tech here, Dee thought as she walked up to the campaign manager to introduce herself and let her know the newspaper was covering the event.

She extended her hand. "Hi, I'm Dee Bennett with the *Claxton Courier*. I mean, I'm writing the story for the paper. I don't actually work there, I—"

"Let me put you on hold," Hensley said, looking Dee straight in the eye as she shook her hand.

"Um, okay," Dee replied.

Hensley touched a button attached to the placket of her blouse and said, "Who are you with?"

"The *Claxton Courier*," Dee repeated. "We publish every day but Sun—"

Hensley raised the walkie-talkie to her face and pressed its button. "No, the Abilene paper's not here yet," she said and walked away, still talking, to collar an assistant whom Dee took to be a college intern.

The candidate had not yet arrived. Dee counted the people. Eleven, including the guy cooking the wieners on the grill. Another assistant removed one of the banners from the gazebo and headed across the street to the pool. Within minutes a line of parents and bedraggled, wet children in swimsuits queued up, paper plates extended for buns and free hot dogs.

A minibus bearing the logo of Carousel Senior Living pulled up, and Hensley and Brek and Django, the interns—Dee had made it a point to get their names—helped the occupants over to the seating area.

At last a black Escalade rolled up to the scene. Rowdy McCorrigan, sporting khaki slacks, a golf shirt in Claxton Cougars black and gold, and penny loafers, jumped out of the passenger front side door as Max Miller climbed out of the back seat on the driver's side, taking a position behind the SUV to shoot a photo.

In less than five minutes, while McCorrigan milled through the growing crowd, shaking hands and introducing himself, Hensley and the interns shepherded the entire hot dog line into seats and then filled plates for the senior citizens.

Another fellow got out of the SUV and retrieved a portable sound system from the back. When the folding chairs were full, McCorrigan strolled over to the pavilion, waited while the sound system guy miked him, and began to speak.

Charley Hensley strolled over to Max, touched his shoulder, and whispered something in his ear. Max began to take photos, moving around the crowd in different angles. Dee had no time for chagrin— she had to focus on her new responsibility. McCorrigan was getting ready to speak, and she positioned her pen to capture his every word.

McCorrigan held up his hands to quiet the group. "Thank y'all for coming," he said, "and congratulations to our volunteers for turning out such a crowd on a holiday. Thank you to the Carousel Senior Citizens Center for being here. It's a fine organization doing good work."

He paused to allow the picnic group to quiet. "It's not easy for a small business to be successful these days . . . with all of the Washington regulations . . ."

Dee paused. Those words sounded awfully familiar.

McCorrigan slowed as though he expected the crowd to boo and hiss. But they were too busy eating their free hot dogs. He flashed his movie-star smile and said, "I hear you. Texans are tired. Too many taxes, too much bureaucracy, too much government."

It was the same speech from Thursday night, Dee thought. The very same speech.

"Too much dependence on foreign oil," he continued. "You and I know that there's plenty of oil right here in West Texas, if Washington will just get out of way with all of this unnecessary red tape—I'm sorry, but we can't hold up energy independence over something like the mating sanctuary of the lesser prairie chicken."

This time one of McCorrigan's laugh lines got a few chuckles. Some of the children had wandered back for a second hot dog by now. Cars had started to pull up and park. The people who got out went straight to the grill—among them some of the customers Dee had seen in Walmart shortly before. Yep, Brek or Django must have gone forth spreading the word.

* * *

Dee hung around until the swimmers and senior citizens had departed before approaching the candidate. She had to catch him before his handlers swept him back into the Escalade, but now he'd turned his back to talk with his campaign manager. "Mr. McCorrigan?" Dee asked tentatively over his shoulder during a pause in their conversation. "Mr. McCorrigan? May have a few minutes of your time?"

"Sure, what do you want to know?"

"I—I just wanted to say, first of all, welcome back to Claxton."

"Thank you," he said, though she could sense his impatience.

"Oh, and I'm Dee Bennett, writing for the *Claxton Courier*."

"Okay. That editor Loveland still in charge?"

"No, he's retired and there's a new editor."

"And you cover what, the society news? Draw the short straw on the holiday?" He seemed to be acting deliberately obtuse. And asking all the questions.

"Not exactly. But Mr. McCorrigan, I would like to get your impression of the kind of reception your hometown has given you."

"Everyone's been welcoming so far, especially the merchant community. Claxton's a great town, always supportive of the Texas way of life." She finished writing out his statement.

"Can you tell me what motivated you to move your campaign here?" Dee asked as her second volley.

"Sure," he said. "So much of the state's oil and gas business is located in West Texas, it made sense to come meet more of the voters I need to get acquainted with between now and November."

"Are you saying you don't need votes in Austin or Dallas or Houston?" she asked before she could think better of it.

"Well, no . . . but I'm already well known in business circles in the capitol and the bigger cities," he replied. "And frankly, I'm enjoying being back here among old friends for a while."

Dee finished scribbling, sensing that her interview subject was growing even more restless. "Okay, well, thank you so much—let me give you my contact information, and I'd appreciate getting yours in case I need to verify anything with you."

"My campaign manager, Charley, will handle all that with you. I think you've met her."

"Sure, will do."

McCorrigan waved curtly and started toward the Escalade, but Dee called out, "Oh, one other thing, I forgot, Mr. McCorrigan. I was supposed to ask you if you'd been in touch with Ricky Jones lately."

He slipped his sunglasses down quickly over his eyes, but not before Dee caught the briefest deer-in-the-headlights look.

"I heard his family moved away. Don't know where," was all he said, shaking his head and shrugging, before continuing toward his vehicle. Dee would've mentioned her connection with Buddy, that she'd only asked because her brother had inquired—but now she was glad she hadn't had the chance. She had an inkling she should follow up.

6
Brags and Sags

To-day no trace of stilted artificiality remains. The tête-a-tête of a quarter of a century ago has given place to the continual presence of a group. A flock of young girls and a flock of young men form a little group of their own—everywhere they are together. In the country they visit the same houses or they live in the same neighborhood, they play golf in foursomes, and tennis in mixed doubles. In winter at balls they sit at the same table for supper, they have little dances at their own homes, where scarcely any but themselves are invited; they play bridge, they have tea together, but whatever they do, they stay in the pack. In more than one way this group habit is excellent; young women and men are friends in a degree of natural and entirely platonic intimacy undreamed of in their parents' youth. Having the habit therefore of knowing her men friends well, a young girl is not going to imagine a stranger, no matter how perfect he may appear to be, anything but an ordinary human man after all. And in finding out his bad points as well as his good, she is aided and abetted, encouraged or held in check, by the members of the group to which she belongs.

—"Friendship and Group System"

THE BI-WEEKLY TUESDAY evening meeting of the Write Stuff hadn't quite gotten underway at the Claxton Public Library when Dee arrived—at five minutes to six she was the first. Even Cynthia was occupied in shutting down the library's computers.

Over the summer Dee had hosted these writers and led them in workshops at the farm in a trade with Cynthia—for after-hours library access to an Internet connection. But everyone had agreed that those workshops would end with summer, and starting in September the group would return to their regular locale and programming. "And don't you think everyone will want to return to an every-other-week schedule?" Cynthia had asked. "There's so much going on during the school year, with homework and football and the holidays to think about." Dee decided that the transition might be easier if she came tonight not as facilitator, but simply as a writer. Each member was to bring a draft they'd been working on since their last meeting, in early August.

For Dee's part, she'd pretty much wrapped up the draft of her book-length study of G. H. Templeton, an early practitioner of creative writing instruction, so she felt at loose ends about something new to tackle. Aside from the regular blog posts, of course. She was waiting for inspiration to strike. Waiting to be visited by the muse. To break through the proverbial writers' block.

R-o-w-d-y M-c-C-o-r-r-i-g-a-n, she typed into the Google search box of her laptop's browser while she waited. The exercise yielded tens of thousands of hits, and it was nearly impossible to tell the legitimate links from those of the fans, the malcontents, and the bitter opponents. But a recent feature in *Texas Monthly* shed some light. Claxton High School, class of 1978. University of Texas, B.B.A., 1982. Wife Gretchen, University of Texas, J.D., 1985. Children Thomas, Laura. Current residence, Austin, West Lake Hills. Current employer, Fox & Ford Government Relations, Austin. She copied, pasted, and saved.

"Been jet-setting lately?" Dee heard Wendell Grover say, as he scooted into the chair across the table from her. Dee glanced at the clock on the wall—5:59. Wendell, the seventy-three-year-old retired Air Force colonel, was never late. He seemed more dapper tonight. His oxford shirt and khaki pants seemed freshly pressed, and Dee thought she caught a whiff of aftershave. Maybe his crew cut even had a fresh buzz.

The Old Spice soon did battle with Estée Lauder and Emeraude as Margaret Strickland and JoAnn Rinehart swept into the room oohing and aahing over baby pictures on Margaret's cell phone. Frances Echols elbowed her way in, getting a peek at the digital photos. Teresa Rivera entered behind them, smiling at their enthusiasm, followed by Hank the teacher and nature writer with the hard-something last name Dee had forgotten.

J. D. Sandifer's boots smelled straight from the horse barn, and there was a whiff of Asiago cheese bread on Summer Jones's Subway uniform. Last to join the group was a dark-skinned man trailing a fresh scent of disinfectant and exhibiting an unforgettable lilting accent. Raul Amey, the hospital nurse who'd seen Mama through her first days of recovery following her disabling car accident three months earlier.

When Margaret was situated beside Dee in one of the straight-backed wooden chairs and Dee had had her own turn admiring the new grandson, the semi-retired features editor of the *Claxton Courier* said, "So I heard you had your Woodward and Bernstein moment yesterday."

"I hope I wasn't interfering with any of your freelance work for the paper," Dee responded.

"Oh, no, honey," Margaret said. "I was the one who told Shannon to call you. I've been reading your blogs. You've got a clear style and an eye for detail. I only take on those assignments to keep my pencil sharp. Mostly I want to make sure the old coots around here don't tear down our historic buildings just because they can, or take advantage of the underprivileged." At this last, she cut her eyes sympathetically in Teresa's direction.

"Margaret, how long have you lived in Claxton?" Dee asked.

"Since God was a baby," the older woman joked, her green eyes sparkling.

Dee had heard that Margaret was a rabid sports fan who never missed a Cougars football game. "Do you remember a football player who was on the same team as Rowdy McCorrigan named Ricky Jones?"

Margaret paused and thought for a moment. "A black kid?"

"Yes."

"Yes, I do. He was a great wide receiver. Talk about underprivileged, though."

"He didn't graduate, right? What happened to him?"

"Ricky came from a tight-knit family with a single mom," Margaret recalled. "His mother was a nurse at the hospital. I think she got a better job in a bigger town, and they moved away."

Dee started to probe more, but Cynthia called the group to order. "May I have your attention, please?" the librarian said, standing at the head of the table. Cynthia adjusted her short-sleeved twin set and left her glasses to hang on the chain around her neck. "I'd like to call the meeting to order," she said. "First, do we have any old business?"

No one offered any. Summer doodled a hangman on her notepad while Margaret stole glances at her cell phone and Teresa sat timidly in the corner, spiral notebook and pen in hand. Dee resisted the urge to leap to the front of the table and draw them out.

"I'd like to introduce two new members," Cynthia said, gesturing toward one newcomer, then the other. "This is Raul Amey—and over here is Hank Hardeberger. We're glad to have both of you."

Everyone mumbled a welcome that sounded halfhearted at best, and the room went quiet again. Cynthia stared at the group, awaiting more.

After a long silence, Dee jumped in. "So, what do you guys write?"

Raul replied, "Dystopian, paranormal, magical realism." Teresa turned to study him, Dee noticed. "I got some Bahama mojo in my blood," he said with a wide smile.

"I seem to recall when we met before," Hank said, "that I told you that I'm a nature writer."

A little prickly, aren't we? Dee thought it was obvious she was being polite for the benefit of the group. "Right, we met that night at the gallery," was all she said.

Cynthia asked all the "old-timers" to tell a little about their writing genres and goals too, for the benefit of Raul and Hank. "I'll start off. Cynthia Philpott, head librarian, writer of the Aunt Martha library mystery stories." Everyone seemed to feel obliged to follow suit and be equally brief. The introductions continued clockwise to one of the group's more experienced writers, with some previous workshop experience, who offered, "JoAnn Rinehart, paralegal, writer of detective fiction." She glanced over at the slender, impeccably coiffed woman to her left.

"Margaret Strickland, retired society reporter and now part-time features writer for the newspaper, and I write contemporary romances. I *do* not go beyond the bedroom door." JoAnn looked as though she were about to say something smart-aleck, then let it drop.

Hank was next, so the baton passed to the wiry, dark-haired woman in the Subway uniform. "Summer. Sci-fi. 'Nuff said."

"Raul."

"Frances Echols. I grew up out in the country near the Bennetts, so I've been around this place a long time, and I have heard a lot of tales growing up. My book is about a murder that happened right here in Caprock County, and—"

"Thanks, Frances," said Cynthia. "We'll keep it concise for now. Wendell?"

"Wendell Grover," said the tall, balding man in jeans, polo shirt, and wire-rimmed glasses. Now that I'm retired and widowed, I'm working on a novel set in the South during the Civil War."

"Teresa Rivera. I write stories, sort of."

"You done already?" said the man next to her, who sported a handlebar moustache and seemed the type to enjoy a good jest. "I am J. D. Sandifer, and besides writin' a little cowboy poetry and some Western tales, the only thing I do now that I'm no longer teachin' ag at the high school is hang out with the Romeos at the coffee shop in the mornings, where m'wife Pauline can't find me."

"Romeos?" asked Margaret.

"Retired Old Men Eating Out." He drew a few laughs with that one.

Dee introduced herself as the new proprietor of the Paragraph Ranch, which was really just her family's cotton farm until J. D. and Wendell had come up with the nickname. "And I'm currently seeking a publisher for my completed book manuscript, if you happen to know one."

"Started anything new, Dee?" asked JoAnn.

"Not yet," she said. "I need to get the boxes unpacked first!"

"Okay, thanks for sharing," Cynthia said. "Any new business?"

"Do I need to go to back to taking the minutes, like we used to?" asked JoAnn. A few members shifted uncomfortably in their chairs.

"Oh, no," Cynthia said. "Dee did such a good job helping us break out of our old habits, we want to continue the momentum. I just have one item of new business before we do our brags and sags."

Brags and sags? What was that? Dee wondered.

"For the newcomers," Cynthia began, "a brag is a writing success you've enjoyed, and a sag is a little setback that the others can help you overcome."

No one said anything.

"No brags?" Cynthia said. "Any sags?"

"Yeah." Summer sat up and leaned forward. "I kind of miss writing at the Paragraph Ranch. I felt like I was making real progress as a writer—not just being a part of some writing club." Summer looked at Dee expectantly.

Dee wasn't sure what she ought to say. At the time they'd gone on hiatus she was relieved to be free of the obligation, but now she realized she, too, missed the creative jolt she received from the regular interaction with this group.

Cynthia spoke up. "Guys, we talked about this. The library needs those community outreach hours that this program contributes to the state data."

"Couldn't it still be held under the auspices of the library," Wendell offered, "even if it met offsite?"

Cynthia smiled and said, "I think we're getting a little ahead of ourselves. Dee was our temporary host—"

"And a damn fine one, if you'll pardon my French," said J. D. "Cowboy Wilbur had a Silver Spur writing award in his sights as long as I could be out in nature on that farm. The words flowed like a stallion out there. Dr. Dee's coaching on dangling participles didn't hurt any either."

All eyes were on Dee now.

"Come on, people," Cynthia said, "you're putting Dee on the spot. Maybe she isn't in a position to continue with the Write Stuff anymore."

"Well?" Summer said, "Cut to the chase, Dr. Dee. Can you be our host and teacher again?"

Dee demurred, though Frances and Wendell were both nodding assent. "The weather won't always be cooperative, you know, and it's a long drive—"

"I found the drive out in the country allowed me to leave my daily grind at the law firm behind," JoAnn said. She motioned to the computers and abandoned carrels in the library. "I sit in a cubicle all day long. I write to escape that—to unplug from technology. Dee's little writing retreat did wonders—although I think it's important that we keep our expectations realistic. I didn't expect her to turn me into the next Janet Evanovich." Even when she was being positive, JoAnn couldn't help but get a dig in.

Dee turned to Margaret. "Oh yes," Margaret said. "JoAnn and I always rode together and sort of did a little mini-workshop on the way." She looked to JoAnn for agreement and added, "We couldn't wait for Tuesdays to roll around."

One last person to check with. "Teresa?" Dee said. "Can you get a ride?"

"I have my own car now," Teresa said, smiling. "The money from the writing contest went for a good cause."

Dee turned to Cynthia. "Up to you, boss. At least there's an air conditioner out there now."

"As long as the library can count the participants in its community outreach data tracking," Cynthia said, "I'm fine with it."

A collective murmur of jubilation passed through the group.

"Now," Cynthia said, "can we finally get to new business?"

They all nodded.

"Texas Writers Online is having its first-ever *offline*, face-to-face meeting in Abilene at the end of this month. They're bringing in agents and editors, and scheduling critique and networking sessions." She consulted her notes. "There'll also be workshops on writing craft, self-publishing, and social media. Registration is only ninety-nine dollars, and if a bunch of us want to go, we can take one of the library's vans. I've got a sign-up sheet right here."

"I'm not sure I got all of that," said Frances. "Who did you say was out of line?"

JoAnn leaned over to her. "Just put your name on the list, Franny. We'll fill you in later."

"Dee," Cynthia said, "would you mind taking over the work-shopping of the writing while I handle the sign-ups?"

"Sure," Dee said, "J. D., let's start with you. Where's Cowboy Wilbur?"

And in an instant, they were caught in the crossfire between Quanah Parker and Colonel Ranald McKenzie as Cowboy Wilbur had gotten lost from his cattle drive en route to the Santa Fe Trail and ended up in the Battle of Palo Duro Canyon.

Dee didn't stop to tell J. D. that she thought Cowboy Wilbur wasn't the only one who was a bit lost—she just let his plot ramble for now. But she took heart that maybe they'd all just taken a step toward recapturing a little writing magic.

7
All the Ships Come In

On the evening before the day of the announcement, the bride's mother either sends a note, or has some one call the various daily papers by telephone, and says: "I am speaking for Mrs. John Huntington Smith. Mr. and Mrs. Smith are announcing the engagement of their daughter, Mary, to Mr. James Smartlington, son of Mr. and Mrs. Arthur Brown Smartlington, of 2000 Arcade Avenue."

If either the Huntington Smiths or the Arthur Smartlingtons are socially prominent, reporters will be sent to get further information. Photographs and details, such as entertainments to be given, or plans for the wedding, will probably be asked for. The prejudices of old-fashioned people against giving personal news to papers is rapidly being overcome and not even the most conservative any longer object to a dignified statement of facts, such as Mrs. Smith's telephone message.

It is now considered entirely good form to give photographs to magazines and newspapers, but one should never send them unless specially requested.

— "Announcement of Engagement"

EARLY THE NEXT MORNING, as the skies threatened rain, Dee found herself back downtown, this time waiting outside of the office of *Claxton Courier* editor Shannon Thomas. The editor's assistant, Becca, had called Dee to arrange the meeting, saying that the three of them needed to sit down. Just why, Dee wasn't sure.

"Hi, Becca," Dee said.

The petite assistant, whom Dee guessed to be a good decade younger than herself, turned around to reveal that she was on the phone and held up a finger. "Okay, I'll tell her." She hung up and said, "Shannon's just gotten out of an economic development board meeting; she'll be here in about five or ten minutes."

Dee lowered her voice and attempted to co-opt the assistant. "Can you tell me what we're meeting about?"

Becca answered in the same tone. "No, I'm not at liberty to say."

A flash of panic swept through Dee's mind. Had there been some issue with her story? Had she libeled the candidate? Ticked off his campaign manager, even if the woman had been an A-number-one bitch? Would she need to write a retraction? And then two further possibilities occurred to her. Were they being sued? Would she be financially liable?

"Would you like a cup of coffee?" Becca offered.

"No, thanks," Dee said, smiling but feeling nauseous. She watched the flat-screen TVs on the wall in the newsroom, where four cubicles stood empty. "Where is everybody?" Dee asked Becca.

"The ad people are making sales calls, and the reporters are covering beats," Becca said, as though that ought to be self-evident.

Dee tried to focus on the TV. Flat screen. Seemed like everyone had one of these, she thought. Even Mama had left her dinosaur of a tube TV at the farm and opted for a contemporary-styled LCD model in her new place. Above the cubicles CNN replayed a seemingly endless loop previewing the GOP convention. "Governor of Alaska to Give Speech Tonight," read the crawl line.

A bell rang on the front door as Shannon Thomas breezed in, and two white-uniformed painters followed her with buckets and tools in hand.

"Hi, Dee," she said. "Start in the back shop," she said to the crew. To Becca, she said, "I thought this place could use a little freshening up."

"Good idea," Becca said, and turning to Dee, added, "We'll meet in Shannon's office."

Shannon took a seat at a small round meeting table in the corner of her office, and Dee and Becca followed suit.

"Dee," Shannon said, "I'll be brief. I'd like to offer you a job."

Dee exhaled, feeling the tension drain from her facial muscles and realizing that her worry must have been apparent.

"What?" Shannon said. "Everything okay with that?"

"I thought something was wrong with my story," Dee said. "I thought there was a problem of some sort."

"Oh, no," Shannon said. "Far from it. Your piece was really good—just what was needed. Becca's here because she also serves as our HR staff, and we'd like to get this nailed down pronto."

Becca nodded, pen poised.

"I don't know," Dee said, "I have responsibilities at the farm . . . but how much does it pay?"

"Because I know that you have responsibilities at the farm, and with your mother, and with the book you're trying to publish," she replied, "it's just part-time and short-term."

"Margaret's been talking," said Dee, relaxing a bit.

"Sorry it doesn't include benefits, because it's only twenty hours a week, but you can telecommute. Once you get Internet service, you can file your stories and blog posts from home."

"Well, what *is* the job?" Dee said.

"Given the local developments on the railroad commission campaign, we're going to need a political reporter," Shannon said. "Since McCorrigan brought his campaign headquarters here, his two opponents have announced swings through Claxton next week and the week after. I don't imagine it's every day that Caprock County becomes a hotbed for a statewide race."

Dee agreed, there. "I don't really have any journalistic training," she said.

"With your background, you'll do fine. What you don't know for this assignment, I can teach you," Shannon said. "You'll do the news gathering and interviews, take some photos, turn in your stories for me to check."

"What does it pay?" Dee asked again.

"Three hundred a week, for nine weeks, through the first week of November."

Dee's heart sank—that wasn't enough. But it was a bird in the hand. "And mileage," Shannon said.

Dee mentally compared the monthly total to her expense side, which was far from extravagant but nonetheless very real and very regular. "I'll need that figure to be four hundred a week, not counting what I'm already earning for the blog."

Shannon raised her eyebrows but punched a few keys on the calculator on the table, then looked up with a smile. "I think we can do that," Shannon said.

Becca looked as though she was going to say something, but Shannon cut her off. "We'll talk later," she said to her. But to Dee, she added, "The first thing you need is Internet at home—like, yesterday—for us to make this happen," Shannon said. "We need to e-mail you your contract, and I'll be sending you some background to read."

"You e-mail me my contract," Dee said, "And I'll have it back to you within the hour." She would make *that* happen if she had to sleep at the library. "And I'll let you know when the Internet installers are scheduled."

"Welcome aboard," Shannon said, extending her hand enthusiastically. A more tentative Becca shook Dee's hand as well and headed back to her desk responsibilities as the editor continued her conversation with Dee.

"I need you to go ahead and mark out a few days on your calendar this week. Saturday morning, Rowdy McCorrigan's campaign bus is going to roll out of here for a four-day swing through West Texas. We'll have a photographer there when it departs, to get a few pictures. But I want you on it."

Dee's eyes widened. "Wow. Okay, I'm free. But how will I know what to do?"

"That's what we're going to talk about. The main thing is, do your homework in advance so you'll know your subject and have your questions ready, and you'll be prepared for eighty percent of what comes your way. Then the other twenty percent that's unpredictable, you can handle."

"Okay—good advice for any situation, I suppose."

Shannon reached over to a bookshelf and took down a paper-back about half an inch thick. "First homework assignment. Are you familiar with the Associated Press stylebook?"

"A little," Dee replied. "I've written lots of magazine features. I know not to use the comma before 'and.'"

"It's more than that. You'll need to bone up on the parts at the back of the book—about libel, sources, and quoting."

Dee nodded. She wasn't unfamiliar with the issues and ethics involved, just unaccustomed to the daily practice. "I'll get on it right away."

"Always remember, get your facts straight and write them down, and if anyone challenges you about a source, come to me first. Then I'll have your back."

Dee sensed the magnitude of what it might mean to be a part of the Fourth Estate—even in a sleepy little place where "news" usu-ally meant Little League scores and church notices.

"Last thing for now," said Shannon. "How much do you know about the Texas Railroad Commission?"

Dee held up her thumb and index finger to indicate a depth of about a millimeter.

"Read up first, then, and let's get together again tomorrow morn-ing to go over your questions. You'll learn more that way."

Dee thanked her new boss, headed out the door into the rain, and went straight for the library—always a sanctuary of calm in a storm.

*   *   *

A hubbub in the genealogy section made Dee set aside her pressing goal for the moment. Behind the glassed-off partition Gladys, the circulation librarian, appeared to be involved in some sort of alter-cation at the computer station with—Mama, and Wendell Grover?

"I was just showing her how to look up some things," she heard Wendell say.

"Does she have a library card?" Dee heard Gladys say.

"I have lived in Claxton for seventy-four years and paid taxes for most of 'em," said Mama. "I ought to be able to use the public library."

Gladys ignored Mama and repeated to Wendell, "Does she?"

Wendell puffed up and said, "We were using *my* library card."

"It doesn't matter," Gladys said, "No one can use the genealogy library without their own library card. The sign on the wall clearly says that."

"Gladys," Dee said, strolling up to the genealogy desk, "So good to see you again. Are you looking for a library card? I have one here."

"Doesn't matter—" Gladys began, but Dee interrupted her.

"I have an unlimited family pass that allows me or any member of my immediate family access to any library services," Dee said, smiling. "I believe you've met my mother, Mary Alice Bennett."

"She still needs her own card," Gladys said. "What if she wants to do some research and you're not here?" Gladys turned on her heel and walked away.

By now Cynthia had emerged from her office to see what the commotion was about. "Just come with me, Mrs. Bennett. We'll get you a library card toot-sweet." Dee gave Mama a quizzical glance as she passed by.

"Just lookin' up some family information, that's all," said Mama. "Mr. Grover uses a program called Ancestry, and he volunteered to meet me here and show me."

While Mama and Wendell returned to their researches, Dee took a second to thank Cynthia for getting Mama her card so promptly.

"I'm the one who should be thanking you for taking on the Write Stuff again," said Cynthia.

"Now that it's just me at the farm, I'm looking forward to the company, and I really enjoyed reading everyone's writing."

"Me, too. So we'll be back out at the farm again on the sixteenth. I have it on my calendar!"

"By the way, I've just landed a new assignment," Dee said. "It's just short-term, but it is writing and it's something totally different from anything I've ever done."

"Really?" Cynthia said. "What's that?"

"Say hello to the *Claxton Courier's* new political reporter," Dee said. "Through Election Day, anyway."

"Shannon's doing such a good job! She definitely has an eye for talent. Listen, Dee," she added, "I've been thinking about something, too. Just promise me you won't be insulted."

Dee didn't know whether she should be. A red flag of worry went up in her mind.

"Our Band-Aid solution of using high school students to help out here at the library hasn't really worked that well," Cynthia said. "About a year ago, when our longtime research librarian retired, the city manager needed to cut budget expenses and made the position part-time. No qualified person ever applied, and we've just used the hours to get the basics done around here. I know your degree isn't in library science, but you've already absorbed a lot this summer, and I could teach you more of what you need to know. This is really beneath your pay grade, Dee, but it would just be temporary until we can recruit another librarian, and it would be a real help to me if you'd consider the job."

"Cynthia, I'm flattered!" Dee said. "I accept."

"I hope you won't go back on that when you hear the pay rate," Cynthia said. "The job's twenty hours a week tops, and some of those hours would have to be on Saturdays."

"It's perfect," Dee said, grateful to the universe. "I'm in. But I do have one request."

"Name it."

"Keep me on the other side of that glass wall from Gladys, will you?"

*   *   *

Wendell was gone when Dee wrapped up her conversation with Cynthia and went to check on Mama, who was thumbing pages in an oversized leatherette-bound volume open on the table.

"I think the dragon scared my *gen-e-ology* coach away," Mama whispered.

"Well, I'm really proud of you for taking the initiative," Dee said. "What are you looking up, anyway?"

"You know, all the years I've lived here, and I have never come down here and read *The History of Caprock County?* You know I'm near about as old as the county is."

"Not so, Mama! I happen to know the county was organized in 1891, and I'm pretty sure you weren't around. But that's cool, that you're reading up," Dee said. "I have some reading to do myself." She told her mother about the newspaper's offer and the library job.

"Well, I'm mighty proud of you, too, then, Dee Anna," Mama said. "Sounds like you've got your work cut out for you. I was about to head back home for lunch, and Teresa's coming for my exercises. Before I go, this came in the mail. It's addressed to me, but I know it belongs to you."

Dee opened the envelope with the Texas Star Energy logo, a design she recognized instantly. The wind power company that had been scouting windmill sites on Caprock County land—including theirs. Hers.

She skimmed the full-page letter then went back to re-read the part that got to the heart of the matter:

> *Texas Star Energy has determined that your property is ideally suited to house one unit in our Spinning Spur wind farm project currently under development.*
>
> *Texas Star Energy's leadership and Landmen have extensive prior experience with leasing and land use management. We pride ourselves in our proven ability to work with landowners toward a fair and mutually beneficial lease agreement and project implementation. TSE understands the issues landowners must face before signing a lease and will work with you to assure that the natural, agricultural and financial values of the land are compatible with the development of wind energy.*

There was a slick brochure enclosed, with more details than Dee could immediately absorb, and another document that looked to be some sort of legal description and disclosure.

"Mama," said Dee, "this doesn't belong to me, it belongs to you. Just because I purchased the farm doesn't mean I should be the one to benefit from an energy lease. And it doesn't look like it's a fortune, anyway, if I understand the terms right."

Mama nodded. "Well, I appreciate that. We'll see. Maybe we ought to divide any of the proceeds up fair and square, four ways."

"Looks like that might net us—hmm, about three hundred dollars apiece on the initial lease. And not until sometime next year at any rate. I wouldn't go spending that all in one place."

Mama considered that. "But you do think we ought to sign it?"

"Why don't we go out and take a look at their proposed site, Mama? Maybe tomorrow, if the rain clears up? And I'll get someone to look this over for us before we decide."

Mama was just about to answer when a voice hissed at them from around the corner of the glass wall. *"Shhhhhhhhhh!"* came Gladys's sharp warning. "Keep it down! It's a library, not a bingo hall!"

Dee and Mama each clammed up to keep from bursting out in giggles. Dee reminded herself she'd have to be vigilant, to keep from awakening the sleeping dragon.

*   *   *

"You remember how, in *The Merchant of Venice,* all of Antonio's ships eventually make it to port, after they think all is lost?" Dee said to Abby, holding the phone with her shoulder while flipping through the notes she'd taken with the other. "That's what it felt like, all in one day."

"Good for you, Mom," said Abby. "So when does your Lois Lane gig begin?"

"Even as we speak! It's like cramming for exams. There's a lot to know before I get on that campaign bus this weekend."

"Wish I was there to help. But I just picked up books for my fall courses today, and you cannot believe the load of reading. Speaking of Shakespeare, I have this doorstop of a *Complete Works,* plus the *Canterbury Tales,* Milton, Dryden, Johnson and Jonson, George Eliot, Virginia Woolf, George Bernard Shaw, and Jeanette Winterson for my British Lit class. Doesn't that sound like a lot of centuries to cover? And that's not counting psychology and calculus, which I am completely dreading."

"I know you'll do fine if you don't have to hold down a job at the same time, honey," Dee said, switching the phone to the other ear.

"Well, about that . . . I had a ship come in too. Don't worry, it's not slinging hash at the diner or anything. I was offered an on-campus internship in the women and gender studies department. It's a really plum assignment, working with a top scholar in the field. It's computer stuff and library research, but it pays a good stipend and it's only twelve hours a week. It'll start when classes begin in a couple of weeks."

"That's great—sounds like a prestigious job."

"I hope so. You know, I really think the summer's experiences helped me get my head on straight. I miss you all, but I'm glad you talked me into coming back here."

"Sounds like you're in for a wonderful year, sweetie. Tell Ian hello from us. Your cat's doing fine. And I'll talk to you later."

"Love you, Mom." The line clicked off, and once again Dee was alone in the dark, old wooden house that creaked with every breath of the wind. Alone was good for now, she thought, but maybe not always. As if reading her thoughts, Cori sauntered down the hallway from wherever she'd been napping and jumped to the tabletop, choosing the stack of papers for her next nest.

"Hey, you rascal," Dee said to the cat. "Wanna learn all about the Texas Railroad Commission?"

The Railroad Commission of Texas, as Dee read in more detail, was the oldest regulatory agency in the state, one of the oldest in the nation and also one of the most powerful. Established in the same year as Caprock County, 1891, it originally did regulate the growing rail industry in the state. Governor James Hogg had gotten himself elected in 1890 on the promise of overseeing wildly varying rates and operations of railroads, terminals, wharves, and express companies—essentially, reining in corporate greed and rewarding improved efficiency. Later, buses and trucks were added. But the monumental shift in jurisdiction happened in 1917, when the three-member commission was granted control of the burgeoning miles of petroleum pipelines, which were designated "common carriers" of goods. By the 1930s the commission gained authority to set oil prices and production quotas in the state, and as went Texas in the oil and gas industry, so went the nation. From that point until the 1960s, when the commission served as the model for the creation of OPEC, the Texas Railroad Commission was the de facto agency in setting worldwide oil prices and policy.

Dee had studied some of this in seventh-grade Texas history, of course, and had to revisit it on a more advanced level in high school. While she was still in school, in fact, in the 1980s, transportation regulation for trains, tucking, and buses had been shifted to the federal government. But what she'd learned she'd pretty much forgotten, and she'd never taken a college-level class that covered the subject. And she'd paid practically no attention when, in 2005, the last of the agency's railroad responsibilities were transferred to the state department of transportation, while its name remained unchanged.

The TRC was still a highly influential body, Dee could tell from the news clippings she'd downloaded and printed in the library. Elections to one of its prime six-year terms in recent years generated vigorous campaigning, hotly contested races, and soaring expenditures. Someone *really* wanted that job this year, she concluded. Three candidates had emerged from the primaries this time around, vying for the one open seat. Well, she'd do her best to ensure that her coverage was fair and thorough. She meant to earn every dime of that four hundred dollars a week.

8
Generations

In cities twenty-five years ago, a young girl had beaux who came to see her one at a time; they in formal clothes and manners, she in her "company best" to "receive" them, sat stiffly in the "front parlor" and made politely formal conversation. Invariably they addressed each other as Miss Smith and Mr. Jones, and they "talked off the top" with about the same lack of reservation as the ambassador of one country may be supposed to talk to him of another. A young man was said to be "devoted" to this young girl or that, but as a matter of fact each was acting a rôle, he of an admirer and she of a siren, and each was actually an utter stranger to the other.

— "Courtship"

"RIGHT DOWN WHERE the fence meets the ditch, Dee Anna — that's where you oughta be able to find that old corner post," said Mama as they cruised along the back road of the farm in the Subaru. Four-wheel drive was always an asset on county roads, which were usually paved in caliche, a white mineral that was firm and chalky when dry but ominously slippery when wet.

"The letter says three hundred eighty feet north-northeast from the southwest corner by the section line," Dee read when they pulled over. "That's, um, a little more than a football field length, right?" She wondered if all this survey information could be any more confusing.

"Your daddy taught me a little about understanding land deeds out here," Mama said. It's real different in the sectioned-off counties than back in East Texas, where the rivers and creeks were used as boundaries." She pointed in a general direction across the field where sorghum stalks stood knee-high. Go see if you can find that corner post, and yeah, I think you're right, look that way about as far as one goalpost to th'other."

"You sure you don't want to come with me? Looks like easy walking once you get to the field."

"No sirree. Might be ant beds in that ditch. Goatheads. Ain't takin' no chance on falling again."

Dee left her mother in the car, engine off and windows rolled down. It was a breezy day that looked to deliver rain later, so the bugs weren't bad. She marched off in what she presumed to be approximately the right direction, weaving her way between the neat rows of grain. When she'd stepped off the approximate distance, she stood and took in the perspective from all angles. The site of the proposed wind turbine was off to the north of the home site, so it looked to her as though the giant windmill wouldn't spoil any of the view. And it would be situated close to the margin of their arable land, a few yards west of the rugged, cedar-wooded breaks and up the slope from the creek bed. There would be little effect on their plowing and planting. She approved. She wouldn't mind it if the company hurried things along, in fact, bringing some of that royalty wealth their way.

Mama was in a talkative mood when Dee returned to the car. "You know it's high time this half section started generatin' something besides a few bales of cotton. You see farther down that hill there?" she asked Dee, pointing east toward the canyon breaks.

"I see those pumpjacks, if that's what you mean," Dee replied. "Uncle Rupert's wells?"

"Still producing after all these years. And it's not like Rupert and Donna ever offered to split any of the proceeds—although they did help out a good deal when your father and I were getting started, setting up housekeeping."

"I remember you talking about how Daddy got the less desirable part when they came to dividing up the land, Mama. That he wasn't too keen on staying put to farm or ranch either one, and he let Uncle Rupert pick his first choice."

"That's right. And whether or not Rupert had any idea that his parcel would end up in the oil patch a few years later, your daddy and I got the half that was the most ideal for farming. So that's what we did. For fifty-five years. I helped him plant even before we were married, our last year in high school, when we got engaged."

"It's hard to imagine, teenagers taking on so much responsibility. Can you just picture that happening now?"

"It was all we had to live on. That, and the little I earned working at my father's cotton gin. In the fifties the gin business was already starting to decline, with so many small community gins consolidating, just like the schools did. The Caprock County school districts went to one big combined high school in 1950, and that's how your daddy and I met."

"I remember. You both lived out in different corners of the county, but you ended up coming to the same school in Claxton," Dee added.

Mama chuckled. "I rode the school bus, but Wilton had this beat-up old 1939 Dodge farm truck. He drove it ten miles from here to town every day. Like as not he was late for homeroom. But on some afternoons when the weather wasn't good for working in the fields, he'd get to stay after school, and so would I. We were in the FFA together, and I was in the camera club. We'd go out in that old truck and get a soda pop, drive around town and country taking pictures, and he'd get me home in time for supper."

"So who took that snapshot of you and Daddy sitting on the front steps of the house?"

"I did," Mama said. "I didn't have a tripod, but I had this Kodak I'd saved up to buy from the Montgomery Ward catalog, and it had a cable you could attach to take the picture. We set the camera on the hood of the truck and posed for it. I thought it turned out pretty good!"

As she and Mama sat in the car and finished their Diet Cokes and sandwiches, Dee thought about the photo albums she'd leafed through when they packed Mama's things to move. There were many photos of Penny as infant and child, some of Buddy, fewer of

Dee. Same in any family, she figured. Baby fatigue must set in gradually. But older photos of their family were rare. She had known her Grandfather Schmidt, her mother's father, because he'd lived to the advanced age of ninety. Both her grandmothers had died young, however, and her paternal grandfather, the first Wilton Eugene Bennett, had also died before she was born.

"Mama, I don't remember seeing a picture of your mother anywhere. I know she died in a car crash when you were young." Dee asked. "What was she like?"

Mama fell silent as she considered the question, then answered, "You know, I have so little memory of my mother . . . after this long, I can't even recall her face. She died when I was two. Everyone said she was smart, and beautiful, and lively . . . at least until she came out to West Texas. Your great aunt Alice and great aunt Sallie used to tell me all about her—that's why I have any image of her at all, I guess."

"And I'm named for her."

"That's right. It seemed like the right thing to do, since Penny was named after your father's mother, Penelope Jean. At least you never had any trouble spelling 'Dee Anna.' To start with you just drew the letter D, back before you could even talk!"

"Well, I suppose I'm still working on that writing thing," Dee said. "And I guess I have to get you back home, so I can do some more of it."

They drove a few more of the farm-to-market roads and checked on the fences, which hardly served a purpose any longer since there hadn't been any livestock in more than a decade, and they checked on the new sorghum crop, which seemed to be flourishing. "You just might have a little profit at harvest time, from the look of things," Mama observed.

"Don't keep saying that, Mama—the crop's another thing that belongs to you. I can't take credit for it, and I sure can't take the proceeds!"

"You won't argue so much when you see what it amounts to, after Hector and Flora take their cut for working it and the crop insurance premium's paid. *You're* gonna be the one with the tax bill next time around," Mama reminded her.

9
Friday Night Lights

So long as Romance exists and Lochinvar remains young manhood's ideal, love at first sight and marriage in a week is within the boundaries of possibility. But usually (and certainly more wisely) a young man is for some time attentive to a young woman before dreaming of marriage. Thus not only have her parents plenty of time to find out what manner of man he is, and either accept or take means to prevent a serious situation; but the modern young woman herself is not likely to be "carried away" by the personality of anyone whose character and temperament she does not pretty thoroughly understand and weigh.

In nothing does the present time more greatly differ from the close of the last century, than in the unreserved frankness of young women and men towards each other. Those who speak of the domination of sex in this day are either too young to remember, or else have not stopped to consider, that mystery played a far greater and more dangerous rôle when sex, like a woman's ankle, was carefully hidden from view, and therefore far more alluring than to-day when both are commonplace matters.

—"Courtship"

UNLIKE MOST FOLKS in Claxton, Dee hadn't planned on attending the biggest event of the week—the Cougars' home football game against a non-district opponent they were sure to beat. But that was before she read two items in the paper. That candidate Rowdy McCorrigan would be on the field with his family from Austin for the coin toss, and that the team they were so highly favored to defeat were the Darrell Dust Devils. Those factors alone decided her. The game would be a perfect opportunity to observe how McCorrigan reacted in a crowd, to see him in action before she had to spend four days on the bus covering him.

What sealed the deal, though, was a phone call from Max.

"Care to accompany a lonesome football fan to Friday night's game?" he asked.

"Well, that would be convenient—but also delightful," she said. "I'm just warning you that Brenda Starr, Reporter, will be on duty, and my brother's coaching the other team. My attention will be divided, and so will my loyalty."

"And I thought maybe we could go to dinner beforehand to celebrate your new job, too. Pick you up at six?"

*   *   *

Dee hustled to get everything in order for her travel, finish the laundry, water the garden and gather the vegetables, study her notes, and make sure that Cori's food and instructions were right where Teresa would find them, while she waited for the Internet installers to arrive.

She also called JoAnn Rinehart, whose experience as a paralegal had come in handy on more than one occasion, to ask what she knew about the ins and outs of wind energy leases.

"Yep, those Texas Star buggers have gotten really busy around here," JoAnn said. "I've heard that some people love 'em, some people oppose 'em."

"Would you mind taking a look at the package they sent me—let me know if we need a lawyer's advice? I don't have any way of knowing if the offer is fair, and I thought some of your courthouse gang might have an idea of the going rate. And of course I'll pay *your* going rate."

JoAnn dismissed the idea of pay. "It won't take me long to sniff around. Let me see what I can find out, and I'll get back to you."

* * *

No sooner had the cable guy finished running what seemed like half a mile of upgraded line and installed a DSL modem on the house phone, than Max was standing on Dee's side porch in jeans and black shirt, his Claxton Cougars ball cap in hand.

"Are you ready for some football?" he mimicked, then whistled as she opened the door and sauntered out in trim-fitting capri pants and a brightly patterned blouse she'd chosen just for the occasion, also taking care that her ensemble included neither team's colors.

"Ready as I'll ever be," she countered, locking the door behind her and welcoming his kiss on her cheek. "You know, all those years in North Carolina turned me into a basketball fan, and I've never looked back. But I may have to rethink that now. With Buddy in sight of a state record and all."

Max walked around with Dee to her side of the pickup, opened the door, and gave her a hand up. "You'll have to look the other way at my jacket tonight, then," he teased her. "All of us officers in the Claxton boosters have to show our Cougar pride."

"I didn't know you were in the booster club," she said.

"I've photographed the team since most of these kids were in grade school," he said. "And as a downtown merchant, I know most of their parents. It's nice to be a part of a community."

Dee understood that longing. The only community she'd ever felt part of, since leaving Claxton, was on campus. When Abby was growing up—when she'd been so focused on her career—there hadn't been time for team sports, clubs, evenings out. And during the years after she and Jacob split up, when Abby had gone to live with him and his new wife, she'd withdrawn into herself, preferring solo activities like writing and kayaking over outings with friends.

Friends—was that how she thought of Max? They'd hardly even made it to the benefits stage, with the constant commotion and full house since she'd returned to stay. Yet the idea of heading down a road toward marriage held no appeal to her.

"I'm glad you've found a place to fit in," she said, as the truck rolled to a halt beyond the gate and he hopped out to shut it.

* * *

The jukebox was playing Faith Hill and Tim McGraw when Dee and Max walked into Jesse Jane's Roadhouse, a favorite watering hole and diner on the Sweetwater Highway. The joint owed its popularity in part to its proximity to the high school football stadium, and on the evening before the first home game it was packed solid. But Max leaned over to the hostess and said something Dee couldn't quite catch, and in less time than it would take for a play clock to run down, Jane had come over from behind the bar to personally show them to a reserved booth for two.

Max winked at Dee and said to the proprietor, "It pays to be on good terms with the big boss, right, Jane?"

"Damn straight. I look after my regulars," she said. "Dr Pepper and a vodka gimlet, right?"

They both nodded.

"And I will never forget the first time *you* came to see me, hon," Jane added, to Dee. "I hope you have a much merrier time tonight."

"Thanks—the bar is low on that one, so to speak," Dee said wryly.

"Well, I'll leave you two lovebirds to your dinner. Your server will be right along with those drinks. I've got a full house to feed. Go Cougars!"

Dee smiled as Max reached across to take her hands in his, a twinkle in his eye. "Is that what we are, lovebirds?" he said.

But before she could respond, a burly man in a gold jacket walked by and paused at their table to say, "Claw 'em, Cougars," making the hand gesture that went with it.

"Hey, Ed, how are you?" Max asked, shaking the guy's hand.

"Fine, man, just fine. Well, oughta be a walk in the park tonight, dontcha think?"

"I expect we'll be off to a strong season start," Max replied.

"Hey, I thought Darrell was six-man. We'll be putting in the JV by halftime."

They don't know my brother, Dee thought.

*   *   *

The sun was still blazing, not quite sunk below the horizon, when Dee and Max strolled hand in hand into Cougar Stadium. A fine night for football, Dee had to agree. If she didn't fully engage in the obsession, she always appreciated the venerable showdown, the pageantry, the sociability, the feeling of being part of something big—and at the same time something very local and intimate.

The band was warming up in the stands and cheerleaders were doing practice tumbles across the grass strip on the sidelines. A short, thin black man called out in singsong, "My name is Levi, come buy a program, Cougars on the prowl, I been here thirty-three years now. Come get your program, we gonna take it to them, programs just three dollars."

Max handed him a five, shook his hand, and said, "Keep the change, buddy."

Buddy, she thought. She scanned the field, but the teams hadn't yet come out yet. She wished that Max had talked more about Buddy and his record-clinching opportunity during dinner instead of the dadgum Claxton Cougars.

The drum corps' rat-a-tat ratcheted up Dee's excitement, and their pace quickened as they reached the bleachers. From the concession stand floated the mixed aroma of popcorn, nachos, cotton candy, and coffee. Under the bleachers cigar and cigarette odors wafted upward—along with a hint of more pungent burning herbs.

As they settled into their front-row seats near the fifty-yard line— Max's usual tickets—the band assembled on field for the national anthem. The announcer directed over the loudspeaker, "Ladies and gentlemen, please direct your attention to the field, and let's give a big Claxton welcome to the Darrell Dust Devils." Many of the locals began to hiss and boo. Dee turned and stared straight at one of the offenders. Max offered a what-are-ya-gonna-do-about-it shrug, which Dee made it clear she didn't appreciate.

The Darrell cheerleaders and the Dust Devil mascot—an eight-foot tall burnt-orange foam cone that did not exactly inspire awe—held up a long butcher-paper poster for their men to run through. As the team burst onto the field, however, full of youthful vigor and confidence, Dee shouted, "That's my brother!" She pointed excitedly to the tall figure in khakis and orange polo. "The coach for Darrell is from Claxton. He's a hometown boy!"

But she was instantly drowned out by the announcer whooping dramatically, "Please w-e-l-l-l-l-l-l-come your Claxton *Cougars*," and the crowd erupted into pandemonium. The Cougars exploded through an illuminated, inflatable wind tunnel complete with fog machine and laser show choreographed to a dance version of the Claxton fight song blaring over the stadium speakers. An imposing line of black-and-gold-clad warriors ran the gauntlet of cheerleaders and stood resolutely on the field as the announcer invited the youth minister from the Methodist church to give the invocation.

The band lifted their instruments again as the announcer said, "Please stand for the national anthem played by the Pride of the West, the Fighting Cougar Band." Max took off his ball cap and held it over his heart. Dee covered her heart as well, as each fan tried their best to sing a creditable "Star-Spangled Banner." Down the row to their right, Dee noticed a well-turned-out, middle-aged woman along with a young man in Vineyard Vines Bermudas and plaid button-down who looked to be her son and a tall, dark-haired girl who must have been her daughter, standing beside the mayor and his wife. More McCorrigans, she gathered. She tried to locate the senior McCorrigan and his sidekick, finally spying them down below, facing the color guard.

At the last strains of "the home—of the—brave," a cheer went up and the field was quickly cleared for the game. "Now, please join us for tonight's coin toss," the announcer said. "Former NFL, NCAA, and Claxton High star quarterback Rowdy McCorrigan will do the honors, and the captains of each team will join him."

Dee caught a glimpse of Charley Hensley, watching intently from the sidelines then holding up her cell phone and stabbing it furiously with her finger. There was a pause in the action on field until the announcer said, "Rowdy is also the Republican nominee for Texas Railroad Commissioner."

The Cougars won the coin toss and opted to receive, and during the first play the kick returner was on the fifty-yard line when a Dust Devil hit him hard and caused the ball to slip out of his hands and take two huge bounces behind him. The Dust Devils recovered on their own forty-eight. When it was the Devils' turn on offense, the quarterback dropped back and threw a twenty-five-yard sideline spiral that the tight end took all the way into the end zone. Dee wanted to jump up and down at their bravado but kept her glee in check. Buddy even went for the two-point conversion—successfully. The Claxton boosters had suddenly clammed up tight, Dee noticed.

McCorrigan joined his family and the mayor down the row from Dee and Max. Charley was not in evidence. Trying to buy off a ref, Dee speculated uncharitably.

The next move by the Devils was on the kickoff, a squibbler of an onside kick that zigzagged across the field. Darrell recovered on their own forty-five.

"Come on, Cougars," Max said. "Get your heads in the game."

Some of the other boosters' language was more salty.

This time the Devils ground out the yardage with a series of quarterback sneaks, end arounds, and sweeps. They never even had to pass, to hit pay dirt once again in the end zone.

"Damn it to hell," Max said, slapping his cap on his knee.

"Maybe y'all should bring in the JV?" Dee said.

"At least it's good for your brother," he said.

Duh, Dee thought, *ya think?*

By halftime, Dee was perhaps the only person on the Claxton side of the stadium who exhibited the slightest pep. As she and Max waited at the concession stand for coffee, she looked back over her shoulder at the sea of grim faces, noticing the McCorrigans and

Charley making their way quietly around to the opponents' side of the stadium.

"Don't be so glum," she admonished Max. "Hey, we could always go under the stands and neck," she teased.

"Hmmm." He squeezed her shoulder tighter and turned to face her. "That might help mend my broken heart. My Cougars are letting me down."

"Game's not over," said Levi the program man, stationed at the fence beside the concession stand with a dwindling stack of booklets to sell. "These little schools have no bench, and wear themselves out. I been watching these games for many years."

The Dust Devils received the kick to start off the second half, and did a touchback in their end zone. At the twenty, the Cougars blitzed with the defensive line and the linebackers, and when the pile of players peeled off the quarterback, he didn't move.

"Time out for Devils," said the announcer.

Dee scanned the field to see who it was, then quickly consulted her program. The downed quarterback, still not moving, was Mitch Mitchell III. She gasped as it dawned on her that their wedding-weekend savior, his father, was probably in the stands opposite them this very second holding his breath. Buddy and the trainer rushed out to the injured player, removed his helmet, then motioned to the EMTs. Medics scurried onto the field, but before they had a chance to bring a stretcher the young man sat up, stood with help, then walked to the sidelines under his own power. The crowd on both sides gave him a relieved standing ovation.

"His backup's a sophomore," crowed a booster behind Dee, and she whirled around and whopped him with her program. Rudeness was one thing, but gross inconsideration of another's misfortune was about more than she could take, thinking how she'd have felt if it were her own Abby out there on the field. Well, that might conjure up another set of absurdities, she thought, but still.

On the next play Dust Devil number 12 threw an interception to the Cougar safety, who ran it all the way back for a touchdown. This time the Cougars went for two and made it.

Both teams spent the third quarter going three and out. Buddy tried to gain yardage on the ground—otherwise, Dee understood, his backup quarterback might throw another interception. The Cougars had been victimized by the infamous Buddy Bennett defense, and they weren't taking any chances now.

A breakthrough for the Cougars came in the fourth quarter, when the punt returner took a wobbly kick that got only to the forty-yard line and ran it all the way in for a touchdown. The extra point brought the score to a tie, 15-15, with five minutes to go.

"Woo-hoo!" Max yelled.

"You've just lost your chance for *any* action under the bleachers," Dee said through clenched teeth.

The stalemate of three and out on both sides continued for four minutes more until a Claxton Cougar fumbled a punt and had to chase it, falling on it on the one-yard line. On the next play the Cougars' quarterback dropped back for a handoff—and was sacked. *Safety,* Dee whispered to herself with satisfaction. *Yes!*

A cheer went up from the clutches of Darrell faithful and the big burnt orange cone did a spiraling dance on the far side of the field, where Charley Hensley shunted her candidate toward the cameras. Dejected Claxton fans poured from their seats with the pace of molasses. Darrell's final tally of seventeen points had just notched another win in the Buddy Bennett column, but when it came to her and Max, Dee sensed full well no one was going to score tonight.

10
On the Road Again

The question of a chaperon differs with locality. In Philadelphia and Baltimore, custom permits any young girl to go alone with a young man approved by her family to the theater, or to be seen home from a party. In New York or Boston, Mrs. Grundy would hold up her hands and run to the neighbors at once with the gossip.

It is perhaps sufficient to say that if a man is thought worthy to be accepted by a father as his daughter's husband, he should also be considered worthy of trust no matter where he finds himself alone with her. It is not good form for an engaged couple to dine together in a restaurant, but it is all right for them to lunch, or have afternoon tea; and few people would criticize their being at the opera or the theater — unless the performance at the latter was of questionable propriety. They should take a chaperon if they motor to road-houses for meals — and it goes without saying that they cannot go on a journey alone that can possibly last over night.

— "The Engaged Couple and the Chaperon"

THE TOUR BUS for the McCorrigan campaign wasn't exactly what Dee had pictured — she supposed the big motor coaches she envisioned were the sort of things that recording artists and rock stars traveled in, not plain old state office–seekers. But it was a sight better than a school bus, too, and she figured if they had to cover fifteen hundred miles over the next four days, she'd be glad for comfortably upholstered seats and a bathroom at the back.

Charley Hensley had checked names off a clipboard as the travelers boarded, though she hadn't bothered to verify credentials. Dee had her honest-to-goodness laminated press pass ready, should anyone ask for it. Also on the bus were the regional reporter and photographer for the *Abilene Reporter-News,* a writer for the *Midland Reporter-Telegram,* and another writer for the *Lubbock Avalanche-Journal.* Besides that, it was only Rowdy McCorrigan, Charley Hensley, the two interns Brek and Django, herself, and the driver; and following the bus was a crew from the Abilene television station. Dee imagined there'd be long stretches of travel during which she'd be expected to pepper the candidate with incisive questions—and she was a little nervous about the prospect. More like terrified.

But so far McCorrigan, seated two rows from the front, had been on the phone constantly. He hadn't even waved as she passed him in the aisle. Dressed in navy slacks and a striped poplin blouse and linen jacket—the best combination of neutral professionalism and travel comfort she could find in her wardrobe—Dee hoped to make a solid impression and do her paper proud. For now she took her laptop and camera bag toward the back, past the real journalists—and sank into her seat to read the laser-printed itinerary Hensley had handed each of them.

SATURDAY

11:00	Arrive community center, Big Spring	Hot dog picnic, community rally
13:00	Depart Big Spring	Journalists' questions for candidate en route
15:00	Hotel check-in, Midland	
18:00	Arrive Petroleum Museum, Midland	Reception and lecture on energy topics
20:00	Dinner, Petroleum Club, Midland	

The itinerary continued, front and back of a full page, in the same vein. Sunday morning, breakfast in Midland with fund-raisers, church in Odessa, visit Jamaica event at Catholic church in afternoon. Gatherings in Seminole, Andrews, Tahoka, Levelland; dinner with campaign supporters in Lubbock; Monday, meetings with petroleum business leaders; Town Hall meeting at Texas Tech; Tuesday, meetings with officials in Amarillo, Plainview, and Snyder before returning to Claxton. How did anyone keep up the pace?

Hensley worked like a dynamo. No detail slipped her grasp. She was on top of every arrival and departure, every appointment. She green-lighted access, steered supporters into the inner circle and hecklers out, directed the flow of people and events like a traffic cop, always with that little electronic receiver wrapped around her ear like a miniature alien invader latching on. She kept Mrs. McCorrigan in the spotlight when the situation was advantageous, and protected her from the media when it wasn't.

Dee took some time to Google Hensley's background, too. Her search turned up only the expected information on the campaign manager's work history, press releases she'd issues, and the like. Plus lots of irrelevant links to *Charlie's Angels, Charley Girl,* and *Travels with Charley.*

Dee mostly kept a low profile, observing everything she could and taking careful notes, and combining them with general press briefings to craft her daily stories each night and file them at the hotel the next morning. She felt fortunate to be working for an afternoon paper—at least that gave her the extra time to write and think that she needed in the evenings.

When Dee at last had her opportunity for a one-on-one with the candidate—somewhere between Justiceburg and Fluvanna on the homeward bound leg—she lobbed a few softballs his way. What did he consider to be the best path to energy independence for the United States? What did he think should be done to keep the price of gas from climbing too high? She avoided topics like hydraulic fracturing that she'd been reading about—she wasn't quite confident of her mastery of the opposing positions and didn't want to get caught looking dumb. She hoped she'd managed to get a meaty enough interview to satisfy her editor.

But before she relinquished the opportunity, there was one other subject she wanted to know more about. McCorrigan's football teammate Ricky Jones, and why her offhand question at the picnic had elicited such a strange reaction. She tried to pick an oblique approach this time. "Mr. McCorrigan," she said, as smoothly as she could manage, "which of your Claxton High classmates would you say was most influential in persuading you to locate your campaign back there?"

"Well, to start with, why don't you just call me Rowdy? I'll bet this won't be the last time you'll have a question or two for me."

"Right. Rowdy."

"So, ah, I don't really know if there are any classmates that . . . ah . . . influenced my decision. I've seen a few since coming back who I was in clubs with, played football with, that sort of thing. But I've been away from Claxton for many years, you understand."

"You're not close to any of your teammates, then? Not even the guy who caught hundreds of your passes, Ricky Jones?"

He seemed to understand where this was going—and deftly blocked the line of questioning. "You know, if anyone ever does find out what happened to Ricky Jones, I'd love to hear of it. I don't think the kid even graduated. Tough home life, all that."

"That's a shame," Dee said. "Too many times people grow and move away and lose touch with their roots. I know I did. That's really why I was asking, because I've been gone from Claxton a long time myself. My brother was reminding me all about the state championship season in '77–'78. You might remember him. Buddy Bennett? Coach at Darrell?"

McCorrigan seemed to thaw somewhat, whether at the mention of the winning season or a familiar name. "Buddy Bennett's your brother? Well, I'll be. Should have made that connection." He relaxed a little more. "Your brother might have hung out with Ed what's-his-name who has the car dealership now. He was younger than me—younger than Ricky and—" He stopped, and Dee noted the pause. McCorrigan might have given Ricky Jones more consideration than he wanted to let on. There was something odd in his reaction, something off.

"I appreciate your time, Rowdy," said Dee, feeling for the first time on a nearly even footing with him. And you're right, I expect there'll be more questions in the future. I'll see you along the trail." She shook his hand and left him to wonder as she strode to the back of the bus. If there was anything to the rumor Cynthia had hinted at, she'd keep on it. She'd prove herself in this job yet. She just needed a little time.

*   *   *

Upon their arrival back in Claxton Tuesday afternoon, weary and road-worn, Dee got her car and headed straight for the paper. Shannon not only expressed satisfaction with all the stories Dee had submitted from the road, but handed her her first substantial paycheck as well.

"You've reached your hour limit in two separate pay periods on this jaunt," she explained. "Friday will be your normal payday, so come in and pick up your check from Becca anytime after noon that day."

"Thanks, that's great," Dee said. "It was a really enlightening experience. I look forward to the next story."

"Unless something unexpected happens on your beat this week, you're free for a few days. Go get some rest. And there's an important date coming up September 25 at the community college—a televised debate with all three candidates. I'm moderating. I'll e-mail you information, but go ahead and mark your calendar."

For now, Dee thought, rest sounded pretty good. Tomorrow she had to put on yet another hat, learn a different job, earn a different paycheck.

*   *   *

Dee reported for her new assignment at one in the afternoon, just as Cynthia was finishing her lunch salad in the library break room. She'd been careful to park in the employee lot out back, relinquishing her usual spot now that she was no longer considered a patron.

"Do I have to get one of those lanyards to wear around my neck now, with a pair of glasses on a ring?" Dee teased Cynthia. "Or at least a little fountain pen?"

Cynthia forced a smile. "Don't be making light," she said. "Do this job for very long, and you'll *need* eyeglasses—do it for five minutes, and you'll wish you had a pen handy!"

"Well, I am in your hands," Dee said. "Put me to work."

Cynthia started with a tour of the reference area, familiar territory to Dee. And yet every library had its idiosyncrasies, its subtle nuances that, in the absence of an orientation, could frustrate even the most experienced researcher. This Dee knew from past explorations in the Boston Public Library, the Library of Congress, and once, even in the British Library—whose catalogues and shelfmarks practically required a course of their own to understand. Even though she had felt at home here since she'd been old enough to read, Dee appreciated Cynthia's discourse on the kinds of reference questions patrons usually asked, and she paid close attention. Stopping every few seconds to pull out yet another bound volume and note on her pad what it was handy for, she soon wished for that pen that would hang, easily accessible, on a chain around her neck.

"Tomorrow we'll spend time getting acquainted with the genealogy collection—more than you already have this summer," said Cynthia. "For now, I've got a backlog of pressing tasks to handle—and so do you." She picked up a stack of computer printouts an inch thick from the reference desk and put it in Dee's hands.

"What's all this?"

"This week's questions. Your job is to find answers," Cynthia said. "They're all yours. Good luck."

Why, Dee wondered, did she get the feeling she'd been sold down the river on this one?

She started in on the stack, taking the first three in the order they came, a process that had her zigzagging through different extremes of the Dewey system before it occurred to here there might be a better way. After taking time to glance over the varied inquiries and sorting them into similar themes, she quickly identified groups of questions that called for similar answers. Either teachers in certain classes were assigning papers with a limited range of topics, she thought, or the demand for services at the Claxton Public Library was much larger than one would ever imagine. A library scavenger hunt assignment—maybe one intended to bring students *into* the library—started to look like the culprit. Dee saved one Word document with the answers, sat down at the computer, and as she composed a reply to each individual e-mail address, copied the relevant portion from her master file into it.

It took her more than an hour to reduce the pile to a manageable three or four clearly dissimilar inquiries, and another hour to track those down.

"Nothing had me stumped for long," she was glad to report when she returned the completed task to Cynthia a few minutes before five.

"You *finished* these?"

Dee explained about the bulk of questions.

"Well, I apologize for the extra work," Cynthia said. "If we'd had a reference librarian in place to answer them as they came in, Gladys would have forwarded them on e-mail instead of printing them all out. We'll set up e-mail access for you tomorrow to rectify that." She clapped her hands together in glee. "And I'll put out the word to teachers that they can start scheduling scavenger hunts for their students once again!"

*   *   *

For dinner, Dee stopped in at the Chinese take-out place on Third Street and picked up a carton of lo mein and some pot stickers. She felt guilty about not calling Mama and offering to bring enough for two, but weariness won out over civility today. She would call Mama in the morning and offer to come for a leisurely lunch on Saturday to make up for it.

Her route out of town took her by Max's studio. She wondered how he was doing down in Houston this week, where it was bound to be hot and humid as a swamp. But as she cruised by and caught a glimpse of a silver Acura MDX with a McCorrigan bumper sticker parked by the curb, she wondered something else. What was Charley Hensley doing on that little-used block? She glanced up to the loft level of the building, where lights were on. Should she call Max? She thought he'd left yesterday morning long before the campaign bus returned. Was there some problem? Was there something he wasn't telling her? It was silly to imagine things, of course. And she didn't feel comfortable calling Max while he was on a road assignment. Clingy wasn't her style.

Still, she slowed down and circled back, taking the shortcut through the alley. No evidence of Max's truck. She lifted her chin, forced the matter from her mind, and drove on.

11
Climate Change

The bride-elect and her mother then go to the stationer and decide
details, such as size and texture of paper and style of engraving,
for the invitations. The order is given at once for the engraving of
all the necessary plates, and probably for the full number of house
invitations, especially if to a sit-down breakfast where the guests
are limited. There are also ordered a moderate number of general
church invitations or announcements, which can be increased later
when the lists are completed and the definite number of guests more
accurately known.

—"The Invitations"

ON SATURDAY, AFTER TWO more demanding afternoons at
the library and a Friday evening chilling out in front of a movie on
her newly acquired HBO channel, Dee was ready for a full day off.
She took her time enjoying her coffee on the porch, appreciating the
slight hint of autumn in the air. That might be exaggerating a little,
she thought. September in West Texas was nothing but an extended
summer, with temperatures still easily reaching the high nineties.
But at some point in the month the hazy skies would start to clear
and the fields of wheat and milo would turn to hues of gold and
rust. She'd know it was really fall when she heard the first flocks of
southbound geese and cranes overhead. She listened; it was early
yet. It was so quiet and still she could make out the squeal of a semi's
brakes far out on the four-lane, the buzz of a small plane somewhere

out of sight, the creaking of a swing set from down the hill where the Woodberrys lived. Otherwise all was calm, and she appreciated her hilltop sanctuary more than ever.

Somewhere, everywhere across the country, tailgate barbecues were gearing up in advance of college football games. Dorms were full of freshmen, professors were grading first rounds of assignments and holding out hope for a rewarding semester. Everywhere, the university enterprise had launched yet another new cycle of activity. Except here. Here, none of that touched Dr. Dee Bennett's serenity. She didn't even sign her name Bennett-Kaufmann anymore. Coming back to Claxton had seemed the right time to drop that artifice, which she hadn't had the courage to do when she and Jake had split seven years ago this month.

She had survived that . . . thrived, even, on her own, had come into her own as a teacher and a person. She drew again on that sense of a new beginning as her thoughts came around again to their persistent chorus these days: *What do you really want to do with your life?*

Right now she really wanted a second cup of coffee. And she had to get moving—Mama would be wondering where she was.

*　*　*

On Mama's small dining table were arranged neat stacks of booklets and computer printouts. Mama's strong German sense of order would never let her leave a work space in disarray. For Mary Alice Bennett, this constituted a mess.

"I left that stuff out hopin' you'd pick me up some file folders and labels, Dee Anna," Mama said as Dee casually flipped through the pages. Census forms, military records, death notices, and deeds, as far as Dee could tell.

"Mama, what is all this?"

"That's some of my genealogy that I've been working on," she replied. "You know I made such a lofty claim at Maddy's wedding about your daddy's family bein' kin to Travis and Houston and all, I thought I better back up my words."

"But that's true, right? You always told us so."

"That's as it was told to me. Your daddy's father, the first Wilton Eugene Bennett, who we named Buddy for, always said his wife Penelope Jean was a descendant of Travis's daughter—and his father was named Samuel Houston Bennett supposedly after *his* grandfather. All those people died before you were born. And before I ever asked any of 'em about their stories."

"Wow, that was a little complicated," said Dee.

"That's why I thought it was time to write it down on paper."

Dee picked up a photocopy of a land grant that appeared to be from the 1800s. "You did all of this by yourself?"

"With a little help," Mama said, sitting up straighter in her chair.

"Why now?" Dee asked, in genuine admiration, coming over to sit on the couch. "You've never documented any of our family history before, have you?"

Mama stopped and looked at Dee as though she was considering the question for the first time. "I don't know," she said. "I think at first, it was because learning about Wilton's family tree helped me feel like he was still with us. You know if you learn something new about someone every day, it's fresh and exciting." Her voice trailed off, and she stared out the window gathering her thoughts. "But after awhile, I just started having a ball learning for learning's sake."

Dee nodded, understanding completely.

Mama looked down and took a sip of iced tea. "You know, I always wanted to go to college," she said. "But my family didn't have the money by then. So I made durn sure that all of my kids went—even if Penny never finished—but I guess a real estate license's is sort of like a college degree."

"Yes," Dee said. "We're all grateful for our educations."

"I love the Internet," Mama said. "I could sit there and learn stuff from it all day. Mr. Grover says it's good company. He e-mails friends and family from all over. He uses genealogy in the stuff he does for your writing group, you know. He was real helpful in teaching me about Ancestry.com. And Rootsweb."

"What's Rootsweb?" Dee said.

"Google it," Mama replied, with a wry grin, getting up to go to the kitchen.

"Well, I just might," Dee replied, continuing to tease her mother. "It's not a porn site, is it?"

Mama scowled in a mock glare and said in a low voice, "The library blocks you from seeing any of those."

"Mama!" Dee said. "How do you know that?"

"Oh, I just run across them by accident."

"That's what they all say," Dee said, and they both burst out laughing and couldn't stop.

When they had regained their composure and Mama had retrieved the goulash from the refrigerator to warm up, she asked Dee, "Seriously, do you think I'm too old to get a computer and get hooked up on the Internet here? I saw on TV where the cable company will come set you up with the connection."

"I think that's a great idea, Mama."

"We're going to have to order the computer off of the Internet," Mama said. "They don't sell them at the Claxton Walmart. I'm not even sure if you can buy one anywhere in town."

"Okay," Dee said. "We'll order you a computer online. Maybe I can come back and help you with it after work next week."

* * *

Dee joined Mama in the tiny kitchen to get their bowls ready. She reported to Mama that Abby had called and her classes were off to a good start; Mama countered that Penny had called and Maddy and Kyle were back from their honeymoon. As Dee was pouring up the stew in their bowls, the land line rang, and she scooted around Mama to grab it.

"Hello, Bennett residence?"

"Is Miss November ready for an encore?" the lively voice on the other end said.

"Give it a rest, Ruby Lee," Dee said. "Fool me once, shame on you—fool me twice and I'll have to kill you."

"So, I was just calling to get Auntie's RSVP. And I was hoping we might persuade Penny and her girls to come to the style show too."

"Your ears must be burning. I was just about to ask Mama. But why don't you talk to her yourself? I'm getting our lunch ready. Mama's legendary goulash recipe."

"I will, but as long as I've got you here, I was going to call you next, to discuss the fee and the rentals."

"Fee?" Were there some hidden costs she was obligated to pay for?

"What the Red Hat Society voted to pay you for using the farm. And what arrangements we need to make for the tents and tables and chairs. The rental company will need to come out and set up a day or so ahead."

"Oh," said Dee, relieved. "The tent company is welcome to come whenever they need to. But I didn't intend for you to pay me anything for using the farm."

"Listen, hon, the Society usually holds this event at the arboretum, and use of their entire facility indoors and outdoors runs us twenty-five hundred dollars. They voted to pay you the same. Don't worry, it's a ticketed event and we'll make it up on sales. And you'll need it, to pay your water bill after all those toilet flushes."

Dee hadn't even thought about restroom facilities for a hundred people. Or where they would all park. Or how to even get their cars up the long, rutted driveway without damage. "Well, then, that is quite generous, and I accept."

"We'll be proud to come out and enjoy the farm," Ruby Lee said. "You've done such a good job getting it back to where it was."

If Ruby Lee considered taking the place from eyesore to mere junkyard an accomplishment, Dee figured she just might be satisfied. It was not exactly *House Beautiful.* What could be done to improve on the situation in a month's time, she didn't know.

Dee handed off the phone to Mama and took their bowls to the end of the table that wasn't covered in papers. She opened the mini-blinds to let in the light and the view.

She paused to note that, since Mama's patio home was the last one on the lane, its east window looked out across the street to a block situated outside the development. Bungalows and brick ranches with modest-sized lawns lined the other side. The one directly across from Mama's place, she noticed, was grown up in grasses and cacti nearly knee-high. And there in the middle of it all, shirtless in cutoff jeans and a bandana around his neck, pruning back a desert willow tree, was Hank Hardeberger the writer–biology teacher.

Mama, hanging up the phone, came over to stand beside her and stare out the window. "Disgusting, don't you think?"

That wasn't the word that was coming to Dee's mind.

"That man has been lettin' his grass just grow and grow ever since he moved in," Mama continued. "Won't cut it."

"Or maybe he's going for something more—natural?"

"At least I don't have to live right next door to that mess like my friend Mrs. Finch. But I do have to look out my window at it ever' morning. He told her it was zero-scape. And I don't like it one bit."

"You don't think it's sort of pretty? Like the prairie?"

"I didn't move away from the prairie into the city only to find it growin' up right across the street from me. That man's yard has ruint the whole block. Them weeds is probably harboring vermin. Probably affected property values too. No telling what Penny would have to say about it."

Dee watched as Hank parted the tall grasses, bending over to pull the occasional weed, sort out the trash and debris. The tall ocotillo and red yucca formed a natural balance with the swaying, silky grasses, and the overall effect was peaceful and artsy. Not to mention low-maintenance. She tried to imagine how such a vista might complement the fruit trees and grape arbor at the home place. She tried to imagine, in fact, what enhancements might be wrought in just a few week's time. She began to hatch an idea.

12
A Pound of This, a Pound of That

Wedding presents are all sent to the bride, and are, according to law, her personal property. Articles are marked with her present—not her future—initials. Mary Smith who is going to marry Jim Smartlington is fortunate as M. S. stands for her future as well as her present name. But in the case of Muriel Jones who is to marry Ross, not a piece of linen or silver in "Ross house" will be marked otherwise than "M. J." It is one of the most senseless customs: all her life which will be as Muriel Ross, she uses linen and silver marked with a "J." Later on many people who go to her house—especially as Ross comes from California where she will naturally be living—will not know what "J" stands for, and many even imagine that the linen and plate have been acquired at auction! Sounds impossible? It has happened more than once.

—"When the Presents Are Shown"

DEE WAS LIKING THE CONCEPT of more frequent paychecks already. As a college professor she had always received her salary monthly, and it seemed there was always too much month left over at the end of the money. Now, she picked up her newspaper check on Fridays, while the library payroll would be direct deposited to her bank account bi-weekly on Thursdays. Even though her combined income was smaller, so were her expenses, and it seemed as though a fresh infusion of funds occurred with more frequency. Furthermore, with Internet readily available at home now, there was no pressure to run to town on short notice for any of her responsibilities.

So she was feeling festive early on Tuesday afternoon before the Write Stuff's return to the farm. Cynthia had relieved her of responsibilities on meeting days, and on Mondays she'd already turned in her blog, so Tuesday was turning out to seem a little like the new Saturday. In that satisfied mood, and with a little extra spending money in her account, she readily agreed when she received an e-mail from Margaret asking if it was okay for the group to turn tonight's meeting into a potluck dinner, with everyone bringing a covered dish or something from their garden.

Sounds great, Dee said, typing her answer. *I'll make a peach cobbler,* she added, thinking of the fruit she and Mama had put up over the summer.

About that same time J. D. Sandifer e-mailed her separately to ask if he could come about half an hour early. *I have an opportunity to bring your way* was his cryptic message. Intrigued, she also gave that proposal a green light. She wondered what the former ag teacher had up his sleeve now.

But if she was going to make that cobbler, she needed to thaw the peaches and get started in a hurry. She dialed her mother's number and caught her after half a dozen rings. "Mama, are you in the middle of something?"

"Just my—therapy exercises," she answered in a strained voice. "Teresa is workin' me hard."

"Well, I'll be quick. I want to make a cobbler out of some of those peaches we froze after the big storm. Do you have a recipe I could borrow? I used to love your peach cobblers when I was a kid."

The other end of the phone line got very quiet.

"You okay, Mama?"

Mama's voice cracked subtly. "I've always dreamed that one of my kids would be nearby, and we could share simple pleasures like this," she said, "but I had given up hope. I guess it's true, Deanna. You really are home."

"Yes, Mama," Dee said softly. "I really am home."

"Then you're going to have to learn how to cook." The feisty M. Alice Bennett returned to form. "Even Abby can cook circles around you. How do you expect to land that Max Miller, if you can't even make a decent chicken fried steak? Teresa, would you bring me my recipe notebook over there? I'm gonna read this out loud to Dee. Can you believe it? Dee Anna is going to make a cobbler?"

Mama read out the ingredients, oven temperature, and directions, then concluded by admonishing Dee, "Now you follow them steps to the letter."

"Okay, Mama, I've got it."

"But even if you don't, well, cobbler's a hard thing to get wrong. There are as many ways to cook one as there are hours in the day, and I think this should even be foolproof for someone like you."

"Thanks, Mama. I mean, really, thanks. For the vote of confidence and all."

"You're welcome," she was in the middle of saying when Dee hung up the phone.

See if I save any for you, Dee thought.

*   *   *

Dee had just put the peach cobbler in the oven and was breathing in the divine aroma of cloves and cinnamon when she looked out the kitchen window and saw J. D.'s pickup come to a stop under the mesquite tree by Daddy's old jury-rigged stock pen. The Dodge Ram towed a small livestock trailer.

Dee wiped her hands on a kitchen towel and headed out the door.

"Howdy, Dr. Dee," J. D. called out, hopping out of the cab and heading toward the rear of the trailer. "I brought you a little house-warming present."

"You brought me a present—in a trailer? You know, I always wanted Santa to bring me a pony, J. D., but don't you think I'm a little old for that now?" she kidded him.

"Oh, you just wait till you get a look at these beauties. You will think it's Christmas in September." He undid the lock and reached around to lower the gate of the trailer. "Best investment you can start with on a Texas farm."

Dee was starting to get a bad feeling about this.

J. D. stuck his head inside the trailer and when he looked back around he was guiding two animals the size of large dogs toward her on leads.

"You brought me—goats?" Dee said.

"Well, I know that you may be between careers," J. D. began, "but animal husbandry can be the first step to self-sufficiency for someone who has as much land as you do. My herd had a very fertile season, so, I want to make a gift to you of one young buck and one young doe. I won't miss 'em."

Dee was caught so flat-footed, she was having a hard time forming words on her tongue.

"Come over here and say hi to Roy and Dale."

Dee proceeded slowly down the steps and over to the truck and gave each of the creatures a soft stroke on the head. *Goats.* Cori the cat had been about all the livestock she'd been prepared to deal with.

"Incorporating dairy goats as the centerpiece of a diversified homestead can be the key to financial independence," J. D. continued. "Even Elmer Kelton himself wrote about how goats saved desperate cattle farmers back in 1957. You ever read *The Time It Never Rained?*"

"J. D., I don't know what to say," Dee said. "I mean, thank you very much."

"I've brought you about a month's worth of alfalfa, and there's lots more where that came from," he continued. "That's about ninety percent of their diets. Otherwise, they eat various grasses and weeds. And it looks like you're well supplied with those."

"Thank you, J. D.," Dee said, still puzzled.

"They're a lot easier to milk than cows, too," J. D. said, "Plus, lots of gourmets like the goat cheese these days. If you've got goats, you'll never go hungry."

"Okay, I'll—I'll learn more about goats," Dee said, not sure whether she should keep the gift. Or whether maybe she already had.

"Good! Then I'll get Mr. Rogers and Ms. Evans set up in your pen over here." He led the animals in that direction, and then stopped and turned her way again. "Oh, and when Pauline heard we were having a potluck, she sent six quarts of black-eyed peas her and I put up, and she's got some warmed up to eat for tonight. There's a cardboard box in the cab there with a crock pot in it, and it just needs to be plugged in."

Margaret and JoAnn pulled up behind the trailer, in Margaret's Buick.

"Hi, Dee," Margaret said, swinging the big driver's side door open. "We've got two bushels of sweet corn, and a tow sack of sweet potatoes. We made some and brought some."

Dee smiled wryly and thanked them—suddenly guessing what was going on. Were these writers giving her a good old-fashioned pounding? Did they suspect she was that impoverished? She remembered, when she was a little girl, that on the day appointed, each member of the congregation of the Second Baptist Church would arrive at the door of the preacher's house with a pound of something: coffee, sugar, flour, butter, honey, what have you. Of course, a pound wasn't always a pound. Someone might provide a ham, a bushel of corn, or a jug of molasses. Many brought canned goods and pickles they'd put up. It was their way of welcoming a new minister and his family and making sure his larder started out full. Poundings were popular as community showers for newlyweds, too, she recalled.

Did the writers think *she* needed all of this? Whatever their motivation, she was touched by their outpouring of thoughtfulness.

Summer brought loaves of bread from the Subway, and Wendell had barbecued two briskets, one to eat and one to freeze. "Look, Dee," Summer said, drawing Dee aside in the kitchen while Margaret and JoAnn filled cups with ice for tea, "we don't want you taking offense, like we were thinking you were a charity case or something. We just figured—we know you're probably going through a thin patch, and we kinda wanted to help you as much as you've helped us."

Dee placed an arm around the young woman's shoulder and said, "I'm touched—more than you can imagine. The pleasure I get from seeing you all so absorbed in writing is reward enough. Now, y'all are going to have to help me eat all this!"

Wendell promptly handed his contribution over to the women and joined J. D. in reinforcing the fence for the goats.

Hank arrived, bringing three cases of Snapple, and Raul brought paper plates, napkins, and plastic cutlery—in five-hundred-count packages.

Teresa came up the steps bearing a pan with six dozen tamales. Frances brought a pound cake, noting that she had already pre-sliced it and measured out exactly a pound, but when that didn't seem like much, she just brought the whole thing anyway.

Cynthia was last with a squash casserole and half a dozen jars of squash relish. "We really had a bumper crop last summer, Dee—I hope you're not allergic!" she said as she placed the foodstuffs on the counter.

Dee wasn't sure how to respond adequately to their largesse, so she simply said, "I guess you guys really want to make sure the Paragraph Ranch stays open for business—so come on in and let's feast."

As the writers filed through the kitchen, Dee said, "Drop your writing samples on the coffee table in the living room, and we'll mix them up and read through a few and workshop them." They let her go first in the dinner line so she'd be finished and ready to start things off.

After fixing herself a plate of brisket, squash casserole, and black-eyed peas, she remembered just in time to turn off the cobbler. She peeked inside the oven. Perfect, if she did say so.

The group picked places around table and coffee table, dining and listening as Dee read. She began with an excerpt from a piece titled "Blood on the Bayou." It didn't take long for the writers to guess whose story it was.

Vampire Bob had been hanging around this bar in Houston since well, Sam Houston had. He had hitched a ride from his native Haiti with the rum runners to the Gulf of Mexico about the time of Stephen F. Austin, and the land grants. Of course, this establishment had gone through a variety of building styles and uses over hundreds of decades. It had been a bakery first, then the Pony Express headquarters, before it started serving alcoholic potations in the last century.

He missed the astronauts. The sixties had been something. The 1960s that was. The 1860s, all that civil war strife—way too much stress. These days, the only thing anyone here seemed interested in was boom money. Oil boom money. His companion, a business acquaintance, arrived only slightly late. No worries, Bob had an endless amount of time.

"Hey, V. B.," his colleague said.

"Buy you a drink?" Bob replied.

"You're not bad for a bloodsucker," the companion retorted.

For a vampire in 2036 the nickname stung. In the decade since his kind had been "rounded up" around the globe and digitally cuffed and essentially, subjected to 24/7 monitoring and observation, he had not partaken of the dark side of his genus.

Not that he ever had. He had always found the black market for blood. Even setting up his own storefront blood bank for a short while at the turn of the 20th Century.

Modern medicine had perfected transfusions and medical compounds. What it hadn't done was to solve the moral and ethical dilemmas, which raged today. Should a species capable of living forever be allowed to?

Dee read to the end of the two-page excerpt, then turned to the group. "So, what did you all think when you read this story?" she said.

"It's got potential," Summer said. "I mean, I love Stephenie Meyer and Charlaine Harris's stuff."

"And Anne Rice," added JoAnn.

"The white women shouldn't have all of the fun with vampires," Raul said, flashing a broad smile.

Teresa echoed his smile and asked, "Speaking of vampires, did any of you catch that new HBO show? *True Blood*?"

Several fans jumped in at once. The conversation threatened to get out of hand with comparisons to all manner of paranormal hits, when Dee brought them back to focus on the written word. "Any other feedback?" she asked.

"I thought the main character was hilariously droll, and the minor characters were funny, too," said Margaret. "Toward the middle, I got a little confused about events. I had a bit of a hard time following what decade V. B. was in, in the present. But I marked some suggestions on the hard copy, and I don't think it'll be hard to revise."

"Keep going," Teresa said. "I love it."

Raul winked at her and said, "Your wish is my command."

"Okay, next piece," Dee said, pulling another one from the stack.

It was the summer of fires and fracking, followed by a fall of the end of affluence as we knew it. The hottest summer on record with West Texas cotton fields burnt crisp, and random grass fires keeping communities on edge. Drought was the word on everyone's dry lips, and there was a new phrase: climate change.

Scientists were saying these new extremes in weather would be sticking around—likely for good.

Sadly, another phrase soon joined the lexicon, "climate change deniers."

And before long, the lemmings had patented their own chant. "Drill, baby, drill."

Reveling in their sarcasm, and scoffing at science and common sense, will they jitterbug off the financial cliff? They are Nero fiddling while Wall Street burns.

Are we seeing the crumbling of our financial system. Sunday, Lehman Brothers, AIG, banks are failing, and pensions, 401ks, and hard-earned retirements are essentially worthless . . . where will it all end?

The group grew somber and thoughtful.

"Hold on a minute," Wendell said. "The stock market will correct itself."

"This is different. I'm writing about things that really matter, because we've got to wake up and speak up," Hank said, immediately outing himself as the author of the piece.

"As for that Drill, Baby, Drill comment," J. D. said, "I guess you'd consider me one of the lemmings. I believe there's plenty of domestic oil if the government wouldn't make it so complicated with all of their regulations."

"You want polluted air, and earthquakes across the state from fracking?" Hank said.

Dee intervened. "Guys—a gentle reminder that, just like fiction, when someone is writing creative nonfiction, our mission here as writers is not to agree or disagree with their premise, but to understand their effectiveness in communication."

"Oh, I think he was pretty effective in getting his point across," Wendell said, shaking his head. He mumbled something else under his breath. "Damn tree huggers running business off to foreign countries."

"What was that?" Hank replied.

"Never mind," Dee scolded.

"I think he was effective," Teresa said. "A little — what is the word I'm looking for, infa—infla—?"

"Inflammatory?" Wendell added.

"Maybe," JoAnn commented. "But if you watch the news, what's going on with Wall Street is not business as usual, and it's a brave thing to write an opinion piece that contributes to the dialogue."

But the group seemed determined to continue debating the issue rather than the expression. "For the president and Congress to say a company has to be rescued to save our financial system is pretty scary stuff," Margaret added.

"Within twenty-four hours of Lehman's going belly up, the credit markets around the world froze. We're no longer talking about mortgages," JoAnn said. "We're talking about car loans, loans to small businesses, commercial paper borrowing by large banks. This is like a disease spreading."

"Ladies, it will be fine," Wendell said.

"I hope you're right," Dee replied, and looked at her watch. "We're going to need to move on. It's after eight and we've made it through only two manuscripts. I have the next one here. Listen up—to the first page of a story titled 'My Father the American.'"

The group grew silent again and paid close attention, drawn in by the simple but elegant rhythms of the sentences. Teresa blushed at the praise her fellow writers heaped on her latest effort, and she recorded their observations in her notebook.

By the end of the session, they'd made it around to portions from all contributors. Swapping hard copies with comments marked and thanking one another for their candid feedback, the writers had managed to morph again into a harmonious organism, Dee felt, a whole that was truly more, and better, than the sum of its parts.

As the participants wrapped up their empty food containers and headed out the door, Dee thanked each one again. What they'd brought to the table, literally and metaphorically, made her not only grateful but proud of their good-heartedness despite a few opposing views.

Hank, last to depart, stopped to ask, "You need any help with the dishes?"

"Look around," she said. "Not a thing to wash! These folks are all about disposable."

"Yeah, I noticed that," he said with a wry smile. "So, hey, I'm sorry for upsetting the apple cart. I can get preachy."

"Don't apologize, Hank—we're here for open sharing of ideas, not censorship."

"Well, I just wanted you to know my heart's in the right place. I really think I can get something out of this group even if I don't agree with the prevailing opinions."

"Give them a chance. They never fail to surprise me," she said. "Now, while you're here I have something to ask you."

"Okay, what's up?"

Dee explained about the commitment she'd made to the Red Hat Society and the embarrassment she felt at offering such an unappealing and run-down site. "I happened to see what you're doing with your yard across from my mother's house—she's in the Autumn Breeze community and she, ah, called my attention to your xeriscape."

"Yeah, I'll bet she talks to Mrs. Finch too. I've already had to defend myself from three city citations."

"I don't know Mrs. Finch, but I assure you, Mary Alice Bennett's bark is worse than her bite. But it's not about that. My hunch is that you know a few things about native plants and trees and things like that. I wondered if you might offer me some tips for sprucing up this place." She nodded generally in the direction of her front yard, which looked a good deal worse than Hank's.

"Oh, absolutely," Hank said, his face lighting up like a child's at Christmas. "I just happened to do landscaping in Austin before coming out here." He reached for his wallet and drew out a business card for her. "Of course, that's a little different from Caprock County. But I think I would have some recommendations, whenever there's a good time for us to take a look together."

"Great," she said. "How's Saturday?"

13
Social Climbing

Here, where the bride and groom are to receive, one can not tell yet what the decoration is to be. Perhaps it is a hedged-in garden scene, a palm grove, a flowering recess, a screen and canopy of wedding bells—but a bower of foliage of some sort is gradually taking shape.
— "The Drawing-Room"

TENDING TO GOATS was *not* the way Dee Bennett had envisioned her post-doctoral career. Traveling to give lectures in interesting cities, check. Meeting a graduate seminar weekly to discuss great literature and great writing, check. Qualifying for prestigious fellowships to exercise creativity in rustic retreat surroundings, check. Seeing name on title page of books cited in important bibliographies, check. Forking alfalfa through fence to ruminant mammals, not even on the list.

She had to admit, the goats were winsome and curious. Their soft brown hides and floppy ears made them seem like oversized pet dogs. But no dog she knew of sneaked around while you were filling its water trough and lifted your cell phone right out of your back pocket.

"Hey, you, gimme that!" she shouted at Roy—or was it Dale?— when she turned to discover what was happening. She dropped the garden hose in astonishment and made a grab for the phone as the animal ducked out of her grasp. She managed to corner him/her with a deft fake and snatched the device from its lips just as it was destined for destruction. "Now you behave!" Stepping backwards gingerly to make sure the goats didn't make a run for it, she tripped over the hose and landed right in the puddle that had pooled up underneath it. She stood up out of the mud, grabbed the hose, and held it ready to let loose if either of them took a step.

Dee quickly exited the makeshift pen and wired the gate shut again behind her. "Try to stay out of trouble while I go clean up for work again, would you?"

*   *   *

Dee was already running late, and nursing a pounding headache, when the house phone rang.

"Hello?" she barked, more sharply than she meant.

"Somebody didn't get enough sleep last night?"

"Oh, hi, Mama. Sorry. What's up? I've got to get into town."

"That's what I called to ask you. I was hopin' you'd take me to the liberry with you today so I can show you some of the things I've been finding. And I need some help with a few questions I'm trying to look up. I'd buy you lunch at the Lot-a-Burger for your trouble."

Great, she thought. The last thing she needed was her own mother as a reference client, on top of the seventh-grade social studies class that was coming in for a field trip. She hadn't slept well, partly worrying about the goats out there at the mercy of the coyotes and partly worrying about getting up to speed on debate protocols, McCorrigan's opponent, and the issues she would be expected to cover next week. But when had her mother offered to include her in any project?

"Sounds great. I'll be by in about twenty minutes."

Cynthia had a meeting with the Friends of the Library first thing, so Dee was glad not to have to explain her activities when she was on the clock. But her companion didn't go unnoticed by Gladys.

"Brought you a new helper this morning, Dee?" Gladys said, as Dee and her mother each entered, notebooks in hand. "That's good, because your middle schoolers will be here at nine-thirty."

Mama just waved at Gladys and said to Dee, "Don't you mind about me. You do your work, and I won't be in your way. I just need to know, do you have a e-mail address?" Dee wrote it on a slip of paper and handed it to her but didn't have time to ask questions— much less answer them.

Mama got herself situated at one of the work stations in the genealogy section, right around the corner from Reference, while Dee prepared for the onslaught.

When Dee had finished the library orientation and directed thirty students where to seek out information about Cabeza de Vaca, the Treaty of Guadalupe Hidalgo, and Spindletop, she sat down at the reference desk, logged in, and started to look up the first item on her own list. Instantly a string of e-mails popped up on her Windows screen—all of them from the address malice@hotmail.com.

She opened the first, which read, *Take a look. Your great-great grandfather.*

Dee hit Reply. *Mama, when did you get e-mail?*

The thread quickly grew with another message landing in her in-box. *Mr. Grover helped me sign up.* Dee peeked around the corner to see Mama absorbed in the keyboard, pausing only momentarily to adjust her bifocals.

One by one Dee opened and scanned the messages. None of them had subject lines—she'd have to teach Mama a few things about netiquette—but each contained a tidbit of information pertaining to the Bennett and Schmidt family lines, their census records, local newspaper items about them, and even a couple of images. She became so caught up in reading the antiquated prose of the news articles—social announcements, wedding write-ups, obituaries, for the most part—that she hadn't seen Cynthia slip in beside her.

She closed the message and offered Cynthia the morning's sign-in sheet, but she could tell Cynthia had something else on her mind. Surely Gladys hadn't found a way to rat her out?

"So the Write Stuff was a smash hit last night, I thought. Were you surprised?"

"Completely!" she said, thinking even more of the gifts on the hoof than those in the pantry.

"Well, I think we got off to a great start at your place again, and I really appreciate it. I hated that Max couldn't make it, though. How's our friend doing, anyway? Heard from him since the gallery opening?"

"Oh, he's fine, I'm sure. Yes, in fact, I had dinner with him right before I had to go on the McCorrigan junket, and before I got back he had to leave on one of those long out-of-town assignments." Dee was still feeling remorseful about the way they'd left things, and especially about letting a silly football game come between them. "You know how it is."

Cynthia smiled thinly. "Yes. I imagine it's a challenge dating someone who's on the road so often."

"It's just part of the job. I think this week he's up at some ranch in the Panhandle doing a spread about quarter horses."

"Really?" Cynthia said.

Dee nodded.

"Hon, this may not be my place and tell me if I need to butt out, but let me show you something I saw last night on Facebook." Cynthia reached across Dee to type a few strokes on the keyboard and brought up a blue-and-white screen filled with photos and text. She used the mouse to scroll down the screen, coming to a halt at one post. She clicked to enlarge the thumbnail, and there staring right at Dee, in living color, were the smiling faces of Max Miller and Charley Hensley together in front of the landmark neon sign of the Big Texan Steak Ranch in Amarillo.

Dee felt the blood rush to her own face. "How did you get this?" she said. "What is this Face Book?"

"Dee, seriously? Are you just hopelessly stuck in the past? Charley's a Facebook friend of the library, so we get her news feed."

"So everyone in Claxton has seen this?" Dee said, her cheeks growing redder.

"Not everyone, just people who are friends with Charley Hensley."

"That can't be too many."

"About a thousand."

"Omigod," Dee said.

Cynthia scrolled through the list. "Looks like most of her follow-ers aren't in Claxton. And see, if you scroll down through the news feed, you can view things she posted—" Dee jerked the mouse out of Cynthia's hand and scrolled down the screen herself, watching the mini-movie of Charley's social life, causes, check-ins.

"Okay, how do I sign up? I think I need to be *friends* with Charley Hensley."

"It's probably nothing," Cynthia said, "but I thought you'd want to know."

Dee muttered her thanks and turned to the new task at hand.

*   *   *

At the Lot-a-Burger, as she and Mama took their trays and found a booth, Dee didn't have much of an appetite. But she tried to put the irritation of the Facebook matter behind her, rationalizing that there were probably half a dozen good reasons why a photographer and a campaign manager might be in the same geographical area in the middle of an election season.

"So, tell me what you turned up, Mama," she said.

"Well, all them e-mails I sent you are like a great big jigsaw puzzle that you don't have the picture for. That's what Mr. Grover says. You start with some facts that are easy to find, like a census record that shows your own parents, because you usually know their names and facts."

Dee nodded, pleased that her mother was understanding, in a nutshell, her whole career. "Like starting with your parents. George Schmidt and Dee Anna Daughtry."

"Right," Mama said, finishing a bite of grilled chicken sandwich. "They can be found in the census for Caprock County in 1930, four years before I came along. He worked as a gin owner, she was a housewife. You can read it right there in the page I sent you. And it says what their parents' names were and where they were born too."

A recent convert to search tools like Ancestry herself, Dee appreciated the wealth of detail that could be ferreted out. "Are you making a family tree online, Mama?"

"Oh, no, I'm too much of a beginner for that," said Mama as Dee poked at her salad. "But you know, I wasn't a bad typist in my day, and I was really fast with the ten-key machine when I kept the books for the gin. Back then everything was in longhand ledger books. You had to be quick with figures."

"Did your mother work in the gin business too?"

Mama looked away out the window. "I don't think that was likely. I was too young to remember her, as hard as I try, but my aunts always said she liked parties and socials much more than the idea of work. She was her father's favorite. I think he spoiled her. And I think your granddaddy Schmidt was probably a fun-loving sort when he met her and married her, too, but that all changed after she died."

"I don't know what it would be like to lose your mother at two," Dee said, and then added, "or at any age."

"I just don't have any memory of her. After she was killed, my aunts wanted to take me back to Mineola with them. But Papa wouldn't hear of it, even though Aunt Alice had a lot more money and Aunt Sallie had a big old Victorian house with plenty of room. He started taking me to the gin with him every day. I grew up at the gin as much as I did at home."

"Maybe all your research will turn up something that'll jog your memory," Dee suggested. "I'm glad you were able to do so much at the library today."

"Speaking of," said Mama, finishing her Coke and wiping her lips on a paper napkin, "somebody needs to put that Gladys woman in her place."

"You're right," Dee said, uncharacteristically not pulling any punches. "I'll say something to Cynthia."

"Well, don't be too hasty about that. Pick the right time."

"Why are you back-peddling now, Mama?"

"Because having that job is helping keep you here," Mama said, "and I don't want anything that would happen to make you leave again."

Dee reached over and squeezed her mother's arm. "Not a chance."

Family, that's what she was here for, she kept reminding herself. Max Miller could eat all the seventy-two-ounce steaks in Amarillo he wanted to with Miss Prissy Pants Hensley. As long as she had her family and her farm, Dee knew she'd be fine.

* * *

Dee finished out her afternoon stint downloading press materials on Ted Maddox, one of McCorrigan's opponents, drafting a reading list for Cynthia on American presidential elections and the Electoral College, and checking out an armload of books with titles like *So You Want to Raise Goats* and *All about Nubians*.

She wished she had already had a chance to read her selections when she returned home that afternoon. On the front porch, sitting in the rocking chairs in a bizarre parody of farm life, were Roy and Dale. Cori paced nervously on the windowsill inside, between the blinds and the windowpane, eyeing them.

How had the critters gotten out? The fence that Daddy had built for his cows from mattress box springs lashed to fenceposts with wire surely should have contained a couple of small goats, she reasoned. But there they were on her porch, just as unperturbed as they could be and looking down on her with those horizontal pupils like they owned the place.

Although she could see no rupture in the fence or gap in the gate, evidence of the goats' jailbreak was everywhere. The kitchen garden had been nibbled to the roots. The squash, cucumber, and tomato plants looked like a Weed-Eater had thrashed them. No, make that two Weed-Eaters. The lower branches of the peach orchard exhibited signs of munching. Only the jalapeño pepper plants had been spared.

As Dee surveyed the ruined plot both nanny and billy leapt down from their thrones and ambled toward her, bleating and looking a little sheepish—if goats could be sheepish, Dee thought. "Why?" she said to them, sweeping her hand around to indicate the scope of the damage. Roy cocked his head and licked her hand. Dale came up to nibble at the tassel hanging from her shoulder bag. "Y'all can stay out tonight," Dee said. "I'm going to bed."

The phone rang as she unlocked the kitchen door. Wasn't this just the way her day had begun? Dee wondered. Groundhog Day in mirror image. She lifted the handset of the brand-new digital model that had been installed along with the DSL service. "Hi, sweetie," she said. "How are you?"

"Wow, Mom, how did you know it was me? Or were you perhaps expecting Max?" she teased.

Dee explained about the upgrade to caller ID.

"Amazing," Abby said. "Finally, you don't have to call the operator and go through the party line anymore."

"Very funny. Don't pick on me. I've had a hard day."

"What happened?" Abby's tone grew concerned.

"The goats have gotten out."

"Goats?"

Dee related the whole episode of the past twenty-four hours, from the pounding party right down to the welcoming committee on the front porch.

Abby was howling with laughter, calling out on the other end, "Ian, come here, you have to hear this," and adding, to her mother, "I'm making cabrito next time I come."

"They're dairy goats. Nubians. I have to figure out how to milk Miz Dale when the time comes."

"Mom," Abby said, "that's great. You can be on the cutting edge of coolness with this whole goat thing. When the writers come to visit you can serve them fresh chèvre."

"Oh, right."

"I'm serious," Abby said. "I would love to do cheese-making."

"You need to be in college. Your thoughts need to be on calculus and the classics, not cheese."

"Well, there are summers and holidays, and I definitely can see the potential of the home place for some trendy country retreat."

"I'm glad you can. I am seriously out of my depth with trying to fix things up in time for Ruby Lee's big event in a couple of weeks. I don't know what kind of miracle it's going to take."

Dee filled Abby in on all the developments in Claxton, and listened to all the news from New England. She enjoyed talking at length and leisure with her daughter, for once.

When she hung up the phone, she dropped her purse and briefcase on the kitchen table and went to the bedroom to change. She slipped on cotton jersey shorts and a tank top, not bothering with a bra. That was one thing she'd always liked about living in her own place, away from the prying eyes of neighbors. Comfort and creativity went hand in hand, as far as she was concerned.

Dee sat down with a bowl of macaroni noodles and her laptop in front of the TV to check e-mail one last time for the evening, sending an Outlook reminder to the address on Hank Hardeberger's card with a note that she was looking forward to their landscape consultation on Saturday. Sometime later she flipped off Jay Leno on the remote, pulled the afghan from the back of the couch over her, and drifted instantly back to sleep. She dreamed of goats, herds of them, coming in through the front door and eating their way from curtains to kitchen, unstoppable.

*   *   *

Friday morning, before her library hours that afternoon, Dee planned to make some headway on the inside of the house—dealing with the last of the boxes that were still lined up in the hallway. She checked on the goats and did feed and water duty before retreating inside and pulling down the attic staircase again. With long planks and cement blocks from the barn that she hosed down and dried off, she planned to construct utility shelving that would hold her file bins and seldom-used books. Of which there were many.

She felt the urge to get her space in order, to arrange working files where she could easily lay her hands on them but leave stacks of current documents out, untouched, before she could even think of drafting

query letters and other dreary tasks she'd been putting off. The immediate pressure to publish *The Working Writer* might have subsided, but
Dee surely hadn't done all that work and sacrificed her entire summer
only to let the project languish. She needed to circle back with that
agent, see if there was something else she should be doing.

She was on the upstairs end of a load when the house phone
rang downstairs, and she scrambled to get it. Although she'd had
the installers run extra wiring to the attic, she hadn't yet bought a
phone to go there.

Breathless, she reached for the receiver and noted the California
number. "Dee Bennett."

"Dee Bennett, this is Elsa Jensen from San Francisco. I hope you
recall our earlier conversation?" asked a cultured, matronly voice.

Her ears must have been burning, Dee thought. "Why, certainly
I do. I'm very glad to hear from you again." The Californian had
given Dee a great deal of the background that had helped her complete her book manuscript over the summer.

"And I hope your book project is coming along well?"

Dee hesitated but didn't want to display a lack of confidence.
"Quite well, thanks—the manuscript is, ah, in the hands of an agent
who's working on finding the right publisher."

"Well, that sounds very promising," Elsa Jensen said.

Dee didn't have the heart to tell her that her efforts in publishing
a book based on her dissertation were actually more firmly stalled
than when they'd last talked. "I've been working on building a following as a writer, so that when the book is eventually published, it
will sell more copies."

"Yes, your platform, as they say. Good idea," she replied. "Now I'm
sure you're wondering about the reason for my call out of the blue."

"Well, yes, though I'm always glad for you to call."

"I've found a document you that might interest you. Tucked
inside a book of no particular significance."

"Go on?"

"G. H. Templeton, as you recall, moved in the circles of those we
now call the Beat writers, in the forties and fifties. Ginsberg, Burroughs,

Kerouac, the whole bunch. You may also be aware of the famous rumors of a long letter from Neal Cassady that Jack Kerouac always claimed inspired him to write *On the Road*.

"You found it?" Dee nearly dropped the phone.

"Not quite that gold mine, I'm afraid," Elsa continued. "But a clue. A tantalizing clue that literary historians will no doubt find interesting. And that a prospective publisher of your book might, too."

"Wow . . . what can you tell me?"

"Right now, only that the note seems to indicate someone named Allan or Allen might have dropped the whole letter in the mail— rather than over the side of a houseboat, as the story goes. The elusive letter could still be out there—somewhere dry and intact."

Dee didn't know what to think. Elsa's information sounded like a game-changer. "Would you be willing to send me a copy? Or even a transcription?"

"You seemed to me a reliable sort. And the right person to entrust with this find, if I may solicit both your pledge of confidentiality and your assistance in making sense of it."

"Absolutely. You have both. When do we get started?"

Dee's hands shook as she replaced the phone in its cradle. Holy crap, she thought. *This* was big.

*   *   *

Dee was on her way back up to the attic when she heard the sound of a pickup truck stop at the driveway gate, then start up the caliche drive. She climbed up and looked through the dormer window to see J. D. on his way to the front door. He was a good-hearted and generous sort, she knew by now, but naively lacking in courtesy. She climbed back down the stairs and met J. D. at the screen door, just as he was about to about to knock. He held a roll of barbed wire under his arm.

"Morning, J. D. What's going on?"

"Morning, Dee. I brought with me—" he held up the coil to demonstrate— "the invention that tamed the West. People get it wrong when they say the six-shooter made this area livable. It was bob war that kept the livestock from roaming, and *that* finally secured the agri-economy. If this artifact could change history, it can surely keep two little goats safe."

"Thank you, J. D. So I guess word got out about the goats getting out?"

"I heard it from your neighbors Jason and Cheryl Woodberry," he said. "Seems they saw your four-footed friends down by the fence line yesterday. They asked me when you'd taken up goat-raising! I thought the least I could do was come reinforce your pen for you."

"That's awfully nice of you, J. D. Come on in. I'll get my work clothes on, and just pour yourself some coffee. I haven't been able to figure out how Roy and Dale were getting out of the fence, but I sure haven't been able to figure out how they were getting back in!"

Dee went out and worked with J. D. for nearly an hour, learning how to cut and fasten the strands as she watched and assisted, and learning about feeding, vaccinating, and milking while he talked.

"Now, the barbed wire's not for keeping the goats in but for keeping the coyotes out," he explained. "Your bedsprings there are surprisingly effective for fencing your enclosure until you can run some woven wire, maybe with a couple of electrified lines to teach 'em their boundaries. But we'll look for any weak places and pull 'em together with baling wire. And the strands of barbed will go across the top to deter the predators."

When they'd finished patching every hole they could find, Dee suggested they go sit on the porch with some ice water and cool off. They sat in Mama's old lawn chairs in the dwindling bit of shade, observing their handiwork, and watched as first one goat and then another found purchase with their hooves on a slightly bulging and slanted part of a bedspring and pulled up step by step until they could balance on the top edge. Avoiding the barbed wide with ease, Dale picked her way across to the corner where the roof of the tool shed was only a couple of feet away—and leapt gracefully onto it. From there she pranced to the other side, jumped down onto the roof of Daddy's pickup parked beside it, and down to the truck bed and onto the ground. Roy followed right behind.

"Dadgum it," said J. D. "Those scheming little critters might as well have just had themselves a climbing wall installed. I wouldn't have believed it."

They got the pair back into the enclosure with a loaf of day-old Mrs. Baird's bread and spent another half hour straightening out the bent side of the fence. "Well, I sure hope that's an improvement," said J. D., "or we'll have to get you a guard dog to keep the goats corralled."

Dee hoped it wouldn't come to that.

*   *   *

After waving good-bye to J. D., Dee climbed the attic stairs once again to turn the lights off, headed back down, and let the attic stairs up. She was running late and rushing to the shower when the phone rang again.

"Hey, Cuz," said the voice on the other line.

"Hey, Cuz, yourself," Dee shot back. "Make it quick, Ruby Lee, I've got to report for duty, and the high school Career Club will be waiting to help me sort books for the used book sale."

"Well, that sounds like an exciting afternoon," Ruby Lee said. "I was hoping to go over details for the style show—you know, theme and decorations, refreshments, parking, and, ah, grounds maintenance. We probably have to start on that right away."

"I get it. You're worried I might not have thought about mowing the yard and trimming the weeds, right?"

"I'm just offering help before things get to the last minute, is all."

"I think I've got it covered. If we could talk about the other stuff early next week, that would be great."

For now that seemed to satisfy her. Good grief, Dee wondered, how was a body ever supposed to think about getting any writing done out here?

14
Getting Over the Color Green

It was in June in the country. The invitations were by word of mouth to neighbors and personal notes to the groom's relatives at a distance. The village church was decorated by the bride, her younger sisters, and some neighbors, with dogwood, than which nothing is more bridelike or beautiful. The shabbiness of her father's little cottage was smothered with flowers and branches cut in a neighboring wood. Her dress, made by herself, was of tarlatan covered with a layer or two of tulle, and her veil was of tulle fastened with a spray, as was her girdle, of natural bridal wreath and laurel leaves. Her bouquet was of trailing bridal wreath and white lilacs.

— "Wedding of a Cinderella"

DEE, WORN OUT FROM yesterday's physical labors, half woke to the tattoo of wood knocking against wood, a sound she was having a hard time placing over the soothing white noise of the air conditioner and the chatter of the television. When she'd fallen asleep on the couch last night, the temperature had still been in the eighties—unseasonably hot in mid-September, even for West Texas. Now she was chilled, her feet sticking out from under the afghan. She leapt up, startling Cori and sending the cat scurrying under the couch, when she recognized the sound as coming from the kitchen screen door. The sun was barely up, but she also made out bleating noises of animals waiting to be fed.

Those damn goats, she thought, and rushed to the front door and flung it open, ready to shoo Roy and Dale off the porch. But there, with the goats nosing around him and trying to get inside, stood Hank Hardeberger. He looked freshly showered and shaved, dressed in a short-sleeved black rayon T-shirt and cargo shorts.

"Dee?" he said. "Good morning?"

"Hank?" was the only thing she knew to reply. She swiftly brushed her tangled hair back out of her face with her hand. "Wow, I'm so sorry, is it eight already? I didn't hear the alarm."

"Oh, shoot, I got a reminder in my e-mail for seven," he said, drawing his iPhone out of his pocket and consulting it. "You sent it to my Outlook a couple of days ago."

"Right, yeah, of course . . . I don't know what I did wrong, but—" Suddenly becoming conscious of her not-ready-for-prime-time appearance, she blurted out, "I've got to get dressed. Be right back."

Before she could shut the door in his face he said, "Did you know your goats are out?"

"Yes," she said. "Talk to them and they'll keep you company."

"If this is a bad time, should I come back later?" he said.

The realization of her unintended rudeness left her more chastised than her state of undress. "No, no. Hey, come on in and have a seat, it's no big deal."

She went back to change quickly into something presentable, washed her face and brushed her teeth, and slipped her favorite kayaking cap on over her ponytail. Picking up her phone from the hall table, she scrolled quickly to the appointment reminder she'd sent. *Eastern* daylight time, she noted, to her embarrassment. An old habit.

She showed Hank her screw-up and apologized for getting him out of bed so early on a Saturday. "And I certainly didn't mean for you to make the coffee," she said sheepishly.

"No worries. How do you take yours?"

She added half-and-half to the cup he'd poured for her. "Well, we'll make an early start and beat the heat, won't we? And I can at least offer you a bite of breakfast."

From the freezer she took a plastic-wrapped package of home-made cinnamon rolls, glad that Abby had left her with a few premade meals, and put them in the microwave to defrost. She slid one of the hot rolls onto a salad plate for each of them and handed Hank a fork.

"This is fabulous," he said, taking a bite. "Yum."

"My daughter's the cook," she said.

"You have a daughter old enough to cook?"

"Don't flatter me," Dee said. "She's a sophomore in college."

"Wow," Hank said. "So just you and your family manage this place?"

"Just me now," Dee answered. "And 'manage' is a relative term."

They took their coffee cups and plates out on the porch, where Dale had now climbed into the windowsill and was peering in at a suspicious Cori. Roy nudged Hank's arm and tried to sneak a bite of the pastry.

"You wanted to talk about shrubs and flowers and things like that," he said to Dee, chuckling, "but it looks like the top priority in your landscape plan is going to be a stronger pen."

"Shall we say, the goats were an unexpected acquisition." She laughed. "But they seem to have made themselves at home." They got the goats back inside the fence and turned to the matter at hand.

"Tell me what plans you have in mind," Hank said, grabbing a note pad from the front seat of his car. "Help me see what you see, short-term and long-term, and I'll make recommendations that get you started in the direction you want to go."

"That's just it, I'm not sure I know," said Dee. "I grew up here and have had this same picture of the place just as it's always been. Some of the trees have grown taller over the years, and some have been lost. The weeds grow up, we chop them down. Otherwise it hasn't changed much."

"Well, then, walk with me and talk about what you always liked about the picture, and what you didn't," Hank said. "That'll help me understand you better. Understand what you want better, I mean." For a guy so vocal about his passion for protecting the environment, Dee thought, he seemed pretty level-headed and laid-back. At least today, on a late-summer morning with a cool breeze blowing over the ridge, nothing about their conversation seemed hurried or fraught with an agenda. She let herself relax and ramble.

"I'm not much of a farmer," she explained to him. "Sure, I always did my share of work in the cotton fields, but I knew it wasn't what I wanted to do as a grownup. So I never did acquire a green thumb or learn the business. I'd be lost overseeing the crops now without Hector and Flora, who handle all the farming."

"But you want to continue that? You want to keep producing cotton?"

"I'm not married to cotton. It might be smart to rotate, just like we did this season with the milo. As long as Mama's alive, I don't see us putting the land to a different use. Hunting, CRP, anything like that. And we're too far from town for residential development, thank goodness, so I'm glad I don't feel any pressure to chop the acreage up into ten-acre ranchettes."

"So you mean to keep it agricultural. That narrows down our focus, doesn't it? To the house and outbuildings and the grounds immediately surrounding them?"

"Yes, that makes sense. You can see that we've never had a fence marking off the lawn, if you can call it that — the rows just come up close to the orchards and the yard and stop. I could certainly see a more generous patch of grass around the house, at least, with some shade trees in addition to the cedars that are already there as a shelterbelt."

Hank smiled wryly. "You know, the writer Wallace Stegner had some wisdom that West Texans often have to take to heart."

"What's that?"

"He said that in order to appreciate the arid West, you have to get over the color green. That out here, it's about geological time, not gardens and lawns, the ideal we're used to."

Dee mulled over the concept. "I can see that, but I don't want to live in the Sahara, either."

"There are some excellent choices of plant material that'll be pleasing to the eye without requiring lots of maintenance or extra water. But if it's a half acre of Bermuda sod you want to see, I'm probably not your man."

"Point taken. So, why don't we discuss some of those short-term solutions for making things look good right around the house first? Something that will have the greatest impact within—two weeks?"

Hank raised his eyebrows, but if the deadline fazed him, he didn't show it otherwise. "And do you have a budget for this phase?"

"Twenty-five hundred dollars," she answered unequivocally. "That's what I'm earning on the event, and I plan to reinvest every dollar of it!"

As they examined each plane of the square wooden house, Hank noted on his pad some suggestions for hardscape and plantings, basing his recommendations on the installation of a rain barrel and runoff capture system that would serve irrigation needs. "This can be done very inexpensively with one length of roof gutter across the back and one downspout, for now. And the barrel's nothing more than a big plastic fifty-five gallon drum with a wire screen over it. A few silverleaf sage bushes would grow up to hide the ugly parts, and they'll give you beautiful purple color most of the year after every rain."

"I like it already."

He continued to sketch out a design that incorporated a field-stone walkway set among river-rock pebbles off the kitchen porch, surrounded by water-wise desert plants like yuccas, autumn sage, and butterfly bush. Standing beside her on the east-facing porch, he pointed out, "This is where I think you want to start, rather than the front, because it's the entrance that's used the most and it's seen the most. It's the one where you greet friends and family. And the viewshed is the best."

"Viewshed?"

"What you can see from here. Your front entrance looks out over that long, sloping driveway and you can see a long way towards Claxton, but on this side the vista is more serene and varied. Plus it's bright in the morning and shaded in the afternoon. And the old wooden windmill is a great focal point."

Dee cast her gaze past the barn and the unsightly livestock pen, trying to see through his eyes. "I do see what you mean . . . the land gets more uneven, with more interesting angles. And more mesquite trees."

"Don't go dissin' your mesquites, honey. Clean out some of the brush around them, and you'll be surprised how well they'll fit in your overall plan."

"I do like what you're saying. Serenity is a good description. I think . . . I think I'd like to see the place in that way, as a retreat, a place to be inspired and create. But who ever considers the flat plains a retreat? People go to the beach, or the mountains."

"You came here, didn't you?"

"Not my first choice."

"But there's something you find inspiring, isn't there?"

Dee looked up toward her one lonely little dormer window off the attic and then back at the *viewshed*. "I get what you're saying. With some renovations to the house, to bring in more light, like that, and maybe an arbor or pergola out here to provide shade—I get it."

"Yes, exactly!"

She turned once more to the barn and its haphazard add-ons. "I can see that the barn could be converted to an inviting meeting space. And there's plenty of open land here, to move a few abandoned cabins and fix them up . . . with pathways between them . . . "

"Don't forget the swimming pool, and we'll just about have reached the limit of your twenty-five hundred bucks," he joked.

"Well, like you said, the long term." She smiled and said, "Why don't you come in and let's have some lunch while we work out the baby steps?"

Over grilled cheese sandwiches and chips the pair whittled down the wish list into phases. Hank sketched and estimated costs and schedule, and Dee okayed the portions she thought were realistic to tackle first. But she let herself bask in the allure of the idealistic, let her mind wander into the "what if" as freely as she liked.

This guy seemed to invite that freedom, to open a door into her imagination. With Max, she was on more of a parallel track of creativity, him with his world of light and shadows and images and her separate one with words and plots and stories. Max was apt to disappear into his world for days, working in solitary pursuits, just like she often did. Hank acted like someone comfortable in whatever environment he found himself.

And just why was she even making the comparison? she thought, chagrined. Just enjoy the moment.

"I have a bottle of wine," she said, in no hurry to bring their session to an end. "Sit out on the porch with me now that it's shady, and join me in a glass?"

Hank looked pleased. "I wouldn't mind that at all."

She opened the bottle of crisp Pinot Grigio, a housewarming gift Penny had sent home with her, and poured two glasses. By early afternoon the east porch was an inviting place, just as he'd so readily recognized. Roy and Dale munched happily on their hay inside the pen and Cori curled around Hank's feet. Dee apologized for the rudimentary seating, tubular aluminum–style lawn chairs with striped webbing that were not retro but the genuine artifact.

She explained to Hank how her father had never thrown anything away, but kept a broken item of any, or no, significance for spare parts and always repaired rather than replaced.

"The ultimate recycler," Hank observed, sipping his Pinot.

"I did not want to come back here into that life, though," she confided as she started in on her second glass. "That sense of meagerness. I wanted to escape the small-mindedness."

"Do you feel that way now?"

"Surprisingly, no. I'm coming to see possibility." She took another sip and waxed expansive. "What if I did decide to stay here in the long run? What if I did build on what we've started with the writers' group? The 'Paragraph Ranch' started out as nothing more than a clever line. What if it could be more than a joke?"

"What if it could?"

"Writers could come for a weekend or a week . . . they would have a wonderful place of beauty in their little bungalows, and then there'd be a great gathering place where we could all share stories."

"*We.* You see yourself as part of this equation in the long run."

"Why, yes, I believe I do." It was a dream she'd never told another soul. An idea she'd never really articulated to herself.

Hank scribbled some more notes and made more sketches in his pad. "I'm seeing the flagstones extended out that way to the barn . . . with more shrubs added to soften the hard lines, a desert willow right about here, for color and shade . . . and low-level solar light-ing for the paths, since I assume guests might be walking around after dark . . . a concrete utility path over this way, for handicapped access . . . taking advantage of a few dips in the ground, a series of drains to make a swale, with an ornamental wooden bridge . . . "

"Now who's thinking outside the budget?!"

"I worked with a lot of clients in Austin who started small and built on it," he said. "Don't be afraid to dream big."

She let the good vibe wash over her as she silently turned the idea over in her mind. Far off, doves cooed in the cedar branches. Crickets chirped in a thicket, nearby. A freshening breeze soughed through the mesquites, rattling the drying seed pods. *This. This is what I want to do with my life. Now it's just a matter of how.*

Hank, who seemed to sense her reverie, said, "I'll leave you to your thoughts—I should be going. And thanks for the refreshments. I'll talk to the contractor and get back to you on Monday, that okay?"

"Sure," she said, clasping his outstretched hand to say good-bye but not getting up from her seat. "You've given me lots to consider, and I'm eager to see the metamorphosis started."

"Yes," Hank said, and then added, "As soon as you get those goats fenced for good."

* * *

Dee polished off the rest of the bottle alone and went in to shower, still riding the crest of her sweeping ideas and good spirits. If she built it, would they come? She took her time as she dressed, then walked through each room of the house to look out a different window and appreciate the changing viewshed. What a great word.

The house itself wasn't large enough to serve as a meeting space for more than a dozen or so, and certainly not functional as a bed and breakfast, given its one bathroom. But that didn't mean that a few cosmetic improvements wouldn't go a long way to make it more inviting, more in harmony with its surroundings and their evolving potential. It had never been anything but a plain white box, inside and out. That could change.

The phone rang, startling and urgent with its new digital ringtone. Maybe she could change that, too. She had grown to appreciate the caller ID feature, however, which saved you from being caught off guard. Nonetheless, her good mood came crashing down when she registered the name and flashed back to that damned Facebook picture.

"Hi, Max," she answered coolly. "Are you back in town?"

"Is that the best welcome a guy gets? I missed you, babe. And I wondered if you were up for company."

"I—sure, I am. And I had been wondering what you were up to, too."

"I'll tell you all about it when I get there. I'll bring dinner, that okay?"

He knocked on her door at seven, sweeping her into his arms with a big kiss and offering up a bouquet of half a dozen stunning peach-and-gold-hued roses.

"What's this?" she asked, immediately suspicious.

"Peace roses. An apology," Max said. "For being such a jerk at your brother's big game and then waiting for two weeks to say I'm sorry."

"Yeah, that wasn't fun," she said, still waiting for any further words of atonement.

"You haven't been around me long enough to know how I am on an assignment, Dee," he said. "When I'm out on the road I'm totally absorbed in the work, and the rest of the world just doesn't exist. That doesn't mean I didn't feel bad about how things went between us. And it doesn't mean I didn't think of you."

She put the flowers in a tea pitcher—all she had for the moment—and said, "I get that way too. And I was churlish about the football game myself. I didn't need to get my nose out of joint."

"I am very proud for your family and Buddy for all he's accomplished. He's a helluva coach. His team played their hearts out and beat a much bigger school. I didn't need to get peeved."

She nodded, noncommittal.

"So hey, are we okay again? Why don't I go out and get the casserole and the wine. And I brought somebody with me."

Brought somebody? She still wondered if he would come clean about the Charley thing. But she was genuinely glad to see him after so long, and eager to regain the easy romance that had started to blossom between them.

She wiped down the kitchen table where she'd left crumbs from her lunch with Hank and heard Max's truck door open. A joyous series of barks ensued, followed by Max's surprised admonition, "Chester! Get back here! What are you doing?!"

Dee looked out the window to see Max's unrestrained yellow lab going for the livestock fence. Roy and Dale began going nuts as the dog circled, leaping nearly to the top edge. She got a laugh at the sight of Max in his freshly pressed Saturday-night duds chasing down the unruly Chester. Served him right for not finding out what had been happening during his absence.

When he got the dog under control and inside the house, he handed her a still-hot Pyrex dish wrapped in a towel, and a bottle of wine. "Goats?" he said, puzzled.

"Max and Chester, meet Roy and Dale. Friends of our buddy J. D. Sandifer."

"Oh," Max said, as if that explained it all.

As she set the table Dee proceeded to tell him all about the Write Stuff potluck and the other events that had transpired, leaving off at this morning's rendezvous with Hank Hardeberger. He in turn related the experience of photographing horses and herds, while he unwrapped the dish and set it, steaming, in front of them, along with a big bowl of Caesar salad and a basket of rolls.

"King Ranch casserole," he said. "Just like my mom taught me to make it."

"It all looks delicious—thank you!"

"So, how's the political beat going?" he asked her as they each tried a forkful.

"Challenging. I have to study something new every day to keep up. Just like college, except there's no syllabus to follow."

"Funny thing, it turns out McCorrigan's campaign bus was in the same part of the state I was last week. I gave him my schedule for the month before I left town, and there we were, the ranch manager and I, having dinner in Amarillo, and in walk all of his folks, with a news team right behind them. He sure gets around."

He's not the only one who gets around, Dee thought. But she pushed that image from her mind.

15
Going to the Candidates' Debate

The groom's mother goes down the aisle on the arm of the head usher and takes her place in the first pew on the right; the groom's father follows alone, and takes his place beside her; the same usher returns to the vestibule and immediately escorts the bride's mother; he should then have time to return to the vestibule and take his place in the procession. The beginning of the wedding march should sound just as the usher returns to the head of the aisle. To repeat: *No other person should be seated after the mother of the bride.* Guests who arrive later must stand in the vestibule or go into the gallery.
—"The Perfectly Managed Wedding"

D.O.D., **READ THE NOTEPAD** sheet taped to the side of Dee's temporary desk at the *Courier* office. Monday mornings, when the paper held its story budget meeting, were usually the only time she made use of it, but by now everyone in the newsroom knew the sign meant "Dee On Deadline." *Do Not Disturb.*

This Wednesday morning, however, was a special case and especially critical, in light of Thursday night's big event. At ten minutes to eleven Dee was racing to finish her advance story on the upcoming debate among the candidates for railroad commissioner, before she had to turn it in and head to her library job. She heard the front door open, and a sweet-sounding female voice asked Becca at the front desk, "Is Dee Bennett available?"

Dee peered over the top of the cubicle wall as Becca said "Ask her yourself," and nearly didn't recognize the visitor. A severely toned-down Charley Hensley turned the corner and said, "Dee, do you have a moment?"

No stiletto heels. No plunging necklines. No heavy perfume. Charley wore jeans, flats, and a gingham shirt. It was as though *Gilligan's Island's* Ginger had morphed into Mary Ann.

She waited for Dee's agreement before sliding into the seventies-style chair next to the big wooden desk. "It's good to see you."

"Sure, you too," Dee said, wondering where the politeness had suddenly come from.

"How's our friend Max?" Charley added.

You've probably seen him since I have, Dee thought, but said, "Fine, just fine."

"Listen," Charley said, "I know you're busy and I don't want to take up a lot of your time."

Dee noticed Phil, the sports reporter, and Suzy, the ad sales rep, lingering over the copier and looking their way.

"What can I do for you, Charley?"

"Oh, I wanted to give you this," she said, handing her a press release. "We actually thought about suspending our campaign in support of Senator McCain, but decided it was best for Texas that we carry on."

Dee glanced at the headline McCorrigan Lauds House for Voting Down Bailout. Oh, crap, she thought, and looked up at the TV monitor airing CNN. Ali Velshi was on a split-screen and the stock market had plunged 770 points since the house decision. Dee felt nauseous—not just for the national economy but for the looming deadline.

"Okay, thanks," Dee said, "but you didn't stop by in person just to give me a press release, did you?"

"Not entirely," Charley said, lowering her voice conspiratorially as though the conversation were a coffee klatch between girlfriends. "We'd like to offer the *Courier* an exclusive on the debate prep tonight. Since the *Courier* is the hometown newspaper for the hometown candidate, of course."

Even with Dee's spotty appreciation of journalistic ethics, she knew that all candidates warranted equal coverage, and she understood that an exclusive could sway the audience in favor of only one. She needed to confirm her instincts with Shannon, but she didn't want to appear as though she had to ask for permission for every move—especially not in front of this woman.

She took a deliberate look at her watch and said to Charley, "I have to submit this story in three minutes. Call you back in ten?" She added, leaning in conspiratorially, "Or maybe I can just message you on Facebook. You seem pretty active there?" Gingham-clad Mary Ann behaved a little less like the ingénue at that one, Dee thought.

In no time Shannon's head appeared over the back side of Dee's cubicle. "Becca texted me that you were getting the hard squeeze from McCorrigan's campaign."

Dee confirmed that was so.

"You played it just right," Shannon said. "Get back to her and accept the opportunity but tell her you'll be giving the other two campaigns the same coverage as well."

Dee suppressed a flash of anxiety over the specter of a suddenly tripled workload and dialed Charley's number. "I'm sure it was never your intention to gain an unfair advantage," she explained, "but if the hometown newspaper were to provide a behind-the-scene profile of the hometown boy it might even persuade locals to show up and cheer for McCorrigan on statewide TV—yep, we've heard that PBS is streaming it in conjunction with the college's channel— and none of us wants to encourage bias, do we?"

"Dee, we don't want to be any trouble," Charley replied. "And we don't want to put you to all that research and work for three stories at the last minute." She paused and backed off. "It was just an idea, no worries. We'll see you and Max there?"

"You bet," Dee said, even though she didn't yet have a clue what Max's plans were. She walked back to the editor's door to tell her boss they were off the hook, and suddenly got it. "You knew that's what she'd say all along, didn't you?"

*   *   *

That evening Dee and Mama dined on grocery-store pizza while watching the national television news. Mama changed the channel from Abilene's local program to CNN, which blared with talking heads and a continuous crawl line. Sensory overload, thought Dee, who'd had about enough of the rhetoric for one day.

"Senator McCain's a good man," Mama said, transfixed by the screen, "but I'm afraid he's not going to win, and then it scares me about what's going to happen to the country."

"We might be headed for another Great Depression either way, from the looks of it, Mama. Did you see about the bank collapsing in Washington and people lined up for their money?"

"Yes, Lordy. It's got me worried. I remember all the stories about my Daughtry grandparents. They were well off—not filthy rich, but I don't think they lacked for anything—and then the stock market crash wiped them out. Not all at once, but just like these folks on TV today, they had money in banks, and tied up in stocks and bonds, and when their assets were devalued and you couldn't even sell cotton for a nickel a pound, their creditors called in notes. They defaulted, just like these businesses are doin'."

Dee focused her attention on a smaller screen, the one on her iPhone, experimenting with the little green icon portraying a speech bubble.

"What's that you're working on over there so intently?" Mama asked.

"Text messaging," said Dee. "I'm determined not to keep letting technology get the best of me."

"I don't know why young folks can't just pick up the phone and call like God always intended. I'm going to have to get that computer just to keep up with Abby. Can't get her to call me these days, now that classes have started."

"I heard from her last night. By text. I think she and Ian are putting in all their spare hours volunteering for the Obama campaign."

"Hmmph," said Mama. "Easier job there than in Texas. Did you ask her if she got that card with the twenty dollars I sent her?"

"No," said Dee, looking up from the iPhone. "The message just popped up on my screen and I didn't how to send a reply back. That's what I'm trying to learn right now."

"I told her to put it on her phone bill. So I guess everything that goes around, comes around."

Dee finished typing her outgoing message to Max's number on the tiny screen. *Will you be my date to the candidates' debate?* She touched the "Send" tab, causing the phone to make a digital *whoosh* signal. Ten seconds later her phone registered a petite little ping and there, in a colored oval, was his reply. She smiled. *If you let me take U 2 dinner after.*

"Yes!" she said aloud despite herself.

"What?" Mama asked.

"I've just figured out the secret to communicating with men and teenagers," she said.

*   *   *

In Dee's mailbox when she stopped at the gate at nearly dark were two things that interested her. One, an oversized postcard inviting graduates of Claxton High School to an All-Class Reunion on the night of the Homecoming football game, October 31, with special guest Rowdy McCorrigan.

The other, a large Kraft envelope, addressed in a spidery hand from Elsa Jensen of San Francisco, California.

Dee shut the gate behind her again, thinking an automatic gate would be the next thing on her home improvement list, but drove up to the house, suddenly revived despite the long work day. She picked her way around the pathway the contractors had started digging out for the flagstones and gravel, and skirted the piles of sand and mulch heaped beside the porch.

She opened the envelope and retrieved a single photocopied sheet, with a note from Elsa paper-clipped at the top. "With hope you can shed light." She turned on the chandelier above the kitchen table and lay the page flat. Cori hopped up to investigate.

"Down, my friend," she said to the cat. "Your attempts to add a footnote to history will not be appreciated."

The note was indeed cryptic—scribbled on the back of a page torn from a 1955 daily diary.

> Allan—
> You might ask for Neal's letter back from Gerd when you go up there. I know it didn't work out with Ace; Wyn's moved on to other things after taking Junky. Bob says there's a place here in Oakland where he ought to submit it.
>
> G.

Dee examined the photocopy closely and made a few obvious guesses. Allan—or Allen—the handwriting wasn't clear—was the easiest. Allan Day Jensen, Elsa's late uncle and a well-known Bay Area jazz musician. Or Allen Ginsberg, most famous of the Beat writers. Neal? That could only be Cassady, if this letter bore any relationship at all to the story that had circulated among literary historians for decades.

She turned the facts over in her mind as she remembered from her college reading. Cassady, Jack Kerouac's outrageous and sexually adventurous friend from Denver after whom Kerouac had modeled his character Dean Moriarty from *On the Road* (and maybe others, though Dee didn't recall the specifics), had actually inspired Kerouac's stream-of-consciousness style by showing him a long typewritten letter—multiple thousands of words—based on semi-autobiographical escapades.

That letter, apparently more of a story-length manuscript that Kerouac encouraged Cassady to publish, was known to Beat circles through a small portion retyped by one of them. The fugitive longer letter, which the writers called "the Joan Anderson letter" among themselves, took on mythic proportions when Kerouac told reporters, after the phenomenal success of *On the Road* in 1957, that someone had lost it the waters of San Francisco Bay—over the railing of a Sausalito houseboat.

She took the piece of paper and her laptop over to the recliner, fully intending to search that strange name, Gerd. But she drifted off to sleep in the chair, waking at midnight Eastern time when the Outlook program lit up her computer screen with a reminder, hastily set for the date and no specific hour, that September 25, in fifteen minutes, the Railroad Commission Debate would take place.

* * *

In the library later that day, a different research question had been nagging at the back of her mind, and there hadn't been time until now to look into it. Where would she start, if she wanted to track down a football player named Ricky Jones who'd played for the Cougars through 1977 and then suddenly disappeared from sight? She checked all the relevant yearbooks for the elusive student who had dropped completely off the radar. From his class pictures, Jones was a good-looking boy, and judging from his extracurriculars a brilliant one. She photocopied relevant pages—anything that listed his name might provide a clue—and soon turned up a few promising leads.

First, the Claxton city directory for 1977 included thirty-six listings for Jones names. She'd track every one down, if need be. Second, she had the names of all the other team members from the yearbook. She could try them too. Third, a skimpy 1979 obituary for a Doris Jones of Dallas listed surviving children Letha Jones McCray of Abilene and Ricky Jones, no city of residence given. There was at least a chance this could be the right track. The current Abilene phone book easily yielded up only two McCrays. She'd cross her fingers that one was the person she sought.

She stepped into the break room to make her call. At the first number there was no answer, but the other number was answered on the eighth ring, just as she was about to give up. A male voice, which she judged by its timbre and rhythm to be aged, answered, "McCray."

"Hi, my name is Dee Bennett, and I'm trying to reach Letha McCray. Do I have the right number?"

"She my niece. What you need wid her?"

"I'd—I'd like to talk with her about a family matter."

"Fam'ly matter. Well, she don' have a listing in the phone book. You gotta call on her cell."

"I understand. Can you give me that number?"

"No, cain't give out no number. You want me to write down yours, I git her to call you back."

"Please do," she said, and provided the information. "She's welcome to call me anytime. And before I let you go, can you tell me to whom I'm speaking?"

"Naw, lady, you don't need my name. Nobody says 'to whom' need to know my name."

*   *   *

Dee and Max arrived early for the debate and took seats close to the front but off to one side of the big semicircle so that she could gauge both the candidates and the crowd. The moderator and panelists were already in place, doing their run-through and mic check.

"Good evening from the Claxton Community College Performing Arts Center. I'm Shannon Thomas, editor of the *Claxton Courier,* and I'd like to welcome you to our debate between the Republican nominee for Texas Railroad Commissioner, Rowdy McCorrigan, and the Democratic nominee, Ted Maddox," said Shannon, following the script on the teleprompter. "The Libertarian candidate, Branford A. Barthels, was unable to attend. We'd like to thank our host, Claxton Community College, and our sponsor, the Claxton County League of Women Voters.

"Let me introduce the rest of the press panel. Justin Dodson from KPBN-TV Midland, Chuck Sherwin from the *Fort Worth Star-Telegram,* and Bill Levy from *Texas Oil & Gas* magazine."

Quiet conversation rippled through the auditorium during the final few minutes before the feed went live. Campaign staffers for both hopefuls finished their last on-stage checks for mic height, water, notepads. No Charley Hensley in sight, Dee noticed.

"I could never go into politics," Max said to her quietly.

"Me either," Dee replied. "Way too much stress."

"But I admire their commitment. Somebody has to do it."

Things were quiet for a minute, and then Dee heard a rush at the door as handlers ushered in the families of each candidate.

Dee remembered Gretchen McCorrigan from the campaign bus. Her no-nonsense style was in evidence tonight. She recognized son Thomas and daughter Laura as well.

Earlene Maddox was classic West Texas—from her peasant dress accented with cowboy boots to her turquoise and sterling silver necklace, earrings, and multiple bracelets. The way Earlene tossed her highlighted blunt cut reminded Dee that she had been the head cheerleader thirty-five years ago in Sweetwater, one county over and Claxton's biggest prep rival. All of the Maddoxes wore boots. The teenaged boys wore bolo ties and western cut jackets, and the young daughter a western skirt like her mom's. Dee had never been much of a political junkie, but she had to admit that it all made for good theater.

The local leaders began to arrive. Mayor Shelton spotted Max and came over and shook his hand. He finally spoke to Dee when Max reintroduced them. Hank Hardeberger walked right to the front row, took a seat behind the moderator, and reviewed what seemed to be a stack of note cards.

The guys from Texas Star Energy went to the back row at the left, Dee noted. Her neighbor Buck Turlock sat at the back, on the right.

"Hello, folks," Shannon said. "I need everyone to come in and take your seats promptly. We'll be shutting down the house lights soon for the cameras."

Soon Dee couldn't tell who was coming in to the darkened auditorium. And then it was time to start. Shannon repeated the intro, and the candidates each made an entrance and shook hands to applause from the audience.

"Gentlemen, I'll be starting the questions tonight. And here's the first one. At this very moment tonight, where do you stand on the nation's financial recovery plan? By coin toss, Mr. Maddox, you get the first answer."

"Well, thank you very much, Shannon, and thanks to Claxton Community College for hosting us tonight and to the Claxton County League of Women Voters for sponsoring us.

"You know, we are at a defining moment in America's history. Our nation is involved in two wars, and we are going through the worst financial crisis since the Great Depression. And although we've heard a lot about Wall Street, I think those of you on Main Street have been struggling for a while, and you recognize that this could have an impact on all sectors of the economy.

"And you're wondering, how's it going to affect me? How's it going to affect my job? How's it going to affect my house? How's it going to affect my retirement savings or my ability to send my children to college?

"So we have to move swiftly, and we have to move wisely. The presidential nominee of the Democratic Party has put forward a series of proposals that make sure that we protect taxpayers as we engage in this important rescue effort.

"Number one, we've got to make sure that we've got oversight over this whole process; seven hundred billion dollars, potentially, is a lot of money.

"Number two, we've got to make sure that taxpayers, when they are putting their money at risk, have the possibility of getting that money back and gains, if the market — and when the market — returns.

"Number three, we've got to make sure that none of that money is going to pad CEO bank accounts or to promote golden parachutes.

"And number four, we've got to make sure that we're helping homeowners, because the root problem here has to do with the foreclosures that are taking place all across the country."

"Mr. McCorrigan, two-minute rebuttal?" Shannon said.

"Oh, it won't take that long," McCorrigan said.

Dee detected a rustling noise at the back of the auditorium behind her as Charley Hensley shepherded a huge crowd of her candidate's partisans down the aisle, sliding in to take places behind the family.

"Mr. Maddox can't even say their nominee's name," McCorrigan proceeded. "He's embarrassed that the Democrat party has nominated Barack Hussein Obama for president. How do you think that's going to fly in Texas?"

As if on cue, the McCorrigan troops laughed and whistled, and whooped and hollered.

"Please, we need to be respectful," the moderator reminded the audience.

The candidates dueled back and forth for another half hour on oil and gas issues, Maddox offering thought-out solutions to questions, McCorrigan zingers.

Shannon shifted the focus to a more personal angle with her next question. "Mr. McCorrigan, there's an increasing demand these days for accountability to an elected official's campaign promises, at any level of government. If elected railroad commissioner, how would you remain faithful to your vows?"

Rowdy McCorrigan hesitated for a second, then rallied to respond, "I have always been faithful to my vows and always will be. I uphold the family values that make our country great."

Max leaned over to Dee and said, "Do I smell a lying sack of shit?"

Dee replied, "I'm beginning to think so." She wondered what Shannon was fishing for.

When the time arrived for questions from the audience, the first person at the mic was Hank Hardeberger. "Where do you both stand on fracking?" he said, leaning in toward the mic and holding his note cards in his hand.

"Mr. McCorrigan," Shannon said, "that question would go to you first."

"I believe that that is a decision for Texans. Rather than pursue a one-size-fits-all federal regulatory approach to energy development, we should empower the states to develop, adopt, and enforce regulations and review processes based on the unique geology, ecology, and concerns of each state and its citizens. From oil and gas to wind and solar development, local regulators are best positioned to understand and thoughtfully address their own unique considerations."

"So are you for it or against it?" Hardeberger said.

"You have my answer," McCorrigan replied.

"Mr. Maddox?" Shannon said.

"The Democratic Party platform has proposed a number of common-sense requirements asking companies to publicly disclose chemicals used in hydraulic fracturing and to protect drinking water sources across 750 million acres of public and tribal lands. And we recommend finalizing standards to require operators of new fractured natural gas wells to use cost-effective technologies and practices to capture pollutants which contribute to smog formation, and air toxics, including benzene and hexane, which can cause cancer and other serious health effects."

Dee was scribbling furiously, trying to capture everything both candidates had said.

Max leaned over again. "Remind me to show you this new invention called a tape recorder."

"Next question?" Shannon said.

A tool pusher from Snyder asked, "Where do you stand on the oil depletion allowance?"

"If it ain't broke, don't fix it," McCorrigan said.

Maddox said, "I don't think the big energy companies need to have oil depletion allowances, but for small, independent oil and gas producers, if they didn't have them to rely on, there'd be even less exploration in America than there is today."

McCorrigan partisans began some low, intermittent booing, which they ceased immediately when the moderator whirled around and glared at them. "I believe we're ready for final statements," Thomas turned back and said.

At the end of the debate, Dee had a strong sense the momentum in the race had shifted. McCorrigan had been the front runner by twenty points. His margin had surely tightened.

16
Texas Writers Offline

Just as it is contrary to all laws of etiquette for the bride to accept any part of her trousseau or wedding reception from the groom, so it is unthinkable for the bride to defray the least fraction of the cost of the wedding journey, no matter though she have millions in her own right, and he be earning ten dollars a week. He must save up his ten dollars as long as necessary, and the trip can be as short as they like, but convention has no rule more rigid than that the wedding trip shall be a responsibility of the groom.

—"Expense of the Wedding Trip"

THE WHITE VAN WITH the county seal and the words Claxton County Library emblazoned on the side idled while Dee pulled the kitchen door shut and locked it behind her. The sky was just beginning to lighten and a couple of coyotes called across the fields to each other. Roy and Dale, already fed and watered, stood peering through the woven wire fence, nonchalantly chewing strands of alfalfa. Dee slipped her suitcase into the cargo area at the back, shouldered her laptop, and joined Cynthia in the front, where the group had saved the seat for her.

"Everybody ready for the big Abilene Adventure?" Dee asked. "Texas Writers Online, here we come."

"We're letting the teacher ride shotgun," Margaret said from the back seat.

"You are way too chipper for me at this hour, Dee," said JoAnn. "I might snooze a little bit back here."

Teresa and Summer, in the third-row seat, were still asleep, heads propped on pillows in their respective corners, with Frances wedged between them.

"Can I help you with your briefcase?" asked Hank from the middle of the second row.

"No, I'm good," Dee said. "I'm going to finish up my blog in the van on the way."

Cynthia announced, "I brought kolaches and a thermos of coffee. I already put cream and sugar in it. I hope that's okay—there are Styrofoam cups right there in the console, Dee."

"Perfect," Dee said. "I'm ready for a second cup."

"Pour it before I turn this boat around," Cynthia replied. "We're in for a bumpy ride."

"I don't see any goat on my side," said Frances. "All clear."

By the time they reached Sweetwater the sun was well up, and Dee had caffeinated sufficiently. She opened her laptop and added the finishing touches to her blog post.

> *Often dubbed the "wettest dry town in Texas," Abilene officially okayed alcohol sales in 1978, following a squeaker of an election eventually decided by the Texas Supreme Court. Residents of Abilene voted 14 times in 76 years to ban the sale of alcoholic beverages, but that year the wets won by 131 votes.*
>
> *As this writer heads to the town nicknamed "The Buckle on the Bible Belt," we celebrate a more innocent time and an eventual acceptance of more tolerance with a toast of a cold libation.*

Dee packed up her laptop and listened as Margaret regaled the group with stories about Impact, Texas, a "wet town" formed by an entrepreneurial turkey farm owner in the 1960s.

"You couldn't buy cold beer in Impact," she said. "The city fathers thought you might drink and drive. It was less than ten miles to

Abilene, but those were their rules. They'd sell you a cooler and ice, but no cold beer."

The group laughed. Everyone was awake now, Dee noticed, though some of their number were missing. "Where are all of the men?"

"I resent that," Hank said with fake chagrin.

"They rode in J. D. Sandifer's double-cab pickup," Cynthia said. "Max wanted to get there early to check the PowerPoint for his presentation, so they left before us."

"I guess I didn't get the memo," Hank said softly.

"Hank, honey, don't you pay them rednecks no mind," JoAnn said. "Politics makes people crazy."

As they passed exits at Stink Creek Road, Trent (home of the Gorillas), and Noodle Dome Road, Margaret recalled the legendary football matchups within the region. That got everyone playing the game of Name That Mascot.

"Okay, how about Roscoe?" JoAnn said, thinking of the town they'd passed through a few miles back.

"Plowboys," said Summer. "My cousin grew up there."

"How about Hamlin?" offered Cynthia.

"Easy," said Margaret. "Pied Pipers."

"Floydada?" said Teresa.

"Whirlwinds," answered Dee, "not to be confused with the Lamesa Golden Tornadoes, the Memphis Cyclones, or my brother's awesome team, the Darrell Dust Devils."

Frances called out from the back seat, "I've got one. Winters."

"Blizzards!" said everyone at once.

As they passed Merkel, Dee said, "We're almost there. Does everyone have their elevator pitches down?" Dee interpreted the murmurs as mostly positive.

But suddenly Summer burst out, "Oh, crap!"

"What?" asked Frances. "Do you need a bathroom stop?"

"Quiet everybody, quiet—I gotta get in the zone," she said.

"Good idea," Dee said. "Everyone should do the same."

But instead of thinking about elevator pitches, Dee scanned her cell phone. She had an additional, ulterior motive for this expedition—if she could still track down Letha Jones McCray.

*   *   *

The rest of their cohort—the other three men—were waiting inside the foyer of the Abilene Civic Center. "I told the check-in personnel we were with the Claxton County group," Wendell said, "and they handed me all of the credentials. That doesn't seem like a very secure process. But perhaps it's because today's terrorist threat code is only at yellow. Here's a copy of the program for everyone—I thought we might want to split up and attend different sessions, then swap intel at our next meeting."

The group seemed impressed by all of the different opportunities that awaited them for meeting "real" writers and editors, and Dee could see them poring through their programs.

"That sounds like a good idea," Dee said. "I'm flexible—except I might need to skip out at some point this morning—" she hesitated and said, "for an errand. But other than that, my schedule is open."

"Actually, Dee, honey," JoAnn began, "it might be better for you to stick around."

Dee furrowed her brow. She wasn't sure she understood. "Is there a problem?" she asked.

"No problem," said Cynthia, glaring at the group over her glasses.

"Guys," Summer said, holding up her arms as though under arrest, "we're busted." She turned to Dee and admitted, "We got a major cool score for you. This major agent dude who's already booked up?"

"Richard Howell Boothe," Cynthia chimed in.

"Right," Summer said. "Seems like every best-selling neurotic memoir starts with this guy."

"Nothing neurotic about your writing, Dee, you understand," Margaret said.

"No, no, no, nothing like that," Summer said. "Just, Boothe is like a huge player in creative nonfiction too. Come to find out, he went to high school in Austin with Hardeberger's sister—long ago before he became hot stuff in the Big Apple. HH got you an hour with the dude at eleven o'clock."

"Wow, you did this for me? I'm stunned and—Hank," Dee turned to face him, "what about your own nonfiction?"

"It's not ready yet," he said, seeming to blush from the attention, while his eyes darted elsewhere in the room. "Besides, you're the one that deserves this, with all you've done for the group and me. I must say we all worked together on this. Every one of us scanned every connection with any editor and agent we might have, and I just happened to have the luck of the draw . . . and I, ah, sent him your chapters that someone who shall remain nameless copied from your workshop last month . . ." he jabbered on a bit more before Summer interrupted.

"Dude, enough, get a room."

Now it was Dee's turn to blush. Did her writers think there was something between her and Hank? Did Max? Did *she*? But before she could consider any of those implications, it was time to disperse for the first session. She recovered her equilibrium and said, "Well, that is very thoughtful—if underhanded—of all of you. Right now we had better *all* pick our rooms."

Hank chuckled as if let off the hook, and the writers went their separate ways.

Cynthia reminded them, "See you at the dinner and open mic tonight, if not before!"

"Sorry to interrupt," Frances said, "but I just checked and there's only one spot left on the sign-up sheet. Are any of you going to read?"

"You go for it, Frances," Dee suggested.

"Oh, not, me," Frances said. She lowered her voice. "The microphone makes my hearing aid whistle."

"Wendell?"

"Ah, I think I'll wait and do a shakedown cruise on this story in our own group. Maybe next year."

With a flourish, Max took the pen and said, "Here, I'll take it."

Dee stared at him, and he winked at her. She wondered what he was up to.

Now, back to the elusive Ms. McCray. Dee checked her incoming calls again. Not a peep. And she still didn't know if she was on the right track. She took her thin folder of notes out of her bag, walked outside for some privacy, and dialed the first phone number again.

This time there was an answer.

"Hi, I'm Dee Bennett, and I'm trying to reach—"

"Oh, you must be the lady trying to reach Letha. My grandfather said someone called and he lost the number. I'm her daughter. What do you want with my mother? Is there something wrong?"

Dee tried to calm her suspicion. At least she'd reached a connection. "I'm looking for some family information. I don't mean to alarm you."

"What is it, then?"

Dee went out on a limb. "It has to do with Ricky."

There was a pause on the other end. "Give me your number."

* * *

Dee waited outside, hoping for a prompt callback. She checked her watch. She had already determined that she could skip the session on romantic mysteries titled "Dying for Love" and the one on poetry—not that she hadn't always found there was something of value to take away from every conference session no matter what one wrote. As the minutes wore on, she pulled out her laptop and looked back over the first few chapters of her manuscript. It had grown cold in the weeks since her last burst of caffeine-fueled revision. Maybe she should spend some time on her own elevator pitch.

At five minutes to eleven, she threw in the towel and returned inside. It might all amount to nothing anyway, even if she did have the correct Ricky Jones. Right now, she had a date with fate.

Dee waited, notebook in hand, at the table bearing Richard Howell Boothe's name on a table tent. The large meeting room buzzed with many conversations, some intense, some friendly, some chatty, as she glanced around to find that she was the only writer still unengaged, as though she were the last patient waiting to see the doctor. At last, seven minutes late, a dark-haired thirtysomething man slipped into the seat opposite her, flipping his phone closed, never looking up. "Sorry," he said. "When Hollywood calls, you have to answer."

"I understand," Dee said, lying. She tried to suppress memories of the dozens of agents who'd had an assistant send a form rejection or never even bothered to answer a query. Now, she had one within spitting distance. She had to keep calm and be professional.

"So, Dawn, what is it you write?" he asked.

Maybe she should spit on him, she thought.

"I'm not Dawn, I'm Dee Bennett. Creative nonfiction," she said. "They told me you went to school with Hank Hardeberger's sister?"

"I'm sorry," he said. "Yes, I went to high school with Dawn Hardeberger in Austin. Did I call you Dawn? Sorry."

She waited again as he shuffled through his papers and drew out her work. He perused the pages as she watched, a process that seemed to take an eternity. She repressed the urge to fidget or talk.

Richard Howell Boothe's gaze rose from the sheaf of papers, his eyes meeting hers for the first time. "I've looked at your submission, and it's quite good. Nice setup of the story, intriguing character, a mystery to be solved. I understand that you've been going back and forth with a publisher and an editor."

"That's about right," she said.

"If you'll send me the full manuscript," he said, "I'll look it over and get back to you. I can't promise speed—it'll a take a couple of months with the backlog I'm facing—but I'll e-mail you with my feedback."

Dee knew it might mean nothing. But she'd never gotten this far with an agent before. "Thank you so much," she said, shaking his hand and gliding from the room on a cloud.

*   *   *

Dee's phone rang while she was in line for the lunch buffet, balancing her plate as she listened to the man behind her describe his book project. "It's literary fiction," he said, "and I know that's a harder sell than mainstream, but—"

She set her plate down on the serving table, grabbed the phone from her pocket, and read the caller ID. "Sorry," she said to her fellow writer. "But when Abilene calls, you have to answer."

She swiped to take the call as she headed out the door for privacy. "Dee Bennett."

"Mrs. Bennett, this is Letha McCray. I apologize that my father-in-law is getting up in years and doesn't remember things. But I understand you were calling about Ricky Jones?"

"Yes," said Dee, out of breath. "Ricky Jones of Claxton. A student in the 1970s."

"What about him?" A good sign.

"I'd like to talk about his high school football career. Do you have a few minutes?"

"I'm at work right now and I don't want to talk on the phone. You got a 919 area code. You're not from around here?"

"I'm in Abilene right now. Can we meet?" When they hung up, Dee had two new tidbits: a number captured in her cell phone, and a meeting at the coffee shop down the street in an hour.

*   *   *

Letha McCray, she learned, was a military nurse stationed at Dyess Air Force Base nearby. Dee bought them both coffee and got right to the point. "I freelance for the Claxton newspaper," she explained, "and someone asked me recently about a player who was crucial to the team getting to the championship in 1977. I thought his contributions to that squad deserved to be remembered."

"I have no comment about anything to do with my brother," McCray replied. This woman had fielded inquiries from nosy media before, Dee could tell. A tall, strikingly beautiful woman with short-cropped hair and dressed in baby-blue scrubs, McCray displayed a discernment and evaluation in eyes that locked with Dee's, unflinching.

168 KAY ELLINGTON & BARBARA BRANNON

"This conversation is background only and off the record," said McCray. "And—I want to emphasize this—I will not be quoted."

Dee's instincts were humming. This was *real*. Something sordid had happened during that storied state title season, and she felt it was her responsibility to find out what. And what it had to do with the man she was covering—Rowdy McCorrigan.

"What do you want to know about my brother's high school football career?" McCray said.

Dee summoned her own confidence and powers of persuasion. "Well, I have all of the stats. Everyone says that Ricky was one of the best receivers to ever play at Claxton High. Do you agree?"

"Yes," McCray said, and then grew silent.

Dee kicked herself mentally for slipping up in her interviewing technique and not leading with an open-ended question.

"What made him such a good player?" she asked, taking another tack.

Ricky's sister seemed to roll the question over in her mind, then eased off a little. "His intelligence. He was smart on and off the field," she said. "I'll bet you didn't run across that information."

"President of the National Honor Society at CHS."

That seemed to make an impression. McCray continued evenly, "And that he made straight A's, and unlike those other ball jockeys, he took philosophy, physics, and all Advanced Placement courses."

"Wow," Dee said, not having had access to academic records.

"And that the coach sent in the plays through him instead of the quarterback, who was too busy with other activities to memorize the playbook."

"Other activities?"

"I thought you just wanted to know about Ricky."

"It all seems relevant," said Dee. "I need some details I can confirm, if I'm going to tell Ricky's story."

"You want to know more about Rowdy McCorrigan, you talk to him about it. I don't imagine he's hard to track down in Claxton these days. Or Blaise Parrish or some of the other players."

"Can you at least put me in touch with your brother? Could I talk with him myself? With a last name like Jones, you understand it's been hard to locate him."

"I do understand. And I think it ought to stay that way."

* * *

Off the record. Dee remembered Shannon's admonition about working with sources and knew she'd have to call her editor in. After her interview's abrupt ending, Dee was sure the matter was more than a hunch—it was becoming a story. But until then, who was Blaise Parrish, and what did he have to do with McCorrigan and Jones? She looked up Parrish's picture on the team roster in her folder. Freckled, medium build, smiling insouciantly in the group photo.

She knew one source who could answer a few questions with no difficulty.

"How's the second winningest coach in Texas today?" she asked Buddy when he answered her call.

"Won again last night, 28-27 against Wink," he said. "Looking good, knock on wood."

"How's Mitch Mitchell III doing?" she thought to ask. "That was a scary hit he took."

"Fine now, thanks. It was a mild concussion and he was back the next week. The backup QB really came through in the clutch, but I'm sure glad Mitchell's back in the game."

"Speaking of backup quarterbacks, I'm looking for some background for a story."

"Okay, shoot."

"Blaise Parrish was the second-string quarterback the year Ricky Jones couldn't make the last two games of the season. You reminded me that you played in those games too."

"That's right. I took Jones's slot as tight end."

"Tell me what you remember about Parrish."

"Well, let's see. His daddy was Dr. Parrish, the dentist. They lived on Bonham Boulevard in the ritzy part of town, and Roxanne was friends with his younger sister. I can't recall that he ever got to play but one or two times early in the season that year. But the thing everybody remembered about Blaise was his nickname, 'Blaze' with a z."

"For his speed?"

"More for his reputation as a pothead. Firing up, you know?"

Now that was interesting. "Well, I know you wild children of the seventies were infamous for experimenting with drugs," she told her brother, "but by the time I came along there was no 'high' in Claxton High. The word was 'Just Say No.'"

"It was only a rumor on the team—an open secret. Nobody ever got in trouble or anything like that."

"Well, everything you've told me is helpful. Anything else I ought to know?"

"You might talk to the principal, Mr. Withers, if you can locate him. I think he retired to New Mexico. Or Mr. Sandifer, the ag teacher."

"I know J. D. Sandifer," Dee said with a wry laugh. "But you don't have time to hear that story right now."

"Too bad Coach passed away a couple of years ago. It would have been great for him to make it to this All-Class Reunion coming up. I hear they're going to do a little ceremony for the thirtieth anniversary championship team. I'd come that night, but hey, I kinda have another game to be at!"

* * *

Dee picked up her pace along the sidewalk, hoping to sneak back into the next conference session with her absence undetected. But the afternoon coffee break time was just ending when she returned to the convention center lobby, and Frances was fidgeting and waiting for her.

"Oh, Dee, so glad you're here," Frances said. "Max Miller was looking for you. He had to go on in to meet the others on his panel," she said, "but he wanted to make sure you were there!"

"Thanks, Frances," Dee said, grabbing a cookie and following Frances down the hall to the breakout room. "I can take it from here."

The lights dimmed as the banquet hall filled with eager participants, all wearing name tags on lanyards and toting their conference bags. A spotlight shone on the dais where the panelists were seated, and the session moderator gave flattering introductions that made each of the presenters sound like Pulitzer winners. The Claxton contingent cheered as he wrapped up Max's bio.

Max went last in the lineup, giving an engaging talk about the experience of publishing a coffee-table book and illustrating it with large-screen renditions of many of the photographs the Claxtonites had seen in his show the previous month. At ten feet high, the windmill images were even more impressive.

"I want to end with the most important lesson this experience has taught me, however," Max said. "The one person absolutely essential to the process is your editor. It doesn't matter how eye-popping your photos are, or how much money you spend on fancy printing, or how much time you put into your blog or your Facebook or your Twitter or whatever." He paused while that last line drew a few laughs. "It won't be worth a hill of beans if your text isn't clear and clean and readable, right down to the last comma."

He went into a little detail about what steps authors shouldn't overlook, from line editing to copyediting, and gave a few pointers about how to locate a good editor. "But I got lucky," he said, "and the best editor in Texas fell right in my lap. So to speak." More laughs.

Dee felt her face grow hot and was very, very glad for the minimal light in the room.

"I want you all to meet Dr. Dee Bennett, writer and editor, from Claxton, Texas—go on, stand up, Dee—and all the members of the Write Stuff writing group—you deserve the credit for making this happen." The spotlight found them around their table, like bugs in a jar, as Max shared his appreciation and the moderator ended his talk by inviting applause for everyone involved in the session. All the Write Stuff members but Dee scattered for the restrooms.

"I think you even managed to embarrass J. D.," she said to Max, laughing, as she caught him in the foyer, where he was preparing to sign books. "And that takes some doing." Dee suddenly found herself surrounded as eager attendees stepped out of the book line to hand her their cards and offer their ten-second synopses.

"Y'all," she said after the third such encounter, "I don't think I'm that kind of editor."

The cohort regrouped afterwards to caravan to the hotel and check in. There was some finagling among the guys about who was sharing accommodations with whom, with J. D. agreeing to take Hank as a roommate. The women had had all their details worked out in advance.

"The mixer starts at six, and then the keynote dinner followed by the open mic," Wendell said, consulting his program once more. "Well, troops, are we ready?"

*   *   *

"Welcome to Open Mic night at what we hope is the first annual TWO "Offline" Conference. Is everybody having a good time?" Cheers and one "hell, yeah" went up. The effects of wine and beer from the cash bar, Dee suspected. "I'm Suzanne Ledbetter, tonight's host, and you know, since this conference has been all about turning our usual expectations around, we're going to do things a little differently, and start from the bottom up on the list. So that would make our first reader—renowned photographer Max Miller out of Claxton, Texas. Come on up and get us started, Max. We didn't know you were a writer too!"

Max strolled to the stage, shook Suzanne's hand, and whispered something in her ear.

"Give us a minute. We're going to have the *next* to last participant read first," Suzanne said, "And then we'll catch up with Max. Will Shirleen Davis of Snyder come up?"

A middle-aged woman in a gabardine pantsuit brought a piece of paper to the lectern. "Hi," she said, in a booming baritone. "Can you hear me? I've always done community theater, so projecting has never been a problem for me."

The crowd laughed.

"This is for all of the poets," she said, and spoke loudly and fervently.

> *I will spin my chrysalis*
> *to protect this caterpillar*
> *en route to evolution and escape*
> *from the toxins of your indifference*
> *Emerging from of the shame*
> *of the ugliness of your rejection*
> *into the beauty of a butterfly spirit . . .*

After another full minute the poet didn't seem to be winding down, but Frances leaned over to Dee, tweaking the control in her hearing aid, and said, "I don't think I quite got all of that."

"Frances," Dee whispered, "no one else did either."

*   *   *

Max took the stage, guitar in hand, and said, "This newest little ditty is for any of you out there who have ever had to deal with animals." A few chuckles punctuated the background conversation. He strummed several chords and tuned his top string. "Big ones, small ones, wild ones, domesticated ones. In your home or on the farm or in the zoo. This one's for you."

He looked directly at Dee as he launched into the first verse, about a pet-shelter cat that leads its custodian into trouble, working in the line *I told her, don't you worry* and ending with "And that's the story of Cori." The Claxton writers exchanged knowing laughs. The second stanza continued in the same vein with the dog's tale, rhyming the terms *pester, test her,* and *stressed her* with "And that's the story of Chester."

After a short bridge he finished with

> Friends and farmers, hear this tale,
> A nanny and a billy broke out of jail,
> Jumped right over the top fence rail,

Ate up all the yard signs on the campaign trail;
So get out the vote but come get your goat!
That's the story—
That's the whole story—of Roy and—Dale.

The crowd howled at the silliness, which seemed to break down some of the barriers of performance anxiety and defuse pretentiousness.

At two a.m. the poets and troubadours and prose stylists called it a day, and the Claxton Library van led the way to a brief night's sleep for them all. Sunday's eight a.m. session on "Ten Tips for Social Media" was beginning to look a lot less appealing.

*   *   *

"I sat through that whole class on Social Media," Frances said as the Write Stuff attendees gathered in the foyer following the awards luncheon and prepared to head home. "But I'm not sure I got much out of it. After all, I'm the one that puts the 'twit' in Twitter," she added good-naturedly.

"Well, I learned a *lot* in the session with the cops talking about police procedurals," said JoAnn. "I've got pages of notes and lots of ideas spinning in my head."

"And what a great way to end the whole event," said Cynthia. "Here comes our award winner now!"

Photo op finished, Teresa Rivera emerged from the banquet hall with her framed certificate to show off, the result of her top-place finish in the organization's regional writing contest earlier in the summer. The writers applauded her again, and Margaret gave her a hug. Raul, who had missed all of Saturday and driven to Abilene after his shift ended at seven a.m., did, too.

"I couldn't miss the big moment," he said, handing Dee his cell phone to take a picture with the honoree.

"Boy, have you got the wrong person for this assignment," Dee said, ready to pass the phone along to someone more adept. Raul took it back and said, "Here, no worries—we'll just do a selfie." He held the camera side of the phone out at arm's length and aimed it towards his smiling face that was pressed against Teresa's, and clicked the button. In a split-second he showed it to Teresa on the screen and pointed out how to post it.

"Selfie?" Max asked.

"Google it, dude," said Summer. "It's a *young* thing."

"Well, everyone ready for a long ride home?" asked Cynthia.

"Sure am, since I have to hit the road again tomorrow," Max said.

"What do you mean?" Dee said, flashing a forced smile.

"Well, Charley called me last night, and we ended up talking about a strategy for targeting Hispanic voters for the McCorrigan campaign, and before I knew it, I had committed to spending a week taking pictures from Brownsville to El Paso."

"Who is Charley, and what did he want?" Frances asked.

"Charley's a she," JoAnn replied.

"Rowdy McCorrigan's campaign manager," Margaret added.

"Oh," Frances said.

"Sounds like the political season has been very lucrative for you and Dee both," Margaret said. Dee rolled her eyes. Margaret, the romance writer, seemed to always be rooting for their united fortunes.

"And I'm going to drop by your place when we get back, and take a look at how the landscaping is progressing," Hank said to Dee. Catching Max's curious glance, he added, "That is, if you didn't already have other plans."

"It'll be fine, come on out," said Dee. "The crews have probably made more progress over the weekend."

"Landscaping, in the middle of a drought?" Max said, looking directly at Dee.

Dee suppressed a haughty smile. "When you get back from your campaign swing," Dee said, "you'll have to check it out."

Hank jumped in. "Actually, right now is the best time to landscape," he said earnestly. "We're implementing a plan to capture runoff and conserve moisture."

"Is McCorrigan already in the runoff?" Frances asked.

"Not yet," Dee replied. "Not yet, Frances."

17
Sí, Se Puede

Conversation is never a fixed grouping of words that are learned or recited like a part in a play; the above examples are given more to indicate the sort of things people in good society usually say. There is, however, one rule: Do not launch into long conversation or details of yourself, how you feel or look or what happened to you, or what you wore when you were married! Your subject must not deviate from the young couple themselves, their wedding, their future.

Also be brief in order not to keep those behind waiting longer than necessary. If you have anything particular to tell them, you can return later when there is no longer a line. But even then, long conversation, especially concerning yourself, is out of place.

—"Wedding Conversation"

ON MONDAY MORNING, to her amazement still drowsy after two cups of coffee, Dee joined Shannon and the rest of the *Courier* staff in the cluttered conference room for the paper's weekly story budget meeting. Though she never spoke up on these occasions, she'd gotten to know all the players by now: sports editor Phil Rios; sales manager Suzy Allen and the rest of her department, which consisted of sales rep Evan Stanfield; lifestyles editor Shirley Temple (yes, that was really her name, she had told Dee on their first meeting); and Becca, the all-purpose utility infielder who seemed capable of pinch-hitting, place-kicking, sprinting, whatever sports analogy seemed to apply in a given week.

Shannon read the topics that had already been slated for the daily budget and the Sunday edition, which published on Saturday afternoons. "Okay, guys, any suggestions?"

"Beautify Claxton is selling mums to area businesses for fall," Shirley said.

"The Texas Star Energy company has announced a public forum for the evening of October 23rd," Suzy said. "I heard about when I was in the Chamber on Friday and thought we might also sell them an ad."

"The county fair's looking for livestock judges," Becca added.

Dee raised her hand.

"It's okay, Dee," Shannon said, "you don't have to raise your hand. You can just talk."

"I know this isn't my beat," she proceeded, showing the postcard she'd brought with her, "but I got this invitation to the Claxton High All-Class Reunion on October 31st—tell me if I'm repeating old news."

Only Phil spoke up. "That's the night of the Homecoming game, but I hadn't heard about a reunion."

Dee continued. "It seems like they're making a big deal of the thirty-year anniversary of the Cougars' state championship season, and I think a lot of that has to do with McCorrigan being here now."

"Okay," Shannon said.

"So I think it would be good to do a sort of 'Where-Are-They-Now' feature about the 1977–78 championship team, since that's the class of '78. I'd do the piece."

"I think that's a great idea!" said Suzy, the ad manager. "We could sell the heck out of that."

"Twenty-two profiles is a lot for one person to tackle. Especially if she works twenty hours a week and covers a political beat too," Shannon said. "Phil, why don't we divide those up among you, Dee, and a couple of your sports stringers," she continued.

"Might not be able to find them all," Phil said.

"Probably won't," Shannon agreed, "but let's cover as many as we can track down."

"Rowdy McCorrigan is easy to find," Dee said, and they all laughed.

Evan, the new kid on the block before Dee had joined the team, chimed in. "We could run the profiles the whole week of Homecoming and the All-Class Reunion," he suggested, "and get multiple days of revenue."

Suzy turned and high-fived him, Becca made notes and ran numbers, and Dee breathed relief at getting a foot in the door for the matter she needed to discuss with Shannon.

"Do you have a minute?" Dee asked her boss as the meeting dispersed.

"Sure, come on in. I'm going to refill my coffee first. How about you?"

"You bet," Dee said, grabbing her mug.

Shannon sat back in her Herman Miller office chair—the only new piece of furniture Dee had seen in the whole place—and said, "What's up?"

"I've got something on something that might be something, or it might just be nothing," Dee said. "But I think it's something."

Shannon moved her hand in a circle to indicate Dee should get on with it.

"There seems to have been an incident with that '77–'78 football team that someone's worked hard to cover up."

"Such as?"

"I don't know yet; I've only been hearing vague rumors that something may have been amiss that fall. Something to do with several players. Maybe including Rowdy McCorrigan."

Shannon set her coffee cup down.

"I thought it was just talk until I reached a person this weekend who met with me and said some things off the record."

Now Dee had the editor's full attention. "Go back to the beginning. You have your notes? I want to hear it all."

*　*　*

With Shannon's blessing Dee launched full-bore into learning more about Blaise Parrish and Ricky Jones. Those two, along with five other Cougars profiles, the editor had assigned to Dee, leaving Phil to pursue an in-depth sports interview with McCorrigan and divide up the rest with his freelance writers.

Google proved to be a dead end, even with a name as unusual as Parrish's. She turned up his father's name in a few hits, but nothing on the son beyond a couple of sports-page mentions in archived newspapers. Apparently he hadn't gone on to a college football career. Or any career, for that matter; no alumni news, no military service, no real estate transactions. No marriage announcement. Not even her go-to Ancestry yielded anything useful. Availability of census records stopped at 1930, and family tree branches for living members were marked Private. Facebook, which she was starting to find quite intriguing, nada.

Continuing her searches that afternoon at the library between hefty assignments for Cynthia, she shifted her focus to Jones. Even combining the names of the two players she'd come up empty, but looking for "Ricky Jones" alone wasn't as bad as going after a needle in a haystack; it was worse. More than a hundred thousand hits, including a black professor and author in Louisville whom she called, then crossed off the list. She'd have to pick it back up tomorrow.

* * *

Dee stopped by Mama's house, bringing takeout cartons from the Chinese restaurant on Third Street for their dinner. She was eager to tell her all about everything that had been going on the past week—the landscaping project, the writers' conference, and the upcoming Claxton High reunion. Standing at the door, her arms full and trying not to spill the egg drop soup, she rang the bell and waited, then rang again. She was fumbling in her purse to find the spare key, panicked that something had happened, when the door opened.

"Sorry, Dee Anna," Mama said. "Come on in—I had this file open on my new computer, and I was trying to save it before I got up."

"You got a computer?" Dee said, following her into the living room. "You really did it?"

"Mr. Grover and J. D. came and put it together for me this morning, and the place was already wired with cable for the Internet. All I had to do was call them and get it turned on."

Dee set the food down on the dwindling empty space on the table, next to a brand-new Dell Inspiron. Mama smoothed down her hair, which was uncharacteristically untidy. "Don't pay no attention to how I look. I sat right here all afternoon, playing with that machine."

"You bought a laptop?" Dee said.

"Mr. Grover said the desktops are dinosaurs. I read up on laptops in a computer magazine at the grocery store last week while you were tied up, and Penny helped me order it."

"Good work," Dee replied.

Dee wondered how using the laptop would affect Mama's healing bones. "Are your arms and wrists better? Did you ask the doctor about it?"

"You know it's seems like moving the computer mouse, and typing is actually helping my agility," Mama said, taking plates down from the kitchen cabinet for them.

"You have a wireless mouse?"

"I hate that touchpad thing," Mama said.

"Me, too," Dee replied, "I just haven't gotten around to buying a mouse."

"Well, when you do," Mama said, "I can show you how to set it up."

"That would be great, thanks," Dee said, shaking her head in wonder.

"When I worked for the gin, I did ten-key and typing both," Mama said. "A computer's kind of like riding a bicycle again. I got used to this keyboard in a hurry."

Mama fixed their plates and set them on the kitchen table.

"Now I have something to ask you," Mama said. "Is your Write Stuff group meeting out at the home place again tomorrow night?"

"When did you start calling them that, instead of the Wrong Stuff?" Dee said, taking a bite of kung pao chicken.

"When I decided I'd like to come," Mama said. "I got to thinking, what's the point in doing all of this genealogy if I don't create more than a bunch of scattered notes? I ought to be preserving these stories for the next generation. It might matter to Abby or Maddy or Mindy some day. Or even them boys of Buddy and Roxanne's, though they don't even bother to remember their grandmother's birthday."

"That all makes good sense," Dee said.

"I'd kind of like to go and find out what it's all about. I just want to listen in, like I did a few times back when I was recuperatin'."

"Why don't you come out early so you can see the transformation in the yard? I could cook dinner too," Dee offered.

"You got plenty of macaroni noodles on hand?"

*   *   *

Dee was thankful for a full day at home without the interruption of driving into town and back. The miles were beginning to rack up on the Subaru, and it wasn't even paid for. But mostly it was the jumping around with the hodgepodge of part-time jobs that was driving her crazy.

As soon as the guys with the Bobcat and the Ditch Witch showed up, though, she almost wished she were back in the quiet of the library. She took her computer upstairs and tried to concentrate on the side of the house where the power equipment wasn't digging, but soon the inside temperature had become unbearable without the window open.

Downstairs she took all her materials to the bedroom, farthest from the construction. She stacked her papers neatly on the small desk she'd had back in high school, closed the door, and began to work—much as she'd done earlier in the summer while plowing through the revision of an entire book-length manuscript.

The first matter she turned to was locating Blaise Parrish. Perhaps if she found him, he'd lead her to his classmate.

That was an idea . . . she signed up for a free trial on Classmates. com and it didn't take long to get information on Blaise Parrish—and many other names she recognized from the team, as well as some students whose siblings she'd known in school herself. But no

Ricky Jones. Not even as an underclassman, except for the yearbook photos she'd already seen and copied.

Blaise Parrish had contributed a short note, about five years earlier, with "Greetings to the Class of '78 from sunny Port A." That would've been his twenty-five-year reunion, she thought in passing. Many of those class members had posted pictures from a gathering in Claxton in June of that year. Parrish did not seem to be among them.

Port A—Port Aransas, on the Gulf Coast—was a familiar and popular place to Texans. That little piece of information provided Dee with the open sesame moment she'd been waiting for. With a narrowed combination of search terms in hand, she landed on a Better Business Bureau listing for the Tiki Torch Bar with Blaise A. Parrish listed as owner. On the bar's website, the About Us link displayed an image of a man in Hawaiian shirt and straw hat, khaki shorts, and sandals, predictably older than in the high school annual but with the same devil-may-care smile. The Contact Us link provided a phone number.

Dee tried the number but reached an answering machine, and she wasn't quite ready to leave a message. Bars, she supposed, weren't known for keeping early hours.

Next on her agenda was teasing out more about the intriguing note from Elsa Jensen. She took some time to go upstairs and consult her dusty volume on the Beat Generation. What she'd recalled about Kerouac and Cassady had been pretty accurate. Further, she read, it was none other than Ginsberg to whom Cassady had entrusted the legendary letter, to shop around for possible publication. Despite the heat, she felt a shiver down her spine. What if . . . what if this unremarkable note from G. H. Templeton's own papers provided corroborating evidence of the story—or even a clue to its true fate? It took her about two seconds to leap from there to the considerable weight it would lend to her scholarship. The dots only she might be in a position to connect.

Whatever bound volumes had languished on Dee's bookshelves for a decade, the computer would certainly shed more light, faster.

She'd learned that lesson the hard way this summer. Returning to the laptop's bright window into the world, she tried a search.

Immediately the screen was flooded with articles. A magazine piece titled "Holy Grail of Beats Destroyed in Watery Grave" pretty much fleshed out the details of the story, doubted by some but accepted as gospel by others. The unfortunate man who had apparently lost the letter had been named Stern—Gerd Stern, Dee wrote on the photocopy when she discovered the full name. And the publisher to whom Ginsberg had submitted the piece was A. A. Wyn, founder of Ace Books, an imprint still going strong today, Dee was sure. The note was beginning to look very convincing. Unless it was an elaborate hoax, which was a disheartening possibility.

"Junky" she thought she recognized as the title of another Beat novel, and sure enough, a combined search of two proper nouns immediately pulled back the curtain on the first novel published by *Naked Lunch* author William S. Burroughs, who'd written under a pseudonym.

"Bob" gave her a harder time at first. But turning to the table of contents of her book on the Beats, she determined it could be poet Robert Creeley, also a friend of Kerouac and Ginsberg.

Now if only she could tease out how the pieces fit together. She emerged from the bedroom to rest her eyes and make a sandwich for lunch . . . only to see that it was past three, and the writers would be arriving at six.

She retrieved her notes and dialed the number in Port Aransas again.

"Tiki Torch," a female voice answered.

"May I speak to Blaise?" Dee said.

"Who's calling?"

"Dee Bennett from Claxton."

In a second, a male voice came on the line. "This is Blaise."

"Hi, Blaise," Dee said, "How are you?"

"Pretty good," he said. "It's not every day I hear from someone back home in Claxton. I remember the Bennetts—especially Penny. She was quite the looker, way out of my league. You were the baby, as I recall. Dee Anna."

"Right. That's me."

"What can I do for you?"

"I'm writing for the *Claxton Courier* now," Dee said. "Say, did you get the word about the All-Class Reunion in October?"

"Nah, can't say that I did . . . I haven't really kept in touch."

"Well, you might be interested to know that the newspaper is doing a big write-up on the state championship football team from your class year. Information about the season, the players—plus a follow-up on what everyone's doing now. It would be great to include you."

"That right?" he said, his tone growing a bit more distant. "Even though I was just the backup quarterback?"

"But you were a team leader," Dee said. "Everyone I talk to mentions you."

"Really." He sounded chillier now, and Dee was sure she'd spooked him somehow.

"So you're a business owner these days," she said, lightening the tone.

"Listen, Dee Anna," he said, "I've had a delivery just come in, and I'm going to have to check the shipment. I'll have to get back to you."

"Okay, here's my number. 919-466—"

The line clicked dead.

*   *   *

Mama called to tell her she'd be catching a ride out to the farm with J. D. and Pauline and Wendell, and asked if it was all right to put on some extra macaroni noodles for dinner. "If not, well, we'll be glad to bring a sack of Lot-a-Burgers," Mama offered.

Dee imagined she could do a little better than that, with the benefit of so many of the canned foods now stocking her pantry and a computer connection to use in locating easy recipes.

When Mama and the trio arrived, Dee was ready to serve up a freshly baked macaroni and cheese casserole with sides of black-eyed peas and stewed tomatoes and okra. It seemed a good, healthy combination for the "last day of September"—a phrase that always stuck in Dee's mind from a kindergarten tune. It made her reminisce of childhood days when Mama might have served a meatless meal like this.

"Your dairy herd's looking good, Dee," J. D. called out as he climbed the porch steps. "Healthy. Happy."

"It's funny how quickly I've become attached to them," Dee said. "I'm glad they're for milk and not meat."

"They're funny little critters," he said, smiling, "and it looks like you're taking good care of them. Keep Roy and Dale happy, and you might have a couple more future milk producers by spring. And our barbed wire is still keeping them safe?"

"So far, so good," Dee said. "But as you can see, we're making a lot of changes out on that side of the yard."

"That's really looking nice," said Pauline, commenting on the changes that were already apparent as brush had been cleared away, limbs had been trimmed, and a new desert willow tree had been set out between the house and the windmill.

Wendell thought the flagstone walkway and pathway lighting were excellent additions for security.

Mama was the last to comment, standing still at the car door where Wendell was waiting to shut it for her. She gazed out to the east, past the windmill, and then turned slowly toward the house, taking in the emerging transformation.

Dee was afraid for a minute that she'd done something terribly wrong. "Mama?"

"It's beautiful, Dee Anna. Just beautiful." Mama took her time in mounting the steps, stopping every few seconds to look around again. Dee watched, too, as the lowering sun cast long shadows across the barn and deepened the canyon breaks in the distance.

"Come on and let's eat, before the others get here," Dee called to her guests. She could have sworn that as she said the words, the moment was an echo of three decades past, a September evening when her mother had said them first.

They finished their meal, with compliments from the harshest critic in the bunch, Mary Alice Bennett. She and Pauline offered to wash up the dishes, and Wendell set up the chairs. Dee asked J. D. to come out and check on a question about the goats with her.

"Everything going okay on your newspaper job?" he asked as they walked toward the pen.

"Yes, just fine. I like it more than I thought I would. But it's wearing. I don't ever need to be rocked to sleep at night."

"I've seen your bylines. Good stuff."

"Thanks, J. D. That's what I wanted to ask you about—a piece I'm writing about the Class of 1978. That includes Rowdy McCorrigan, of course. And Blaise Parrish. Ricky Jones, too, from the class of '79."

"You know they were all students when I was still teaching."

"That's what Buddy said. Were any of them in your classes?"

"No, I never taught a one of 'em. But McCorrigan was in my homeroom."

"What was he like?"

"Well," he paused. "Rowdy was never one of my favorites."

"What do you mean?"

"People can change and grow up, and I imagine he has. But he had an arrogance about him, seemed like he thought the world owed him success on a silver platter. I don't know why. His daddy was a tool pusher with Hughes and had a drinking problem. Poor fellow, killed himself and McCorrigan's mama in a DWI crash right after Rowdy was drafted into the NFL. Seemed like the boy never played as well after all that happened."

"Is there anything else specific that you recall from his senior year? Now, remember, I'll want to use what you say for the story if you'll let me."

"Let's just say, I think Rowdy might have acted entitled because he was such a good football player, practically from the time he could walk. But he might've inherited his father's addictive personality."

"You mean drugs?"

J. D. didn't answer.

"I'll have to try to get the truth another way."

"I can't rat out a Claxton student. Not for something nobody could ever prove. Rowdy was Teflon. Nothing ever stuck to him. Still doesn't."

"Does that go for Parrish and Jones too?"

The rest of the group had started to arrive. JoAnn waved in their direction.

J. D. paused for a long moment then said, "Somebody with pull was watching out for those boys. I just never knew who."

*　*　*

On the table was a fresh stack of writing Dee hadn't seen. There hadn't been time. But they were getting past the point now where the leader had to read and comment on every piece—they could be trusted to do that respectfully among themselves as Cynthia distributed their blind drafts on e-mail during the off weeks.

"I think we were all inspired in Abilene," Cynthia said.

Wendell seconded her observation. "I'm ready to debrief on the sessions, if you are."

"Before we get started," Hank said, "I've brought some Obama yard signs if anyone would like one."

"None for me," Wendell said. "I think national security is at risk if that Muslim gets elected."

"He's not a Muslim," Raul said, and suddenly the free-for-all was on.

Mama, never one to hold her tongue where race was concerned, couldn't resist joining in. "I think he secretly hates white people," she said. "Did you see what his so-called preacher Jeremiah Wright said?"

Teresa retorted, "He's half white. His mother was white. I don't think he hates white people." Mama glared at her erstwhile home health aide as though a serf had decided to challenge the queen.

"Folks, this is a county-sanctioned event," Cynthia said. "We can't be discussing partisan politics here."

"Cynthia makes a good point," Dee said, though she wasn't certain of the accuracy of the statement. "Hank, leave your signs on the front porch."

He looked at her quizzically but complied.

"Thank you," Cynthia said.

When Hank returned, Dee said, "This is a very special group, and I can see significant improvement in your writing. But we have to work as a team and focus on your creative product. We're going to have our differences about politics, religion, and even football, but let's leave our personal views at the door."

The writers, chastened, nodded.

"Now, in the spirit of collaboration, which would you rather do—debrief on what you learned in Abilene? Or dive into the new stuff?"

"Dive," Summer said, a sentiment the majority echoed.

Hamilton thought he'd never feel that way again. She made him feel young, smart, even, sexy. If a person can be sexy at fifty-four. He'd felt like a widower—even though he was still married—for years. Numb to life and his own body.

His wife's one true love was her work. She'd be gone for days at a time on the campaign trail.

Could it have been twenty-seven years ago that they had been married? They seemed like different people back them. With their late-night rendezvous of reckless lovemaking?

Now the only thing they seemed to jointly anticipate was the absurd antics of their grandchildren.

His career seemed like a prison sentence to him to be served until social security kicked in.

He looked in the mirror. He was still a handsome man, and he felt like this new woman truly appreciated him. He could feel her eyes on him as she passed by his corner office.

He admired his profile in the new tailor-made suit. The hue of his tie brought out his blue eyes and silver temples.

He'd felt his wife had been committing adultery with her career for years. What could a little harmless flirtation hurt anyway?

"Whoo, whose was that?" Margaret said.

"A little hanky-panky from Hanky?" Summer teased.

"Not mine," the accused replied.

"Guys," Dee said, "remember when a writer submits her or his work for critique anonymously as this one is, it's to encourage everyone to give honest and candid feedback."

"I liked it," Margaret said. "Infidelity can be to a career as well as a person. That's why it's important for couples to work at keeping the sizzle."

The writers generally tittered at any degree of hotness, though so far in Dee's experience none had come forth with anything really risqué.

"Interesting," Dee said, "this entire new batch of excerpts were submitted blind."

"I think we all preferred it that way," Margaret said. "Fewer hard feelings. Even if you knew it was your writing being scrutinized, no one else did. It wasn't personal."

Dee agreed to read the next one for them. "But after this week, maybe we should rotate reading aloud, too—so that everyone gets some practice. And you don't always want to listen to *my* voice!"

Ricki Rocco didn't start dating the EMT guy just to get referrals for her fledging legal practice, but it did come in handy. Some people called lawyers ambulance chasers, but in her case she was an ambulance texter.

Especially at night.

Her beau J.T. would text her from the hospital emergency room. D&D. Will need counsel. That was short for drunk and disorderly.

She'd head straight to the law enforcement processing center, and before the defendant even had the chance to make a phone call, Ricki would be there to slip her business card into his hand.

It helped that her law office, home, and mode of transportation were all one and the same—a 1998 Winnebago Winnie.

When Dee finished reading to the end of the scene, the group applauded.

Dee just smiled. JoAnn, the paralegal, had reason to be proud of her progress. She was developing a distinctive style and a shtick that worked.

They read a few more samples, some improved, some less so, and as the group broke up for the evening, JoAnn said, "Dee, if you've got a minute, I have some information on the wind energy agreement for you."

"Hey, that's great. Just a second—Mama should hear this too."

JoAnn explained that, contrary to what the company implied, the lease fee was not set in stone. She'd heard of a few property owners who had held out for a larger figure, citing unknown future impacts on their land and farms. "That initial lease is the only thing you'll have any control over," she advised them. "Once they start generating electricity, the kilowatt-hour rate is standard."

"And what about them big transmission high-lines and towers?" asked Mama.

"That's an issue landowners need to keep an eye on, Mrs. Bennett. You might not be able to fight eminent domain in the end, but if they want to run those lines run across your property you'll want to know before they show up with the backhoes."

"We appreciate it, JoAnn. Will we see you at the community forum?" Dee said.

"Sure will," she said. "Just remember, honey, everything's a negotiation."

"Spoken just like Ricki Rocco," Dee said.

"How did you know?" JoAnn said, smiling.

"You've come a long way as a writer."

"You've helped."

Mama bid everyone good-night and headed down the steps with the group she'd come with. And Dee had another of those flashes of role reversal, recalling a long-ago double date when she'd gone with her friends to a waiting car, her mother watching, like a guardian, from where she stood now.

18
Fashion Sense

Later, at the house, there is not only a floral bower under which the bridal couple receive, but every room has been turned into a veritable woodland or garden, so massed are the plants and flowers. An orchestra—or two, so that the playing may be without intermission—is hidden behind palms in the hall or wherever is most convenient. A huge canopied platform is built on the lawn or added to the veranda (or built out over the yard of a city house), and is decorated to look like an enclosed formal garden. It is packed with small tables, each seating four, six, or eight, as the occasion may require.
—"The Most Elaborate Wedding Possible"

FOR TWO SOLID WEEKS Dee had given as much attention as she could spare to the work on the home place, which was taking more of it than she'd bargained for. The French drain system had had the north and east sides of the yard looking like the site of trench warfare, but Hank had assured her all the un-sexy infrastructure had to be completed before the other features or the rest of the plantings could be put in place. While that was under way, he'd suggested, why not work on the barn? Remove the unsightly lean-to shed from it, reattach loose batten strips, paint it?

Dee had let him talk her into it, springing to have the whole thing pressure-washed and spray-painted. "And instead of an ordinary red," Hank had put out there, "why not consider a Tiffany green, to coordinate with the metal roof of the main house?"

She had to admit, the effect was stunning. Hank really had an eye for those artistic details, while she leaned toward the practical. It was a relief this morning—only two days till Ruby Lee's big event—to see it all come together. Hank would get to see the finished product for himself this afternoon. Since the high school had their Columbus Day break and the teachers had a work day, he'd promised to come out later and review the punch list with the contractors. They would finish up in the nick of time for the tent rental crew and the decorators to show up tomorrow.

But she couldn't stand around all day and moon over her emerging paradise. She'd had no luck getting Blaise Parrish to return her calls. Anyone else she'd asked casually, including the four other teammates whose profiles she had now almost completed, either didn't know or didn't care what Parrish had done in high school, or with the rest of his life.

All was quiet on the McCorrigan front as the candidate completed his borderlands tour, and Charley had made herself scarce too.

And no one was talking about Ricky Jones.

* * *

After Monday's story budget meeting, Dee said as much to Shannon.

"Sometimes a journalist runs into a dead end," her editor said. "If everyone's keeping mum for the moment, eventually there'll be a breakthrough."

"That's what I wanted to tell you. An opportunity may have presented itself. Charley Hensley texted me this morning to let me know about another media event next week—three days on the Texas coast to tour an offshore oil platform. Several journalists have been invited, travel is by charter jet, and it could provide a chance to nail down Blaise Parrish."

"Go ahead and accept, then. Be smart in your questions and observe closely. But don't beat yourself up if nothing comes of it.

For every sensational exposé, there are a hundred routine stories that don't uncover anything more exciting than paint drying."

With no library duties—city and county offices were closed too—Dee headed back home to wrap up the last investigative task of her day, a report to Elsa Jensen about what they had come to call "the Neal Cassady note."

Low clouds moved in from the west and a sprinkle of rain splashed on the windshield of the Subaru, and a teensy seed of worry sprang up in her mind about the style show. Of course Ruby Lee had a Plan B in case of rain—the tent would accommodate a hundred and fifty people, and the backup script for everything from food service to the fashion models' path from ad hoc green room to catwalk had been shared with all participants. But rain would certainly prevent guests from enjoying the full splendor and effect of all the weeks of preparation. Dee wondered in passing how anyone in the wedding planning business ever survived the anxiety. She'd be a basket case in a role like that.

The rain continued as Dee took her computer up to her writer's garret. She opened the window to let in the fresh air and clean scent, and began typing a lengthy e-mail.

> Dear Elsa,
>
> You asked me to give my assessment of the hand-written document you were generous enough to share with me, and you asked for my recommendations. I'm outlining the finer points below. But in brief I believe you are in possession of a potentially valuable piece of literary evidence, and your first step should be to have a handwriting expert compare known letters in G. H. Templeton's script with the Neal note and confirm what you and I already believe—that Gineva wrote it. And not to Allen Ginsberg as most scholars would first guess but to her husband, Allan Jensen.
>
> Regardless of the outcome of that evaluation, I agree with you that this note sheds no additional light on

the questions of whether, or how, Cassady's legendary Joan Anderson letter was destroyed. The world may still never know.

Nonetheless I believe the literary world will be interested in learning of this note. When even a small scrap surfaces unexpectedly after it has lain unseen inside a book for more than half a century, scholars and readers gain new insights about the personalities and events involved, and they can add their own, just as we are doing now.

I'd appreciate the opportunity to write the first article about the Neal note, if you're able to authenticate it. And I'd be eager to come to San Francisco and see the real artifact, and to meet you in person at last.

Dee outlined carefully her speculations regarding personalities and events, citing the numerous sources she'd consulted and attaching relevant documents, and sent it to Elsa's e-mail address. There, she thought—closure on one project, at least.

*   *   *

"You've really pulled off a miracle," Dee said to Hank as they huddled under her big golf umbrella and picked their way around puddles. "I had no idea so much could come together in such a short time."

Hank appeared pleased, too. "You and me both, frankly," he admitted. "I've overseen some larger projects, but that was always with a staff. This may be the most ambitious thing I've designed solo."

"Don't be surprised if your services are in great demand after this week. And you'll have to start charging a lot more than you did me!"

They walked over to inspect the low deck platform situated between the house and the back of the barn, another of Hank's inspirations that would serve as the event stage for now and, in due time, the base of the shade pergola. "Work looks good to me," Hank said, bending down to feel that the stain sealer had dried before the rain started. "I think this'll be ready for use by Wednesday."

The new livestock enclosure looked strong and functional, with its own shed area where Roy and Dale were now huddled to keep dry. Gone were the bedsprings and barbed wire. And she'd enlarged on her initial plans at J. D.'s suggestion, allowing space for milking in the spring.

The grapevines had been trimmed back and the homemade arbor reinforced to disguise its origins as a clothesline. Dee felt it would make a natural focal point for the tent location, and the plantings of pampas grass and sage had been ingeniously designed to lead the eye there.

The drain system also appeared to be doing its job. Patches of standing water were few, and they could find no rivulets that would eventually create erosion. Runoff water was pouring gently down the slope from the swale that had been designed to collect it. "Now aren't you glad for a little rain shower?" Hank asked Dee, his face close to hers as he held the umbrella for them. "Nature's own dress rehearsal."

She slipped her arm around his waist and hugged him—an impulsive gesture that felt comfortable but with no tension or romantic expectation on her part. He seemed to take it in the same spirit.

*   *   *

Rain continued off and on through the night as Dee, lying awake, listened for the rumble of thunder and soothed Cori, who was mewling piteously under the edge of the bedcovers. She'd thought that pets were supposed be a companion and comfort to their owners. But it was turning out quite the other way around.

She slept as late on Tuesday as the cat would let her, then took her coffee to the computer and checked the newspaper's website for the day's stories. She was not going to drive all the way to the gate in this downpour just to get yesterday afternoon's print edition. She was certain she wasn't the only reader with that reaction. Soon, she mused, every transaction of their lives would be tied to the computer. Libraries, archives, classrooms, books, banks. She'd already given in to a great extent.

As if mirroring her thoughts, an e-mail alert pinged and a message popped up on her screen. Dee finished off her coffee as she read. Elsa was amenable to having the Neal Cassady note examined by specialists locally. She'd insist they keep it quiet until Dee Bennett could publish an essay. But for all their benefit, if the document proved real, they should proceed with alacrity. *Alacrity,* Dee thought. Only Elsa would think to use such a formal term in e-mail. But that's what governed all their lives these days. The need for speed.

*   *   *

The rain let up around four, but it had already put the tent rental guys way behind. Dee's phone pinged with a text message—a medium she'd discovered would transmit even when her voice service wouldn't, out in the boonies—from Ruby Lee. *Running late C U @ 6.* Dee was learning to decipher the shorthand of this texting thing, too. *Hope U R OK,* she texted back, pleased with herself.

She figured they'd manage, with the Write Stuff session going on inside and the party setup outside. They'd just have to, now.

She'd had no time to let the writers know in advance, though, when the circus began. The arriving Write Stuff members were busy admiring Hank's handiwork and about to head into the house with their bundles of manuscripts when the first big truck arrived, following Ruby Lee's SUV through the gate, and Dee realized she'd seriously underestimated the situation. She was definitely not prepared for the second SUV in the caravan, a silver Acura MDX with a McCorrigan bumper sticker.

Ruby Lee pulled over beside the barn, hopped out, and guided the truck with the confidence of a teamster. Charley Hensley stepped out with the demeanor of a cop at a crime scene and began shouting to the onlookers, "Excuse me—you all are going to have to move these vehicles. We have to unload here."

"How the heck did she get in charge?" Margaret asked Dee, who was already headed down the steps to fend off damage to the new plantings. Ruby Lee said, "I see you've met my new helper, Charley Hensley."

"Yes, Charley has a way of not going unnoticed," Dee said, as the writers scrambled to move their cars further down the hill. Mama and Pauline leaned over the porch rail and watched in wry amusement.

"She's a former model," Ruby Lee explained. "And as a political organizer she knows everything about putting on events. I recruited her when I met her at Max's show."

"I see," Dee said.

"You've done wonders with the farm," Ruby Lee said. "You've got to give me the name of your landscaper."

"Later," she said.

Charley Hensley called out from beside the peach orchard. "I think we should put the tent in over here," she said. "We can set up a little cabana beside it, and that'll provide more room for wardrobe changes in case it rains."

"I think Dee wanted it by the grape arbor," Ruby Lee said.

"Too crowded there," Charley responded.

The workers were struggling to fit the tent into the area by the vines, and Dee had to admit Charley was right. The woman did seem to be very good at her job. Dee couldn't compete with that kind of chutzpah.

Cynthia, who was also adept at crisis management, said to Dee, "It looks like you have your hands full. Why don't we cancel tonight's workshop?"

"We can use all the hands we can get, to get this done," Charley said to Cynthia.

"I'll help," Summer said. "Put me to work."

"We all will," Wendell said. "What do you need?"

Within minutes, Wendell, J. D., and the party rental guys had hoisted and staked out the tent near the orchard. Raul and Hank unloaded and set up eighteen round tables underneath it. Teresa,

JoAnn, Margaret, Frances, Cynthia, and Summer placed 144 chairs. The set decorators pulled up in a flatbed loaded with hay bales, bundled cornstalks, and pumpkins. The sound crew arrived with their DJ trailer.

Ruby Lee and Charley turned the smaller tent into a dressing room, and Dee helped by shuttling the models' outfits from hangers in Ruby Lee's vehicle to a portable clothes rack. As Hank strung white lights around the inside of the tent roof and hung the spotlights from atop a ladder, Max arrived to scout out photo angles. He waved cordially as the younger man looked down at him, and he offered a curt "Howdy."

Finding Dee and Ruby Lee frantically moving back and forth like buses swerving to miss each other on a busy highway, Max asked, "Anything I can do to help?"

Dee could only shake her head and keep moving. "I think we're about finished."

"Well then," he said, "I guess so am I." Dee watched him return to his truck and depart but had no chance to catch him.

As the sun set and Ruby Lee flipped the switch to test the lights, the party truck and the flatbed rumbled back down the hill and turned toward town.

"Y'all are done," Charley said to the Write Stuff members. "Thanks." She turned back to Ruby Lee and said, "Let's reevaluate that table décor, shall we?"

Margaret rolled her eyes and walked with the others down to their cars.

"Thank you all," Dee said to the writers as she saw them out.

"Get some rest," JoAnn said to her, and whispered in her ear, "and kick Miss Bossy Britches out of here."

Dee texted Max later, after she had helped Ruby Lee complete the table centerpieces and set them in the kitchen with the tablecloths for the caterers to find. Whatever else Ruby Lee was out checking on in the tent, Dee had reached the limit of her strength. Wearily, she collapsed into the recliner and pulled out her phone. There was already a message waiting for her. *C U tomorrow, Miss November.*

*   *   *

Dee woke the next morning feeling about as stiff and sore as Mama during her recuperation, and headed straight for the coffeepot in her pajamas. Ruby Lee lay snoring on her couch under the afghan. Her cousin hardly stirred as Dee started the coffee, set out a package of muffins and some butter, and hit the shower.

Ruby Lee had roused by the time Dee was finished, and Dee offered her a spare bathrobe for her own shower.

"Sorry to crash on your couch," Ruby Lee said, "but I did not have the energy to drive home. I am so glad my luncheon ensemble and makeup are already in the car!"

Barefoot and in bathrobes, towels around their wet hair, Dee and Ruby Lee filled their cups in the kitchen.

"Care to join me on the verandah, Dame Bargeron?" said Dee.

"That sounds lovely, Lady Bennett," said Ruby Lee.

The pair enjoyed their breakfast at Dee's brand-new bistro table and seating, which had taken the place of the folding aluminum chairs. The air was fresh and crisp, the sky the clearest blue she'd ever recalled in West Texas. The new shrubs and the old trees looked equally vibrant, revived by the rain. Any trace of dust had been washed away.

"This is a beautiful vista," said Ruby Lee. "I don't know that I've ever sat here. You can see all the way down the hill practically into town."

"Let's take our coffee and stroll the grounds before the guests arrive, darling," Dee said, standing and crooking her pinkie. "Between Hank's landscaping and your fall decorations the home place looks like a resort. At least the yard part does . . . the house needs a new coat of paint and could definitely use central heat and air."

"Hush, you, it's gorgeous, just gorgeous," Ruby Lee said. "There's not a cloud in the sky. And no wind. In West Texas, no wind! I haven't checked the forecast, have you?"

Dee shook her head. As they said hello to the goats and returned to the house to dress, Ruby Lee said, "Aren't you glad you came back?"

"Yes," Dee said, and meant it.

*   *   *

The tranquility of their repast was short-lived. Ruby Lee, in her black pantsuit with three-quarter length jacket and a long draping scarf in fall colors, showed the caterer and florist their drills and left the kitchen to them. Dee answered the phone, made sure there was extra toilet paper accessible, pointed out locations of electrical outlets when asked, things like that. On Ruby Lee's advice she also monitored the weather app on her iPhone, surprised to see that it was possible to learn the current temperature and the forecast right from her pocket. It concerned her to see the word "wind," even preceded by the modifier "light."

Ruby Lee's husband, Barge, came early and brought Mama, and that was a good thing since J. D. came early and brought Pauline, and Dee didn't think she needed that kind of help. She let J. D. check over the goat pen carefully with her to verify it had been escape-proofed, and Barge took over with car-parking and golf-cart shuttle duty. Charley, who was set to model a flowing red cocktail dress, had abdicated her Bossy Britches role and was practicing her runway walk on the deck, a move that got J. D.'s attention. "You know," he said to Dee, "they say McCorrigan's race is tightening up, and he's got a tough contest ahead of him, but I wouldn't mind being in his position if I had a little filly like that to look at every day."

"Don't you let Pauline hear you talking that way!" she teased him, while pointing the florist in the direction of the closest water faucet.

"Why do you think I'd rather gab with the goats?" he said, laughing.

*   *   *

But it was not Charley's attire that received the most applause from the red-hatted crowd, after all was said and done. The fall fashions on display ran the gamut from business suits, a cheerleader outfit, hunting gear in pink and gray camouflage tones, a fur-trimmed dress for Christmas, a black velvet evening ensemble, coats for all occasions, and a candlelight silk wedding dress for autumn. Next to last, right before Charley Hensley's grand finale with her dress and

New Year's 2009 ruby tiara, Margaret Strickland stole the show as Professor McGonagall from the *Harry Potter* movies, complete with red-accented witch's hat, a wand, and a white stuffed owl on her shoulder. The applause from Margaret's fellow Red Hatters was still going strong when Charley did her strut, the light breeze lending the former model's hair and the flounces of her dress a flair worthy of a high-fashion magazine spread.

At the mic, Ruby Lee held tight to her red fedora as she brought back all the models for an encore. Max continued snapping frames and the audience rose for a standing ovation.

When she called on Margaret to take her bow, a sudden gust of wind lifted the witch's hat and detached the stuffed owl from her getup and sent both flying into the goats' enclosure, where Roy and Dale immediately discovered the unanticipated snacks. Luncheon guests whipped out their own phone cameras to capture the scene. Max was turning to follow the action with his camera when another stiff breeze lifted Charley's skirt à la Marilyn Monroe and he stayed with that view instead. And Dee, who had had about enough of Charley's shenanigans, was just about to thwart Max's shot with a tablecloth when a windborne tumbleweed did the trick for her.

Charley dodged the rolling weed, wedged her heel between the deck boards, and went sprawling toward the camera. Max managed to save both Charley and his Nikon from a harder fall on the flagstones, but several amateur shutterbugs caught the moment as he held her in his arms.

Other red hats went flying before quick-witted Barge let down the flaps on the north side of the tent. Ruby Lee thanked everyone for coming and said she hoped they'd all visit Ruby Lee's Treasure Chest in Poplar Grove for the Christmas Tree extravaganza starting Thanksgiving weekend.

Dee saw Charley's Acura peel out of the field they'd used for a parking area and head back down the hill ahead of the guests. Max was nowhere in sight. Margaret, Cynthia, Frances, JoAnn, and Pauline set about assisting with collecting stray cloth napkins and bundling up trash while Ruby Lee and Mama bid guests farewell.

Margaret came over to the tent beside Dee, slipping out of her Hogwarts gown and laying it on the table along with the hat she'd retrieved. "The owl was a goner."

"Funny how the Woman in Red was all about giving everyone directions for setup," Pauline noted, "but didn't stick around for cleanup."

"Oh, but she's a *model,*" Margaret said.

"If she was a model, then I was a ballerina," JoAnn said. "Charley Hensley may act patriotic now but she was *ex*-otic then."

"Seriously?" Dee said. "Are you saying what I think you're saying?"

"Never mess with a paralegal if you have any skeletons in your closet," JoAnn said.

"Tell us more," Dee said.

"While Charley Hensley was earning her degree in poli sci, she worked the pole instead of the polls, if you know what I mean?"

"How did you find that out?"

"A quick search of the online police blotter—a trick I learned from the guys in Abilene. There was a drug bust at a place called the Purple Lion, and no charges were ever filed against her, but it was still in the database. In all honesty, you'd be surprised how many smart, capable college girls earn their tuition money that way."

"What other dirty laundry did you discover?" asked Margaret.

"I thought the party people were washing the tablecloths," said Frances.

Dee turned to Pauline and said, "Do you think you and Frances might carry these centerpieces down to Ruby Lee's car?"

When the coast was clear, JoAnn continued, "I think everything else pretty much matches up with her public resume. Graduate school at Georgetown. Clerked for a Houston Congressman for a couple of terms in DC. Spent time at a think tank in Washington for a couple of years. Worked for McCorrigan when he was an energy lobbyist in Austin after that."

"I appreciate the scoop, JoAnn," said Dee. "I'll have the pleasure of Charley's company on an assignment again the rest of this week. At least I can make sure she's not throwing herself at Max—literally."

Margaret added her own advice. "I sure wouldn't let a hussy like that steal *my* man, if I had a man like—"

Max peeked into the tent, zipping his camera bag closed, and said, "Had to go make sure this baby was still in working order. Did I miss anything important?"

19
Railroaded

His first actual duty is that of packer and expressman; he must see
that everything necessary for the journey is packed, and that the
groom does not absent-mindedly put the furnishings of his room in
his valise and leave his belongings hanging in the closet. He must see
that the clothes the groom is to "wear away" are put into a special
bag to be taken to the house of the bride (where he, as well as she,
must change from wedding into traveling clothes). The best man
becomes expressman if the first stage of the wedding journey is to
be to a hotel in town. He puts all the groom's luggage into his own
car or a taxi, drives to the bride's house, carries the bag with the
groom's traveling suit in it to the room set aside for his use—usually
the dressing-room of the bride's father or the bedroom of her brother.
He then collects, according to prearrangement, the luggage of the
bride and drives with the entire equipment of both bride and groom
to the hotel where rooms have already been engaged, sees it all into
the rooms, and makes sure that everything is as it should be. If he
is very thoughtful, he may himself put flowers about the rooms. He
also registers for the newly-weds, takes the room key, returns to the
house of the groom, gives him the key and assures him that everything at the hotel is in readiness.

—"Best Man As Expressman"

DEE HADN'T BEEN to the Texas coast since she was a sophomore
in high school. But the two yellow school buses hauling sixty hyper
teenagers at fifty-five miles per hour across the state for a marching
band competition back then had nothing in common with her mode
of transportation today.

The Cessna Citation glided low in sight of the Harbor Bridge out-side Corpus Christi at dusk as McCorrigan's flight touched down and taxied to the general aviation hangar of CRP. The autumn sunlight glinted on the water, turning it to gold. Unless you lived in Texas you could never believe it was possible to find such a lush tropical paradise in the same state as the dry, dusty flatlands and breaks near Claxton.

Dee thought of the shrimp boats she'd spotted, gracefully returning towards the marina, dolphins leaping behind in hope of some morsel.

That's sort of how she felt about this trip. Could she get a tidbit of evidence to sustain her pursuit of the McCorrigan-Jones matter? Or was she looking at the wrong story? Something felt fishy about this junket already.

In the charter jet that could accommodate ten passengers, there were six other people aboard—along with Rowdy McCorrigan and Charley Hensley and the two interns were Jimmy Gilliam, the owner of JDG oil services in Midland and their host on this coastal swing, and another reporter besides herself, Ralph Begedovitch, the *Midland Reporter-Telegram* writer whom Dee had met briefly on the Panhandle bus trip. The Abilene guy had had to back out, and Ralph looked eager to corner every spare minute of access freed up by the cancellation.

"And I'm very disappointed that our PR photographer, Max Miller of Claxton, couldn't make it," Charley said as she went over the itinerary. "It appears he was already booked for a five-day horse-back trip through the South Texas brush country, so we'll be picking up a local stringer in Corpus who comes highly recommended."

Dee gritted her teeth at that last detail. How was it that this woman always seemed to know as much about her guy as she did? There, she'd said it. To herself anyway. *Her guy.* Maybe it was time she made that possession a little clearer. But for now she had to listen up and keep her eye on the ball.

They would all meet up in the morning with Carl Daniels, a reporter from the Corpus Christi TV station, and Billy Franks, the foreman of the offshore drilling platform that Gilliam wanted McCorrigan to see, and that, Dee presumed, that McCorrigan wanted the press to see that he wanted to see.

Wednesday was marked as fundraising meetings, personal visits that were closed to the press, then on the way back on Thursday, the plane would touch down in San Antonio for a breakfast meeting and San Angelo for a luncheon speech. Something about that seemed odd to Dee—who keeps a bunch of reporters and interns at loose ends when you could be making better use of their coverage?—but she could handle only so much intrigue at a time. And besides, their closed-door meetings might just provide her an opportunity to slip away to Port Aransas, where she hoped she'd find Blaise Parrish.

A town car arrived to take the group to the hotel, and it was apparent they wouldn't all fit in one vehicle. Dee seized the opportunity. It was only a matter of hanging back a wee bit while bags were being stowed in the trunk and then stepping forward as though she meant to take the last seat in the back. Ralph cut her off swiftly, and she shrugged as though maybe she'd get luckier next time. "You all go on," she said. "I'll just get a cab and catch up with you later at the hotel." Well, that would be true eventually.

When the car pulled out of sight, Dee rolled her bag over to the National counter. "How much for a sub-compact car, one day only?" she inquired.

"That'll be . . . $25.95 plus insurance and tax, ma'am. But keep in mind, those are all manual-crank windows. Right now we're running a special on intermediates."

"How much?"

"$23.95 plus insurance and tax."

"That sounds like a good deal."

"Plus if you sign up for our loyalty program and reserve intermediate or higher, you can pick any car you want from that row."

"Really? Any?" she looked around at the inventory. "Sold."

*　*　*

Zipping up the coast to Port A in the silver Sebring, its top down, was the most divine experience Dee could recall since her return to

Texas. Maybe ever. The fall temperature was perfect. She slipped on the blingy sunglasses she'd acquired from Ruby Lee's shop and let her hair whip loose around her face.

The forty miles between Corpus and Port A flew by too fast, in a haze of white dunes and sparkling waves and beach cottages, but it was dark when she pulled into the parking lot at the Tiki Bar. A two-story establishment with a wood-shingled façade and a marina-front view, the Tiki Bar looked like the sort of place that would appeal to locals. The lights were low and a Jimmy Buffet tune played over the speakers. The décor consisted solely of neon bar signs. Dee's pupils struggled to adjust.

A horseshoe-shaped bar filled much of the room. On one side a group of guys huddled to watch *Monday Night Football.* Dee wondered if there was any night of the week in the fall when there wasn't some kind of football contest on TV? She took a seat far enough away to scan the scene. Reconnaissance, Wendell Grover would've said.

"What can I get you, hon?" said a young blonde woman who didn't look old enough to be a patron of the bar, let alone its bartender.

"Tito's and tonic with lime, please, and a bottle of water." Dee scoped out the crowd. There weren't too many in the off season, and that made her job easier. She was pretty sure she recognized the proprietor holding forth at the far end of the bar, sporting a Tommy Bahama shirt, cargo shorts, flip-flops, and the ruddy complexion of a buzz well under way. He puffed on a cigar and alternately sipped from a rocks glass half full of dark liquor. She waited till the bartender refilled it.

A DJ set up a chalkboard sign on the small stage "Karaoke 9 p.m. Sign up here." The hands on the Clydesdale clock indicated eight-thirty, so she knew she had to act fast.

Dee topped off her drink with the water, slipped the bottle into her shoulder bag, and took the glass with her toward where Blaise Parrish sat and slipped in, leaving one bar stool between them. She pretended to watch the game.

"Mark my word," Parrish said to a couple of his Tommy-Bahama–and-flip-flops comrades. "Texas will go into Lubbock next week and lose to Tech."

"No way," the other two said.

Parrish looked at Dee and said, "How about you little lady? Are you a football fan?"

Dee smiled demurely and took a sip of her vodka. "A little bit," she said.

"Who do you like in Saturday's game—Texas Tech or Texas?"

"It depends," she said.

"On what might that be?"

"Tech. The O-line has to protect Harrell to get the sideline patterns to Crabtree and the throwaways to Batch. If Brandon Carter can win the right-side matchup, it'll be okay. McNeill's defense has got to keep the pressure on Colt McCoy all afternoon—especially with third-down conversions. That forty percent rate is asking for disaster with the 'Horns."

"Hello, I think I'm in love," Parrish said, sliding over onto the stool next to Dee. "I'm Blaise. This gin joint is mine."

She pulled out a business card and handed it to him. "Hi, I'm Dee Bennett with the *Claxton Courier*. And yes, I know. Nice to meet you."

He roared with laughter, and his two friends managed to slip out the door.

"You never did return my phone calls, Blaise darlin'. And here I thought you'd be flattered."

"No wonder you know all about football. You're Buddy Bennett's little sister. Now, you're a *lot* better looking than Buddy," he said, and then in an aside to the bartender, "Give her another—on the house. Bourbon on the rocks for me."

Dee let the barkeep bring her the drink but kept nursing the first.

"So you came all of the way here to talk to me?" he said loudly.

"Actually I'm a political reporter covering Rowdy McCorrigan's campaign," she said.

"Damn," Parrish said, "this *is* like old home week. That sum-bitch's not in my bar, is he?" He looked around.

Before Dee could answer, Parrish fell into a coughing jag that seemed would never stop. She sipped her second drink and casually watered it again while he was distracted. He eventually recovered and stubbed out his cigar in a Lone Star ashtray.

"McCorrigan's not here," Dee said. "He's in Corpus."

"Good, even that's too close."

"What's the issue?"

"Slimy sumbitch stole my starting QB's job right out from under me," Parrish said.

"I see."

"But that was a long time ago," Parrish said, "I suppose if I had worked harder and partied less I might could have gotten it back."

"I'm working on a feature about the state championship team—"

He interrupted her, slurring his words. "I remember you telling me that over the phone."

"But one player that I can't seem to learn anything about is Ricky Jones."

"He was a great tight end," Parrish said. "One of the best to ever play at Claxton."

"That's what I hear," Dee said, "Why is it no one wants to talk about him?"

Parrish inhaled and tossed back the rest of his liquor. He seemed to consider the question for a moment and turned serious. "I think it's out of respect for his family. He was raised by a single mom, and she had really made a good life for her and her kids. She was a nurse. But even the best of kids can turn bad."

"Do you know what happened?"

"Not really. Poor black kid who's a football superstar gets in trouble with the law, and his career's over. How many times have we heard that one?"

"I haven't found any evidence of a record," Dee said.

Parrish snorted. "And you're never gonna." He snorted again and called for another Wild Turkey. "Did I just say that?"

The karaoke contest had started up in the far corner, and Dee was having a hard time following Parrish.

"Listen, Blaise, I don't want to print anything that casts any of the team in an unflattering light years after they left Claxton. Like your story, for instance. Hanging out in a bar instead of passing the bar. I don't want to write a story like that. So do you know how I might locate Ricky Jones so I can talk with him myself, or not?"

"Not a thing," he admitted, and he sounded sincere. He shrugged. "He was this talented sixteen-year-old kid who up and walked right out of our lives. What can I say?"

He motioned for the bartender to refill his drink.

"Besides, what does it all matter now? Why smear a good kid's name? Why embarrass his family?"

He nuzzled toward her, overwhelming her with the smell of Bourbon and cigar smoke. "Why not, as they say, just let sleeping dogs lie?"

*   *   *

Dee, reeking of unpleasant bar odors and eager for a shower, returned the rental to the airport at nearly midnight and caught a cab to the hotel. Her mind was still on what had transpired in Port A as she rolled her suitcase quietly down the carpeted corridor. Blaise Parrish was lying—that much was clear. *Why* was yet another conundrum. All she knew now was that she was no closer to Ricky Jones than she had been when Buddy first mentioned the boy's name weeks ago. How *could* a talented sixteen-year-old kid just walk right out of their lives?

She had almost reached her room number, key card in hand, when a door on the opposite side opened and out stepped a slightly disheveled Charley Hensley, nearly walking into her.

Dee raised her eyebrows and Charley coolly patted down her hair. "Long strategy session," the campaign manager said. She looked Dee right in the eye and wrinkled her nose. "Where have *you* been?"

"Enjoying the beach," Dee replied just as coolly. She watched as Charley turned and walked to the end of the hallway, to what Dee assumed was her own room.

*   *   *

Tuesday night after dark, following their exhilarating helicopter flight out over the Gulf of Mexico and an amazing tour of the oil rig, Dee and the other reporter, Ralph, returned to the hotel with the interns while the candidate and his manager stayed behind with their host to talk fund-raising turkey. They'd be traveling together to Houston and back in Corpus Christi tomorrow. Dee planned to use those free hours tomorrow to finish her story before their return to Claxton. So much technical information and so many detailed statistics danced in her head, she wanted to be sure to get it down in writing before her first impressions faded.

"It's fascinating to learn how offshore production works, up close," said Dee, jammed into the back of the taxi between Brek and Django. "I had no idea what was involved."

"Come on, Dee, stop being such a Pollyanna," Ralph said, turning around from the front passenger seat. "Where've you been all your life?"

"Well, it *is* new to me. But I expect I'll digest it quickly and write a good story," she shot back. The senior writer's condescension stung. He'd probably observed how carefully she'd taken notes and cell-phone photos, asking for clarification on numerous occasions about the finer points of energy policy. Guys like Ralph had probably been covering the oil and gas industry since the dawn of the drill bit. But he was harmless enough. Her real challenge was going to be delivering a story for the Claxton paper that would validate Shannon's faith in her—and the hours she'd been allowed for this trip.

"Yeah, I imagine you'll hit your stride," he said. "So, what do you all say to a drink at the bar when we get back? I'll buy the first round."

Brek took a quick glance at Django and said thanks, but they'd pass. Dee had a feeling their refusal might have something to do with the club down the street—which looked to be a lot more their scene than the Blue Moon Bar at the hotel. She felt sorry enough for Ralph that, against her better judgment and the ache in her tired feet, she took him up on the invitation.

Ralph was already waiting in a curved booth, Scotch in hand, when she joined him after changing clothes and wiping the hint of salty-air residue from her face.

"What can I get for you?" he asked, waving the waitress over. Dee found his old-school chivalry a bit charming. She took him to be somewhere in his fifties but probably pushing closer to the retirement end of the gauge. His slightly stooped shoulders conjured up years of hunching over a keyboard. He reminded her a little of her father, except more talkative. She let him order her vodka gimlet.

He laid his arm across the back of the banquette behind her. "Gimlet? What kind of a drink is that for a journalist?"

"Teacher by profession, journalist by accident, you mean," she countered. "But hey, what do the ink-stained wretches drink these days? Absinthe? Mead?"

"A good Scotch never goes out of style."

"So, Ralph, why did you come along on this excursion?" she asked as the bartender brought her drink. "Are helicopter trips and offshore tours just everyday happenings for you, or are you covering a particular angle?"

He let out a chuckle. "Helicopter rides and offshore tours are more ordinary than you might think, when you've worked for an oil-town newspaper as long as I have," he said. "But I always have something specific in mind."

She looked at him, expecting more, but he kept his counsel.

"As I suppose your editor did in sending you here, too. I don't imagine it's every day the Claxton newspaper budgets for a reporter to go on the road."

"It's only because McCorrigan's relocated to our back yard," Dee said.

"Yes, that was a pretty bold move on his part," Ralph said, taking a whiff of his Scotch, followed by a generous sip.

"Well, having him back on his own turf has really stirred up the activity in town. Not to mention the effect that Charley has had!"

Ralph laughed his knowing laugh again. "I'll bet. I've been watching her turn heads for years."

Dee saw an opportunity to dig for some useful intel about the previous night. "What do you know about her past? I mean, anything juicy?"

"Nothing that matters a whit in the news, if that's what you're asking. Hell, there are always rumors floating around."

Dee nodded and baited him, not to be outdone. "More than rumors."

"Even if it's true I can't see any of it having any bearing on how well her boss does his job. I frankly don't care who he sleeps with as long as he does right by the citizens of Texas—if he gets elected, of course."

"Are you saying what I think you are?" Dee said.

Ralph looked at her more directly and laughed out loud this time. "I'm not *saying* a thing, sweetheart. But how many guys in his situation, with his looks and his luck, wouldn't have a little something on the side? I've known lots of businessmen over the years, covered 'em in the office and the boardroom—and do you have any idea how long my sources would've kept talking if I told everything I knew about what they did in the bedroom?"

"But he's running for office," she objected. "Doesn't the public have a right to know?"

"Honey," he said, "if the public has a right to know about the personal lives of every two-bit commissioner and judge and board member in Texas, you're going to need lots more hours than Shannon Thomas is giving you and a hell of a lot more proof. And you're going to have to ask yourself whether the public gives a damn in the first place."

Well, they just might, thought Dee, and she'd bet the farm that Ralph Begedovitch wouldn't hesitate to cheat on his wife too. But she had to agree that she had nothing stronger to nail McCorrigan with than circumstance and hearsay, and she didn't relish the idea of serving up scuttlebutt like some New York tabloid anyhow.

"Charley and I go way back, Dee. I won't deny a little crush on her myself. There are always tales. Just like the one circulating about her and this guy from Claxton right now." He pulled a BlackBerry out of the pocket of his jacket and flipped to a postage-stamp-sized Facebook photo of Charley Hensley in a red cocktail dress, cradled in the arms of a smitten-looking photographer. "Someone you might know?"

*   *   *

Dee didn't know whether Ralph the Reporter was trying to get her goat—picking on a greenhorn—or what the hell was going on. But she intended to get to the bottom of it. Paying her half of the tab and begging off on account of the late hour, Dee left Ralph in the bar, took the elevator straight upstairs to her room, and dialed Max's mobile number. After ten rings her call went to voice mail, but, too furious to leave a message, she hit End quickly. Deciding that was stupid—whenever he finally did retrieve his missed calls, he'd see her number and worry that there had been an emergency—she called back. This time she spoke smoothly and controlled her emotion. She thought.

Hi, Max, this is Dee and I hope your trip is going well. Call me as soon as you get this. Or you don't have to call the minute you get this, it's not urgent, I mean, it's important and I'd like to talk to you. 'Bye.

Now that was *really* stupid. Not only had she sounded like a whiner, she'd been as clear as mud and also managed to come across with all the romance of a rock.

She watched the iPhone's glass face, waiting for it to light up with an incoming number, for half an hour before turning on the television and clicking through the channels in search of a movie to take her mind off the image of that red dress.

That dress Charley had worn to the Red Hat Society Style Show. Oh, she hadn't forgotten the dress. But how did Charley get hold of a photo to share? And that look in Max's eyes . . . even on that tiny digital window she could read his concern . . . his what, affection? His *lust.*

Dee picked up the phone and started to dial again. Lust. Yes, that's exactly what it had looked like. She was right in the middle of figuring out how to redial the previous number when the ringer announcing an incoming call made her drop the phone. She picked it up off the carpet, not noting the caller.

"Hello?"

"Mom—what's that loud noise?"

"Jeez, Abby, sorry, sweetie," she said. "Let me turn down the TV."

"Are you at Gramma Alice's?"

Dee flipped the TV completely off. "What's going on?"

"Just—checking in and, I kinda had a question to ask you."

"What's that?" After midnight "I kinda had a question" always put her on high alert.

"How do you know when a guy's the one?"

*   *   *

Between the Facebook drama and the long conversation with Abby about Ian, Dee was drained the next day. She was never happier to enjoy a view of the beach from inside her lodging. She ordered room service and, wrapped in the hotel's plush white robe, pounded out her story on McCorrigan's visit to the oil rig. She found herself using especially forceful verbs and excising more modifiers than usual. This was slash and burn.

Max's number did not appear on her screen. Nor did it the day after, on the group's return flight, when Dee buckled herself in as far from Ralph and Charley and Rowdy McCorrigan as the ten-seater would allow. She stared out the oval window of the plane and wondered how on God's green earth she was going to get through ten more days of travails with Charley, trying to salvage both her relationship and her job.

20
Hide and Seek

If a young man and his parents are very close friends it is more than likely he will already have told them of the seriousness of his intentions. Very possibly he has asked his father's financial assistance, or at least discussed ways and means, but as soon as he and she have definitely made up their minds that they want to marry each other, it is the immediate duty of the man to go to the girl's father or her guardian, and ask his consent. If her father refuses, the engagement cannot exist. The man must then try, through work or other proof of stability and seriousness, to win the father's approval. Failing in that, the young woman is faced with dismissing him or marrying in opposition to her parents. There are, of course, unreasonable and obdurate parents, but it is needless to point out that a young woman assumes a very great risk who takes her future into her own hands and elopes. But even so, there is no excuse for the most unfilial act of all—deception. The honorable young woman who has made up her mind to marry in spite of her parents' disapproval, announces to them, if she can, that on such and such a day her wedding will take place. If this is impossible, she at least refuses to give her word that she will not marry. The height of dishonor is to "give her word" and then break it.

—"First Duty of the Accepted Suitor"

WHEN THE JET TOUCHED down in Claxton, Dee stepped off the stairs, took her bag as the airport manager handed it to her, and wheeled away without a word of good-bye.

Behind her back she heard Rowdy McCorrigan ask Charley, "What's up with her?"

"Oh, I'm not certain," his campaign manager answered. "But I heard it had something to do with a late night at the bar."

Dee had no time for innuendo. In fifteen minutes she had to pick up Mama and get to the high school auditorium for the wind energy forum. Dee had the sense a lot was riding on this meeting—for the farm and for Caprock County.

They made it with minutes to spare, Mama quizzing Dee the whole way about the big offshore adventure. Dee was still in no mood for small talk.

"Well, I don't understand why that photographer boyfriend of yours isn't here tonight," Mama said as they headed up the school walkway, a path Dee had not taken since the final day of her senior year.

"He didn't part ways with the Texas Star folks on the friendliest terms, if you recall," Dee responded.

"We'll, I'd-a thought they might patch things up, considerin' how well that book's been doing. I know lots of folks have bought copies."

"I'm not privy to Max's book sales figures, Mama," Dee snapped, just as a voice called out to her, "Wait up!" She turned to see Hank Hardeberger jogging toward her, notebook in hand.

He caught up to them and said to Mama, "How are you, Mrs. Bennett?"

"I'm doin' fine, Hank. You found a yard man yet?"

Before Hank could offer her mother a straight-faced answer, Dee stepped in. "I know none of us wants to miss the start of the program. Don't let us hold you back, Hank."

"Oh, it's no trouble, Dee," he said, slipping a friendly arm around her shoulder. "You look like you've had a long day. Let me get that door for you."

She was suddenly very grateful for someone who showed a little kindness. Someone who never placed an expectation on her or mysteriously disappeared for days at a time or caused her the least worry. The only time Hank ever seemed to get riled was when he was defending the environment, and she supposed you could

218   KAY ELLINGTON & BARBARA BRANNON

hardly fault a guy for standing up for a better world. She and Mama preceded Hank through the double doors and walked down the sloping aisle to the front, so that Mama could follow every part of the presentation, and Dee motioned for him to join them.

Dee slumped into a squeaky fold-down theater seat between Mama and Hank, then took out her phone and turned it off. Still no reply, that she could see. She pulled out a pen and a small spiral notebook from her purse, opened its cover, and uncapped her pen in a series of actions that so precisely mirrored Hank's, they both laughed. The irritations of the past days crumbled, and Dee sat back to listen and absorb new information.

Mayor Shelton and the chairwoman of the city council, a land-owner named Jessica Cater, introduced the Texas Star Energy panel. Among the guests were two representatives who'd called on Mama and Dee previously.

"Where you think them other sorry cusses are, Dee Anna?" Mama whispered.

Dee recalled their unexpected visit from the pair of landmen, and they just about broke out in giggles. Dee caught Buck Turlock's eye and waved across the room, but Buck just nodded back at her.

"Friends of yours?" asked Hank.

"I doubt it," said Dee.

The mic squealed as the mayor handed it over to the first represen-tative, a Mr. John Olbermeyer. "Thank you all for coming out tonight," he said as the amplification was adjusted. "There, that better? Okay. At Texas Star Energy, we are committed to clean, renewable energy resources that bring economic prosperity to our communities. Most of you are here because you've received our packets in the mail or have talked with one of our landowner liaison staff."

"Landowner liaison, my foot," said Hank under his breath. Dee could see the evening getting longer already.

The first man wrapped up his spiel about the company and its financial backers and corporate ethics and community support, and the second, a Mr. Grinstead, took the mic. Good cop, bad cop, Dee thought, as Grinstead described the way the leasing process would work, when construction of the turbines would begin, how land-owners would be compensated, when energy production would go online, and the like. Mama, Dee noted, was listening intently. Across the aisle from them Margaret Strickland, who had been covering the Texas Star Energy story for the paper from the outset, had her tape recorder going.

"Now I'm sure you all have lots of questions," said Grinstead. "We want to get in as many as possible, so please try to state them briefly and myself and John here will do our best to answer clearly."

The first few questions seemed simple enough, and so did the responses. Margaret raised her hand, and Olbermeyer called on her. "Margaret Strickland, *Claxton Courier.* I understand that there is some concern for the impacts of the giant turbines on people and the environment. Can you tell us how these machines will affect, say, cattle herds, bats and migratory birds, and even humans living nearby?"

"Thank you for bringing up that important issue, Mrs. Strickland," said Grinstead. "Bird and bat mortality is a concern that we continue to study and monitor, especially since we know that other tall structures, such as radio and TV towers, smokestacks, and even tall buildings, have been associated with bird and bat kills. But when it comes to the safety of human life, we must keep in mind that wind turbines do not produce air emissions or contribute to smog, they don't burn fossil fuels, and they use very small amounts of toxic fluids such as lubricating oils, so the risk of contamination is quite slim compared to what you get with other forms of energy production. Even solar has its risks."

Margaret took notes and did not offer a follow-up question. But Hank's hand shot up for the next one.

"I for one believe that wind energy is one of the safest and most sustainable options available to us," he said. "But I wonder what alternatives your company has considered to building more high-lines and transmission pylons across the landscape?"

Olbermeyer fielded this one. "I'm glad you asked that, too, Mr.—?"

"Hardeberger. I teach biology here at Claxton High."

"Well, Mr. Hardeberger, then as a scientist I'm sure you fully appreciate the challenges we face with long-distance electrical transmission—moving power from remote parts of Texas and the West to the parts of the country where demand is highest."

Hank nodded.

"At Texas Star, we fully support research currently underway to develop supercooled underground electrical cables," said Olbermeyer. "That plan would bring the added benefit of being better protected from terrorist threats. But it's expensive, and probably still a long way off."

Buck Turlock spoke up. "Until then, I'm kinda like everybody else on this subject. 'Not in my backyard'!"

Mama nodded. It might be the only matter she was likely to agree with him on, thought Dee.

After a couple more questions having to do with complex rights issues, the Texas Star staff seemed ready to pack up as they'd received a smattering of applause, when a loud voice came from the center of the room. "I'm J. D. Sandifer from Claxton, Texas. I got plenty of cattle out on my land, and I don't think they're gonna be fazed by any old pinwheel blowin' over their heads. I'm ready to sign and start making some electricity. All those people that say 'Drill, Baby, Drill,' well, I just say, 'Blow, Baby, Blow'!"

J. D.'s opinion seemed to find wide agreement. "Most of our neighbors are signing their leases and saying 'show me the money,'" Pauline Sandifer told Mama as the crowd poured out of the auditorium like an uphill lava flow. "We couldn't think of a good reason not to."

Dee hung back, waiting for Margaret, while Mama went on out with J. D. and Pauline. She sighed loudly and pressed her temples, feeling a headache coming on.

"Really tough week, huh?" Hank asked quietly.

"You have no idea," she said.

"Well then, I have only one piece of advice to offer you. *Noli illegitimus carborundum.*"

"What's that?" Dee asked, looking at him with a skeptical grin.

"Don't let the bastards get you down."

"You're an original, Hank," she said. "See you Tuesday night, right?"

Margaret weaved through the aisles to reach Dee just as Hank was leaving. "Well, that went pretty smoothly, I'd say, wouldn't you?"

"I think we finally found something in Claxton that Hank approves of," Dee said.

Margaret looked up the aisle, indicating where he'd exited. "You're not getting—interested, are you?"

Dee started to say no but hesitated, considering the question herself.

"Dee," Margaret said, "not that it's any of my business. But you and Max Miller seem like a perfect fit, to me. And if there was a woman like Charley Hensley circling around my man, I'd tighten his leash and fend her off. You might do well to consider the same."

Dee laughed, rubbed her temples again, and said, "I'll bear that in mind. But I think he keeps slipping his collar."

*   *   *

As Dee cranked the car and backed out, Mama said, "You're not gonna get tangled up with some tree hugger, are you?"

"Don't be silly, Mama."

"Well, I did have to agree with one thing he said tonight."

"What's that?"

"I don't think you want one-a-them big high-lines running across the place neither. I know they have to go somewhere. But as I figure it, the best way to make sure the company doesn't eventually come take your land for the power line is, sign up and let 'em build a windmill on it. Not like they're gonna come tear it down later, is it?"

"Well, you might have a point there. JoAnn says we might consider holding out and negotiating the lease price."

"I think she's right. And I think I have an even better idea. But you're tard, I can tell. Let's talk about it when you're rested up."

Dee pulled up to Mama's place and walked her in, making sure all was in order before locking the door and driving the ten miles to the farm. She remembered, first, to switch her phone back on. A voice mail message was waiting. *Hey, babe, just now back in phone range. I hope you're okay, and I miss you like crazy. I'll be back home Friday. Lots of great photos to show you.*

*   *   *

The following morning Dee woke with Margaret's words repeating in her ears. She'd endured a string of strange dreams, in which Blaise Parrish slid into the seat beside her on the plane and offered her a cigar but Charley Hensley, wearing a slinky red dress, took it from her and Margaret Strickland came down the aisle in a flight attendant's uniform and reminded them there was no smoking on the flight, and about that time the aircraft went into a spiral dive and a baby started crying.

If there was a woman like Charley Hensley circling around my man . . . she heard again, before the sound of Cori's whiny meowing drowned out the thought.

Dee opened her eyes just a slit, shooed the cat, pulled up the covers in a room that had grown icy cold overnight, and reached for her phone. She knew exactly what she was going to do. This was the time to test the magical powers of texting.

Lying here in bed thinking of u, she sent to Max's number, hoping she'd struck the right note.

The reply came back in a flash. *Sounds naughty. Wish I was there.*

Were, she thought. But then, who took the time for grammatical niceties when carrying on a conversation over a screen the size of a cake of soap, for crying out loud?

She texted, *How about a date 2nite? Up for another game?*

He texted back. *Who r u rooting for?*

She responded. *Cougars all the way.* Was that too suggestive? In for a dime, in for a dollar, she thought. She tightened the leash and hit Send.

Pick u up 6? Max texted back.

It was time to get some answers.

* * *

Dee welcomed Max at the door, genuinely glad to see him but certain of what she had to do. "Home is the wanderer," she said, welcoming his kiss on her lips but stopping him there. "Get in here before you freeze!"

"It was a long drive and an even longer drive back," he said. "You start to understand how the pioneers felt, going for weeks on the trail without a letter."

"You like that, don't you? That throwback to the open range?" She motioned him over to the couch, where a bottle of chilled champagne and two flutes awaited on the coffee table.

"Sure, there's something in me that needs to be alone every so often. But not this moment." He reached for her hand, and she let him hold it.

Dee filled their glasses halfway, waited for the bubbles to subside, and said, "What shall we drink to?"

"To an injury-free evening," he said as they each took a sip, then added, "on and off the field." He set his glass down, took her chin in his rough hand, and kissed her longingly. He ran his other hand down the smooth nap of her velour pullover, and she could feel the shape of his fingers through the fabric. She had to put those thoughts aside for now.

"I have to ask you something," she said. "I have to know."

"What?"

"When did you stop seeing Charley Hensley?"

"Seeing her, as in, on jobs? Well, I guess, I haven't stopped seeing her. I have an assignment with her on Monday."

"And when did you start seeing her?"

"I met her at the show opening, when you did," Max answered, looking increasingly confused. "Or I assume when you did. Maybe you technically started seeing her first."

"And when did you last sleep with her?"

"*Sleep* with her."

"Yes, sleep with her."

"Now you're telling me to sleep with her?" he mocked her.

"No, of course not! I'm asking, when did you have sexual relations with Charley Hensley?"

Max laughed and wagged his finger at her in a bad imitation of Bill Clinton. "I have never had sexual relations with Charley Hensley."

Dee stood up and pulled her cell phone out of her pocket, scrolling to find the damning photos Ralph the Reporter had showed her. She held the screen out toward his face. "Where were you on the afternoon of Wednesday, October 22?"

"Two days ago? I was in Kingsville, Texas. Packing up and getting ready to drive back here. To see you, of course."

"I heard on the news that there was a huge wreck on the Interstate. Traffic blocked both ways for hours. Must have been difficult traveling."

"Is that so? I took the back way through Alice and George West." He was having a hard time keeping the corners of his mouth from twitching.

"You didn't return my phone call that day. So I am sure you are hiding something."

Max raised his eyebrows and took the phone from her, scrolled and clicked a couple of times. He turned it and showed Dee the record of incoming calls—twice a day from his number, all week. "Now it's my turn for a question," he said. "You flew to Corpus Christi, right?"

She nodded.

"Did the pilot by any chance ask passengers to put phones in airplane mode? This little icon right here?"

"Um, yes . . . "

"That setting that keeps transmissions from coming and going?"

"So that's what that does," she said, suddenly getting it.

"All right, then, what's up with all the silly questions?"

Dee reached into the drawer of the end table beside her recliner and handed him the book. *Interview and Interrogation Techniques, 3rd Ed.* "I've been polishing my journalism skills," she said. "You never know when you might need to catch a liar."

"The Volatile Conundrum." Max held back the laugh he'd been suppressing, and Dee collapsed on the sofa beside him, laughing till she cried. "I *was* in the military, you know," he said. "They taught us a few things about interrogation. But you really thought there was some intrigue going on between me and the Wicked Witch of the East?" he asked.

"Well, there have been photos," she said, wiping a tear from her eye.

"From the day at the style show, when blue-haired red-hats from all over the county captured us in what only looked like compromising positions? Come on, surely it takes more than that to make you doubt me."

"I don't think I dreamed I saw Charley's car in front of your house once while you were gone."

"Spying on me, huh? I asked her to feed Chester on several occasions. It hardly seemed fair to ask you, while she was living around the corner."

She let out a sigh. "You must consider me a lunatic for behaving like this," she said.

"It's touching that you're jealous. I'm flattered," he said, enfolding her in his arms and kissing her fully and passionately. She gave in, sinking into his embrace and putting all thought of scheming campaign managers aside.

It had been a long time since she'd felt such reckless abandon with Max, not since that night under the stars all those weeks ago. But they heard the clock strike the hour, and disengaged reluctantly.

"Kickoff is at seven-thirty," Dee said, "and your boosters will be waiting."

"The wind is really howling out there. I hope you have a warm coat—I've got blankets and a Thermos."

At Cougar Stadium, while Max bought their tickets and Dee snuggled in close to him in the line, she heard a familiar voice over the wind.

"My name is Levi, come buy a program, Cougars on the prowl, I been here thirty-three years now. Come get your program. We gonna take it to them. Programs just three dollars."

"Max," she said as soon as he had tickets in hand, "I'm starving. Will you get us some hot dogs?"

"This minute?" he said. "The concession stands are packed."

"I'm really hungry," she said.

"Whatever you'd like," he said.

"I'll wait here—and thank you so much! I'm suddenly famished!"

When Max turned his back and disappeared into the crush of fans, she pushed through the crowd to Levi's corner.

"Program three dollars," he said.

She handed him three singles. "Levi, you've been here thirty-three years?"

"Yes, ma'am."

"Then you remember Ricky Jones?"

A funny look came over his face. Dee was beginning to expect that look whenever she mentioned the young man's name. "Why do you want to know?" Levi asked.

She pulled the muffler back from her face to be heard clearly. "Because from everything I've heard, he seemed like a pretty amazing kid who deserved better than he got. I want to talk to him. Do you know how to find him?"

Levi looked around as if he might be overheard. "Come back and see me when I get off work. I settle up with those folks in there." He pointed toward the concession stand with his head. "I'll be around after the game for a bit."

He turned away and resumed hawking his wares. Dee scanned the crowd for Max but had lost sight of him.

"Dee!" She heard a man say, and she turned in his direction. She almost didn't make out Hank's voice, bundled up as he was in pea coat and nattily wrapped beige plaid muffler.

"Hi, Hank? Wow, what a night!"

"Did you come alone?" he said to her.

"No, she's with me," Max said, appearing at Dee's side with two hot dogs and a steaming hot chocolate to share.

Hank greeted Max and said, "Those guys and girls you see walking through the stands peddling chocolate bars are from the Science

Club. So, if you feel like dessert?" He pulled his gold toboggan further down on his brow, waved, and walked off.

"There's something different about him," Max said. "Why does he always manage to be where you are?"

"Life is full of coincidences," Dee said.

They squeezed into their seats through the mass of down and wool and GoreTex, and could see that although Claxton had taken control of the game from the opening kickoff, the Winters Blizzards were battling back each time. Dee appreciated the chance to huddle close to Max, whose figure shielded her somewhat from the wind.

By the end of the half the Cougars had managed to score twice—failing the point after each time as the wind frustrated the kicker's best efforts. The Blizzards had likewise scored twice, but made good on one of theirs. As the teams left the field for their respective locker rooms at the half, neither away nor home marching band seemed keen to take the field for the shows they'd worked so hard to perfect. The baton twirlers had it worst of all. A Claxton head twirler managed to launch her rubber-tipped baton with a nice spiral only to have a sudden gust whip it out of control and send it plummeting like a spear. The cheerleaders, dance team, and twirlers ran for cover as clouds began to swirl overhead and snow fell, if you could call it that, in horizontal waves.

Max and his booster buddies scratched their heads nervously as the second half began, alternately leaning forward in the bleachers and holding their fists to their mouths in the "Thinker" position. Dee, meanwhile, was absorbed in framing the different questions she should ask Levi the program guy. If she didn't do any better with him than her bush-league lie detector questions for Max, though, she would probably blow the best shot she had at this.

Late in the fourth quarter Winters kicked a field goal to widen the gap. While it wasn't enough to clinch the win with four minutes left on the clock, Claxton fans began swarming out of the bleachers and heading toward the gate.

The freak snowstorm was tapering off by the time the Cougars quarterback slipped and slid his way through a maze of blockers who fell over and got up again like prairie dogs popping up on the prairie. He ran the ball all the way in for another six—but the kicker missed the extra point.

With a minute left in the game the score was Claxton 18, Winters 16.

Eighteen to sixteen, Dee thought, jumping up in the stands as though it were the biggest victory of the year.

"I know it's a close game, but I've never seen you that excited about the score," said Max.

"I'm going to hurry down to the ladies' room to beat the line," she said. "Wait for me at the exit gate."

"Now?" he said, as the band whipped the bleachers into a frenzy with a musical chant rising a half step in pitch each round.

"When ya gotta go, ya gotta go," she said, and was gone.

Dee didn't want to jinx her hunch or waste a second now. She peeked around the gate. No Levi. She walked all the way around the concession stand. Had he gone home early? Had he gotten cold feet? But in a flash she saw the man wave for her to join him behind the concession stand, where there was a big gas heater going for the smokers. Dee and Levi now had the warm spot to themselves.

"I'm a reporter with the Claxton newspaper," Dee began.

"I know who you are," he said. "You Buddy Bennett's little sister who been tailing McCorrigan's butt all month."

"What do you think of Rowdy McCorrigan?" she said.

"Not much."

"What did he do to Ricky Jones?"

"I can't prove anything."

Dee sighed. She'd tried to avoid closed-ended questions, but this was going nowhere. Max would come looking for her any moment.

"But I can tell you what the scuttlebutt was at the time."

"What was that?"

"Three players. One had money, one had talent, one had a fast car. Two got busted, one took the rap."

She knew it. She'd guessed the last part, anyway—that a juvenile case was involved—that's why Blaise had said she'd never find a record. "Because he was a juvenile and the other two were already eighteen, right? But what was the crime? And why would Jones take the fall for something he didn't do?"

"He was poor and money talks."

"Omigosh. What happened to him?"

"Ask him yourself."

"How?"

"Seek and ye shall find."

What was that supposed to mean, in this context? Why was Levi the program man quoting scripture to her, posing riddles out in the cold while the football fans disappeared into the night?

The tall stadium lights shut down and the field was left in darkness. Levi leaned toward Dee and said in his rhythmic singsong, "Then he is gracious unto him, and saith, Deliver him from going down to the pit: I have found a ransom."

At the far exit gate Dee spotted Max, anxiously pacing, his arms full of blankets.

"I got to finish settling up. I got stuff to do. Seek and ye shall find. God bless you."

"And you, too Levi." She thanked him. But what she might do with what he'd revealed to her, she wasn't sure.

By the time she caught up with Max her teeth were chattering. He wrapped a blanket around her shoulders and teased her as they hiked toward his pickup, "I lost you there for a while! Did you decide you had to have some of Hank's candy?"

"What? No," she said, then remembered. The conversation about the science club chocolate bars seemed eons ago. Dee smiled at Max though she felt chilled to the bone. "So, now who's jealous?"

"Let's get you home and warm." He nuzzled her neck. "And maybe we could finish up where we left off."

* * *

"It's serious business, Max," Dee said once she'd begun to thaw out and she repeated Levi's words to him, confiding what she'd been after. "I think it's a lot more than a profile in the football section of a small-town newspaper."

"If I get what you're saying, you're looking at a cover-up that's stood for thirty years."

"I think it's big. And I have to tell my editor the latest. But first I have to figure out just what it is I'm telling her."

"I'll help if you like. Maybe an outsider's perspective will be useful."

At the farm, Dee turned up the heat and put on a pot of coffee. She brought her computer and her file of notes to the kitchen table and walked Max through the facts to the extent she knew them.

"Here's Rowdy McCorrigan," she said, laying down one enlarged yearbook photo at the top of an imaginary triangle. "We have plenty of background on him. Born Claxton, Texas, October 22, 1959. Played varsity football for the Cougars three seasons, leading the team to the state championship in December 1977. Has an older sister and two older brothers. Parents deceased. Married since 1982 to Gretchen Marks of Austin. Two children."

"What more do you know about his high school days? Especially senior year?" asked Max.

"Lots of his teammates I talked to for the newspaper feature recalled Rowdy's car. A gold Camaro. In a town where any self-respecting teenaged boy back then drove a pickup—where they still do—that car stood out in people's minds. One of the guys remembered Rowdy taking a trip to Mexico in it the summer before senior year—kind of a crazy lark with Ricky Jones and Blaise Parrish." She laid Parrish's photo at another corner of the triangle.

"Drugs involved, then?"

"Surely so. Parrish was the one with the reputation as a stoner. My own brother told me as much, and so did others. And I think—if Levi's description means anything—he must have been the one of the trio with money, since everyone describes Ricky Jones as smart and talented." She completed the figure with his yearbook picture from the sophomore class. "And here's the thing: the birth certificate I obtained gives Jones's date of birth as January 2, 1961, so he's the youngest of the three. The only one who hasn't turned at least seventeen in fall of 1977. The perfect way to hide any evidence of wrongdoing—by burying it in juvenile court. In Texas, those records are sealed, and can even be expunged later. There's no paper trail."

"And Levi says Ricky took the fall for a crime he didn't commit," said Max. "Must have been some powerful persuasion. Like blackmail, or a hefty bribe."

The wind continued to whip around the porch, rattling the branches of the cedars in the wee hours. "Are you sure you can stay?" Dee asked. "Are you sure you want to keep on with this?"

Max cradled Dee's weary head against his chest. "I'll be here anytime you need me. I promise. I was thoughtless to go off and not even let you know my plans."

"They're your plans," said Dee. "I don't have any claim on your time."

"But if you want it," he said, making the point, "I'll gladly give it. And you know I wouldn't say that to just anyone."

She nodded. "Let's keep on, then." Max refilled their coffee cups.

"I've been thinking more about those Bible verses Levi spoke," Dee said. She wrote them down on another piece of paper. "At least, I think they're both from the Bible. This second one is an odd phrase. Old Testament, I think. But where to even start?"

"You know there are plenty of websites you can use to look it up, right? Any version you prefer. My mother doesn't even use her old leatherbound King James anymore."

"Let's check, then."

Dee's assessment that the verse was from the Old Testament was on the money. From the book of Job, a sobering prophecy if ever there was one. "Elihu rebukes Job's three friends," read the annotation above the scripture.

A chill ran down Dee's spine. She stared at the screen for a few minutes before seeking the next connection. Searches for various combinations of the words turned up nothing that appeared relevant. The hour was dulling her faculties. Nothing was making sense.

Her fatigue was not lost on Max. "Hey, babe, why don't you get some sleep?"

"I need . . . I need to figure out . . . "

"Come on, to bed with you," he said to her, guiding her up from the chair and down the hallway, and the last thing she remembered before wearily changing into her pajamas was Max's kiss on her forehead and the kitchen door clicking and closing behind him.

21
Skeletons in the Closet

Popularly supposed to have been a frightful orgy, and now arid as the Sahara desert and quite as flat and dreary, the bachelor dinner was in truth more often than not, a sheep in wolf's clothing.

It is quite true that certain big clubs and restaurants had rooms especially constructed for the purpose, with walls of stone and nothing breakable within hitting distance, which certainly does rather suggest frightfulness. As a matter of fact, "an orgy" was never looked upon with favor by any but silly and wholly misguided youths, whose idea of a howling good time was to make a howling noise; chiefly by singing at the top of their lungs and—breaking crockery. A boisterous picture, but scarcely a vicious one! Especially as quantities of the cheapest glassware and crockery were always there for the purpose.

The breaking habit originated with drinking the bride's health and breaking the stem of the wine glass, so that it "might never serve a less honorable purpose." A perfectly high-minded sentiment! And this same time-honored custom is followed to this day. Toward the latter end of the dinner the groom rises, and holding a filled champagne glass aloft says: "To the bride!" Every man rises, drinks the toast standing, and then breaks the delicate stem of the glass. The impulse to break more glass is natural to youth, and probably still occurs. It is not hard to understand. The same impulse is seen at every county fair where enthusiastic youths (and men) delight in shooting, or throwing balls, at clay pipes and ducks and—crockery!

Aside from toasting the bride and its glass-smashing result, the groom's farewell dinner is exactly like any other "man's dinner," the details depending upon the extravagance or the frugality of the host, and upon whether his particular friends are staid citizens of sober years or mere boys full of the exuberance of youth. Usually there is music of some sort . . . and the dinner party itself does the singing. Often the dinner is short and all go to the theater.

— "The Bachelor Dinner"

DEE WOKE ON SATURDAY to bright sunshine and frost on the windowpanes. She showered quickly, letting the steam bring her back to life as she pondered Levi's riddle. Every search of either scripture had brought up thousands of sermon texts, Sunday School lessons, even an old book by the title of *Select Works of Thomas Boston, with a Memoir of His Life.* But nothing remotely connected with Ricky Jones.

She toweled dry and dressed.

Returning to the Bible search portal she'd left open a few hours earlier, she typed in the verse from Matthew again. Chapter 7, the Sermon on the Mount. Wise admonitions for those of any faith, she had always believed. *Judge not, lest ye be judged.*

A judge . . . there had to have been a judge who had heard the Ricky Jones case, even in juvenile court. And a docket, and a disposition of the case. Was it not possible to discover what wasn't there by the records you could locate, of what was? Anywhere a gap appeared in the record, you might narrow the field. But that would have to wait till Monday, and time was running out. Monday morning would be her deadline for the football profiles she'd been working on for weeks now. If she could show her editor something for her efforts on Jones, she might just get to stay on the story—and get to the truth that McCorrigan and Parrish were hiding.

At random, she typed in search string combinations from the facts at her disposal. She'd become pretty good at that during her short stay on the library reference desk. And suddenly it hit her. Just choose the most relevant words out of all the possibilities. Not arcane, endlessly recombined phrases. Just three words. *Seek. Jones. Ransom.*

Dee's computer screen delivered up the website of the Traditional Values Network, a Christian cable broadcast headquartered in New

York and with studios in Houston and Dallas, and headed by one Ransom Jones, whose picture was featured prominently above the scriptural motto, *Ask, and it shall be given you; seek, and ye shall find; knock, and it shall be opened unto you.*

She read on for a few paragraphs then ran to retrieve the TV remote and search for the right channel. She watched and listened, transfixed, at what she knew in her heart were the visage and voice of Ricky Jones, late of Claxton, Texas.

Mr. Jones—she could not tell whether he was an ordained minister—anchored a weekend segment called "Faith and Finances" while a stock market ticker ran underneath.

Dee brought the laptop over to the couch. Sometimes Jones interviewed captains of industry who had ties to the Christian market, but for the most part his topics concerned personal finance. How to improve your credit scores. How to shop for a mortgage. What to look for in credit card offers. How to negotiate buying a car. How to build your savings. How to plan for retirement. That sort of thing. A black male Suze Orman, Dee thought. It all looked like practical and sound advice to her.

Jones's message was a simple one. *God takes care of those who take care of themselves.* Seek, and ye shall find.

His brief bio on the station website said he'd grown up in a small Texas town—bingo—and graduated from the London School of Economics. He had returned to the states and worked on Wall Street in hedge funds for a while before leaving to help form a Christian credit counseling service in Brooklyn. This latest enterprise, on a Christian cable network, seemed to be fairly recent.

Dee hammered out an e-mail to the founder of TVN.

> Dear Mr. Jones:
>
> First of all, I'd like to say that I've been watching the archives of Faith and Finances and find it to be very valuable, especially during these times of economic uncertainty. Quite impressive for someone who got their start at Claxton High.

I am writing a story on the 30th anniversary of the Cougars' state championship football team, and would like to talk with you about your experiences in that historic year. I am on a tight deadline, since the section closes day after tomorrow and the team reunion is scheduled for this Friday night's game in Claxton.

Sincerely,

Dee Bennett

Claxton Courier

Dee called Max to describe what she'd found, and he said he'd bring lunch and remain at her disposal as long as she needed. They ate quietly, did the dishes, and went out to make sure the bedding for the goats was sufficient for another cold night. She didn't want to wander far from the computer. But one day turned into another with no response from Ransom Jones. Not a word.

*   *   *

On Monday the mood in the newsroom was electric, as the final week of election season dawned. The story budget meeting ranged from how much play the *Courier* ought to give national stories, to how much coverage the paper would devote to football during Homecoming week. There seemed to be no other topic worth consideration.

Dee had posted a blog about energy and conservation issues in the state. Drawing on her newly expanded knowledge of the workings of wind, water, and wells, she had crafted a post that she hoped would be provocative. In a good way.

She'd submitted her completed team profiles, to add to the batches from Phil and his writers that would begin running that afternoon. Shannon's strategy would be to start with the defensive players and work gradually to the offense and close it out with the quarterback. A full tabloid section, jam-packed with ads, would run on Thursday afternoon, repeating all the profiles. "Good work," Shannon added as they wrapped up the meeting. "We'll have a final

tally on our ad revenues next Monday, when we'll also put the finishing touches on our plan for election-night coverage."

Dee met with Shannon behind closed doors afterward to fill her
in on all she'd learned about the whereabouts of Ricky Jones. "It
wasn't enough, though," Dee said. "After all that I came up empty. I
guess we'll just be running that yearbook photo and a few stats for
him on Wednesday. And I'm baffled that the other angle has grown
into one big dead end."

"Don't kick yourself. This whole feature was a terrific idea.
Advertisers have eaten it up. And readers will, too, as soon as papers
start hitting their front porches in a few hours."

Dee promised to keep her boss posted, if anything should change.

At about four that afternoon, as she toiled away on the next scavenger hunt assignment in the library, it did. But not for the better.
She heard the swoosh on the phone in her pocket that indicated
incoming e-mail.

> Dear Dee Bennett:
> Ransom Jones forwarded your inquiry to me
> regarding a story about a town called Claxton.
> You must have him mistaken with someone else.
> Apologies that he is not the person you are seeking.
> All best,
> Jessica Klepper
> TVN Publicist

If this was not the guy, Dee thought, wouldn't he have just
e-mailed her himself? Why delegate the task to a subordinate? The
whole response smelled to her like an attempt to dodge an interview.

Dee logged into the reference desk computer. She plowed back
over every scrap of information she recalled from Jones's bio. But
she located nothing new from his hedge fund days. Nothing connected with the London School of Economics. Nothing from his stint
with Christian Credit Counselors except a string of press releases
that led to a defunct website and an e-mail address that immediately

bounced. When she added the URL of that old website to her search, however, a document opened with detailed instructions for exhibitors at a financial trade show CCC had put on in Queens—including a mobile phone number for vendors to call if they encountered issues. She dialed it.

After about three rings a surprised voice said, "Hello?"

"May I speak to Ransom Jones?"

"Speaking. Who is this?"

"My name is Dee Bennett and—"

"Listen, I don't know how you got this number," he said, "and I believe my assistant has already responded to your message." So he *had* seen the e-mail.

"I understand. I only wanted to say that in preparing for the All-Class Reunion in Claxton this Friday—"

He cut her off, over-polite. "I'm not the person you're looking for."

"Have you never lived in Claxton, Texas?" *Chapter 6, Phrasing Questions to Throw Interviewees Off Balance.*

"I'm going to hang up now," he said. "Please do not contact me again."

*   *   *

On the drive home Dee had an inspiration. Sitting down to a bowl of canned chicken soup—the prospect of which enticed Cori to jump into the dining chair beside her as if waiting to be served—she pulled out the number of Blaise Parrish in Port Aransas again. She dialed it and caught the proprietor himself.

"Hello, Blaise, hon?"

"Yeah?"

"It's Dee Bennett from Claxton, and I'm only calling to say how much I enjoyed our little get-together at your bar last week. It was nice of you to see me."

"Ah, sure. Me too," he answered.

"Listen, I had some news for you in case you still weren't certain about coming up to Claxton for that reunion Friday night."

"Naw, I can't come. I've got plans."

"Even if Ricky Jones were coming?"

The line went quiet.

"So Blaise, I sure am sorry you can't make it, but let me give you some details just in case anything changes at the last minute. Let's see, kickoff is at seven-thirty against the Sweetwater Mustangs. There'll be a special recognition of the class of 1978 at halftime. And then the All-Class Reunion will be downtown in the old Kress store—you remember that, right? on Second Street next to where the Western Auto store used to be? Oh, and it's a costume party, of course, because it's Halloween."

"I appreciate it," said Parrish.

"Just thought you might want to know. We'll sure miss you."

With that seed planted, she moved down the row to dig another hole.

"Hi, Charley, it's Dee Bennett. Sorry to bother you after hours, but I just had one teensy little thing to check on, about that football profile on Rowdy."

"Make it quick," Charley said.

"You know, the main story is going to run on Thursday. But what if we were able to get even more coverage out of that angle?"

Now she had Charley's interest. "What if, on Friday night at the football game and the class reunion, we were able to get a picture of McCorrigan together with Blaise Parrish and Ricky Jones?"

Charley's voice shot up about an octave. "They're coming?"

"The invitation has been extended. But that's all I know for sure."

*   *   *

Though the bitter temperatures of the previous week had grown more temperate, Tuesday morning's warming trend brought high winds and more rain. On the newspaper's website, comments ran high on whether the weather would affect Friday night's big game. But to Dee a rainy day seemed the perfect occasion to decamp to her attic hide-away and immerse herself in the evening's Write Stuff submissions.

E-mail notices were popping up like fish jumping on a lake. JoAnn volunteered to read aloud from her Ricki Rocco story. Raul, never shy, offered up a new chapter of Vampire Bob. *And I'll be happy to read a couple of pages in character, mon.*

J. D. wrote to say he had set Cowboy Wilbur aside for the moment; he was attaching a new poem and wanted to get the group's reaction. Wendell was coming close to a finished draft of his Civil War novel but didn't think he had anything quite ready to read. He wondered if he could yield his time to Dee's mother, who might have something to share but didn't know how to send it on e-mail.

Mama? That should be interesting, Dee thought. She reminded herself to exercise professional detachment, just as she would with any other writer.

*   *   *

As the scribes arrived at the farm that evening, they had to battle a blustery norther with intermittent rain, wind, and lightning—and the vibe among them seemed as charged as the electricity in the air. "One week away from a new day and a new way, W. G.," Hank teased Wendell as they walked in together, shedding raincoats in the kitchen, where he found their host making a pot of coffee. "I liked your blog from yesterday," he said to Dee.

"Well done," Wendell added, looking in Hank's direction, "without being partisan."

Frances, who had given Mama a ride from town, said, "I sure am glad I already did early voting. That makes it a lot easier."

"Well, I still like to go on Election Day," said Mama. "In case something happens to make me change my mind at the last minute." The muffled sound of rain drumming on the roof grew quiet for a few minutes.

"Who all's going to the All-Class Reunion?" Margaret asked, coming through the door behind JoAnn.

"Frances and I actually started out at Kemp," Mama said, "before they consolidated our school into Claxton." Frances nodded.

"That shouldn't keep you from going to the party," J. D. said, as he came in. "Might be your last chance to see some of these soreheads.

Pauline and I are going for old times' sake—we spent lots of years on chaperon duty!"

"I think I'd rather stay home and give out Halloween candy," said Mama. "I didn't ever get to do that out at the farm."

Raul, Teresa, and Summer arrived last, drenched from the latest downpour.

"Y'all come in out of the rain," Dee said. "I've made coffee. Grab a cup to warm up."

The stack of manuscripts on the coffee table was taller than ever, the living room full to capacity and buzzing with interesting talk. Dee dried her hands on a kitchen towel and considered the moment. As a teenager growing up—alone, for the most part—she'd never imagined that this little farmhouse could be a gathering place for people of all sorts to come together in creativity, in ideas—and yes, in friendship.

Dee pulled up a kitchen chair and called for everyone's attention. Frances said, "So, what is it we're supposed to be doing?"

When Dee explained that writers who wished would be reading from their own work tonight, Frances said, "Okay. I'll go first!"

"Take it away, Frances," said Dee, and none of the others who had volunteered in advance seemed to mind. She was proud of the easy give-and-take they'd developed, for the most part. She knew they all wanted to encourage Frances, the quintessential late bloomer.

Frances sat up straighter on the edge of the sofa, adjusted her glasses, and held up her paper-clipped batches of pages. She cleared her throat.

Katy would never forget the day she heard that June had gone missing. It was a miserably hot August, and she and her brother, Sonny, had been hired by Missus Ferguson to chop cotton for thirty-five cents an hour. They had been excited by the opportunity. In one hour, they'd have enough money to go to the picture show and get a Coke and candy bar. Chopping cotton. That's what they called it—even though it was the weeds they were hoeing. They were hurting and thirsty and hungry and miserable when the sheriff had pulled right up to the field and said, "Can you Gabbert kids tell

me where your Pa is? I need to talk to him about his sister, June." Sonny
told him he was plowing on the other end of the Ferguson place.

*Katy jumped in and said, "Take us in your car, and we'll show you right
where he is. You got anything cold in there to drink?"*

*"Katy!" her brother yelled at her. "Don't pay her no mind. She talks too
much."*

*The sheriff laughed and said, "Climb in," and I had just stopped at Hal's
and gotten a cold Coca-Cola. "Y'all can have the rest of it if you aren't afraid
of my cooties."*

*"No, thank you," Sonny said, but Katy was already in the back seat and
was halfway through the Coke, when her brother jumped in after her, and
grabbed the soda bottle out of her hand.*

*Katy thought she was going to be sick. Not from the heat or Coke
cooties, but for her Aunt June. She never called her Aunt June. June was
only twenty, and Katy adored her. June was fun and taught Katy how to
jitterbug. She wore make-up and smoked cigarettes and drove a little red
Corvair—until she married that preacher, Raymond Franks.*

*For the past week June had been missing. Katy had heard her Ma and Pa
talking about it in low tones at night after they'd gone to bed.*

*She'd found one comment from her Ma especially chilling. "He stood up
there in the pulpit bawling that he had had nothing to do with it. No good's
gonna come out of this, I can just tell."*

Frances laid her pages back in her lap, shrugged, and said, "It's
a work in progress."

The other Write Stuff members applauded.

"Any feedback for Frances?" Dee asked.

Before anyone could answer, a loud clap of thunder shook the
house. A bolt of lightning flashed, the lights flickered, and the house
went dark.

"Woooo," said JoAnn. "Powerful stuff!"

Dee stood and felt her way around the chairs.

"There should be candles and coal oil lamps in the hall closet, Dee
Anna," Mama said, "unless you've moved them." Before Dee could

reach the closet, though, Summer, Raul, and Teresa pulled out their cell phones and tapped their screens to turn them into flashlights.

By the instant cell-phone light Dee quickly located the emergency supplies and lit a pair of large tapers that had been wedged into vegetable cans with floral foam.

"Candlelight will be perfect for a reading from the romance writer," Margaret said. "If everyone's open to continuing?"

Heads nodded in affirmation as the drumming of the rain grew louder over their heads. No one was eager to head back out in the storm yet.

"Go for it," Dee said, using a long match to light one of the oil lamps.

Margaret began.

"Late bloomer," Susan typed into the Tell Us About You section of the online dating service. Who was she kidding? Late bloomer sounded like an autumn flower, but in the world of romance Susan Timmons felt like a weed—a fraud, even.

As a florist and wedding planner by trade, she felt the victim of some huge practical joke in life, as she faced the day after her thirtieth birthday. She hadn't had a date since. Well, let's just say, since her twenties.

Susan hit the escape button on perfectmatch.com. She needed an adventure, and she returned to her romance novel from last night, and curled up under the blanket on the couch. Frank the cat hopped up and found his favorite snuggling spot between her ankles.

Tonight's read was The Yellow Rose, *a grocery-store paperback whose cover showed a cowboy and ingénue locked in an embrace. But Susan couldn't focus on the story. Tomorrow was Valentine's Day, and she'd be slammed with deliveries. In Buffalo, New York, where they were expecting three feet of snow.*

Why? she thought. What was she doing with her life? There had to be a better way. She put down the book and walked over to her computer and typed in Jobs at Dude Ranches. And then Best Careers to Meet Men. Followed by Opportunities in the Peace Corps.

The group applauded and Margaret took a bow.

Summer raised her hand with a question. "So, Margaret, this is a brand-new story, right? It doesn't fit into the novel you're working on?"

"Well, it might—Susan is a minor character in the book, but she sort of took on a life of her own. I let her star in this episode, which I think could be its own short story."

Teresa said, laughing, "Well, that first page makes me want to learn more about who she's going to meet."

"Maybe it will be a—*vampire!*," said Raul dramatically, sending Teresa into giggles.

"Okay," Dee said. "Who wants to go next?"

J. D. read his poem as rain poured outside the windows. Everyone had to agree the weather lent a dramatic edge to his account of a drover caught out on the range in a storm. Several alternatives for images and rhymes were suggested, but everyone thought J. D. had a winner, that he should try to perform at the next cowboy poetry gathering.

When there was no other volunteer, Cynthia said to Dee, "I think that means the rest of us chickens would like you to read. Just pick one."

"Okay," Dee said. "Here we go."

This fall I turn twenty-one. I was born into a family of immigrants, and everyone I love misses a place I do not know, may never know because the place of their past is gone. The town is still there, but the era, their culture, their history is nothing but memories.

I was born into a city where my family has no history, and every day people tell us that we do not belong here. I came into the world in the same hospital as the mayor and attended the same schools as the city council, but because my parents did not know how to attain a piece of paper, I am supposed to be denied all rights, all dignity. In the words of my native tongue. No mas. When I turn 21, I will finally stop feeling like an outsider. I can legally help my father become a citizen. I feel like I will be able to lift this veil of shame from family with two words.

"Happy Birthday."

Mama reached over and patted Teresa's shoulder.

"Well, there were a couple more writers who had volunteered for tonight," said Dee, "so maybe it'll be best to hold those for our next meeting, in November. What's your pleasure?"

"Mine can wait," said Raul. JoAnn likewise agreed she could be flexible. But none of the writers made an explicit move to leave, and Wendell spoke up. "There's one story that ought to be heard, because it's from someone who's a veteran of our group, in a manner of speaking, but has submitted some of her writing for the first time ever. I think we need to hear from Mary Alice Bennett."

"Y'all have been kind enough to get me started on computers and the Internet," Mama said, "so I want to show you some of what I've been doing with it." Margaret shone a flashlight over Mama's shoulder onto her printout. Dee glanced around and decided the darkness was probably useful, helping relieve any awkwardness Mama might have felt at reading her first story in what had up until recently been her own house.

Rain started east of Abilene and it was coming down heavy by now. She had left early that morning but it was already getting late in the day. She was glad the windshield wipers on her old green Packard still worked just fine. She had only been on this road once, and that was coming out here with George in 1928. That time he drove, right after they were married. He brought them to their new home in Caprock County, far away from her parents and sisters in the green forested part of Texas.

She kept her eyes on the two-lane highway ahead of her and tried to remember what this part of the state looked like from the train. The steep hill at Ranger was hard even for the locomotives. There were other stretches ahead like the wild Palo Pinto country and the narrow trestle bridges across the Brazos River that scared her. She always wondered what would happen if the train broke down on one of those bridges, or if the brakes failed while the engine was coming down the mountain.

She was sure that steep drop-off was somewhere ahead, it was coming up soon. The rain was not letting up. She could hardly make out the headlamps

of the oncoming cars. There ahead she spotted the big lighted sign of a ser-
vice station. It said Ranger Hill in giant letters. She wondered if she ought
to pull in and rest. She didn't need gas because she had stopped in Abilene,
but she thought maybe she ought to have the brakes checked. She could get
a cup of coffee, or even check into one of those little tourist cabins for the
night. No respectable woman did that alone. She was so tired.

But if she stopped at all she might decide to turn around and go back.
She might lose her resolve. She might drive right back to their failed farm
and their wrecked marriage. She might return to George and never get up
the nerve to leave him again. It was better to keep on the direction she was
going, ask her sisters for help, and then come back to get the child.

She drove on past the brightly lit station and the diner and the cozy
little cabins. She would not stop and spend a dime on a cup of coffee or a
penny on a postcard.

She turned the big curve and started down the hill. Suddenly a truck
coming the other way hit a puddle and doused the Packard. She tried to keep
the car in the lane, looking to her right to avoid the guardrail. She saw the
center yellow line to her left and was relieved. When she saw the treacher-
ous hill ahead she tapped the brakes like her papa had told her, to slow down,
and she put in the clutch and downshifted. But the car continued to pick up
speed. She tried the brakes again. There was no response. She could see that
the curve would straighten out in a few hundred feet, and if she could reach
the straight part of the road she would be okay. But she was going too fast.
The curve was too tight. Heading directly toward the side of the cliff on the
other side, she swerved to avoid a car in the eastbound lane. The Packard
left the road and plunged toward the valley hundreds of feet below. Her last
thoughts were not about George, but about the child. Her two-year-old baby
girl she would never see again. Thank God, she thought, she had left little
Mary Alice sleeping back home safe in her bed.

Margaret let the flashlight slip out of her hand, and it crashed to
the floor. Dee, startled, let out a gasp. Then, in the candlelight all was
silent except for the sound of someone struggling to keep from crying.

The lights came back up, the furnace kicked in, and the refrigerator began to hum again.

Wendell slipped his hand away from where he had patted Mama's knee. Frances, wiping tears from her face, said, "My goodness. Now, was that fact or was it fiction?"

Mama, seeing that all eyes were on her, replied, "Well, I don't think anybody could ever know for sure what the woman was thinking. But there's no disputing the details in my mother's death certificate from March 20, 1936."

*   *   *

Though no one returned her calls the next day, Dee made damn sure the airplane mode didn't accidentally get switched on. Elsa Jensen, however, emailed with the big news that the verdict was back on the Templeton letter, which appeared by handwriting comparison and contemporary paper swatches to be authentic.

Dee immediately dug out Boothe's card from her Abilene conference folder and composed a note.

*   *   *

"Cheer up, cowboy," Dee said to Max as hundreds of dejected fans trudged to their cars and trucks, dodging puddles left by a week of rain. She slipped her arm through his. "There's always next year."

"I know," he said. "At least I'm not like those hard cases who live or die by whether the team makes the playoffs. We just thought this might be the year again, is all." Claxton's unexpected loss to Sweetwater in their Homecoming game had dashed postseason hopes. Not since the storied season that had been celebrated at halftime tonight had Claxton come this close to another run at the championship. And now, they would have to wait again.

"I'm glad the pressure's off," she said. "Now I might get to spend some time with you away from the fifty-yard line."

"And I am equally glad election season's nearly over," Max countered. "I might get to spend some time with you away from all this campaign intrigue."

All around them fans rumbled and grumbled about a couple of bad calls in the second half, combined with an unlucky Cougars fumble in the clutch. This bunch were not gracious losers.

Dee had to admit that she felt a strange sense of letdown herself. No amount of cajoling and no clever interviewer's tricks had brought her any closer to understanding what had happened to Ricky Jones. Of the original 1977–78 championship team, only thirteen players had bothered to return for the reunion. Despite having Rowdy McCorrigan as their standard bearer during the halftime show, they looked like a motley and mostly out-of-shape bunch. And despite the success of the newspaper's promotion, Dee felt she'd come up well short of a first down.

"Well, it's Halloween night," Max said. "What do you say we wave a magic wand and pretend there was never any football game, and just go enjoy the party?"

"I like it!" said Dee. "Let's get out of here and go change. And I will cast my Have-A-Good-Time spell!"

At Max's loft above his studio, they each changed into the costumes Dee had gathered for them that week from Claxton's thrift stores. In his trench coat and fedora complete with press pass tucked in the hatband, and carrying a vintage bulb-type camera, Max looked the part of news photographer straight out of the *noir* era. As she finished pinning her hair up, grabbing her satchel, and adding the Victorian houndstooth cap and her own press pass to a stylishly steampunk ensemble, Dee asked him, fretting, "Do you think anyone will get it? Will anyone recognize my costume?"

"Not a chance, babe," he said, laughing. "You'll be completely incognito."

*   *   *

Claxton's deserted downtown streets seemed especially ominous on All Hallows' Eve as Dee and Max walked the three blocks to the hulking Kress department store building, a two-story relic of the 1920s that had stood vacant for a decade. Streetlights cast eerie shadows on the damp, red-brick streets. Silhouetted figures converged on the tile-paved vestibule, ghost shoppers from days gone by. A banner had been hung over the entrance proclaiming "Welcome to Cl AXE ton." Dee expected to spot Jack the Ripper over her shoulder at any moment.

But inside, she entered an even more surreal scene. Cleopatra in a headdress and long golden gown welcomed them at the door, along with her co-host in black tailored shirt, aviator Ray-Bans, and penciled-on moustache. "Marc Anthony, get it?" he said, pointing them toward the bar. The store's former main sales floor, with its terrazzo staircase leading up to what Dee recalled as clothing, music, and toy departments, had been transformed into dance floor with a DJ. Toward the back, where tools and hardware had once been, were the refreshments and bar.

Max led Dee in that direction, past Dracula and Dolly Parton dancing to a George Strait tune while Batman and a sexy nurse chatted animatedly over the music with Cinderella and the Great Pumpkin. A guy wearing a cardboard table with dentures soaking in a glass of water, a book, and a lamp secured to his shoulders circulated, beer in hand. Max gave the reveler an odd look, to which he extended his hand and replied, "One Night Stand, Class of '86. How about you?"

Princess Leia swept by them, bearing a tray of sandwiches. A couple of Wookiees followed with more.

"Hi, Summer," Dee said over the music. "Great getup."

"Thanks. Gotta get these to the food table. I heard supplies were running low."

There did not seem to be any shortage of alcohol, however, as fans arriving from the game slipped in brown bags and the back door opened for the arrival of another keg. Max fetched Dee a vodka tonic and himself a Coke. "Any sign of your football players?" he asked her.

"Oh, I wasn't really counting on that. But who can tell anyhow?"

"You make a good point."

"So, what about any of your old classmates?" he shouted over the music.

"Who would know, in this craziness?" she replied. "I thought I might run into some of the yearbook staff, but I haven't seen a soul I recognize from my class yet. I'm pretty sure Cynthia is here somewhere, too—she graduated from Claxton a couple years after me. Penny said she might come, but I haven't seen her—and Buddy was, you know, tied up with Darrell's game." All of a sudden she felt alone and friendless, feeling that *all* her classmates were old, and realizing with chagrin that her own date hadn't yet asked her to dance.

The DJ started up a Bob Wills tune as J. D. and Pauline took the floor in cowboy-and-cowgirl finery, leading the crowd in an impressive Western swing dance. Others of the older generations joined in, including Dolly Parton—whom Dee at last recognized as her cousin Ruby Lee—and her husband, Barge, a Claxton graduate of 1969.

At the sight of the dancers, Dee leaned against Max and let a feeling of warmth wash over her. She was remembering how much she'd enjoyed the waltz with him at Madison's wedding, and putting her blue self-pity behind her, when a man in dark wig and white polyester suit suddenly appeared at her side.

"May I have this dance?" he said to her, and then, to Max, "If you don't mind, I'm cutting in with Nellie Bly here." The stranger swept her onto the floor as the music changed to a funky Bee Gees number.

"Jesus!" Dee said in a panic.

"Nope, John Travolta." She finally recognized his voice.

"Wait—Hank—I'm a terrible dancer!" She didn't know which caught her by greater surprise, his skill in twirling her around the floor or his correct identification of her character.

"Stick with me, baby, and we'll boogie all night long!"

"Have you been drinking?"

"Hasn't everyone?"

The room moved around her in a blur. Thing One and Thing Two shook their booties. She thought she caught a glimpse of Sarah Palin and Barack Obama—in addition to Max's bemused grin.

The song came to an end and Dee gratefully let Hank escort her back to Max's company. "Catch you later, Dee," said Hank. "Gotta make sure none of my Science Club students are trying to sneak back in."

"Well," said Max. "I imagine I owe the lady journalist a dance now. But your *Saturday Night Fever* friend's a hard act to follow!" He led her by the waist to a more restrained number, Etta James's sultry "At Last."

"Should we consider this our song, do you think?" Dee asked him, the earthy vocals and the drink going to her head. "'Cause I'm awfully glad *you* came along."

"My love," Max said into her ear. "Suits me."

The air around her grew close and hot, and she wondered if she had heard right. Love? A word she thought had disappeared from her life. She savored the moment, letting him kiss her, their costume hats providing a shield, as they swayed to the music.

Their private universe was rudely interrupted this time by a red-headed devil in a slinky red bustier, short skirt, heels, and fishnet hose. Charley Hensley smoothly lured Dee's guy away, leaving her standing blankly on the sidelines.

Determined not to give Charley the opportunity to gloat, Dee marched off to pour herself another drink. She gulped it down and stomped upstairs, away from the loud dance floor.

In a corner of what had once been the books department, the drama club had set up a fortune-telling booth as a fund-raiser. There she spotted Teresa Rivera and Raul Amey waiting their turn, right behind Princess Leia. "Come on, Dee, don't you want your palm read?" Raul teased her.

"I'm not sure I want to know what's in the crystal ball!" she said.

"Oh, come on," Summer agreed. "It'll be fun. Here, you go in front of us."

Before she knew it Dee was seated in front of the tall, mysterious Madame FiFi VuDu, outfitted in kabuki makeup with a purple velvet turban, peacock shawl, and full-length caftan in a kaleidoscope of colors.

"Welcome, my child. You must cross Madame's palm with silver if you care to learn your future," said the fortune-teller. Dee looked back at her friends, who were urging her on. She dug into the bottom of her costume carpetbag and came up with a five-dollar bill.

"Paper will do just as well," said FiFi VuDu, tucking the money into a pocket of the caftan. "Now let us see." She took Dee's hand in her own gloved one and said in a throaty voice, "Your life line is long, that is good. And I can see that you work with your hands, as well as your head, no?"

Dee, feeling quite foolish, nodded. Teresa and Raul edged closer. Summer leaned over them.

Madame FiFi continued. "You are dogged in your pursuit of truth. Let's see . . . you must be . . . a news reporter!"

Dee glared into Madame FiFi's eyes, trying to detect which of her insiders was pulling the stunt. She recognized no one. "Close enough," she replied.

"You are pursuing three men. Fugitives from justice. And you are pursued by another. Stay on the path and you will find what you seek."

Dee drew away her hand as if she had touched a live wire. She jumped up and ran to the rail of the mezzanine, fanned herself and drew in a gulp of fresh air. Teresa came to her side. "You okay, Dee? It was all in fun!"

"I know, Teresa," she said, regaining control of her senses. "This costume . . . is just too tight. I'll be okay."

Downstairs the volume was turned town and the emcee from the class of '78 stepped to the mic amid whoops and applause. Dee remained at the rail to watch.

"We hope you're all having a great time at the Claxton High School All-Class Reunion!" he said, and roars and applause went up from every corner. "We have lots of special guests here, including the chaperons we all knew and loved, Mr. Sandifer and his wife—" the emcee paused for groans, laughter, and clapping— "and now, our own Claxton Cougars of the nineteen-seventy-eight state championship team!" The DJ turned up the volume as thirteen football players burst into the spotlight in Cougars jerseys, making their grand entrance to Queen's "We Are the Champions." Rowdy

McCorrigan raised his helmet and motioned for his wife to join him. Gretchen didn't look terribly pleased to be the center of attention in a cheerleader outfit, Dee thought.

Rowdy took the mic, thanked his classmates, and said to the crowd, "You know, it's times like this that make us proud to be Texans." She tuned his speech out, scanning the sea of costumes from her vantage point.

Princess Leia nudged her and indicated the direction of the bar. There Dee picked out Charley Hensley in her slinky devil's costume, handing the bartender her empty cup for a refill. Max was not immediately in evidence.

"Talk about typecasting." Dee heard a voice behind her and turned to find Margaret Strickland in her witch's garb, scanning the crowd below.

"Having a good time?" Dee asked her.

"Just fine, thanks, although I'm having a hard time keeping my hubby in line, between the booze and the bimbos!" she said. "Listen, I was looking for you," she added as quietly as she could over the party noise. "I just had a call from an old news buddy in Austin. I think he was fishing for some local details. But apparently the *American-Statesman* is onto something big about McCorrigan that's about to blow."

"Something I should know about?"

"I think so. Let's go over here and I'll tell you the details."

"Wait," Dee said, staring down at the bar. "I'll have to catch you later."

"But—"

Nellie Bly left Professor McGonagall gathering her robes and trying to keep up as she dashed around to the stairwell and down the steps. For there, at the bar, was a middle-aged guy in a Tommy Bahama shirt, quaffing a margarita, a fake parrot perched on his shoulder and a paper cutout of a shaker of salt duct-taped to his back.

* * *

"Yeah, that quarterback slot oughta have been mine," Blaise Parrish was telling Charley Hensley. "Your guy there—you work for him, right? You're his, like girl Friday or something?"

"Campaign manager," she said icily.

"Yeah, your boss there. His folks were just white trash. But everybody thought he was the big hero. Yep. Ronald "Rowdy" McCorrigan could do no wrong. Started at quarterback every game. With that cocky receiver Ricky Jones. Every Friday night, the Rowdy and Ricky show."

Dee hung back from making her presence known and slipped into the shadows to eavesdrop. Margaret fell in behind her.

Parrish took another drink of his margarita. "But you know what chapped my butt most of all? It wasn't keeping the bench warm every Friday night, only getting put in late in the fourth quarter if there was a double-digit lead."

Charley stared at him, finished off her own drink, and said, "You think I give a shit?"

Parrish continued, undeterred. "What really got to me was when his sidekick Jones started going out with my girl. Can you just believe it? She's over there right now in the Goldilocks costume. Debbie Taylor. Or that was her name back them."

Charley followed Parrish's gaze. Dee saw the woman, too.

"After Rowdy and Ricky and I came back from Mexico with that load of pot, I knew I had the way to nail him." Parrish started to cry. "It was a cheap shot. I ruined a boy's life just because I was jealous."

At this, Charley looked concerned. Dee could see why. There could be real consequences for McCorrigan—if anything unsavory were to surface on the eve of the election. "Blaise," she said sweetly, "would you like for me to get Rowdy over here, so you can tell him all this yourself? He's right over there. Let me get him for you."

Parrish made himself scarce, heading for the back door, before Hensley could take a full step toward her boss.

Dee turned to follow Parrish. "Margaret," she said, "I lost Max in the crowd. Do you think you could track him down and come find me?"

*   *   *

Out back of the Kress store, Parrish leaned on a Dumpster to rest, pulled a joint out of his pocket, and lit up.

Dee cleared her throat and said, "Is that a good idea?"

"Well, if it isn't the lady reporter herself. You called, I came." He coughed when he tried to laugh. "It's medicinal, you know."

"This is no joke, Blaise. What were you telling Charley Hensley about setting up Ricky Jones? You let him take the rap for a crime?"

"It's no joke that I'm dying of cancer either. Go ahead, ask me anything you want. I'm a dead man anyway."

"You're drunk, Blaise."

"Yep. Plan to stay that way."

The back door opened and Margaret came running, with Max right behind.

"Everything okay?" Max called out to Dee as he came over to check on her.

"Miss Lady Reporter and I were about to have a conversation—off the record," he said, then turned back to Dee. "Ricky didn't have anything to do with it except going along with us to Mexico. Never even took a toke, as far as I know. Rowdy was the one selling. Nickel-and-dime stuff, no real harm. Just enough to get him busted if someone knew to tip off the cops."

"Which you did?" said Dee.

"It looked like a good way to get Rowdy suspended so I could start. And make Debbie forget all about Ricky," Parrish said. "I never meant for him to go to prison." He took another long draw on the joint, then held his arm to his waist as he started coughing again. The coughs dissolved into jagged tears.

"I don't understand," said Dee. "I thought you said Ricky was innocent."

"Nobody knew my old man was going to get Mitch Mitchell involved."

"Mitch Mitchell?" asked Dee in alarm, catching the look in Max's eye too.

"Mitchell Senior, the big guy. He's dead now. But back in the day he was known as a fixer. Somebody in Texas had a problem, they called Mitch Mitchell, Senior. Especially if a certain university's most eligible blue-chip potential recruit was about to be busted on drug charges." Parrish coughed again, recovered, and continued. "Of the three of us, Ricky was the only one who would've been charged as a juvenile. When Mitchell realized that, he gave us all our marching orders. He didn't ask us, he told us."

"You and McCorrigan went free, then, while Ricky went to prison?" Dee said, coming closer to Parrish and trying to look him in the eye.

"Just for six months. And when he got out, he had his pick of any college he wanted, so long as he stayed scarce. Mitchell paid for it all."

"Let me guess," said Dee. "London School of Economics."

"How'd you know that?"

"I didn't," she said. "You just told me."

Parrish laughed. "Naw, I didn't know it for sure. It was just rumor that he got out of the country. None of us knew what happened to Ricky. We were afraid he'd been killed in prison or something. Do you know what it's been like to live with that, all these years?"

"And Ricky's family? What happened to them?"

"They moved away the next day. I heard something about his sister going in the army. That was the last word I knew. None of my black friends would say a word. Not even Levi the program guy. Eventually everyone I knew turned their backs on me."

"What about McCorrigan, are you protecting him?"

"That piece of shit? Hell, no, he didn't even speak to me tonight. He was too busy fighting with his wife. God only knows what she was saying to him."

Parrish slid down the side of the trash bin and buried his face in his hands. "You know what the real irony is? McCorrigan got to finish out the season anyway, I never saw another minute of game time, and I never went on another date with Debbie. It all ended right then and there."

Parrish slumped to the ground, blubbering about making things right before he died.

Dee shook his shoulder. "Come on, Blaise. We can't just leave you here in the alley." She turned to Max and Margaret. "What do we do, call the EMTs, or the police?"

Max picked up the burned-out roach Parrish had dropped. "With this?"

"Not the police," said Parrish, revived.

"Come with us to the newspaper," Dee said. "We'll get you some coffee. And there's someone there who can give us all some useful advice. Max, let's get my car, if you'll give me a hand. Margaret, we'll meet you there."

"That's an excellent idea, Dee," Margaret said, fumbling for her keys, "and you haven't even heard what I have to say yet."

22
Día de los Muertos

It is unnecessary to say that an engaged man shows no attention whatever to other women. It should be plain to every one, even though he need not behave like a moon-calf, that "one" is alone in his thoughts.

Often it so happens that engaged people are very little together, because he is away at work, or for other reasons. Rather than sit home alone, she may continue to go out in society, which is quite all right, but she must avoid being with any one man more than another and she should remain visibly within the general circle of her group. It always gives gossip a chance to see an engaged girl sitting out dances with any particular man, and slander is never far away if any evidence of ardor creeps into their regard, even if it be merely "manner," and actually mean nothing at all.

—"Etiquette of Engaged People"

"GOOD EVENING, LADIES," Shannon said, looking up from a computer in the four-cubicle newsroom. Phil and two student assistants were also there, taking scores and game calls from high school coaches. The Lubbock television station sportscast ran on one wall TV, the one from Abilene on the other, both with volume down.

Max stayed behind in the parking lot to make sure Parrish didn't get up and leave.

"Why don't y'all come on in my office?" Shannon said. "Nice duds, by the way."

"Crap," Margaret said, removing her hat and cape. "I forgot I still had this on."

Dee set the houndstooth cap aside.

Shannon shut the door behind them.

Margaret spoke first. "Y'all need to let me talk now," she said. "This is breaking as we speak. Gretchen McCorrigan has gone to the Austin newspaper with the claim that Charley Hensley is having an affair with her husband."

"I for one am not surprised," said Shannon. "Though that's not exactly the affair I'd heard about."

"And there's—" said Dee, but Margaret waved her off.

"Someone anonymously tipped Mrs. McCorrigan off, and told her to check the phone and hotel records from her husband's birthday, October 22. She went to Verizon with his social security card and driver's license as his spouse, and they ported all of the texts, calls, and pictures from a phone she didn't even know he had to a new one she bought."

"Damn, that's good," said Shannon.

"And it wasn't pretty. It's not just the indiscretion, apparently, but the fact that McCorrigan used campaign money for the, um, trysts."

Shannon turned to Dee. "Did you have any indication of this when you were on the last trip with them?"

"Nothing like that, no—but when I witnessed Charley's walk of shame at the hotel I started to wonder who she was seeing. I guess I should have brought it to you."

"Looks that way," the editor said. "But let's deal with the situation as it stands now. Has the *Statesman* filed a FOIA paper to get what's on the phone?" she asked Margaret.

"I don't know," said Margaret.

"But there's—" said Dee again, anxiously looking toward the front door.

"Y'all hold on," Shannon said, dialing her desk phone. "Let's get our attorney on speaker."

Dee whispered to Margaret, while Shannon adjusted the volume on the speaker phone. "What's a foyapaper?"

"Freedom of Information Act request," Margaret answered, as much on the sly as she could manage. Dee nodded her thanks.

A man's groggy voice answered, "Hullo?"

"Sorry to wake you, Stan," Shannon said, "but we need to file a FOIA."

"Tonight?" he said.

"Yesterday," Shannon said.

"Okay, hit it," said the voice on the speaker phone.

"Stan, you remember Margaret Strickland. I also have Dee Bennett, our political reporter, on the line. Margaret, tell it again," Shannon said.

She did.

"What's our next move, Stan?" Shannon said.

"Pray McCorrigan bought the extra phone with campaign money too, so it's public record," the lawyer said.

"There's only one way to find out," the editor said.

"I'll draw up the paperwork," the attorney said.

"Wait," Dee said. "About that other matter you and I were working on, Shannon, there have been new developments tonight." Dee indicated to Shannon that she should mute the speaker phone for a second.

"And one of the new developments is outside in the car." She raced through her account of Blaise Parrish's off-the-record confession.

"Dear God," said Shannon. "Get him in here." Margaret went for Max. Shannon pressed the speaker phone button again. "Stan, I'll need a FOIA for Claxton district court records for the month of November 1977, too."

"That might take a little longer," he said.

"I take it juvenile is sealed?"

"That might take a miracle."

"What about Mitch Mitchell, Junior?" Shannon suggested. "His late father was supposed to be a wheeler-dealer who might have dealt on the shady side, but Junior's supposed to be legit all the way. Maybe he'd cooperate and give access to his father's papers if he knew anything?"

Dee added, "Ransom Jones's ministry will be damaged if any of this comes from any source besides him. I could call him again. He might talk."

"Especially if you lay out all of the facts correctly," Stan said. "I'm going to call the Claxton D.A. and the district judge at home and tell them to expect these FOIAs."

"I don't want Austin scooping this Gretchen McCorrigan story out from under us, especially in our own hometown," Shannon said.

The attorney replied, "I'll leave the journalism to you guys. But all of this could be made a little easier if someone could get hold of Mrs. McCorrigan. As for me, I have to wake several people at midnight on Halloween and make their lives miserable. I'll report back in an hour."

The phone went dead.

"You—" Shannon said to Dee, but before she could get the assignment out, Dee said, "I think I can reach Gretchen McCorrigan." She turned and nearly ran into a bleary-eyed and bumbling Blaise Parrish, escorted by Max in his costume and Margaret, who all paused at the editor's half-open door.

"Who are you?" Shannon asked Max sharply.

"I'm her ride," he said, pointing to Dee.

"And you—you're Blaise Parrish, Claxton High School Class of 1978?" Shannon asked him.

Parrish nodded.

"Have a seat right out there if you like, Mr. Parrish. I understand you have a story to tell us?"

He rubbed his head and said, "You can't use my name. I don't care what happens after I'm dead and gone. But right now, I've had enough shit to deal with. And—" he suddenly looked green around the gills— "I think I need to use your bathroom."

Max got him out just in time.

"I think there's bottled water in the fridge," said Margaret. "I'll go get it."

To Dee, Shannon said, "Well, what are you waiting for?"

* * *

Dee scrolled to the phone number she'd saved weeks ago on the bus trip. Please let it be a mobile, she thought. She didn't fully know what happened to texts that went to wrong numbers. She tried to think of a delicate way to broach the subject in case it fell into the wrong hands.

Gretchen, I met you on the campaign bus. Thank you for telling people the truth. I know it's hard when you have children. CH has tried to sabotage my relationship too.

Within two minutes, a reply came back. *Who is this?*

Dee thought carefully and responded. *Dee Bennett. My boyfriend has been a photographer for the campaign from time to time.*

This time the response was instant. *Max Miller?*

Yes.

She told us Max was her boyfriend.

The words stung, but Dee felt she understood what was going on now. She wrote back, *I think that would be news to Max.*

Thank you. You have confirmed for me that they were lying.

Call me at this number? Dee texted.

When the phone rang, Dee answered in her most solicitous tone. "I'm very sorry about the situation, Mrs. McCorrigan. But if you want people to know what's been happening, the *Claxton Courier* would like to run the story you offered the *American-Statesman*. And understand we'll check it just as carefully as they would."

"What's your e-mail address? I'll send you everything I sent them."

"I think we've got the Gretchen McCorrigan story," Dee called out to Shannon from her cubicle. She forwarded each of Gretchen's messages as they arrived.

"I'm rolling Becca out of bed," Shannon shouted back. "We'll want her to get this on the web ASAP."

Now Dee just needed to get corroboration of Parrish's story. "Margaret?" she called blindly around the corner, where her part-time colleague was sitting in the borrowed sales rep's cubicle, keeping tabs on Austin.

"Yep?"

"Doesn't the newspaper keep an archive of old issues, you know, stories that go back farther than you can search online?"

"You mean in the morgue?"

"Yes, the morgue. Even if the court records Parrish alluded to were sealed, wouldn't there have been an arrest record?"

"The paper wouldn't have run the name of a minor, either," Margaret replied.

"But it seems like I remember reading news briefs that just listed the crimes."

"The police blotter, sure." Margaret peeked around the edge of the cubicle wall and said, "The police blotter! That's something, at least. So when would this have been?"

Dee jotted down the narrowed range of dates and handed it to her.

"Walk with me."

The morgue bore no resemblance to the coroner's cold room on the TV shows that the word always conjured up for Dee. Instead, it was a back hallway lined with shelves the depth of a newspaper broadsheet, with giant bound volumes labeled by month and year. Margaret started with November 1977, based on Dee's estimate of the last Cougars game in which Ricky Jones had played. She quickly landed on the item they sought, confirming that officers had stopped a juvenile on suspicion of possession of a controlled substance. "It wasn't a frequent occurrence in Claxton back then, I'll tell you," she said. "So you're probably onto something. Still, it's only circumstantial evidence, so you'll need more than that."

"Like the testimony of an eyewitness?" a booming voice called out from behind them.

Dee shrieked, and Margaret cried out, "Good Lord, where did you come from?"

Behind them in the corridor, Madame FiFi VuDu pulled off her wig. "I am not the Lord, madam, but I do serve Him." The fortune teller removed the caftan, revealing a man's business suit. "Ransom Jones, formerly known as Ricky. How can I be of help?"

* * *

"It wasn't difficult to persuade the volunteer at the fund-raising booth that I was there to spell her," said Ransom Jones. "You knew I wouldn't risk McCorrigan and Parrish undoing all the years I have put into this work. There was no telling what Parrish might say. I had to find a way to keep an eye on them," he added as he continued to wipe the makeup off his face with a tissue. "It wasn't hard to follow you here, either."

"You overheard everything he said in the alley?" asked Dee.

"For someone who lied thirty-one years ago to protect his own interests," Jones said, "he seems to have done a remarkable job with the truth last night."

"Parrish told us his side of the story off the record," said Shannon. "Does he know you're here?" she asked.

"I don't think so."

"I don't think he knows anything right now," said Margaret. "He's passed out cold on the couch in the lobby. Max is keeping an eye on him."

"And McCorrigan?" Shannon asked. "Did he know you were coming? Have you talked with him?"

"I didn't tip my hand," said Jones. "But I will tell you my side of the story, and you may feel free to record it, and check what the others say against it."

"Why now?"

"When Dee Bennett here was successful in tracking me down," Jones explained, "I knew others would, too." He glanced in Dee's direction. "No aspersions against your research skills, of course. In fact, in all those years no one has located me—or no one has tried to."

Shannon said, "Becca? Call Rudy and Juan and get them up here to start the press. I want them on standby to print a four-page bull-dog extra. Then we'll come out with the rest of the weekend edition at its regular time on Saturday afternoon. Who do we know that can help throw papers?"

Margaret switched on the digital recorder while Ransom Jones talked.

"I did not know, when I made the varsity football team as a sophomore, what that fateful event would cost me," he began. "It was a thrill to hang out with teammates a year or two older. By the summer that Rowdy McCorrigan and Blaise Parrish were rising seniors, I was still a rising junior, but they considered me one of their bunch, and for a kid without a car in a white-bread Texas town, that was a pretty big deal. I was also a year younger in age than most of my classmates, because of my January birthday and my early start in school.

"Rowdy was the one who got the idea to go to Mexico that summer of 1977. He had that muscle car, that gold Camaro. But Blaise got the inspiration to buy marijuana. His father was a dentist; he knew a little about drugs, and he had money. And the stuff wasn't difficult to buy. It wasn't even difficult to bring back over the border.

"Rowdy couldn't keep his mouth shut about the stash. He kept it in his car. He dealt small amounts to the team; he gave it away if he wanted a favor. Everyone was loyal; no one broke the confidence. I was one of the few who didn't partake." He paused in his story for the anticipated skepticism. "Seriously. I didn't inhale, didn't light up, didn't touch the stuff. My mama had big plans for me. My big sister would have read me the riot act if I had even mentioned drugs.

"One day in November, just after we'd clinched the district in football and knew we were going to the playoffs, Rowdy and I were leaving Blaise's house about nine in the morning. The police pulled Rowdy's car over. They searched it. Sure, I know now they shouldn't have been able to harass us or search him without a warrant. But can you imagine how terrified we were, the star quarterback and the sixteen-year-old black kid, neither of whose parents had any pull in the community? We cooperated. You bet we did.

"But Blaise's stunt backfired. Yes, I eventually figured out he'd set us up. The police saw whose house we had left. And everybody knew we were inseparable anyhow. They were bound to talk to his parents. Dr. Parrish had the kind of connections that could make an episode like that go away. Next thing you know, Mitch Mitchell, Senior, arrives from Midland, and he makes all the arrangements. I never saw Rowdy or Blaise that day, or ever again; Mitchell spoke to us separately. Rowdy went completely free, I heard. As if nothing had ever happened. Blaise walked, too, in exchange for his testimony. And I, the least able to defend myself and the only one under age seventeen, was escorted off to jail, tried as a juvenile, sent to prison, released, and bribed to keep quiet.

"There are so many things you don't know in that situation. That juvenile court records are sealed once you've reached majority—as long as the convicted felon requests so in writing. I had a close call over that. But juvenile records can also be expunged, and you can be sure not a trace will be found today.

"I like to believe that my brief time in prison only made me stronger. I emerged with a deeper faith and a mission to help others avoid the same trap I had fallen into. God had ransomed me, and by His grace I knew I could still live a full and useful life. Job's friends accused him of doing evil; but God's way will be revealed in time."

He reached the end of his statement and said, "If the past is going to come to light, I want it to be from my lips, and not from those of short-sighted Job's comforters."

Not a sound was heard in the newsroom for long seconds until Margaret reached over and clicked the recorder off.

"Thank you for coming forward, Mr. Jones," said Shannon. "Now, I believe we have a story to write and a short time to do it in."

Margaret hooked up her headphones and transcribed the recording, even while Dee began writing, with Shannon standing over her shoulder and reminding her to make liberal use of the phrase *Jones alleges*. They used Margaret's transcript to verify quotations, and read them back to Jones for accuracy. A copy of the story went to Stan the attorney via e-mail.

Becca had the website ready at 3:45 a.m. with both stories lined up side by side at the top. For art she'd had to use publicity shots of Rowdy and Gretchen McCorrigan, and the press photo of Ransom

Jones from his TVN webpage. Rudy made up the page for print and Juan started their clunker of a web press.

Half an hour later, Hank Hardeberger and the Science Club showed up at the newspaper office. Armed with bags of rubber bands, they rolled newspapers as copies came off the press. Dee and Max, along with JoAnn, Margaret, Summer, and Teresa, loaded up the bundles in several cars and delivered them to subscribers.

At six that morning, when the major daily serving the state's capital city hit Austin doorsteps with the scandal concerning one particular candidate for railroad commissioner, readers of an afternoon six-day newspaper three hundred miles away with a circulation of 4,983 already had the scoop about their golden boy.

*   *   *

Dee and Max collapsed on either end of the big leather couch at the home place an hour before dawn, still in parts of their costumes. In her Subaru, filled with rolled-up newspapers, they'd taken the rural routes on the east side of the county, slipping their last paper into Buck Turlock's tube around five a.m.

"Come on in and get a few hours' sleep," Dee said to Max. "We'll figure out the rest of it later." Though Dee was exhausted, she only dozed. There was an adrenaline, an electricity coursing through her veins, a feeling that she had been a part of a team committed to virtue for its own sake. She'd never experienced that before.

Academia, she mused, was hardly a team sport. Every professor was his or her own one-trick pony. She tried to bury those useless thoughts in the throw pillow so she could sleep. She wondered if Max had felt the same rush she had. But he slept the sleep of the dead.

That was okay. They didn't have to be carbon copies of each other. They didn't have to be joined at the hip. But he had supported her in every way this night, and for that she was truly grateful.

Charley Hensley had tried to use Max as a decoy to cover her own extracurricular activity. Or McCorrigan's; she still didn't have a sense of who had instigated the affair. But Dee shuddered at the thought of someone as manipulative and powerful as McCorrigan's campaign manager interfering in their lives. McCorrigan, she thought, surely wouldn't win now.

*   *   *

Morning light brightened the room, emphasizing the splitting headache that had taken root between Dee's temples. She crawled off the couch, went to the bathroom, and took some aspirin.

She pulled off her costume, pulled on a pair of stretch pants and sweatshirt, washed her face, and brushed her teeth. She was preparing to make coffee when she heard a pounding on the front door. It was certainly high time to get a doorbell. It might sound a lot less jarring.

She padded down the hallway in her loafers and peeked out the front door curtain.

There stood Charley Hensley, waving the *Courier* edition with its screaming EXTRA headline in her hand.

"Dee Bennett, I know you're in there," Hensley shouted. "You can't put this garbage out and not face me."

Dee threw the front door open and pointed at the paper through the screen. "Don't call the work of these journalists garbage."

"And good morning to you, too," Hensley said, working herself into a frenzy. "We're suing this rag and you personally. You can say bye-bye to your sweet little family farm because it'll take everything you own to fight a million-dollar lawsuit."

Dee had been reading up on press law and libel. She now knew the kind of insurance the paper carried, too. She let the woman rage on.

"Yep, too bad this suck-egg town is going to lose its newspaper, too," Hensley said, pacing back and forth on Dee's front porch. "Because the Claxton Claptrap won't be able to keep its doors open when we're through with you."

"Is this on the record, Charley?" Dee said, arms crossed on her side of the screen door.

"Ha! No, bitch, this is *all* off the record," she said. "In fact, I don't even work for McCorrigan anymore. The whole Claxton operation was shit-canned at sunup."

"Can I quote you on that?" Dee said.

"No," Hensley screamed, jamming her finger toward the screen door. "Don't you ever ask me that again! You—you—you bush-league schoolmarm pretending to be a journalist at this two-bit, rinky-dink, second-string, small-time pathetic excuse of a newspaper!"

"Charley," Dee said, "why are you here?"

"I want to know why you did this to me. Why you did this to Rowdy."

"We simply reported the truth," Dee answered.

"The truth?" Charley said. "You did it because you were jealous of me and Max Miller. And *that's* the truth. Max and I have been sleeping together for weeks. All this time you've been making calf-eyes at your precious photographer. In fact, we slept together last night."

"That could have been challenging," said a voice behind Dee, as Max opened the door and stepped out onto the porch.

Charley Hensley stared at both of them. "Small-town rubes," she said. "You deserve each other."

Turning on her heel, storming down the steps, and striding off toward her car in a huff, Charley threw the newspaper down as though she meant to stomp it. But she dropped her key chain from her hand as well. Keys scattered, and she bent to retrieve them. Roy, foraging unseen on the pampas grass next to the porch, spotted the opportunity for a tasty morsel of newsprint and bounded toward the visitor. Dale, taking the stranger for an oddly shaped, moving rock, leapt onto Charley's back and began chewing on her red hair.

"Get off of me," Hensley screamed, wriggling free. "Omigod, you have *goats*? You disgusting hayseeds! All of you."

"Goats," Max said to Dee. "I've heard they'll climb anything."

"Yep. Not picky eaters, either."

Hensley scrambled into her Acura, slammed the vehicle into reverse, and peeled out down the driveway, leaving scorched earth in her wake.

* * *

After watching the dust settle all the way down the road, Dee turned to Max and said, "I guess I should see what McCorrigan's up to."

"You work," he said. "I'll shower and make breakfast."

"If you're tired of that Walter Winchell ensemble you've been wearing for twelve hours, there are still some of Buddy's old shirts and jeans in the closet in there. Help yourself."

The *American-Statesman* website, Dee noted, had run a sidebar with a statement from McCorrigan. *Due to a change in management I have closed my Claxton office. My Austin staff will be handling the campaign from this point. Please allow me and my family the privacy we need to address these personal matters, which do not reflect on the campaign in any way. As for fabricated claims by high school classmates, I expect to be fully vindicated and have no comment.*

The *Statesman* website noted that the new campaign manager—for the remaining seventy-two hours—was Bob Payne, a seventy-year-old GOP operative whose first job had been with a 1961 Senate race.

Dee took particular pleasure in visiting the websites of every major newspaper in the state. Each referenced both stories with attribution to the *Claxton (Tex.) Courier.* She found the discovery exhilarating but depressing at the same time. She relished the role of truth teller that the newspaper afforded her. She just hated how truth disrupted lives. She thought of Gretchen McCorrigan and her two children. Ransom Jones. Even Blaise Parrish.

Once she had told their stories, though, she knew none of them wanted to hear from her. She was a cog in the machine, the conduit through which news flowed, then shut off when it was done. She thought Shannon Thomas deserved a real victory lap, too, but if she knew her editor, the woman was probably back at the paper already planning tomorrow's coverage.

A delicious aroma wafted from the kitchen. Dee closed her eyes and imagined that Abby was home again, making a meal for Ian and Mama and her. Or that Mama was up cooking breakfast for a hard-working farm family.

"Hungry?" Max said, holding up a plate of bacon and eggs.

"Starving."

She brought her laptop to the table and said, "In case you want to get up to speed."

"No, thanks," he said. "I think I've had enough drama for a while. What about you, do you have to go back in to work?"

"No," she said, "I don't think so."

"Did McCorrigan concede?"

"Not likely," she said. "If I've learned one thing about him, he always believes he's a winner, no matter how dire the scoreboard is looking."

"What do you think Charley will do next?"

"I don't know. Maybe the circus needs a lion tamer?"

"Well, let's hope she's angry enough to wipe those photos off Facebook," he said. "I was pretty dense not to realize she was using me as a smoke screen." He took Dee's hand and kissed it lightly.

"I was a fool for ever doubting you," she said.

"So, I suppose," he said, his eyes twinkling, "that I don't have anything to worry about with you and Hardeberger?"

"I think Hank has the makings of a true-blue friend," she said.

"Yep. And after seeing him dance, I've begun to think we're not playing for the same team, either." He took her other hand and said, "But I don't want to talk about any of that."

"Oh?"

"Tomorrow someone has a birthday. A big one."

"Please don't remind me," she said.

"I understand it's a big work day for you, but I was hoping you'd save some time for dinner with me?"

"You got it, cowboy," she said.

"Forty's the new thirty, you know," he said. "I can tell you from experience, it's not as bad as you think."

"Promise me, no over-the-hill decorations or black armbands?"

"You got it, Nellie Bly."

23
Election Returns

The groom, having changed his clothes, waits upstairs, in the hall generally, until the bride emerges from her room in her traveling clothes. All the ushers shake hands with them both. His immediate family, as well as hers, have gradually collected—any that are missing must unfailingly be sent for. The bride's mother gives her a last kiss, her bridesmaids hurry down-stairs to have plenty of rice ready and to tell everyone below as they descend "They are coming!" A passage from the stairway and out of the front door, all the way to the motor, is left free between two rows of eager guests, their hands full of rice. Upon the waiting motor the ushers have tied everything they can lay their hands on in the way of white ribbons and shoes and slippers.

At last the groom appears at the top of the stairs, a glimpse of the bride behind him. It surely is running the gauntlet! They seemingly count "one, two, three, go!" With shoulders hunched and collars held tight to their necks, they run through shrapnel of rice, down the stairs, out through the hall, down the outside steps, into the motor, slam the door, and are off!

The wedding guests stand out on the street or roadway looking after them for as long as a vestige can be seen—and then gradually disperse.

—"Here They Come!"

SHANNON FANNED OUT the print editions of a dozen Sunday papers across the conference room table like a giant deck of cards. "Read 'em and weep, guys," she said. "Top-notch teamwork from the Little Paper That Could."

The staff of half a dozen clapped, as Phil regaled them again with the part about FiFi VuDu showing up at midnight.

The cowbell attached to the front door clanged, and Becca got up and went to the lobby. She was back in a jiffy with donuts and gourmet coffee delivered from Wilson's Bakery down the street. "The boss thought we deserved a little treat," she explained. "And a sugar rush to get us through the next two days!"

"I also thought we should take a minute to wish our newest staff member a happy birthday," Shannon said.

"And soon to be former staff member," Dee added. "It feels weird to celebrate at the start of my final week!"

"We all appreciate your contributions to the paper's coverage, Dee," said Shannon. "Don't be a stranger. Now, let's finish the budget and parcel out assignments for tomorrow. Dee, you'll be at the polls early to get exit interviews and man-on-the-street comment," she said.

"And woman on the street," Dee added, feeling her oats today.

"For election-night parties, the Republicans will be at the country club. Who wants to cover that?"

"I will," Margaret said, and Dee was relieved.

"I also hear there's to be a so-called nonpartisan gathering that the Democrats are hosting at Jesse Jane's—"

"I'll take that one," Dee said, before Shannon could finish her sentence.

*   *   *

Dee stopped to see Mama for lunch, which consisted of homemade potato soup and crackers. "My favorite!" she said, giving her mother a hug and sitting down at the table to catch up on the events of the past week.

"I about thought you'd forgotten your old mama, I hadn't heard from you in so long. But I saw your name in the paper a lot."

"In a good way, I hope," Dee said. "I wouldn't want my name in those pages this week if I were Rowdy McCorrigan."

274   KAY ELLINGTON & BARBARA BRANNON

"Aw, folks will forget all about it in no time. Don't nobody care about what the railroad commissioner does these days as long as he doesn't steal our money. Them politicians like to talk all about family values, but when it comes down to it, they only think with their p—"

"Mama, I know you weren't about to say what I think you were!"

"So, I've been tuning in to watch this Ransom Jones fella on TV. He's got a good head on his shoulders. I think he and I might see eye to eye on some things. But I never would have believed he was that same Ricky Jones from Claxton if you hadn't wrote the story."

"Speaking of writing stories . . . that was a doozy you read at the Write Stuff. I hadn't had a chance to ask you about it. That was really Dee Anna Daughtry, who ran her car off the road?"

Mama nodded soberly. "That was as true as I could tell it. We'll probably never know for sure if she intended to leave her husband and never come back here. I imagine life would have turned out a lot different if she had of."

"George and Dee Anna might have gone back to East Texas together. Or moved to another town. You might not have stuck around here to marry Daddy, and had Penny, and Buddy, and me."

"That's right. You might not have come into this world on Sam Houston's birthday, on that night the gin almost burned down, when your daddy just about didn't get me to the hospital in time."

"Why, Mama, it sounds to me like you're turning sentimental in your old age. I've never known you to dwell on such matters."

"Well, it just comes from spendin' so much time online, research-ing that family tree stuff. Makes you appreciate details you never realized."

They finished their soup while watching the last half of Ransom Jones's financial planning show, then switched over to CNN's non-stop election-eve news until it was time for Dee to depart for the afternoon shift at the library.

"I just don't know what's going to happen with this country," said Mama. "Used to be, every soul in Caprock County voted Democrat. The farmers and ranchers stood solidly behind FDR, all the way up through Lyndon Johnson. But Mr. Grover says American values have changed. That the Democrats have got too liberal and the Republicans will keep the country going strong."

"I, for one, am ready for a change," Dee said. "I'm ready for health insurance again. I'm ready for fairness and equality. I'm ready for war to be over with."

Mama shook her head. "I bet McCain still wins."

"I tell you what, Mama," said Dee. "It's my birthday and I'm feeling lucky. I'll take your bet. McCain wins, I'll buy you and Mr. Grover dinner anywhere you like. If the other guy succeeds, the two of you have to come celebrate at Jesse Jane's tomorrow night!"

"You're on, Dee Anna," said Mama. "Now, before you go, I did get you a card and a little something for your birthday. It's on the table by the door there. Open it up."

There was a distinctly non-sentimental card with a funny line about cats. And Dee unwrapped the small package to find a Walmart blister-pack containing a wireless computer mouse.

"Just helping keep you up to date with technology," Mama said.

*　*　*

Dee returned home early to feed the goats, check the mail and the paper, and get ready for her birthday-night date with Max. He hadn't indicated what he had in mind. And with Max, she'd learned, "surprise" could involve anything from suit and tie to shooting match.

In the mailbox was a padded envelope from Abby containing something shaped exactly like a book. Sure enough, Dee thought, opening the package to find a guide to making chèvre and other home dairy products from goat's milk. Well, that would have to wait a few months, she thought, though it was never too early to study up.

She laid the rest of the mail on the hall table, impatient to put the bills out of her consciousness. She didn't want to face the reality that her two sources of income, meager as they were, would come to an end within days. It had been an amazing ride, and she was grateful. She had to leave it at that.

It was in that belt-tightening frame of mind that she answered the phone when it rang. "Dee Bennett," she said.

"I'm glad to have reached you, Dee Bennett. Not Dawn. I hope you'll forgive and forget that gaffe."

"Richard Howell Boothe, I presume."

"Indeed."

"What's on your mind? It happens to be my birthday, and I'm preparing to celebrate."

There was a pause, then Boothe continued. "Well, you must have made some wish today, Dee, because I'm calling to say I'd like to represent you. Your work is solid. I like it."

She held her breath. "And you think you can sell it?"

"I know so. I already have."

"What?!"

"On the strength of the note you described. That one tidbit of literary arcana has stirred up a feeding frenzy. You won't believe the figure I'm about to mention to you, and if you'll sign the agreement I'm sending your way, I'll put your book out for auction this week."

"Auction." Dee sat straight down on the couch. "Auction, you said."

"Check your e-mail, Dee," Boothe said. "Sign it, send it back, then go pour yourself your favorite drink and toast yourself from me."

"Vodka gimlet," she said under her breath, laughing and letting her head loll back on the cushion.

"What?"

"Never mind. You'll have to read the book."

*   *   *

Max arrived at six, while Dee was sipping her gimlet on the porch and gazing out at the mutli-hued sunset. "I see you've got your boots on," he said as he climbed the steps and came over to kiss her warmly. "You'll need them."

"Whatever did you have in mind, Mr. Miller?" she asked. "Is it branding time?"

He sat down beside her and leaned back in his chair.

"Not exactly. But you just sit right here and make yourself comfy. Keep your feet up. You'll want the rest."

She looked at him quizzically. What was he up to now?

In a few minutes, about the time the sun was fading on the horizon, a vehicle that reminded Dee of the ice-cream truck she used to love to see in town pulled in through the gate and rattled up the hill. As it came closer she could see it was hardly an ice-cream truck, but a custom-equipped van with a colorful graphic design. "Dusty Land and His Cowboy Band," it read, and no sooner did it come to a halt than Dusty and the boys jumped out and began setting up their instruments and equipment.

"This where you wanted us, over here, Max?" called the good-looking guy Dee assumed to be Dusty, the front man. The ensemble found their places beside the deck platform. On cue, when Max walked over to a switch hidden beside the desert willow tree, the band struck up "Waltz across Texas" and a thousand little lights strung across Dee's newly landscaped yard transformed the place into their own private dance hall.

Max took Dee's hand in his, slipped an arm around her waist, and moved with her to the easy, inviting tune.

"How lovely!" she said. "I'm beginning to like this dancing idea."

"This could be the first of many out here," he said.

"I only want to know," she wondered, "how you got the weather to cooperate?"

"The contingency plan was in the barn. But I'm glad we didn't have to resort to it."

After they'd two-stepped to a couple of Hal Ketchum tunes Max led Dee back up to the porch. The band continued as he fetched a brown grocery bag from the pickup. "Buck's Barbecue Barn," he said. "It's what's for dinner!"

"You get no argument from me," said Dee. The band took requests as she and Max savored their brisket and fixin's, ending with her all-time favorite tune, "San Antonio Rose," and her all-time favorite dessert, German chocolate cake.

"This might be the best birthday ever," she told him, strolling the grounds with him while the band packed up. "And if this is what forty looks like, I won't dread forty-one at all."

* * *

On Tuesday morning, reporter's notebook ready for her final assignment, Dee drove Mama to the polling place to cast their votes. Neither revealed their decisions. Throughout the day Dee visited Claxton's various precincts, where she saw long lines of voters—especially younger generations and minorities. A text message arrived in her phone from Abby and Ian, with a selfie of them assisting Massachusetts voters to the polls—and a note that, like all good operatives, they had voted early in order to be available to help turn out the vote on Election Day. Sentiment in Caprock County seemed to be trending about even among the two front-runners—so by afternoon Dee still figured the outcome was anyone's guess.

The curious, the certain, and the early cocktail set began drifting into Jesse Jane's Roadhouse around four. It was easy to spot the location from the Obama bumper-stickered cars, and by the Yes We Can! and ¡Sí Se Puede! signs staked around the perimeter of the building.

Dee wandered in and searched out a good vantage point. The TV set in the bar was on as usual, set to the regional news, but in the main dining room an installation crew was still struggling to set up a 52-inch set for watching returns all evening.

"This is gonna be something," predicted Jane, decked out in a cowboy hat with an Obama button pinned to the front. Her partner, Jess, helped out tending bar. "And if I'm goin' to watch history being made, I want to watch it *big!*"

Dee said, "Well, I have to admire that kind of enthusiasm."

"Now, if you want some real dinner off the menu, Dee, go ahead and order it now. We're closing down the kitchen soon and setting up the buffet over this way." Jane indicated where the fajitas, popcorn, and hot dogs would be served in the side dining room, courtesy of the local Democratic party. "The karaoke stage will be used for announcements throughout the evening. And of course, the cash bar will be open. Get you anything to start off with?"

"Just an ice water, thank you. I'm on the clock, you know."

"And I just wanted to say, you are doing a really good job at the paper," Jane shouted, already on her way out of the room.

"Thanks," Dee yelled back, settling into a booth with a good view of the door, the stage, and the TV—and room for anyone who just might be joining her.

More patrons started to arrive around seven, when the local polls closed. Max found her and slid into the booth beside her, bringing soft drinks and baskets of popcorn. "Saving those other two seats for someone in particular?" he asked, and Dee told him about her bet.

"I won't be surprised if the old Colonel has to eat his hat," Max said. "Me, I've always leaned Libertarian, but in a national race you have to admit it comes down to a two-party system." The restaurant continued to fill with friends and strangers. JoAnn waved, and

Wen and Lee Huan, the Vietnamese couple who now owned the donut shop, made their way over to say hello to Max.

Over the din, Jane grabbed the remote and rushed up to the TV. "Hush, y'all," she yelled above the hubbub, "something big is happening." And the crowd quieted to listen to the TV audio.

"Obama's just won Ohio, Michigan, and New York," Jane yelled. "He's halfway there!"

Cheers, whoops, and hollers went up from the group.

As the returns became known, and Obama passed milestone after milestone, winning Ohio, Pennsylvania, New Hampshire, Iowa, and New Mexico, friends started pouring in. Hank, Teresa, and Raul arrived around eight when many of the Eastern state polls closed and Obama had begun to build a sizeable lead.

"Amazing," Hank said, when their bunch found Dee and Max. "A hundred and fifty years ago, this man might have been a slave in this country. Now it's likely he could be president."

"Pull up a chair, Hank," said Max, who went to fetch a couple more from the corner. The two places in the booth remained empty, reserved with a couple of menus on the seat and the target of covetous eyes. When many of the Central time zone state polls closed, and Obama's Electoral College votes soared, Raul said, "It gives us all hope."

"Anyone in this country can do anything," Teresa said.

Dee spotted Margaret and J. D. and Pauline entering around nine and shouldering their way through the standing-room-only crowd. "It was dead at the country club," Margaret shouted. "The Grand Old Party turned out the lights at nine and shut it down. So we decided to come on over here."

"Whether you voted for him or not," J. D. said, "it is historic." It was impossible to hear the TV over the crowd, but everyone could see the screen as state after state lit up in blue.

At last Dee saw the door open to admit two more figures, the ones she'd been waiting for. Wendell Grover entered the packed room tentatively, making a path for Mama. Dee jumped up, waded through to them, and showed them to the places she'd struggled to save. "Mr. Grover's still holding out hope," said Mama, "but I can see the writing on the wall."

When Washington State's eleven electoral votes put Barack Obama past the magic 270 number needed to win the Electoral College, the crowd erupted with excitement. Jane and her partner embraced and kissed, then passed out packages of confetti for revelers to throw. Max gave Dee an encouraging hug as a group somewhere in the room broke out in "Happy Days Are Here Again."

Wendell Grover stood up from the booth and indicated he'd be right back. Dee watched as he made his way not toward the restrooms but to the raised stage a few feet away. He stepped up and took the mic. "Is this thing on?"

The room quieted a bit; apparently it was. The crowd pushed back to see what was going on, and the group in the booth had a clear sight line. The Colonel spoke clearly, his words unmistakable. "Alice Bennett, this seems to be a night when anything can happen." The room went completely silent as he got down on his knee and looked directly at Mama. "So—do you think it might be possible for someone like you to marry someone like me?"

No one said a word as Mama, registering first astonishment on her face and then determination not to be nonplussed in front of a crowd, rose and made her way over to where Wendell waited, took the microphone from him, and offered up a single word: a regal "Yes." Her suitor stood again, stepped down from the platform and kissed her on the lips, and escorted her back through the crowd toward their seats.

Dee picked her jaw up off the floor. "Well, sweet jumping Christopher," she said to no one in particular.

Teresa leaned over and said, "I knew that was his story in the writing group!"

Max stood and shook Wendell's hand and hugged Mama as she retook her seat.

Dee reached across, smiling, and took her mother's hand, then pulled out her phone and dialed Penny's number. When her sister answered, Dee shouted over the noise, "Mama's here with me at the election night party. And she has some news for you."

*   *   *

By the end of the night, as the last of the crowd departed, McCain had won Texas by double digits. Votes were still being counted in an unexpectedly close race for railroad commissioner.

"I think you should get some rest, sweetheart," said Max. "It's been a roller coaster."

"Yeah, it's been an evening of surprises, all right," said Dee.

He kissed her forehead as he walked her to her car. "That's really great, for your mother and Wendell."

She nodded. "Tell me truthfully. Did you ever see *that* coming?"

"I sort of thought Mary Alice and the Colonel had more in common than their Civil War ancestors. They're each tough in their own way. They're survivors. I expect they'll do well together."

"It never ceases to amaze me, where true love might spring up."

"That so? I didn't take you for a starry-eyed romantic."

She looked up at the multitude of brilliant stars in the Texas sky, taking in their myriad sizes and colors and combinations, then smiled at him. "Tonight was proof that just anything might be possible."

24
Engagements

The marriage of a widow is the same as that of a maid except that she cannot wear white or orange blossoms, which are emblems of virginity, nor does she have bridesmaids. Usually a widow chooses a very quiet wedding, but there is no reason why she should not have a "big wedding" if she cares to, except that somber ushers and a bride in traveling dress, or at best a light afternoon one with a hat, does not make an effective processional—unless she is beautiful enough to compensate for all that is missing.

—"The Second Marriage"

"WATCH YOUR STEP on those flagstones," Dee cautioned as Buddy carried the precious cardboard box from Halfmann's Cake Cottage along the walkway and up the porch steps to the kitchen. "I had to go all the way to San Angelo for that, and I don't think we could find a substitute on a holiday if anything happened to it!"

As friends began to arrive and Dee's siblings unloaded the last of the covered dishes they'd brought from Mama's house, Dee took one last look around to be sure every detail was perfect. Ruby Lee had worked her usual magic, with silver gauze ribbon and coral-hued roses. Abby had scrubbed and polished and vacuumed the day before, while Ian made sure the grounds were in tip-top shape. Penny and her daughters had overseen the party menu and the Thanksgiving meal preparation—all in Mama's kitchen at her patio home. "You didn't think I was going to take any chances on an occasion like this, did you?" Mama had said when Dee tried to talk her into leaving the cooking to others.

There was never any doubt in Mama's mind, though, that the wedding would happen at the home place. "It's the perfect thing for bringing families together," she'd declared.

Out on the lawn near the grape arbor, Buddy's sons and Kyle and Ian showed guests to their seats in white folding chairs. Wendell's daughter, son-in-law, and granddaughter from Abilene circulated, getting to know their newly expanded roster of kin. The setting was simple: only the arbor was draped in roses as a backdrop, accented with more of the silver gauze ribbon. There were no other flowers, no boutonnieres or corsages, no bouquet. "Just for all of y'all to be here, that's all the decoration we need," Mama had said.

The ceremony was equally simple, with Brother Roy, the Baptist minister who'd said Wilton Bennett's funeral service the previous December, joining the new couple together in matrimony. Mama looked resplendent in the silver silk ensemble she'd worn to Maddy's wedding, Dee thought, and Wendell Grover cut a fine figure in a charcoal pin-striped suit and coral-colored tie.

Neither Dee nor Penny, sitting on Dee's right, could hold back sniffles when they heard the timeless words "I do" repeated. Whether brought on by an unsuppressed sorrow for their late father or joy for their mother, Dee wasn't sure. Max, on her left, squeezed her hand.

After applause for the new Mr. and Mrs. Wendell Grover, Penny brought the cake out to the porch and set it on the coral-draped bistro table for the couple to cut. Guests watched from the yard and walkways as the stiff-backed colonel offered a dainty morsel to his bride, who finished it, licked her lips, and then said, "Now I know it's not the usual thing to have the dessert first, but everybody come line up in the kitchen and don't be shy, because we've got a whole Thanksgiving feast to enjoy before Mr. Grover and I depart for our honeymoon."

Guests laughed and speculated on the couple's plans.

Luncheon plates were piled high with turkey and dressing and cranberry sauce, green beans, and sweet potato casserole. "All my favorites that Auntie Alice used to cook," Ruby Lee said to Dee as they went through the line. "Nobody can make dressing like your mama."

Ruby Lee's father, Rupert, stage-whispered to Dee, "I'm surprised your mother didn't wait the full year of mourning. Not that I have any problem with it, no sirree. It just doesn't seem like Mary Alice to jump into anything."

"You hush, Daddy," said Ruby Lee, overhearing. "Auntie Alice told me herself, when you get hitched at her age, who's got time for etiquette?"

After the meal and cake, the time came for the couple to say farewell to their guests. Wendell tapped his glass and announced that he and Alice were headed to the Caribbean for a three-week tour of the islands. Penny admitted to helping her mother expedite the passport process on the QT. Buddy added that Mitch Mitchell's private plane was waiting for them already at the Claxton airport to whisk them off to their connecting flight from—where else? Love Field.

Dee saw her mother off with a tearful hug. Max shook Wendell's hand and congratulated him.

Whit Bennett put an arm around his mother's shoulder and said, "*Now* can we go watch football?"

*   *   *

Penny and her family returned to Dallas that afternoon, so as not to miss the Black Friday sales the next day.

Buddy, likewise, rushed back to Darrell with Roxanne and the boys, to make sure his Dust Devils continued to toe the line in practice for the playoffs. The stats were looking good for him to cross the elusive .850 win percentage mark, thanks in part to Claxton's Halloween-night loss.

Mama and Wendell would be back the week before Christmas, with plans to host a small holiday gathering as they figured out how best to combine households.

Teresa had found it an opportune time to give notice on her job with Helping Hands and enroll in the community college for spring semester.

Hank Hardeberger picked up a landscaping commission from an unexpected client, his neighbor Mrs. Finch, who decided if you couldn't beat 'em, join 'em.

Shannon Thomas had called Dee in to her office the previous week to gauge her interest in continuing in the newsroom. "It's all contingent on first-quarter projections," she explained, "but the possibility is looking good after the first of the year."

Margaret covered the news that the Texas Star Energy Company was being sold to a conglomerate out of Kansas. That same week Dee received a letter indicating the new owners would be eager to act promptly on the option she'd granted to Texas Star — since, on her mother's advice, their parcel was the only place on the ridge that was still holding out when the company changed hands.

Ransom Jones's TVN numbers soared as his story circulated nationwide.

Rowdy McCorrigan clinched the seat on the railroad commission based on the sizeable lead he'd gained in early voting, while ultimately winning with less than two percentage points, far beneath any other GOP candidate on the Texas statewide ticket. The Texas Ethics Commission wasted no time in issuing a subpoena for his campaign expense records.

Charley Hensley was quickly snapped up as deputy chief of staff in the office of the governor of South Carolina, a state where no one seemed to care about a little peccadillo far away in Texas. Ransom Jones's TVN numbers soared as his story circulated nationwide.

Abby and Ian were cleaning up the last of the dinner dishes while Dee relaxed on the sofa, her feet stretched out over Max's lap. Chester lay on the rug beside his master, while Cori lounged lazily across the spine of the sofa. Dee switched off the remote when the football game ended, and all was quiet.

"You know, I've been thinking," she said. "I realize it's not good luck to spend your windfall until the check is in hand, but I can't help but dream about how I want to use that book advance."

Ian came over and sat down in the recliner, and Abby slid over the arm of the chair into his lap.

Abby offered a guess. "You're finally going to install central air, right before the weather turns cold?"

"That can wait till spring," Dee said. "But I don't see why we couldn't get started on finishing out the barn. There ought to be enough money for enclosing it, sheetrocking it, updating electrical and heat, things like that."

"Those aren't challenging jobs at all," said Ian, "since you already have a concrete foundation, strong framing, and a good roof."

"It would make a great place for the writing group to meet, and we could hold a weekend retreat, and we could host events to generate some revenue."

"Are you sure you're not getting a little ahead of yourself?" asked Max. "What kind of events?"

"Well," said Abby, more demurely than usual, "I think Ian and I could be the guinea pigs. We've been talking . . . can I tell them, babe? . . . about a June wedding. The bar is already high with Gramma Alice and Wendell, you know, but here at the Paragraph Ranch would be awesome!"

Dee looked around at her daughter from the sofa and reached a hand over to touch hers. She propped up on her elbow and said, "Sweetie, that's the best news I've had, in a day that's already been full of good things. We can start planning tomorrow."

Not to be excluded, Dale peeked in through the living room window, then hopped up into one of the rocking chairs. Roy was not far behind. The golden beams of a late November afternoon played on the polished wooden floorboards, and far off down the hill a train sounded its evening benediction.

Acknowledgments

WE ARE GRATEFUL to the many readers who have traipsed through the Paragraph Ranch since the first novel in the series. You gave us the courage and determination to keep pursuing the dream. We are similarly grateful to the Abilene (Texas) Public Library and the West Texas Book Festival, for inviting us to take part in their 2014 event with our first book. You provided the perfect launch venue and paved the way for others to feature us too. To friends and kinfolk who came from all over Texas to hear us, you made it a special celebration indeed!

Once again, we owe tremendous thanks to those who helped out with this volume: especially Cathey, Lori, Kara, and Betty, some of the keenest beta readers we know; to the Ad Hoc Writers' Group of Lubbock, Texas, whose members have continued to offer invaluable critique and encouragement; to our Booktrope publishing and marketing team Kenneth Shear, Katherine Sears, Jesse James Freeman, Kate Burkett, and Adam Bodendieck, and our extraordinary Booktrope creative team, book manager Stephanie Konat, designer Greg Simanson, and proofreader Cecile Jagodzinski (are we square now?); and to other friends, family members, and fans who have commented, praised, corrected, and, not least, purchased.

The election season of 2008 was one of the most important turning points in American history. When it came down to decision time, our nation did not shy from electing a leader of mixed race, one who promised change. The real-life backdrop in which this work of fiction is situated honors President Barack Obama and acknowledges the doors that opened with the advent of his administration. The availability, at last, of affordable health insurance and equitable care for all made it possible for at least two authors to complete a goal they'd long wanted to pursue. The system isn't perfect, but we're headed in the right direction.

We appreciate all the real institutions, the towns, the people, and the events that inspired the fictional landscape in which the Paragraph Ranch books are set. We hope our truest love and respect for them shine through.

ALSO BY KAY ELLINGTON & BARBARA BRANNON

The Paragraph Ranch (Fiction) A motley group of writers and a cast of small-town Texas characters prove that maybe you can go home again, and find love in the unlikeliest of places.

Give a Cup of Water

A Paragraph Ranch novella

by Barbara Brannon

The citizens of Claxton, Texas, are justifiably possessed with a healthy thirst — on the dusty plains of West Texas, they're in the midst of a seven-year drought when the town finally votes to go wet. The opposition faction, and its leader, Miss Jessica Cater, manage to shut down the promotion beer-store owner Buck Turlock has cooked up just in time for the Fourth of July celebration. But will Buck's schemes lead Miss Jessie to rethink her position?